The Innocent Dead

By Lin Anderson

Driftnet
Torch
Deadly Code
Dark Flight
Easy Kill
Final Cut
The Reborn
Picture Her Dead
Paths of the Dead
The Special Dead
None but the Dead
Follow the Dead
Sins of the Dead
Time for the Dead
The Innocent Dead

NOVELLA
Blood Red Roses

The Innocent Dead

. . . are always the first victims

LIN ANDERSON

MACMILLAN

First published 2020 by Macmillan
an imprint of Pan Macmillan
The Smithson, 6 Briset Street, London EC1M 5NR
Associated companies throughout the world
www.panmacmillan.com

ISBN 978-1-5290-3364-9

1 3 5 7 9 8 6 4 2

A CIP catalogue record for this book is available from the British Library.

Typeset in Meridien by Palimpsest Book Production Ltd, Falkirk, Stirlingshire
Printed and bound by CPI Group (UK) Ltd, Croydon, CR0 4YY

Visit www.panmacmillan.com to read more about all our books
and to buy them. You will also find features, author interviews and
news of any author events, and you can sign up for e-newsletters
so that you're always first to hear about our new releases.

For my father
DI Bill Mitchell

The past is what we decide it to be.

1

Karen had been feeling odd for days. Her current world consisted of vivid, insistent and disturbing memories, some of which she would rather not revisit, others that she couldn't believe had happened to her at all.

The mind played tricks, she reminded herself. Especially at her age. Like the recurring dream she'd had over the years.

In it she was ten and visiting a house with her dad. The house was near a railway line and there was a garden with raspberry bushes. She'd climbed up onto a footbridge to watch a train chug past.

Yet when Karen had asked her dad who'd lived in that house, he'd told her that she must have imagined it. That they'd never had friends or relatives with a house like that.

It was just a dream, he'd said.

But the current memory wasn't a dream.

It featured Karen's older sister's wedding day. Eleanor, all in white, looked beautiful dancing round the floor with her new husband, who was tall and handsome, but . . .

Karen shuddered. There was something about his eyes. The way he would stare at Karen, before leaning down to whisper in her ear.

The memory suddenly switched to another white dress. This time the wearer was small, Karen's height but with dark hair. It was her childhood pal, Mary McIntyre. She too wore a veil just like a bride.

The image almost made her heart stop.

No, she thought. *I don't want to think about that day. Not now. Not ever again.*

It was then she heard a cawing sound coming from the hall or the far sitting room. She tried to recall whether she'd left the porch door open. Could one of the garden birds be trapped inside the house?

Opening the kitchen door, she found the hall empty and the porch door shut. So nothing could have come in that way.

She was about to check the sitting room, when the next memory swept over her like a tidal wave, halting Karen in her tracks.

In it she was walking along the path to the den that she and Mary had built in the woods. Suddenly a crow, disturbed by her approach, abandoned the blood-splattered body of a lamb to rise squawking in front of her, furious that she'd disturbed it at its feast.

A feeling of revulsion swept over Karen, and she reached out to steady herself against the wall.

Why had such a horrible memory come back to haunt her after all these years?

Striving to regain her composure, she contemplated the closed door of the sitting room.

She didn't go in there much any more. Not since Jack had died. It was too full of memories. Plus Jack had been the one to light the fire and Karen couldn't bring herself to do that. So she'd taken up permanent residence in the kitchen by the oil-fired range.

'Don't be a fool, Karen,' she said out loud. 'You have to check.'

Steeling herself, she reached for the handle.

The sitting room didn't get the sun at this time of day. Also, being at the gable end of the house, it was rarely warm, even in midsummer. Nevertheless, Karen was perturbed to find that the air that rushed out to greet her was cold. Icily so.

Had she opened a window sometime earlier to air the room and forgotten to shut it again?

Glancing around, she noted that the window was closed and there was no immediate sighting of a trapped bird.

Jack's voice suddenly came to her.

Remember when a pair of crows fell down our chimney? Lucky the fire wasn't on.

Emboldened by Jack's internal reminder, Karen decided to check out the fireplace.

It was at that moment she had the strong sense she was being watched. The feeling was so powerful it stopped Karen in her tracks.

Someone or something was in there with her.

Forcing herself to turn, she found a pair of beady black eyes glaring at her from the back of the sofa.

The image of the crow was as threatening as in her earlier memory, and the resulting scream froze in Karen's throat.

Okay, she tried to reason, her heart pounding her chest so hard that she could scarcely breathe. Jack had been right. A bird had fallen down the chimney and that bird just happened to be a crow. She turned back to the window and, releasing the lock, pushed it wide open. She would need to find a way to shoo the crow out, that was all.

It was then the cat appeared round the side of the house to cross the drive in front of her. Big-bodied, jet-black with a white splash on its chest, there was no doubt it was Toby.

Stunned, she released the window and it immediately shut with a bang. Expecting the noise to startle the crow into cawing, she turned to find the bird no longer there.

In that moment Karen knew the reason for the torrent of memories, the images of white dresses, the appearance of the black crow and the sighting of her dead cat Toby.

It was all about Mary. It had to be.

2

The resurfacing of memories, the imagined crow and the vision of Toby marching across her path had all happened for a reason. What that reason was, Karen had no idea. If Jack had been here, he would have made sense of it all.

As she started up the loft ladder, the pain of his loss gripped Karen and she had to wait until she could draw air into her lungs before she continued her ascent.

She'd never expected to be a widow. She'd always presumed she would be the first to go. Jack's father had lived into his nineties, faculties intact. His mother had preceded her husband by only a few months.

As for her own parents, they hadn't been so lucky.

Dust motes, disturbed by her entry, danced before her as she made her way to the box near the leftmost skylight. Jack, in his tidy manner, had labelled the box KAREN MISCELLANEOUS and dated it with the year she'd left home. As such, it had seemed a suitable resting place for what she now sought.

Having extracted it, she headed back down to the kitchen, at which point she put the kettle on and made a pot of tea. In past times, during Jack's illness and after his death, when anxiety had beset her, she would have sought refuge in a glass of wine.

Not any more.

Settling herself beside the range, mug of tea alongside,

Karen opened the old school jotter, hoping whatever was in there hadn't faded with time.

She had written the diary in pencil. In the lead-up to that day the entries were brief, like 'practised spelling for test tomorrow' and 'Stephen fancies Mary. He sent her a love letter in class.'

Everything changed on the first day of May.

For a moment Karen was back in her old bedroom, sitting at the desk by the window. The street she'd lived in had houses on one side only. On the other side were two newly built primary schools. One for Catholics. The other for Protestants. The school grounds were separated by an area of open land and a small wood.

That's where we built our den.

The road outside her house was steep and mostly empty of cars. A few delivery vans drove up and down. An ice-cream van. A rag-and-bone cart.

We played in the street all the time.

Until that day.

It was so long ago. How could she possibly remember what she'd felt like back then? Yet, she could. As Karen read the words she'd written, the horror of that day, so long buried, rose up to engulf her.

Diary entry of Karen Marshall aged 11
1 May 1975

It was sunny today. I practised my skipping.

> *Mary's in the kitchen*
> *Doing a little stitchin'*
> *In comes a bogeyman*
> *And out goes she*

Mary's my best friend. The bogeyman is the man who waits near the shops to show us his willy. Mary and I always run past trying not to look.

I was waiting for Mary to come and have her photograph taken in our front garden. She would be wearing her white confirmation dress and veil, which are beautiful.

I want a dress like Mary's, but I can't be confirmed, because I'm a Protestant. Mary says there's a seat in heaven reserved for her because she's a Catholic.

I imagine a packed cinema like the one we go to on Saturday mornings, all the seats filled by Catholics, and wonder where I will go when I die.

The sun shone all day and it got late and Mary never came to have her picture taken.

Then my dad arrived home and told me to go inside as Mary wasn't coming.

When I asked why, he didn't answer. Just took me in the house, shouted on my mum and they went into the kitchen together and shut the door.

Standing outside, I heard my mum crying.

That's when it all began.

3

The April sun was bright, but not strong enough to have made any difference to the temperature of the lochan.

In an attempt at bravado, Dougal had waded in already, wearing nothing but his trunks. Julie knew he didn't like swimming anywhere other than a proper swimming pool, where he could see what lurked beneath him. A calm sea was also manageable provided he wasn't required to venture out too far *and* he could see the sandy floor.

A dark-brown loch, on the other hand, was Dougal's idea of a horror movie, in which he had a starring part.

So to get him to come here, Julie had had to agree to an evening doing exactly what Dougal wanted. Julie had no problem with that, since Dougal's romantic plans for tonight pretty well matched her own.

Without a wetsuit, he won't last long enough to enjoy the water, Julie thought as she watched him wade in cautiously. Once the tingling in his upper body moved from mild to severe pain, Dougal would be back on shore quicker than he went in.

Ready now, Julie walked in slowly, enjoying the sensation of the water entering her wetsuit to form a warm protective film against her skin. Launching herself forward, she began to swim, feeling the soft peaty water enclose her like brown silk.

Much as she loved swimming in the sea in all seasons, there was nothing to beat a freshwater loch whatever the time of year. Turning, she floated on her back and closed her eyes, enjoying the gentle slurp of water in her ears.

It was Dougal's sudden shout that disturbed this dream-like state. Julie turned over and took a look, assuming the cold had got to him by now. It certainly appeared that way. He was swimming, seemingly in a great hurry, back to the strip of sand where they'd undressed earlier.

'Froze your balls off, did it?' Julie shouted. 'I warned you.'

Having reached the shore, he rose, swore loudly and pointed at the opposite bank.

'What?' Julie said, unmoved by his antics.

Dougal was a joker and he'd caught her out on numerous occasions, so her first instinct was to ignore him.

'Fu-ck-ing l-l-look!' he stuttered, his face white, his body starting to shiver.

He was putting on a fine performance, Julie had to admit that. Next, no doubt, would come the theme tune from *Jaws*. He'd tried that one during one of her wild sea swims.

'Get dressed before you freeze to death,' she shouted back. 'There's hot coffee in my rucksack.'

'Julie, I'm not kidding. There's something over there in the fucking bank.'

Due to the long dry spring weather, the water level in the loch was the lowest she'd ever encountered, leaving the raised peat bank on the far shore exposed.

Although still suspicious, Julie turned and made for the spot where Dougal continued to point.

At first glance, the bank looked normal, although some of it had crumbled away, exposing the twisted form of heather roots.

'There!' Dougal shouted, panic still in his voice. 'There's something there.'

Julie got closer, treading water, and reached up for the odd bulge made by the knotted roots. Her touch sent more dry peat to detach and plop into the water alongside her.

The tingling cold surged into her own upper body, making her gasp. Yet it wasn't the length of time she'd been in the water that caused her sudden drop in temperature, but horror at what she now saw.

Free of earth, the leathery finger poked through the tangle of roots to beckon her, as though in desperation.

4

Rhona exited the main door of her flat into bright spring sunshine. She stood for a moment, letting the sun warm her face, before she set off down the steps that led into Kelvingrove Park. Six months ago she had believed herself incapable of either being back living here or walking through the park to Glasgow University and her lab of a morning.

Yet here she was.

Her sojourn on Skye after the sin-eater case had set her on the road to recovery, but it had been her time at Castlebrae, the police treatment centre, that had taught her to properly deal with her PTSD.

As a result of the care she'd received there, the nightmares had eased and the claustrophobic flashbacks diminished in power. Plus she'd heard stories from her fellow inmates which had helped put her own experience into perspective.

The past is always with us, but it need not define us, had become her mantra. Or as Chrissy McInsh, her forensic assistant, was wont to say, *Shit happens, but so does fun.*

Rhona smiled at the memory of Chrissy's face when she'd turned up for her first day back at work. Standing outside the door of the lab, Rhona had been besieged by doubts about her ability to do her job again, despite what they'd said at Castlebrae.

Then she'd heard Chrissy inside and smelled the usual pot

of morning coffee and, without a doubt, the scent of filled rolls, Glasgow-style, which Chrissy always brought in with her.

Square sausage, tattie scone, black pudding and an egg.

Maybe Chrissy had heard her outside, or maybe it was just that second sense Chrissy often exhibited, but the door had been flung open and the joy on Chrissy's face had propelled Rhona inside. That and Chrissy's firm grip on her arm.

'Perfect timing. I got you the full works this morning,' Chrissy had informed her. 'Plus I've purchased a few more condiments to complement your breakfast roll.'

Chrissy was a ketchup gal on pretty much everything. Even the haggis rolls she'd bought from the van at Kilt Rock on the island of Skye, before she'd abseiled down the cliff face and presented herself to Rhona at the bottom.

After the months of hiding out on Skye at her adopted parents' former home, Rhona's heart had lifted at the unexpected sight of Chrissy flourishing those haggis rolls. As a result, she'd heard herself laugh properly. Something that hadn't happened in months.

Pouring out two mugs of, no doubt, strong coffee, Chrissy had plonked Rhona's roll down before her with a smile.

'Welcome back, partner!'

And in that moment, Rhona was glad to be back.

The daily walk through the park held its own memories, none more so than the body they'd discovered near the ancient yew tree. A glance in the direction of its gnarled trunk now no longer brought forth the heavy scent of yew needles mixed with death.

Should she require to walk through the dense undergrowth that surrounded it, Rhona now knew she could handle it. By far the worst symptom of her incarceration had been her panicked reaction to suffocating spaces. That had been her biggest obstacle in returning to work, because working in confined spaces was a necessary part of the job.

She thought of one of the participants she'd met during her stay at Castlebrae: a forensic pathologist who, after working on the terrible site of a major plane crash, had taken to writing her own name on every part of her body before she could climb on a plane.

Trauma took on many guises.

This morning, being crisp, sunny and dry, brought forth runners, walkers and cyclists to populate the paths of the park. In the distance, the red sandstone of Kelvingrove Art Gallery and Museum glowed through the budding trees, watched over from the nearby hill by the Gothic magnificence of Glasgow University.

Crossing Kelvin Way, she made for the path that led up to the face of the university, which was already busy with students set on the same destination. At the top, Rhona stopped for a moment to take in her favourite view of the city of Glasgow which, along with the Palace of Kelvingrove, also included the golden dome of the nearby Sikh temple and the skeleton beauty of the giant Finnieston Crane, a memory of Glasgow's great engineering past, and still in perfect working order.

When she arrived at the lab, she found Chrissy was there before her. A usual occurrence, broken only for a short while after the birth of Chrissy's now toddler son, wee Michael, named after DS Michael McNab.

The familiar smell of coffee on entry was, however, not accompanied by the usual and much-anticipated filled rolls. Rhona found herself perturbed by this, since her brisk walk through the park had definitely given her an appetite.

Chrissy's hair colour at present was a deep auburn. Rhona

13

harboured a suspicion that she was attempting to replicate the DS Michael McNab look. Not the chin stubble, of course, but definitely the hair tone.

DS McNab was a hero of Chrissy's, having shielded her pregnant self from a gunshot, the scar of which he still wore on his back, although it was now cleverly disguised by a skull tattoo.

'What? No rolls?'

Rhona looked about in the hope that the familiar paper bag might be on view, just not yet opened to allow the hot aroma to escape.

'I thought we'd try something new for breakfast for a change,' Chrissy said, rather sheepishly, it seemed to Rhona.

'What exactly?' Rhona demanded.

'Porridge pots,' Chrissy offered. 'And you have a wide choice of flavours.' She pointed at a line of the pots. 'Cinnamon, apple, banana, honey, syrup. All very healthy,' she added.

'What's going on, Chrissy? Since when have you been health-conscious?'

Her forensic assistant looked mightily offended by that remark. 'Since I had wee Michael.'

'I'm talking about *your* eating habits, not what you feed your son.'

Chrissy shrugged. 'People change. They get older. They get wiser.'

'You've joined a gym,' Rhona accused her.

'Never,' Chrissy replied with gusto.

'What then?'

There was a moment's silence before Chrissy admitted, 'I've taken up running.'

'Really?'

Rhona was impressed if it were true, although Chrissy had 'taken up' things before now, only to discover her enthusiasm waning after a while. Usually because the guy she was joining on such pursuits had lost his appeal.

'Who is it?' Rhona demanded.

'No one,' Chrissy said categorically. 'Just me. So, what's your poison?' She gestured at the line of pots.

Trying not to look too downhearted, Rhona chose a pot, hoping this new plan of how to start the day was simply another one of Chrissy's fanciful ideas, like changing her hair colour regularly, and would soon be abandoned.

'Right,' Chrissy said, pouring what Rhona prayed was still strong coffee. 'There's a message for you from Bill. He wants you to call him after breakfast.'

DI Wilson, or Bill as she and Chrissy called him, had been Rhona's mentor since she began in this job. He'd been on duty the night she'd attended the scene of a particularly brutal murder of a teenage boy – a boy who had looked so like her that Rhona had imagined he might be Liam, the son she'd given up for adoption seventeen years previously. In the end, Liam had found her and they'd eventually come to an understanding regarding why Rhona, when still a teen-ager herself, had given up her baby.

She'd confided in Bill back then, how personal the death of that teenager had been to her, and how it had prompted her to search for her own son. Bill, with two teenage children of his own, had known exactly what she meant.

'It's my biggest fear,' he'd said. 'That one day I'll turn up at a scene of crime and one of my kids is the victim . . . or the perpetrator.'

His inclusion of perpetrator hadn't just been a way to lighten the tension of that moment. Every parent worried about their kids getting into trouble, police officers probably more than most. They knew that kids from supportive families could go down the wrong path just like the ones who didn't have the same advantages.

Bill too had been the one who'd never given up on his quest to get her to go to Castlebrae. *How she had fought him on that.* Rhona smiled in silent thanks that she'd finally listened to his wise advice.

'You like the porridge pot!' Chrissy said, thinking the smile had indicated that.

Rhona didn't correct her.

Two cups of strong coffee later, Rhona made the call.

'Good morning, Dr MacLeod. How was your porridge?'

'You know about that?'

'I was given full details this morning. I'll take a bet and say you went for plain.'

'You know me too well. So, what's up?'

'Wild swimmers spotted what they thought was a human hand in a raised peat bank next to Advie Lochan, south of Glasgow. We sent someone up to take a look and they confirmed the sighting. Since buried and hidden bodies are a speciality of yours, we'd like you to excavate the site.'

'Okay. Can you send me the location?'

'A police car will lead you out there. It should be with you in ten minutes or so.'

As she rang off, Chrissy appeared. 'We're off then?'

'We are,' Rhona said. 'An excavation by Advie Lochan. South of the city.'

'Cool. I'll get organized.' Chrissy paused for a moment. 'I take it we're in the wilds up there? Do I need to take a food supply just in case?'

'Just not porridge,' Rhona said firmly.

5

They're still looking for Mary. So am I. I've been to all the places we like. The den was first. She always went there when she was happy. I imagined her sitting in her white dress, but she wasn't there.

Dad's a detective, so he's looking for her too. The police are going to every house in the street to ask questions. Nobody came out to play Kick the Can tonight. Dad wouldn't even let me go outside the garden to skip on the pavement. I had to play ball against the side of the house.

When I was going to bed Dad asked me if Mary might have run away.

I know about Mary's dad. How angry he gets if Mary, her big brother or sister don't come in when he whistles on them. There's a big belt he uses hanging up in their kitchen.

Mary never seemed to mind that, although she got the belt sometimes. The belt wouldn't have made her run away. She had been confirmed in her white dress and veil. She was saved now and had a seat reserved for her in heaven.

When I told Dad that, he didn't seem to understand about the dress. But the dress was the most important thing in Mary's life. She would never go anywhere she might dirty her dress.

6

The scene on arrival had immediately reminded Rhona of a black-and-white photograph she'd seen of Saddleworth Moor, near Manchester, when the police had been searching for the bodies of three of the children killed by Ian Brady and Myra Hindley in the mid-sixties.

Under a clear April sky, though, this Scottish moor looked benign, empty and majestic. On closer inspection, Rhona could make out dark burnt patches among the heather and mosses, indicating it was being used for driven grouse shooting. Despite the intrusion of man, this was still a perfect spot – just like Saddleworth Moor – in which to hide a body that would never be found.

Whoever had buried the body she and Chrissy were preparing to expose could never have imagined that folk would be mad enough to ever wild swim in the neighbouring dark waters of Advie Lochan, never mind in early April.

Even then, had there not been a long dry spell – had the water level not fallen, exposing the bank and allowing it to dry out – there would have been nothing to see, even for the determined and curious wild swimmer, which had been Bill's description of the young woman who'd alerted the police to her find. Despite the shock, Julie had fetched her mobile and, swimming back, had taken a number of images to back up her gruesome discovery.

Rhona had already set up the time-lapse camera, with a cover to protect it from any change in the weather. Although, according to the forecast, there was a chance that they might avoid rain for the next twenty-four hours.

Once they were ready to begin, she would set the camera to take an image every ten minutes of excavation. That sequence of shots would eventually be put together as an MP4 video, which she could use in court if required. This type of work required daylight, so that the different-coloured layers of the soil might be registered, hence no forensic tent.

En route to the locus, Rhona had called Jen Mackie, her forensic soil scientist colleague, regarding their destination and had discovered that the co-ordinates of the locus were likely to be in an area of raised bog. If true, that would affect what they might find during the excavation.

'I was involved with the Woodland Trust in 2012 survey-ing areas of raised bog across Scotland,' Jen had told her. 'Where you're heading is one of the areas we mapped. I'll email you the report. It makes for interesting reading.'

Rhona had put the call on speaker in the car, so Chrissy might listen in.

'So what does that mean exactly for the state of the remains?' Rhona had asked.

'The chemistry of raised bogs would suggest you may find more than just a skeleton. I'll be in touch when I get back from Paris,' Jen had promised. 'I'm currently being driven through the streets in an armed police convoy to give evi-dence in an enquiry.'

At this news, Chrissy's eyes had lit up.

'When can I go to Paris to give evidence?' she'd whis-pered.

'When you come to work for me,' Jen had told her with a chuckle, having obviously heard Chrissy. 'You'll send me images?'

'I will,' Rhona had promised.

At that point, Jen had wished them good luck before they'd heard the whine of a siren, and she'd rung off.

'Does she have to give her evidence in French?' Chrissy said.

'With the degree of complexity involved there'll be an interpreter, although Jen's quite fluent in French,' Rhona had told a wide-eyed Chrissy.

'I'd better get started on the Duolingo then,' Chrissy had announced with a characteristic grin.

The emailed piece from Jen on raised bogs *had* made for interesting reading, particularly in the current circumstances.

The specific acidic and oxygen-poor conditions which are present allow for the mummification of the body's soft parts such as skin, hair and stomach contents. However, many other conditions must also be fulfilled in order to prevent micro-organisms from breaking down the human body. The corpse must be sunk in water or dug into the ground and covered quickly. In addition, the deposition of the body must occur when the bog water is cold, in the winter or early spring, otherwise the process of decay can begin. Examples of raised bog bodies include the Woman from Huldremose, Grauballe Man and Tollund Man.

'Cool,' Chrissy had pronounced on reading it. 'So that's how we become famous. We unearth a five-thousand-year-old body, perfectly preserved, and have to go around the world giving lectures on our discovery.'

They'd exchanged looks at that point, signifying their mutual hope that it would in fact be a prehistoric mummy they were heading towards, rather than a more recent burial.

Had it been warm, damp summer weather, rather than a cool, dry spring, disturbing the heather cover near the designated area would have resulted in a concentrated cloud attack by the resident midges. There were still some about, many of which found their way to the areas of Rhona's face not covered by the mask. Chrissy had determinedly flapped at a few herself before heading for her bag to bring back a supply of midge repellent.

Rhona smiled her thanks as she sprayed her exposed skin.

Once the mix of grass, heather cover and associated roots were removed to expose the underlying peat, they began laying out an alphanumerical grid round the suspect area at 0.5-metre intervals.

There had been nothing definitive on the surface in the form of vegetation to suggest a recent decomposition below, although the heather had given way to grass in part. If it was indeed an ancient burial, then the ground cover would have had time to recover.

Rhona had already studied the fingers visible in the bank, just short of a metre below the surface of the peat. They belonged, in her opinion, to a human hand, either that of a small female or a child. Its time in the ground would only be determined when the excavation was complete. Once the remains were fully exposed, should they appear to be prehistoric, like the other bog bodies found in Britain and Europe, then archaeologists would be called in.

As she became absorbed in the careful removal and sifting of the layers of earth, Rhona recalled the last time she'd been involved in such an excavation. Then, they had been called to the Orkney island of Sanday where a digger, breaking up the tarred playground of a former island school, had unearthed a human skull. The site had been very sandy, much like the rest of the island, although as exposed to both the wind and the weather as the current locus.

Of course, Orkney was rich in archaeological sites, so the first thing they'd had to confirm was that they weren't digging up the bones of some Viking ancestor, a common enough occurrence and definitely the province of archaeologists.

Rhona found herself quietly wishing that what they were about to unearth might prove to be what Chrissy desired – another bog man or woman – rather than the discovery of a child's body, like the scene she'd recalled from Saddleworth Moor.

Eventually the hope she'd been nursing began to evaporate. Chrissy knew it too, but said nothing, although Rhona could read it in her eyes as she carefully extracted the last of the peaty soil to expose their first full view of a naked and mummified body.

Possibly a female, she lay on her back, a stuffed plastic bag placed under her head, seemingly to act as a cushion.

They knelt in silence for a moment, the monstrosity of what they had just unearthed overwhelming them.

'When did supermarkets start giving out plastic bags?' Chrissy said quietly.

'Sometime in the sixties, I think.'

'So we have a time frame at least,' Chrissy said.

Jen had been right about the effect of the raised bog locus. The exposed body appeared well preserved, the quality of the soil allowing for the mummification of the skin and hair – and, hopefully, the stomach contents.

'It's every parent's nightmare,' Chrissy said, and Rhona knew she was thinking about her own toddler son, wee Michael.

'We can raise the tent now,' Rhona said. 'Then you can take the soil samples to the van. Get the SCO to give you a hand. Best to give Bill a call too and tell him what we've found, while I do a closer examination.'

'You're okay to be here alone?'

In the silence that followed Chrissy's question, the memory of what had happened during the sin-eater case passed between them.

'I'll be okay,' Rhona assured her, although she wasn't at all certain that she would be.

Well, this is how I find out.

After the tent had been raised, Rhona began to take a series of her own photographs at close quarters, noting the careful laying out of the body and the cushioned head, seemingly at odds with a violent end, although there were marks on the pubic area that suggested stabbing might have played a part.

The long, dark, peat-reddened hair looked carefully arranged on either side of her face, the setting of her arms at a sixty-degree angle to her side resulting in the fingers of the left hand protruding from the dried-out bank.

Something the gravedigger hadn't anticipated, Rhona thought.

Focused as she had been on the body, she had managed for a while to blot out the strong smell of disturbed earth. Scent, she was acutely aware, lingered longest in the mind and was the most likely sense to trigger a PTSD flashback, and so must be avoided.

Despite her best efforts, the scent now rose to engulf her

and with it came the memory of soil raining down on her, to clog her throat and blind her eyes.

Focus on the victim, she told herself. *I am her witness, and that's more important than anything that's happened to me.*

Eventually her brain reacted to her command and the tidal wave began to retreat, slowly at first, but then more swiftly.

And then it was gone.

Rhona released the breath she hadn't been aware she'd been holding and set about taping the body in situ, as there was always a chance that she might recover something other than soil. Once on the mortuary slab, all this would happen again, but in the movement between here and there, something vital could be lost.

It was time to write up her notes. Climbing out of the grave, Rhona settled down with her notebook. She felt strangely calm now, knowing the emotional storm had passed. Having weathered it, she could feel more confident about working in confined locations again.

It had grown cold as the early April sun had started its descent. Having now bagged the remains for the journey to the mortuary, the locus would be covered, and they would return to it in the morning. A careful study of the soil beneath the body was as important as the material removed from above.

'Are we just securing the plastic bag and its contents?' Chrissy asked on her return.

'We'll check inside and bag the items separately,' Rhona said.

Rhona carefully opened the bag, noting how resilient the plastic had been. It was no wonder that the world was groaning under an ever-increasing accumulation of plastic in the time since the plastic bag had become a shopping essential.

The first item she extracted turned out to be a plastic tiara with a stained veil attached. Next came the remains of a white net dress and underskirt. Finally, a pair of small black pumps with a bow.

The clothing was, of course, circumstantial but it did point to their initial thought that they were likely dealing with a young female.

As each item was recorded and bagged, the air of sadness between them grew.

'That might have been the outfit I wore when I was confirmed,' Chrissy said, a catch in her throat. 'Except for the shoes. Mine were white.'

'How old were you back then?' Rhona said.

'Eleven. What are you thinking?' Chrissy added, noting Rhona's thoughtful expression.

'I was wondering what happened to her underwear.'

7

Diary entry of Karen Marshall aged 11
3 May 1975

Today was Mary's birthday. We were meant to have a party. But she hasn't come home and the police are still searching for her. When the news comes on, Dad switches off the TV.

I heard Dad tell Mum the police think Mary was abducted?? On her way back from chapel after her confirmation. Probably by a man with a car.

What man? No one round here has a car except Father Feeney.

I thought about the man at the shops, but his coat is ragged so I don't think he has a car.

Dad came up when I was in bed. He told me not to talk to strangers. Especially men in cars.

I asked about Mary. Why would a man take Mary away?

Some men are bad, Dad says.

I wanted to ask, how do I know if they're bad, but didn't.

Did I know any bad men?

And then I thought of one.

8

The narrow road that led to the red-brick Victorian prison that was HMP Barlinnie, more commonly known in Glasgow as the Bar-L, went straight through a housing estate. Perched a little higher than the rows of neat houses, it provided little to no possibility for parking unless you managed to get a space in the official car park, which was anything but large enough for the task.

Thus Professor Magnus Pirie had arrived early for his morning meeting, with the slender hope of finding a space.

And, amazingly, it seemed he was in luck.

A small van was in the process of exiting a parking bay near the gate. Drawing to one side, Magnus let him depart, before doing a swift reversal just as another car entered and assumed the vacant space might be for them.

Not for the first time, Magnus, in his psychologist role, wondered how many fights had originated outside Barlinnie over a parking space rather than inside the halls of the vast and imposing prison.

Locking the car, he made for the visitor entrance. Despite the early hour, there was already a stream of people entering or leaving through the glass facade.

This wasn't his first official visit so he knew the drill. Ignoring the reception area, Magnus crossed instead to the heavy metal door on the opposite wall and pressed the buzzer.

'Professor Magnus Pirie come to visit Alec McLaughlin.'

The buzzer sounded and Magnus pulled on the heavy door. Inside was the gathering area for those who were bound for locations not accessible to ordinary visitors – the halls behind the walls. Security was tight here, and wherever you went would involve an accompanying prison officer and a great deal of locking and unlocking of doors.

Magnus's allotted officer for today would likely be Archie Urqhuart, who he already knew from previous visits involving his current research.

After giving his name and the reason for his visit, Magnus was asked to sign in before being handed his security pass, but he still had to wait until the four folk in front, two men and two women, went through the usual scanner bag and body checks.

Entering a prison was much like trying to go through security at the airport. You were required to show photo ID and negotiate the screening process, the difference being that you weren't allowed to take any personal items into the jail and especially not your mobile phone.

Listening in on their chatting, Magnus realized the four were there to run the recovery cafe. The Recovery Community Network in Glasgow was something Magnus both knew about and supported, having been invited on occasion to talk to groups about the psychology of recovering from addiction. These four advocates were chatty and in high spirits and obviously knew most of the staff on duty.

One of them, Magnus realized, he'd met before. Tall, in her thirties, with a blonde ponytail, Magnus remembered the woman as being a recovery development officer for a group he'd visited in Raploch, Stirling.

'Pat?' he tried as he emerged from the scanner.

'Magnus,' she said in surprise. 'What are you doing in Bar-L? Not on remand, I hope?' She gave the throaty infectious laugh he remembered.

'Carrying out some research,' Magnus told her.

'Can I ask what about?'

'Education and the Sexual Offender,' Magnus admitted, with a wry smile.

Pat grinned. 'So you know they're the ones who take all the education classes?'

'You have a theory about why that is?' Magnus said.

'Interview me sometime and I'll tell you all my theories on the subject,' Pat promised.

'I may well take you up on that.'

Recovery development officers like Pat had their own experience of addiction. Pat had been quite open about hers – alcohol, with a good measure of cocaine thrown in. Her back story was as varied as any of the other women he'd met in the sessions he'd attended. What had struck him most during his visits was the mutual and safe support system the women had created for one another. This had given them the confidence to speak out and the stories of how they'd ended up in addiction were informative, if rarely pretty.

Many had involved manipulative and often violent men. Not dissimilar to the men Magnus had been interviewing for his current research. Watching Pat depart with the group's allotted prison officer, he found himself contemplating giving her a call. Barlinnie wouldn't be the only prison she'd visited, so her opinions on the uptake of education facilities could be useful.

At that point in his thoughts, Archie appeared.

'Hey, Prof, you ready for the fray?'

'Morning, Archie. I am.'

'So it's Old Alec this time?'

When Magnus nodded, Archie said in a serious voice, 'Just remember, Old Alec's a highly intelligent and skilled liar. That's how he managed to rape and sexually abuse weans for years before he was caught.'

Archie wasn't normally as blunt as that about his charges, so Magnus decided to take his warning seriously.

'Thanks for the reminder,' he said.

'One other thing. He's at the end of his sentence. Out in a couple of days. As a criminal profiler, you know all about modus operandi and the fantasy worlds men like Alec create for themselves.' Archie looked Magnus in the eye. 'In my opinion, McLaughlin won't change his sexual habits, despite his age or all the qualifications he's managed to acquire while inside.'

Passing the educational unit, Magnus saw the long line of men waiting to go in for the morning sessions, the majority of them wearing the red fleeces indicating they were convicted prisoners. The blue signified those on remand.

'I've got a room for you in another block. As you can see, the Ed unit's pretty full this morning.'

A few minutes later, Archie ushered Magnus into a small and sparsely furnished room where he found an elderly man waiting for him.

Magnus had chosen a selection of men to interview based on the length of their sentences and the educational courses they'd picked during their incarceration. Alec McLaughlin was one of the long-stay prisoners who'd worked his way through three Highers and on to degree level. Interestingly, the degree he had been taking through the Open University was in Magnus's chosen area of psychology.

The white-haired man sporting a small, neatly trimmed beard was, according to his details, approaching sixty-one. The red cheeks, bulging waistline and welcoming smile only added to the image of a jolly Santa Claus, which was further enhanced by the red fleece.

As Magnus entered, his interviewee rose with some difficulty and, leaning on the walking stick in his right hand, extended his left in welcome.

'Professor Pirie. Alec McLaughlin. I'm delighted to meet you. I am so enjoying reading your work on psychopathic personalities, especially your study of the Reborn dollmaker, Jeff Coulter.'

When Magnus didn't immediately respond, he continued, 'I wondered if you truly ever came to a decision on whether Coulter was a psychopathic personality, pretending to be ill. Or was he in fact in remission due to the drugs administered in hospital for a debilitating mental illness?'

It was a valid question, although not one Magnus particularly wanted to respond to. His whole research around Coulter had been to try and establish either a psychotic illness, treatable in part by medication, or an untreatable psychopathic personality.

Jeff Coulter had been imprisoned for killing his baby son. Locked up in Carstairs and treated with drugs, he had re-invented himself as the Reborn maker, fashioning realistic baby dolls modelled on actual photographs of dead infants for their grieving parents. His work and apparent rehabilitation had made him something of a cult figure. Magnus remembered Coulter's Reborn workshop, the wall festooned with photographs of the dolls he had made, pictured with their loving and grateful parents.

It was a case that haunted Magnus to this day.

'My conclusions are in the research paper, so I presume you know them already. Besides, I'm not here to discuss Jeff Coulter, but to talk to you about your studies.'

Alec sat back at this point and for a moment Magnus caught a disgruntled look, which was quickly masked.

'So,' Magnus began, 'can you give me a potted history of your involvement with the educational unit here at Barlinnie?'

Alec did just that, succinctly and with occasional self-deprecating humour. He'd had very little formal education as a child, he told Magnus. Abandoned by his mother, he'd been put in a Catholic orphanage from the age of two to five.

'Then my bitch of an aunt took me in. As for her husband . . . They had no kids of their own, so they could concentrate all their love on me,' he said in a tone that suggested the experience had been anything but pleasant.

He'd skipped school a lot and suspected his various teachers were rather glad about that.

'They said I was disruptive. I wonder why?' He paused at that point as though he anticipated an interruption. When that didn't happen, he continued.

'I was in and out of short-term sentences. Back then, there wasn't any desire to educate inmates in Her Majesty's prisons. It wasn't until I had a substantial sentence that that became a possibility. I started with the O-level equivalents in English and Maths and went on from there.'

He paused and examined Magnus. 'Can I ask you a question, Professor Pirie?'

Magnus nodded. 'Certainly.'

'Why are you so interested in sexual offenders and their thirst for knowledge?'

Magnus wasn't sure he had a straight answer to that, so

instead he said, 'May I turn the question round and ask why the more intelligent prisoners tend to be in here for sexual offences?'

Alec gave a little snort of derision.

'In my childhood, so-called sexual offences, just like domestic violence, weren't regarded as crimes. According to the Bible, women were created for the pleasure of men, and children and wives were the property of their husbands. To do with as they wished.' He smiled. 'Maybe the sexual offenders in here just haven't caught up with the changing nature of society.'

'But that doesn't explain why, in general, they are so keen on education,' Magnus tried.

'Most men in here are Neanderthal in nature and have one set of thoughts and actions they repeat *ad infinitum*. Also, they don't favour the educational unit, but in some misguided sense of moral superiority, they dislike those who do.'

They spoke for another ten minutes or so about Alec's choice of psychology at degree level. After which Magnus was left with the idea that Alec was viewing his subject specialization as a training ground in mind manipulation, rather than as a way of understanding human behaviour.

By then Archie had reappeared.

'Time's up, guys.'

At this, Old Alec rose more swiftly and easily than at the beginning of their meeting, leading Magnus to think that his earlier difficulty had been merely for show.

'So glad to speak with you, Professor Pirie,' he said, as though he were the interviewer and Magnus the inter- viewee. 'Next time let's discuss that Catholic orphanage and what was regarded as right and wrong in there.'

Archie ushered Magnus out, leaving Alec with his own guard.

'So,' Archie said as they crossed the open space between the halls, 'what did you think of Old Alec as a fellow psychologist?'

'He's as intelligent and manipulative as you led me to believe,' Magnus told him.

'Don't know if you're into true crime podcasts and documentaries, Professor. But I watched an American documentary where a paedophile priest in charge of a girls' school gets himself a certificate in psychology which he then uses to manipulate the girls even more than he did with religion. I can't help but think Old Alec, who the guys in here call Secret Santa, has something similar in mind when he gets out of here.'

'He'll be on the sex offenders list and monitored though, won't he?' Magnus said.

'I've a feeling he's already working out a way around that,' Archie said. 'And we're probably helping him.'

They walked on in silence across the now-deserted yards to the high wall and exit door. The clunk of the lock just served to remind Magnus of the imminent departure of Old Alec, released back into the world again. A world he hadn't been in for close on fifteen years.

As Archie said goodbye before ushering Magnus through, he gave him his final thoughts on the matter.

'You know this idea that men who abuse children do it because they were abused themselves? Well, just imagine if all the girls and women who've ever been abused decided to do the same? Where would we all be then, Professor?'

9

Karen checked her watch for the umpteenth time. Was she going or wasn't she? Her indecision had grown with each passing moment. She'd risen at the usual time, determined to go, despite having had so little sleep.

In fact, her brain had been turning like a concrete mixer all night, churning memories and thoughts together much like it had done after Jack's death. The problem was, occasionally there was a moment when she thought that what she was remembering might be the truth.

It was as though the imagined sighting of the crow in her sitting room, followed by the dead shadow of Toby, had opened a gate to the past. Just a little, but enough to tell her that there was more to come.

And that was what Karen was afraid of.

The kettle having boiled, she made herself a mug of tea and switched on the radio. It had been her lifeline since Jack died. It provided voices to listen to rather than focusing on her own traumatized thoughts. If it hadn't been for the radio, her drinking would have been even worse than it had been. And that was bad enough.

She'd started drinking as Jack's health had deteriorated. It had been the way she got through the days and the nights. Jack, in his dementia, had swiftly forgotten who she was. Every attempted conversation had left Karen with the feeling that they had never met. That she was as much a stranger to their life together as he undoubtedly was.

That maybe she wasn't even real.

But occasionally, just occasionally, the light in his eyes would shine and he would see her again and say her name. *My Karen*. Those moments were precious but grew few and far between.

Alcohol had blurred the horror of her world enough for her to deal with it. Plus she kept telling herself that there was a way out for her. When Jack went, she could go too. But, in the interim, she had to stay alive to look after Jack. And to do that she needed to drink. After he went from her, she would be free to choose her own end.

She'd carried on, though, after Jack died, drinking even more, putting off her decision on what would happen next. The days and nights met one another in an endless cycle until, one morning, she made up her mind to stop. It had happened after a particularly powerful dream featuring Jack. Not the frightened Jack who didn't recognize her, but the real Jack. Her Jack.

'What are we going to do about you?' he'd said. 'Well, first things first. You're not a drinker, Karen. Never have been. Tomorrow you're going back to being you.'

So she'd tried, because Jack told her to.

The memory of that dream and Jack's words had taken her as far as the recovery cafe. The women she'd met there had done the rest.

With her mind made up to go to today's gathering, Karen carried her mug to the sink to rinse it. As she did so, the news bulletin came on the radio. Karen paused in her reach to switch it off, knowing the announcer was saying something she had to hear.

And there it was.

A child's body had been unearthed on moorland south of Glasgow. It was thought that it may have been buried there for up to fifty years.

Fifty years. A lifetime.

As her thoughts swung back in time, Karen knew. This was what yesterday had all been about. The rush of memories, both good and terrifyingly bad. The knowing that something was about to happen. The certainty, by the images alone, that it had something to do with Mary.

And here it was.

As the mug slipped from her hand, Karen watched the remaining tea fan out like blood and thought of Mary's disappearance, and her own part in it.

10

McNab emerged after his workout, not convinced that a gym membership was doing anything for his love life or his career.

No time for early-morning sex any more *and* he was already knackered by the time he got to work.

It was his colleague DS Janice Clark's remark that he'd put on a few pounds recently that had forced him down this road. McNab liked to blame his current contented love life for his lapse into the fat bastard model of himself. Plus he hadn't run after, or run away from, some mad Glasgow headbanger for a while, which could mean he was out of condition . . . but only just.

So he'd taken up his SPRA membership and joined a gym as close to the police station as possible. When he'd told Ellie of his decision, he'd been shocked to note the smile of satisfaction on her face. Which meant she already thought he was a fat bastard, or she no longer looked forward to their morning couplings.

When McNab had pointed out he would have to rise pretty early to fit in the gym before work, thus depriving Ellie of his company, she'd merely laughed.

'Going to the gym will give you more energy,' had been her reply. Which sounded okay in principle, although the only result for McNab so far was a desire for more sleep and pains in muscles he'd forgotten he possessed.

Also, why did Ellie think he required more energy?

There were compensations, however. From his experience of being in public spaces, he was wont to spend far too much time scanning for faces he recognized from the Glasgow criminal underworld, usually identifying at least one. Happily, he was yet to spot anyone in that category during his early-morning workouts, although there were some very attractive ladies also pumping iron.

McNab hadn't mentioned the eye candy to Ellie because, let's face it, he had no intention of following up on any of it. Still, their presence did, if he was honest, urge him to work harder when he was there.

The after-workout swim followed by a hot shower was then enhanced by two double espressos from the machine in the cafe, and he was ready for the day. Hence he'd arrived bright and sparkly at the station this morning, which was causing the desk sergeant to crease his brows in consternation.

'I'm not sure I like this version of you,' he said.

'You can't please everyone all of the time,' was McNab's retort. 'What's happening?'

The sergeant continued to scan McNab as though he were a fake version of himself.

'A lot. Dr MacLeod unearthed a body on moorland south of Glasgow.'

Whatever he'd expected in today's news, it hadn't been that.

'Is it anyone we're looking for?' McNab said, immediately thinking of the current status of organized crime in the city.

'Strategy meeting on it shortly. Best go up there and find out.'

McNab took a detour past his desk to check if his partner, DS Clark, was about. Janice was seated in front of her computer, staring at something she obviously found interesting.

McNab took a look over her shoulder to discover it was an article about bog bodies with a gruesome photograph of a twisted, blackened corpse lying in a grave.

'You've heard, then,' she said, catching sight of McNab and sitting back to give him a better view.

'If it's one as old as that,' McNab said, 'then we're not involved. No one left alive to jail for it.'

Janice gave him one of her withering looks, of which there were a multitude to choose from.

'Word is there was a plastic bag under the head. So a little nearer our time,' she told him.

'Mmmm. A time-frame clue. No longer available once we ban all plastic bags in this brave new green world.'

By the look on Janice's face, his attempt at humour wasn't welcome in the circumstances, which might suggest she already knew more about this than he did, a thought McNab wasn't comfortable with.

'Let's go,' he said.

The room was already busy, most of the assembled audience studying the visuals of the excavation site. McNab was a little taken aback by the images of the body. Although it was a similar colour to the one on Janice's screen, that was, to his mind, where the similarity ended.

The child-size body wasn't twisted into a weird shape like the bog man, but had been laid out on its back, with the head placed on what had to be a makeshift plastic bag pillow. A pillow that was revealed in other images to have contained clothes.

And if the clothing belonged to the victim, the body was that of a young girl. Suddenly McNab's earlier jokes regarding bog bodies seemed totally inappropriate.

The impact of the photographs on the officers in the room

was palpable. Any abduction of a child was horrific. The discovery of their remains even more so.

The boss appeared at that point to give them an update. On DI Wilson's entry the babble of voices fell silent.

'As you're no doubt aware, we received a report yesterday from Julie Black, a wild swimmer who, with her partner Dougal Thompson, discovered what they thought was a human hand protruding from an exposed peat bank at Advie Lochan, south of Glasgow. An officer confirmed the sighting and Dr MacLeod began an excavation of the site, the result of which is shown here.'

He continued, 'The remains are mummified due to the chemistry of the location. Raised bogs are fairly rare now in Scotland. Bog bodies, as you probably know, have been found across Europe and identified as being thousands of years old. However, not in this case.

'Plastic bags began being issued in supermarkets in 1965, which provides us with a much more recent time frame. The clothing in the bag included what looks like a white confirmation dress, tiara with veil and black shoes, suggesting the child, probably a girl but yet to be confirmed, may have been abducted sometime close to when she had taken her confirmation, which gives us another lead. However, there is no firm evidence at the moment that these are in fact the victim's clothes.

'From 1965 onwards a number of children have disappeared across the UK. Without another explanation for their disappearance, we must assume the probability that they were abducted and killed.

'There are a few Scottish ones among these, but we can't say for definite that this child wasn't taken from elsewhere in the UK and brought north of the border for burial.

'The post-mortem will hopefully provide us with more, and Dr MacLeod is back on site at the moment so there may be further forensic detail to follow. I want the identification of this child to be a top priority. So let's get on with it.'

The boss's look fastened on McNab and Janice at this point, indicating he wanted to speak to them in his office.

Once in and the door closed, he said, 'I'd like you two to visit Jimmy McCreadie, who was a DI around the time we're looking at and dealt with a missing child enquiry. I spoke to him on the phone earlier and he's happy to talk to you. Unfortunately, a number of the investigation files on missing persons around then were lost or destroyed, so anything he can tell you may prove invaluable.'

McNab tried to do a mental calculation on the age of the old bloke they were about to visit.

As though reading his mind, the boss said, 'Jimmy was the youngest DI on the force, but he managed to annoy the big brass by doing his own thing. He succeeded in getting himself demoted, took umbrage at that, departed the police and joined Special Forces instead. Despite all that he became a bit of a legend for the cases he broke open back in the day.'

The boss's expression directed at McNab said even more than the words, alluding, as he suspected they did, to his own demotion from DI to DS in the wake of the Stonewarrior case. He, however, hadn't left the force, although he'd contemplated it at the time. If DI Wilson hadn't been his boss, he likely would have.

'Did he say anything on the phone we should know about?' McNab said.

'He asked if the body was that of a girl wearing a confirmation dress.'

42

11

McNab had reluctantly agreed that Janice should be the driver on their jaunt to see former DI Jimmy McCreadie. It wasn't that his partner was a bad driver, although she was a mite too cautious for McNab's liking. It was just that he preferred being the one in charge of the wheel.

He remembered how, before he'd got his own Harley, Ellie, his current biker girlfriend, had suggested a pilgrimage to Netherton Cottage, ancestral home of the Harley-Davidson brothers. Horrified that he wouldn't be the one in the driver's seat, McNab had almost turned her down. Which, he recalled, would have probably meant the end of their relationship.

Luckily realizing this at the time, he'd consoled himself with the idea of hugging Ellie for the couple of hours required to head up the A90 to their destination. It was, McNab recalled, one of the best decisions he'd ever made.

However, today's trip definitely wasn't in that category, nor was there any consolation prize, except perhaps to avoid getting grief from DS Clark. So rather than dwell on being a reluctant passenger during the said journey, McNab decided to see if Wikipedia had heard of Jimmy McCreadie, and was surprised to find that it had.

The entry opened with McCreadie's time as a police

officer, followed by his service with Special Forces, after which it was all about his current career as the crime thriller writer known as J. D. Smart.

Something the boss had definitely not mentioned.

'I know that name,' Janice said, when McNab told her. 'I've read his books. They're good.'

'You read crime novels?' McNab responded, open-mouthed.

Janice nodded, obviously unperturbed by his reaction.

DS Clark often surprised him, despite the length of time they'd worked together, but this was something else entirely. McNab wanted to ask why the fuck a police officer would do such a thing.

'What?' Janice said, noting his expression.

'I thought you would have gone more for fact than fiction, that's all,' McNab lied.

'Fiction is the lie through which we tell the truth,' Janice informed him.

'Who the fuck said that?' McNab demanded.

'Albert Camus.'

Having heard the name but with no idea to its significance, McNab decided to steer the conversation in a different direction.

'Well, if McCreadie's so good at making stuff up, how can we be sure that what he tells us isn't fiction?'

'You once told me, despite Professor Pirie's research on the subject, that a good detective can always spot a lie.' Janice shot him a glance that reminded McNab of all the times he'd been lax with the truth himself.

At that point he decided to shut up and observe the passing countryside instead.

Having negotiated their departure from Glasgow, they were now heading north-east. Apparently, the wayward cop-turned-soldier-turned-writer hadn't retired to his home city of Glasgow after leaving Special Forces.

McNab wondered why. Perhaps McCreadie, aka J. D. Smart, hadn't wanted to bump into old enemies, on either side of the law. That was something McNab *could* understand. Or maybe it was easier to reinvent himself as a novelist elsewhere.

So he'd taken up residence a little further north. According to the Google map, his current abode was a substantial stone villa on the outskirts of Stirling, just below Castle Hill, with a view over an area of parkland known as King's Knot.

'The writing game must be paying off,' McNab said as they eventually drew up outside.

'We're not interested in what he does now.' Janice pulled on the brake. 'Just what he knows about our case,' she reminded him in her usual forthright fashion.

Entering through a wrought-iron gate, the manicured lawn and well-tended flower beds indicated that J. D. Smart was either a keen gardener or else had help in that department.

Which certainly seemed to be the case on the housekeeping front.

Obviously expected, they were shown by a woman McNab presumed was the housekeeper to a conservatory at the rear of the building, which apparently was also the all-important writing room.

Smart McCreadie, as McNab had already fashioned the former detective, rose to greet them from his seat in front of a keyboard and three large screens.

'DS Clark and DS McNab, I presume?'

They all shook hands, McNab registering the slight tremor in McCreadie's grip.

'Dodgy tendons,' he explained. 'Viking DNA, I'm reliably

informed, although how they continued to wield a sword once the tendon shortened I have no idea. My eyesight's going too, hence the big screens.'

'Why three of them?' McNab asked.

'I have three different characters' viewpoints on the go. I switch from one to another as the plot develops. Plus I need to remember what each player knows about the others at any given time.'

'So, just like a real crime, only with fewer players?' McNab said, trying to keep sarcasm out of his voice.

By McCreadie's response, his attempt was unsuccessful.

'Ah, I see DS McNab is not a fan of the genre. And what about you, DS Clark?' McCreadie said.

'I enjoy your books,' Janice told him. 'Along with a few other crime authors.'

'Dare I ask who my rivals are?'

'You can, but I won't divulge the names,' Janice said with a conspiratorial smile (or at least McNab thought that's what it was).

'Not giving anything away. I like that,' Smart McCreadie said with a glance at McNab.

He gestured to a nearby sofa and took a seat himself on a big leather reclining armchair. The spring sun was hitting the glass and there was a scent of something in the air. McNab took it to come from the climber with white flowers that stretched across part of the glass roof above them.

'Winter jasmine,' McCreadie offered, as though reading McNab's mind, 'which flowers here in spring. If it gets too bright, I'll close some blinds. I like the light. If I was an artist, I'd paint in here.'

Once settled, a tray arrived via the housekeeper to be placed on a table between them.

After a quick, 'Thank you, Lucy,' McCreadie said, 'I can offer tea or coffee. If you'd rather a soft drink, I have some in the little fridge over there.'

Both McNab and Janice opted for coffee.

'You like yours strong, DS McNab,' McCreadie said with confidence. 'I sense another caffeine addict. As for DS Clark, there's hot water in the jug if you need to dilute it a bit. Can I ask you to pour? My tendons don't allow me to lift a heavy pot.'

Janice did the honours and McNab took a long swallow of the strong and delicious coffee.

'Better, I imagine, than what gets served up at some vending machine at the station?' McCreadie suggested. 'In my day, it was big pots of stewed tea that kept us going, especially on all-nighters.' He paused there as though fondly recalling his former life for a moment.

He's trying to get us on side, McNab thought. *And it's working as far as Janice is concerned.*

'Okay,' McCreadie was saying. 'Fire away.'

'When you spoke to DI Wilson you asked if we'd found a wee girl in a confirmation dress. Why?' Janice began.

McCreadie sat back in the leather armchair. 'Because it's the one that haunts me the most. The one I gave up my job over.'

A story McCreadie, no doubt, was keen to recount. McNab didn't ask him to elaborate, but with a glance at Janice, proceeded as planned.

'No autopsy report to confirm as yet, but the well-preserved body Dr MacLeod unearthed is thought to be that of a girl, aged somewhere between ten and fourteen, both sex and age still to be forensically confirmed.'

'Is that Dr Rhona MacLeod, the forensic scientist involved in the sin-eater case?' McCreadie immediately asked.

McNab nodded, made uneasy by the sudden and unexpected detour.

'I followed that case closely,' McCreadie went on. 'The accessibility of forensic science to the general public, and of course by extension to the criminal world, is a concern of mine.'

McNab wondered if this sudden declaration was for his benefit. If McCreadie had done his homework like the detective he'd been and perhaps still was, then, McNab realized, he would likely know two key things about him: that he'd been demoted (like McCreadie) for going his own way in the Stonewarrior case; and that he believed making forensic knowledge easily accessible was putting the police force at both a disadvantage and, in Rhona's case, in danger.

Unwilling to respond in a way that indicated his own feelings on the matter, McNab carried on as before.

'The body was unclothed but there was clothing in there with her,' he said, making no mention of the plastic bag.

'A white dress and a veil?'

When McNab didn't respond, McCreadie said, 'A wee girl called Mary McIntyre disappeared after her confirmation on May the first in East Kilbride, 1975. Her father reported her missing when she didn't appear back at the primary school with the rest of the big group of pupils going for confirmation that day.'

He fell silent for a moment and from his expression he wasn't having happy memories.

'We put out a big search, but there were no sightings of her and we never found a body.'

'Any suspects?'

McCreadie gave a sharp laugh. 'From memory, quite a

few, including her father, who had a fierce temper and liked to use a leather belt on his kids sometimes. There was a teenage boy who lived in the same street. An altar boy at the church. Even, for me at least, the family priest, Father Joseph Feeney. Didn't like the man. There were more but they're the ones I remember.'

'And you never settled on one in particular?'

McCreadie looked as though he might say something, then shook his head.

'Was she picked up in a car?' McNab went on.

'Well, if she *is* your bog body, someone transported her to the moor from the south of East Kilbride, but at the time there were no reported sightings of a suspicious vehicle in the vicinity. In fact, there weren't many vehicles on the road back then.'

He continued, 'It was a new council estate built on open land. Vehicles around the place were mostly ice-cream vans, the milkman, coal lorry, et cetera.'

'How far did the search extend?'

'For miles around. There were no sightings after the children went into the chapel to be confirmed.'

'Was the girl actually confirmed?'

'The priest, Father Feeney, said he thought so, but there were eighty kids that day, two classes' worth from the nearby primary school. Hard to imagine quite as many these days, either in a class or in the chapel.'

It was a bit before his time, but there were similarities with McNab's own childhood. He suddenly recalled his march to the chapel with his schoolmates, all wearing wee jackets and smart trousers. God knows where his mother had got his outfit. Probably borrowed it from someone, because he'd never seen it again. Thank God.

McCreadie went on, 'There should be records and what little evidence we collected, if it wasn't thrown out over the years. Oh, and I have something that might be of use.'

'What?' McNab said, his ears pricking up at this.

'I liked to make my own notes in detail. I still have my personal notebooks about the case. They're useful when I'm thinking up plots and characters.'

McNab suddenly imagined himself appearing as a character in a subsequent J. D. Smart thriller, and was not enamoured by the idea.

McCreadie had risen, somewhat stiffly, from the chair. It was at this point McNab wondered how old McCreadie must be.

'I'm seventy next week,' he said, seemingly reading McNab's mind yet again.

He retrieved a cardboard storage box from below his desk and brought it to the coffee table. 'I was the youngest DI in the force back then, although I didn't last long in the job.' He gave McNab a swift glance, as though they might share that in common, then placed the box in front of him. 'Take a look in here.'

McNab lifted the lid. Inside was a collection of standard black covered notebooks.

'I'd like these returned, of course,' McCreadie said. 'There could be inspiration in that lot.'

The housekeeper appeared again at that precise moment, causing McNab to think the timing had been pre-arranged to let them know the show was over.

'Apologies,' McCreadie said with a half-smile. 'I have a deadline looming. Publishers, eh? Worse than my bosses of yore,' he added with a short laugh.

McNab wasn't convinced they'd heard everything Smart

McCreadie had to tell them. However, like any good thriller writer, he would likely choose to hold on to his secrets for as long as possible.

When they reached the door, as though on cue, McCreadie suddenly recalled something else as a parting gift.

'Mary McIntyre had a pal called Karen Marshall who lived two doors down from her. The kid was a mess when her pal disappeared. Could hardly speak at all. Her dad was a detective constable himself. I heard he died maybe ten years after Mary's disappearance. Karen might still be around, with luck. I always thought the wee lassie knew more than she said, but back then kids weren't believed in principle. They were seen as unreliable witnesses. You'll find my interviews with her in there.'

And with that, their chapter in the tale he was weaving ended, and they were dismissed.

12

When she'd been drinking heavily, the car, Jack's car, had remained in the garage. When still caring for him, she hadn't needed the car, because she never left the house. Ever. Even to buy food.

Karen wondered now whether the nice man who'd brought the shopping she'd ordered online had spotted just how many bottles of wine she was consuming. If he had, it was never mentioned, not even in a joking fashion.

He always asked after Jack though. Told me his mum had gone the same way.

It was the dead Jack who had pointed out, in one of their many silent conversations, that now she was sober, she might drive the car again.

It was after she'd first seen the advert in the local paper about the women's recovery cafe, and was wrestling with herself as to whether she should go. As usual, she could find plenty of reasons not to, including working out how she might actually get there.

As she'd mumped on about buses, Jack had silently countermanded her excuses by telling her to start driving again. And he'd been right, both about driving and about going to the recovery cafe meetings, Karen acknowledged, as she turned left onto the Raploch Road, with the Stirling Castle rock rising steeply on her right-hand side.

The car had become a lifeline to a world outside the self-made prison she'd shared for four long years with a man who was no longer her husband.

Raploch Community Campus sparkled in the midday sunshine, although looking north clouds were gathering over the Ochil Hills. Passing the community centre, Karen turned left and parked outside the church.

Having got here, her doubts now returned in earnest, despite all her attempts at positive thoughts. She would be unable to disguise her current state of mind from the other women. That was certain. Someone would spot that something was wrong, probably Marge.

The point of coming to the cafe was to be honest with herself and with the other women. Could she still do that?

Well, she was about to find out.

The feeling when Karen did step over the threshold was one of relief. Just getting here at all after the shock of the news bulletin was, she told herself, a success in itself.

'Is that you, Karen?' Marge's booming voice came from their meeting room. 'Tea's made and Joyce has brought home baking.'

All six faces turned to greet her with a smile, springing tears in Karen's eyes.

'Hey,' Marge said, quickly rising and coming over to her. 'What's happened, Karen?'

And so she told them. Not everything, of course, most of which she couldn't say out loud – questioning, as she was, her own sanity.

'And you think the wee girl they found is your pal?' Joyce asked quietly, when Karen had finished explaining about the news item.

She nodded. 'I'd been thinking about her a lot recently.

And I read some of my diary entries about when she disappeared. It was as though . . .' She halted there, not sure about saying she'd felt Mary reaching out to her in some fashion. 'Anyway, I switched on the radio and suddenly there it was.'

'I heard it too,' Shona said. 'It was horrible. All those years, and her family never knew what had happened to their wee girl.'

'Have you talked to the police?' Marge, always the sensible one, asked. 'If it turns out to be your pal, they'll want to talk to you about what you remember from back then.'

Which was exactly what Karen was afraid of.

'I can't go back to all that,' she said. 'Just reading a bit of the diary . . .' She stumbled to a halt.

'The police have trauma counsellors,' Marge said, patting her arm. 'And one of us would go with you, if you wanted us to.'

'I'll wait and see,' Karen declared. 'If it's not Mary, then I don't need to go to the police.'

She was prevaricating. She knew that, but the memories that were bubbling up both tortured and horrified her.

Marge was studying Karen, her face showing her concern.

'You're remembering stuff you wanted to forget?'

The circle of concerned faces confirmed that everyone in that room had something awful they wanted to forget. Which was why they'd all ended up here.

Karen nodded. 'And I don't know if what I remember is true or if my mind's going, just like Jack's.'

There. She'd said it.

The silence that followed her announcement almost convinced Karen that she was right, until Marge said with conviction, 'You're talking rubbish, my girl. You're not losing your mind, but if you don't deal with what's going on, you just might.'

What Marge said was true. Karen knew that, and Jack's silent voice in her head confirmed it.

'What if I do know what happened to Mary? There were things I didn't realize back then because I was just a wee girl and I didn't understand.'

'You didn't understand what?' Marge said.

How to tell the bad men from the good.

13

'That's it,' Chrissy confirmed as she handed Rhona the last bag of soil from the grave. 'Now we have to sift through that little lot.'

The layer of soil below the victim, just like that which had covered the victim, would be examined in detail in the lab, along with the clothing and the plastic bag. They also had a full recording of the excavation to pore over, including details of the tool marks from the sides of the grave.

As Chrissy made a move to climb out, Rhona asked her to wait, because she'd just spotted something else.

'Where?' Chrissy said.

'There.' Rhona pointed at the side nearest the lochan. It was most likely the end of an exposed root, of which there had been many already, but they should check just in case.

Chrissy turned and crouched for a better look.

After a moment's study, she said, 'Can you hand me down the tweezers?'

Rhona's view was obscured as Chrissy worked to extract whatever it was from the side wall of the grave.

'Well, well, well!' Chrissy said as she examined the small object caught in the forensic tweezers.

'What is it?' Rhona demanded.

'See for yourself, boss.' Chrissy dropped the object in an evidence bag and passed it up.

Rhona glanced inside, and then she too broke into a grin. She'd known by Chrissy's expression that it had to be good. But it was better than good.

'Well spotted,' Chrissy said, extending a hand for help in getting out. 'Assuming it was discarded by whoever dug the grave, we might have a lead on the killer.'

Whoever had shovelled the soil over the child's body had smoked a cigarette during the burial and tossed the end into the grave. Someone who, fifty or so years ago, had no fear of leaving behind such evidence of their presence, because DNA fingerprinting hadn't come into existence until 1986.

As Rhona and Chrissy emerged from the tent, they discovered the sky had darkened considerably while they'd been working.

'Forecast was for heavy rain later today,' Chrissy said, glancing at the sky. 'It looks like it's early.'

'Let's get the remaining soil bags to the van before we get caught in it,' Rhona said.

Spotting them beginning their trek to the vehicle, the crime scene manager came to assist.

'I was on my way to warn you, Dr McLeod, that the heavens were about to open.' DS Strachan gave a nod to the swiftly encroaching rain clouds, which appeared to be circling them. 'Are you all finished here?'

'We just need to take these soil bags and our gear to the vehicle, then we're off,' Rhona told him.

There was little doubt from the CSM's expression he was pleased about that, because it might mean he didn't have to spend another night out on the moors.

As they passed the lochan on their final trip, raindrops were already beginning to puncture its flat brown surface.

Jumping into the van just in time, they watched as the sky opened and deposited what it had held back for the past three weeks. Even now, seeing how swiftly the small stream that fed the lochan appeared, they knew how quickly its water level would rise.

'The peat bank will be submerged again soon,' Chrissy said as the windscreen wipers tried to throw the rain off as swiftly as it fell. 'It's weird. It's almost as though we were meant to find her. And we were given just enough time to do that.'

Rhona had the same feeling herself. 'Seamus Heaney wrote a poem . . .' she began.

'"Bog Queen",' Chrissy said. 'I studied it for Higher English.

'I lay waiting
between turf-face and demesne wall,
between heathery levels
and glass-toothed stone.'

The drumming on the roof seemed to grow louder, drowning their thoughts and Chrissy's quietly spoken words. On a nearby rocky outcrop, two crows who'd watched them load the van now rose cawing into the air.

Rhona and Chrissy waited in silence for the downpour to lessen, before Rhona started up the engine and began to tackle the now-muddy track to the main road.

'Can we drop the evidence at the lab, then go for a drink?' Chrissy suggested. 'I think we deserve one.'

Rhona had it in mind to head back to the flat and go over the photographs and her notes from today.

Chrissy, reading her like a book, said, 'No way. Remember what they said at Castlebrae? You must leave time for yourself.'

Rhona thought of Skye and the time she'd spent walking in the hills and on the beaches, and how good that had been for her.

'Okay,' she relented. 'I'll come out tonight and take some time off tomorrow.'

As they crossed the moor, heading back to Glasgow, Rhona's mobile rang.

'It's McNab,' Chrissy said, reading the screen. 'Whatever he's after, it's not changing our plans,' she added in a determined fashion, before switching the call to speaker.

'Rhona?'

'We're both here,' Chrissy informed him. 'Rhona's driving.'

'You're finished at the locus then?'

'We're on our way back to the lab with the soil from beneath the body,' Rhona said.

'Anything further I should know?'

Chrissy told him about finding the cigarette butt.

'That could be useful,' McNab agreed. 'Also, we may have a lead on the identity of the victim from a former detective who worked a missing child case in our time frame.'

'Who's that?' Chrissy asked.

'Former DI Jimmy McCreadie thinks it might be eleven-year-old Mary McIntyre, who disappeared from her confirmation ceremony, East Kilbride, May first, 1975.'

Chrissy and Rhona exchanged looks.

'That would account for the confirmation outfit buried with her,' Chrissy said. 'We're dropping off the rest of the evidence bags at the lab, then heading to the jazz club. You could meet us there and fill us in on DI McCreadie.'

'Aka J. D. Smart, crime thriller writer,' McNab said, rather sarcastically.

Chrissy gave Rhona a wide-eyed look. 'You're kidding me?'

'I don't kid about things like that.'

'Cool.' Chrissy nodded her appreciation.

'You've heard of him?' McNab said suspiciously.

'You mean you haven't?' Chrissy sounded shocked.

Rhona guessed that her forensic assistant was taking the mickey. Now Chrissy's wicked grin told her she was right.

'I'll maybe see you at the club,' McNab said. 'If not, I'll see you at the PM.'

Chrissy grinned at Rhona as McNab rang off. 'He's so easy to wind up.'

'And you do it so well.'

Having made swift work labelling and storing the evidence, Rhona had a quick shower and found something in her locker to wear. Chrissy was ready before her and, as usual, outdid Rhona on the outfit front.

Chrissy had also donned make-up, which suggested that her assistant's desire to go to the jazz club held more meaning than Rhona had anticipated.

'Mum's staying over with wee Michael tonight,' Chrissy told her as they headed out. 'So it's my night off.'

'Mmmm,' Rhona said. 'And you certainly look the part. Have you got a date?'

'Not exactly.'

'Someone at the jazz club I should know about?'

Chrissy smiled sweetly but said nothing.

Ashton Lane was busy despite the puddles on the cobbles from the earlier downpour. After all, Glaswegians were used to rain in all its forms since the Scottish weather could have four seasons in an hour, never mind a day.

'Sean's on tonight,' Chrissy said.

'You seem to know more about Sean's schedule than I do,' Rhona said wryly.

'It's open mic night,' Chrissy informed her. 'Sean encourages young musicians up on stage and accompanies them. Don't you two ever talk?'

'When we do meet up, we don't discuss work,' Rhona told her.

'Mmmm.' Chrissy raised an eyebrow. 'So things are good between you two?'

Rhona wanted to say 'for the moment' but that might have sounded mean, so she just nodded.

She and Sean Maguire, the Irish part-owner of the jazz club, had been in an on–off relationship for some considerable time. During the sin-eater case, things had got pretty fraught between them, which had more to do with her than Sean. Despite all of that, he'd welcomed her back from Skye and supported her in her recovery.

Chrissy was reading her expression. 'Sean's a keeper. I've always said that.'

Yes, but am I? Rhona left those words unspoken.

The bar was already busy with the after-work crowd. The open mic session had yet to begin, although the stage was obviously being set up for it.

Chrissy was scanning both those on stage and the audience, but seemed disappointed by the result.

'You're here to see one of the performers?' Rhona said.

'Maybe,' Chrissy admitted coyly.

They took up their usual place at the bar, where there was no sign of McNab, nor was he the first of their colleagues to arrive. It had been a long time since Rhona had seen DI Wilson in the jazz club, although he was a firm fan of Sean's saxophone playing. In fact it had been at Bill's fiftieth birthday party that she'd first met Sean Maguire and decided to take him home with her.

Since Bill's wife Margaret had passed away from cancer, Bill hadn't socialized much, so Rhona was delighted to see him there, as he was her.

'So we're both venturing out into the world again,' he said as he greeted her.

Rhona knew Bill well enough to gauge his real reason for their meeting up tonight, and it wasn't strictly social. Bill got round to the anticipated question as their drinks arrived.

'How was it up there on the moor?' he said, quietly enough for only Rhona to hear.

It was something that needed to be asked. Being back in a grave, even if it wasn't her own this time, had been traumatic, but she'd survived.

'It was okay,' Rhona said honestly.

Bill looked relieved.

'You were taking a chance sending me out there,' Rhona said.

'More of a calculated risk,' Bill admitted. He fell silent before asking, 'McNab told you about McCreadie?'

Rhona nodded. 'You knew he'd become a crime author? Quite a famous one by all accounts.'

'Yes, although I didn't warn DS McNab.' Bill smiled. 'In truth, McNab reminds me of McCreadie, or at least the stories about him. Has difficulty with authority. Brilliant detective but inclined to go his own way.'

It did sound like McNab.

'McCreadie left under a cloud during the McIntyre case,' Bill went on. 'I suspect the cloud was manufactured to get rid of him. Rumour was that McCreadie uncovered something that those in power back then didn't want exposed.'

'What sort of thing?' Rhona said.

'Whatever it was, it's definitely not in the files. I've already pulled them. Maybe, just maybe, us finding the girl now might provide some answers.'

At this point, Rhona heard Sean's voice from the stage. Turning, he spotted her and threw her a surprised smile, before introducing their first performer of open mic night.

Rhona didn't have to be told that the young man who stood next to Sean was the real reason for Chrissy's visit to the jazz club that evening.

14

It looked like Ollie in IT had done okay in the short space of time between receiving McNab's email and his arrival in person at the Tech department.

Some of the players in the Mary McIntyre story given to McNab by former DI McCreadie were listed on the computer screen for McNab's benefit, together with what was currently known about them, dead or alive.

DI Wilson had already retrieved the old physical files from storage but, according to the boss, they were incomplete. So McCreadie's notebooks might just prove to be by far the best source of information on the case.

It was from the first of them that McNab had pulled the family details, plus a list of suspects identified by McCreadie, which he had then forwarded to Ollie to check out. Handing over his current offering (or inducement) to Ollie of a large coffee and a Tunnock's caramel wafer, McNab settled himself down to take a closer look at Ollie's findings.

First up was their possible victim, with the photograph published at the time of her disappearance. McNab saw a wee girl, slim, with long dark curly hair and a wide smile. She was eating an ice cream, with a beach behind her, on one of the few days in Scotland when the sun had shone.

Her date of birth was 3 May, so she'd disappeared just two days short of her twelfth birthday. Ollie had also dug up a class photograph from her primary school. Those being the days of large classes, McNab had had to search for Mary among the many, eventually finding her in the middle of the second row from the front.

There wasn't a photo of the dad or the mum, just dates of their deaths. Dave McIntyre had died almost ten years to the day after his daughter had vanished. Her mother, Evelyn, had followed two years later. There were no details as to how they'd died.

Two more photographs: one of Mary's big brother, Robbie, who was fourteen when his wee sister went missing, and one of her sister, Jean, who was sixteen. You could see the family resemblance, despite Robbie's scowl and Jean's smile for the camera.

Ollie, tucking into his caramel wafer, was watching as McNab scrolled down through the details he'd unearthed in the short period of time he'd been given.

As McNab reached Robbie, Ollie added, 'The brother has a criminal record. He went to Borstal for a spell, then prison for a short time. Both happened soon after Mary disappeared. Nothing on him since then. I've emailed you the details.'

'And Jean?' McNab said.

'She married a Samuel Barclay two years after Mary went missing. As far as I'm aware, they're still married and have two girls, now adults: Marianne and Lesley. Oh, and the good news is Jean and Sam Barclay's current address is the family home in East Kilbride where Mary was brought up.'

So I have at least one survivor to talk to, McNab thought.

'The best friend, Karen Marshall. Nothing on her?' McNab said, realizing he'd reached the end of Ollie's search results. After what McCreadie had told him about the pal, McNab was very keen to know of her whereabouts.

'Sorry, I haven't got anything on her yet,' Ollie said apologetically.

'What about Karen's dad?' McNab said. 'McCreadie said he was a detective constable at the time. There must be something in the records about him?'

'I'm sorry. That's as far as I've got.'

Ollie was much too polite to say, 'Fuck's sake, I've only just been given the job', although McNab read it from his expression.

'So can we carry on looking?' McNab made his request sound like a plea. 'We could order in a pizza if you're hungry.'

When his offer was followed by a studied silence, McNab suddenly woke up to the fact that Ollie was keen for the off. Since he usually seemed to live in the IT suite pretty well permanently, this was unusual, to say the least.

Then it dawned on him why Ollie might be so keen on leaving.

'You've got somewhere important to be?' McNab raised an eyebrow.

When Ollie flushed, McNab gave a low whistle. 'If you have a date, I sincerely hope it's with the lovely Maria from the canteen?'

'We're going for a pizza,' Ollie admitted.

'So that's why you blew me off? Well, don't forget who introduced you two,' McNab reminded him as Ollie rose in somewhat of a hurry now that he had been officially released.

Watching Ollie exit, McNab smiled. Ollie had been helping Maria in the canteen for months with her digital devices, never cottoning on to the fact that she was only asking for help because she fancied him. Something McNab had set about fixing. And apparently it had worked.

McNab congratulated himself on getting that relationship right. As for his own, it too was in fairly good nick for the moment. He checked his watch. Ellie was working tonight and he'd told her he would come to the Rock Cafe later and they could go home together. A date he didn't intend to miss.

He set the alarm on his mobile, just to be sure.

After his earlier meeting with the boss, McNab now knew a little about DI McCreadie's fall from grace. It hadn't passed his notice that McCreadie's story read a little like his own, although DI Wilson hadn't put that into words. McNab had also picked up on the fact that McCreadie's colleagues had believed him to have been hard done by.

It appeared that the former DI's departure had a smell about it that hadn't gone away with time. Maybe it was just legend. Good cop versus bad cop, with a whiff of something rotten at the top, bearing in mind that they were talking about the world of the seventies, when paedophiles were being sheltered by the state, whether as famous disc jockeys, politicians, members of the upper echelons of society or even priests.

McNab hoped times had changed, but he wasn't yet convinced that they had.

Something about the whole McIntyre story rang bells with McNab. Brought up by his single mum, the Catholic Church had been a big part of his life back when he was a boy, although he'd removed himself from its sphere pretty soon after adolescence.

And the main reason for that had been Father Barry.

True, he'd continued to act as though he was going to

mass, for his mum's sake, then walked round the block instead. He suspected his mother knew what he was up to. If nothing else, Father Barry probably ratted on him, but if he had, his mother never challenged her son about it.

What remained from all that religion was a lasting memory of the power the Church had over people, and children in particular, especially via priests like Father Barry.

As a ten-year-old from a single-parent family, he'd been taken on a free week's holiday to the seaside with the priest. There had been eight boys in total, all between the ages of ten and twelve. They'd had a great time on the beach and in the amusement arcades. The Church had even presented them with pocket money for the trip.

They were put up in a boarding house where the food was good and the woman who ran it unfailingly cheerful, despite having eight boys under her roof. They'd all slept together in a dormitory, and that was fine too. There was just one weird thing about it. At night, before they went to sleep, they were required to lie on their beds with their bare feet sticking over the end, so that Father Barry could inspect them in some detail.

The excuse for this being, he didn't want any smelly or dirty feet.

At age ten, the idea that a priest had a foot fetish involving small boys would have seemed ridiculous if presented, although they'd all thought the practice strange and a little creepy too. But basically, if a foot inspection every night was required to avoid being sent home, then no boy in that room would have refused.

But what if the required favour in order to stay had been something more than that? And maybe it had been, just not for him.

McNab had never mentioned Father Barry's interest in small boys' feet to his mum, because he somehow knew she would have been upset. And, after all, for him at least, it had gone no further than that. Later, he'd heard Barry had left the parish somewhat abruptly, having been transferred elsewhere. At that point his mum had questioned McNab about the priest and that holiday. By the worried look on her face, he'd wondered just why the priest had gone. Even then he hadn't had the courage to tell the tale.

The name following Karen's father on the list was Father Joseph Feeney. McCreadie had been fairly cutting about the priest in his notes, so he was definitely worth checking out.

McNab briefly contemplated doing a search for his own Father Barry, just to see what had happened to him, then decided against it when the alarm on his phone reminded him that it was time to depart.

Having come to work on his Harley, he decided to leave the bike where it was and make his way to the Rock Cafe by other means. Ellie always went to work on her bike, so he could have a drink and she could run them back to the flat together.

As he passed the desk, the sergeant called after him.

'DS McNab. There was a guy in here earlier asking after you. I thought you were out.'

'I was up in IT. Did he leave a name?'

The sergeant handed him a slip of paper with a number on it. 'No name, but he asked if you could give this number a call. A snitch, maybe?'

McNab had built up a few informants over the years, but checking the number, he knew this wasn't one of them. There was, of course, one way to find out who it was. He hesitated for a moment, then stuck the paper in his pocket.

Whatever it was, it could wait. He had other non-police-related plans for tonight.

When he arrived at the Rock Cafe, the row of motorbikes parked outside suggested it was as busy as usual.

Heading downstairs, he stopped halfway so that he might observe Ellie in her place behind the bar. She had her hair up, so the tattoos that encircled her lovely neck were in full view. McNab knew every one of them by now in minute detail. Her skin was a story he loved to reread. For every picture painted, there was an accompanying story of why Ellie had chosen to be inked with that particular pattern.

As for McNab, he had only one story and one tattoo . . . on his back, where a bullet hole had become the empty eye of a skull, and it had been Ellie who had been the one to ink him. It was the sweetest pain he had ever endured.

Spotting him on the stairs, Ellie waved him over.

'Just in time,' she said, in a voice that suggested she might have been giving up on him. 'I finish in fifteen minutes.'

'I know,' McNab said with a suggestive smile. 'I left my bike at the station.'

'So I'm running you home?'

'I hope so, or else I'm walking.'

'So what are you having?'

'A single malt,' McNab told her.

'A bad day at work?' Ellie said.

McNab smiled. 'Forgotten already.'

'Is that a promise?'

'It is,' McNab reassured her.

Seated at a table with his dram, curiosity got the better of McNab and he fished for the piece of paper the desk sergeant had given him and dialled the number. It rang out only once before a male voice said, 'Is that Detective Sergeant McNab?'

'It is,' McNab said cautiously.

'McCreadie told me to contact you. He says you're working the Mary McIntyre case.'

McNab's ears pricked up at this. 'Who am I talking to?'

The caller skipped the name request, saying instead, 'It's about who killed wee Mary McIntyre.'

In the seconds that followed, McNab contemplated the possibility that he had a nutter on the line who had not yet given his name but could somehow get in touch with a former DI who was now a crime writer.

'Name?' he demanded again.

'Robbie McIntyre. We need to talk.'

15

Extracting herself from Sean's arms, Rhona grabbed her dressing gown. Her sudden departure from the bed, she knew, had little chance of waking Sean.

His untroubled and easy sleep was something she envied him for. It was said that to sleep well, it was better to sleep alone. That didn't appear true for Sean, but it was for her.

Sean always offered to go to the spare room after they'd had sex, knowing her sleeping habits very well. Last night Rhona hadn't wanted him to desert her, and it had been obvious how much that had pleased him.

The previous evening, her intention hadn't been to stay late at the jazz club, but she'd become captivated by watching things develop between Danny, the young jazz guitarist, and Chrissy. Eventually, realizing just how late it was, she'd got ready to leave, only for Sean to offer to walk her home, if she would stay a little longer.

Rhona had been intent on going over the notes she'd taken at the locus despite what she'd told Chrissy, but suddenly Sean's company had seemed preferable to that. Perhaps it was the wine, or maybe because a faint sense of dread still beset her when she thought of entering the flat alone late at night.

It was a feeling she'd hoped would eventually fade, and for the most part it had. But today's excavation had stirred up such thoughts again. So she'd agreed to wait a little longer, had ordered up another glass of wine and had watched as Chrissy and her latest conquest left together.

It had been, Rhona realized, like the night she'd first met Sean. Not a jazz fan herself, she wouldn't have chosen to spend time in the club had it not been for Bill having his birthday party there. When the tall, dark-haired Irish musician had asked if he might join her at the interval, Rhona had gladly agreed, because she'd wanted them to get together as much as he obviously did.

Rhona had discovered fairly soon after their first coupling that Sean's way of dealing with the world was pretty much the polar opposite of her own. Chrissy said he was a keeper, but Rhona had never been certain of that. There was always a posse of available women with an eye for the saxophonist, and she had decided early on in their relationship that Sean was probably playing the field.

Much like herself.

Rhona definitely wasn't looking for a life partner, and most of the time she liked to live alone. Despite this, Sean had always been there for her when she'd needed him most. Particularly during the sin-eater case.

'So,' Sean had said as they'd eventually headed out onto Ashton Lane. 'What did you think of the open mic night?'

There had been five participants, all probably good, but to Rhona's ear, most jazz was impenetrable.

'I liked Danny and his guitar the best,' she'd said honestly. 'And that's nothing to do with Chrissy's interest in him,' she'd added with an amused smile.

'I think it was definitely mutual.' Sean had caught her eye at that point, reminding her, Rhona knew, of the evening they'd first met.

They'd walked on then in companionable silence, crossing the wide tree-lined Kelvin Way still busy with groups of students, either heading home or perhaps only now going out for their evening's entertainment.

Entering the park, they'd made their way down towards one of the many bridges that crossed the River Kelvin on its way to its bigger sister, the Clyde. The surrounding trees, for the most part, were still awaiting the arrival of their summer foliage, but the scent of growing things, particularly after the rain, had been pungent. Rhona had stopped midway across the bridge.

An underground tributary of the River Kelvin had saved her life during her incarceration, and she rarely traversed the park without offering a silent thank you to its swirling waters.

'I heard on the news about the child's body found buried on the moor,' Sean had ventured as they'd started on their way again.

'I can't discuss it,' Rhona had said shortly.

'I wouldn't expect you to.' There had been no rancour in Sean's voice despite her sharp reply. 'I just thought that dealing with the scenario might have been difficult.'

'All crime scenes are traumatic. Especially when a child is involved.'

She hadn't said *unborn child*, but that was what had been in her mind. And Sean knew her well enough to understand that.

She'd turned away from him then to take back control of her feelings.

That's what it will always be between us, Rhona thought. *Too much emotion. Too many memories.*

Before she could walk away though, Sean had encased her in his arms.

'It doesn't have to come between us, Rhona. Nothing does. Nothing will.'

She'd turned and kissed him then, knowing they would end up in bed together, and by doing so, they might close the still-open wounds between them, for a short while at least.

Now, on the threshold of the kitchen, Rhona halted for a moment. The remembered horror of what had happened there in her home had faded, aided by what Sean had done with the room during her absence on Skye. With the new colour scheme and new fridge, he had changed her much-loved room, just enough for it not to replay too many bad memories for her.

Rhona filled the coffee machine, then set up her laptop, keen to look again at the evidence she'd gathered on the moor.

Pouring herself a freshly brewed mug of coffee, she settled down to view all the images she'd taken on site, and the notes she'd recorded beside the grave.

Two thoughts had come to mind in the interim, and the more she examined the images, the more she thought they might be pertinent. Rhona pulled up the notes she'd made while reading Jen's report on the preservation of bog bodies.

To preserve a bog body, specific acidic and oxygen-poor conditions must be present, thus allowing for the mummification of the body's soft parts.

Many other conditions must also be fulfilled in order to prevent micro-organisms from breaking down the human body.

1) The corpse must be sunk in water or dug into the ground and covered quickly.

2) The deposition of the body must occur when the bog water is cold, in the winter or early spring, otherwise the process of decay can begin.

For the child's body to be so well preserved, it would have been deposited when the bog water was at its coldest, in winter or spring. According to McNab, Mary McIntyre had been abducted on 1 May 1975.

Up on a Scottish moor in May, the temperature of the bog water would have still been sufficiently cold to prevent the process of decay, and checking the weather of 1975, Rhona had found that snow had fallen as far south as Portsmouth during the first week of June.

Returning to the measurements she'd taken of the body, she now considered the dress they'd extracted from the plastic bag. The post-mortem would result in more precise estimates for the measurements of the victim, but in Rhona's judgement, the dress buried with the girl looked on the small size to have been worn by her.

When she'd carefully compared the size of the shoes and the remains of the feet, she wasn't convinced that they would fit either.

Maybe the clothes weren't those of the victim at all.

Sean's voice broke into Rhona's thoughts.

'Hey. Can I smell fresh coffee?' Sean padded across in his boxers and poured himself a mug. 'You hungry? I can make us some breakfast?' he suggested.

'There's food in the fridge?' Rhona said, surprised. Not a cook herself, she relied mostly on takeaways unless Sean cooked for them.

Sean displayed the contents. 'I can offer you sliced sausage, eggs and tattie scones.'

'You're joking? I haven't been to the shops recently,' Rhona said, amazed.

'I took the liberty of stocking up for you when you were up on the moors with Chrissy,' he said, almost apologetically.

'You didn't happen to buy rolls?' Rhona said.

Sean opened the bread bin and flourished a pack at her.

'Chrissy's taken to feeding me porridge of a morning,' Rhona explained her excitement.

'I know. Hence the contents of the fridge. Fancy doing something together later?' Sean suggested as he brought things out.

Rhona knew what she intended doing, and she had no intention of including Sean in her plans. Judging by his expression, he was picking up on that.

'You have to work?' he said.

'In a way,' Rhona admitted. 'I'm going to take another look at the locus.'

'I thought Chrissy said you'd finished up on the moors?'

'I'm not sure we are yet,' Rhona said.

Noting her expression, Sean nodded. 'Fine. It was just a thought. Well, if you're heading out, I'd better get frying.'

'You don't have to leave when I do,' Rhona offered.

'I know,' Sean said with an easy smile. 'And I'll make sure Tom's inside before I go.'

The cat normally had access to the flat roof of the tenement block via an open kitchen window. Despite Sean's entreaties about Rhona shutting the window at night, she'd usually failed to do so, preferring to give Tom free range as to when he went out. Something that, since the sin-eater case, no longer happened.

'If you would.' Rhona smiled her thanks.

*

The weather had reverted from heavy rain to spring sunshine. The drenching had brought the moor to life, as though the prolonged downfall had been exactly what the mosses and heather had craved.

Having agreed that DS Strachan could leave the locus the previous evening, all that was left of their excavation was a roped-off area.

The grave was part-filled with water from yesterday's rain, with softened peat reshaping the sides she and Chrissy had so carefully dug out. Rhona wasn't concerned by this. They had, she believed, retrieved all the evidence that had lain there.

Making her way onto the small stretch of sand that bordered the northern end of the lochan, Rhona undressed and pulled on her short wetsuit, before fixing her head torch and wading into what felt like ice-cold water.

The little stream she'd watched spring to life with the downpour had dwindled again in strength, but the water it had fed into the lochan had raised the level by at least half a metre.

As the water filled her wetsuit, Rhona felt a warm layer begin to form. Wading further in, it took only a metre before she had enough water to swim. She stopped after a couple of strokes to feel again for the bottom, but it was no longer there, indicating the probability that the lochan had a deep core.

She suspected, once she'd dived a little to confirm this, that the incoming stream, when in spate, had succeeded in carving out the peaty soil from the deepest area, and what she could see and touch there was in fact bedrock.

Moving towards the bank that lay between her and the grave, she had to submerge again to look for the cavity that had housed the tangled roots interwoven with the fingers of the victim. Filled again with soil, had she not mapped its location, she would never have identified its position.

As Chrissy had said, the window of opportunity in which the body might be discovered had been small, relying as it had done on the long spell of unseasonably dry weather, plus the presence of a wild and curious swimmer.

Rhona, diving again, began to slowly map out the underwater world of the lochan. What she was looking for she had no idea. If asked, she could have only declared it as a hunch. But, as Magnus Pirie often said, intuition was just psychology in action.

Ever since she'd acknowledged, to herself at least, that the outfit and the victim were possibly not a match, Rhona couldn't avoid the thought that more than one child might be involved. Maybe the Saddleworth Moor episode had influenced her thinking on that. Then again, child killers rarely stopped at one child, and generally went on killing until caught. And Mary McIntyre's abductor had never been identified, let alone apprehended.

If she gleaned any evidence to suggest there might be more than one gravesite in the location then she could ask for a fuller search of the surrounding area. Recent advances involved using small unmanned aerial vehicles (UAVs) for aerial photography, which could examine the surrounding area for anomalies. Nutrient flush might be spotted where greener grass had come about because of leachate, a product of water passing through a deposition site.

Peat vegetation in general took a long time to get back to normal, although if the area had been heavily grazed, chances were it would all look similar over time. On her trips up here Rhona had seen no grazing sheep, but that didn't mean there hadn't been any in the intervening years.

Although she'd begun to feel the cold, she submerged once again, to cross and recross the small yet deep loch, her reasoning being that since the fingers had managed to exit the grave, something might have escaped with them.

She had all but given in to the cold when the beam from her head torch glinted back at her. Going closer, Rhona saw a circular object, likely tarnished metal, wedged between two stones. Prising it free, she rose to the surface, desperate for air.

She now swam towards the beach, knowing she'd stayed in too long and was seriously chilled by her time in the water. Securing her prize on a stone, she quickly stripped off the wetsuit and got dried and dressed. After which, she poured some coffee from her flask and, nursing the cup, warmed both her hands and her insides.

When her teeth had finally stopped chittering, Rhona fetched her camera from her backpack and photographed the item she'd retrieved from the floor of the lochan.

It was clear what it was, despite the tarnished appearance. The vintage-style sterling silver bracelet, once popular as a gift for a child, had likely been a celebratory present for the special event in a little girl's life, her confirmation into the Roman Catholic Church.

16

Despite the chill in the morning air, Magnus was having his morning coffee on the balcony so that he might watch the boundless flow of the River Clyde as it wound its way westward to the Irish Sea.

Living in a city that stood on a river, in an apartment that overlooked the river, wasn't the same as living in a stone house on the shores of Scapa Flow in Orkney, but it was a decent enough substitute.

Especially on mornings like this, Magnus decided.

After the sudden downpour, it was as though the earth had sprung to life around him. Spring had already arrived, albeit a little tentatively. With a sunny spell followed by a plentiful water supply from the heavens, everything had decided it was time to sprout. Even his meagre selection of plants that occupied the balcony space with him.

Magnus's thoughts turned back to Orkney and when he might next visit his island home. He was particularly fond of spring, when the mayflowers appeared. Known in Glasgow as primroses, they weren't as abundant here as in Orkney, where they turned the roadside verges into a bright blanket of dancing yellow.

From his home at Houton Bay he also had a great view of the hills of Hoy on the other side of Scapa Flow. Here in Glasgow, the scene across the river was undoubtedly urban, but impressive nonetheless. Gone were the huge shipyards that had made Glasgow famous, and in their place were landscaped green living spaces for the new city dwellers.

Magnus loved this gregarious and garrulous city, its friendliness to strangers easily equal, in his opinion, to that of his homeland of Orkney.

Refilling his coffee mug, he resumed his outdoor seat to further enjoy his positive mood, which, he acknowledged, was as much a product of having finally completed his current stack of student marking, the topic being: 'High-risk young people with developing personality disorders – a possible treatment.'

Although there was no established treatment for psychopathy in adults, his own university of Strathclyde was home to the Interventions for Vulnerable Youth project, which his criminal psychology students were currently studying.

That thought led immediately to another, featuring the man he'd recently interviewed in Barlinnie. Alec McLaughlin, in Magnus's opinion, had a psychopathic personality, which old age, Magnus feared, had neither diminished nor improved, despite a long jail sentence and the further education courses he'd successfully taken while incarcerated.

Having drafted his piece on Old Alec, Magnus had harboured no desire to see the man again. However, that was before he'd received a message on his university email stating that Alec McLaughlin had been released on schedule and that he would like to meet with Professor Pirie to talk further. He was happy to come to the university to do so, if that suited the professor.

When Magnus had replied politely that he had all he needed for his paper on the topic they'd discussed, Alec had responded that he wanted to talk to Professor Pirie on another matter entirely, which had arisen from the recent news of the discovery of a child's remains buried on the moor south of Glasgow.

Magnus had yet to answer that particular email, which had arrived late last night. His first instinct was to advise Mr McLaughlin to speak to the police, but he also suspected that Old Alec would do no such thing, having just been released after serving fifteen years in Barlinnie Prison.

Sitting here, his eyes resting on the slow-moving waters of the Clyde, Magnus decided he would agree to meet Alec again, who was after all a free man now, and see what he had to say. Then, should such a meeting warrant informing the police, he would contact DI Bill Wilson, with whom he'd worked as a profiler on a number of occasions, and ask his advice.

His mind made up, he went through to his office and sent the required email, suggesting today at 1 p.m. would be a suitable time to meet, and that Alec should come to reception at the Graham Hills Building and ask for him. The email brought an almost immediate response, confirming that Alec would be delighted to come along today at that time.

The morning passed without anything else of note. Magnus delivered a couple of hour-long lectures, then decided to have a light lunch in his office, only to discover a queue of students who wished to talk to him personally about the marks posted on their recent papers.

Magnus agreed times to speak to each of them, and by then it was almost time for Alec's arrival. He now found himself intrigued by what might occur during their meeting, plus relief that he would have a break from justifying his student scores to their recipients.

Checking his watch, he noted he had thirty minutes left to review what information he had on the body on the moors, or at least what he'd gleaned via the press and TV reports. For his own interest, he'd already looked through old newspaper articles around the time when the burial was mooted to have occurred.

Being a professor of psychology, Magnus was even more aware than the general public that neither the newspapers, websites or television channels were renowned for telling the truth, then or now, relying as they all did on capturing and entertaining an audience.

He'd briefly contemplated calling Rhona to enquire what she knew regarding the recent discovery, or even DS McNab, with whom he had a chequered history, but had decided rather to wait and hear what Alec had to say first. After all, he'd not been invited as yet to become involved as a criminal psychologist in the case, so they would be reluctant to give out confidential information.

The current news reports had made two things plain at least: the body was believed to be that of a child and it was likely connected to an unsolved case from up to fifty years ago.

It hadn't taken long after that to unearth (an unfortunate term) the missing children's cases in Scotland in that time frame. And the disappearance of Mary McIntyre just north of the deposition site, after her church confirmation in 1975, appeared the most likely match to the body that had been found on the moor.

Which was certainly the train of thought favoured by the press.

Armed with this information, Magnus headed for reception as soon as the call came through that he had a visitor.

Having discarded the prison's red fleece, and also the

walking stick, Alec McLaughlin looked a different man, and definitely younger. The personal details Magnus had been given prior to his interview with McLaughlin had stated his age at sixty-one, which meant he'd been incarcerated at the age of forty-six. Magnus hadn't been given the exact details of his conviction, although his own research had provided some answers.

As Archie had said, it had taken a long time to catch him, but they finally had through the three children of a former partner. The two girls and a boy, now grown up, had accused McLaughlin of numerous counts of rape during their childhood. At the time these had occurred, McLaughlin had been in his thirties. Archie had suspected there had been many more assaults on children which they hadn't yet discovered or proved.

Spying Magnus's exit from the lift, Old Alec had come swiftly towards him, hand outstretched. 'Professor Pirie, I am delighted to meet with you again. Thank you so much for agreeing to see me.'

Magnus saw no sign of the stiff gait he'd noted in their prison encounter. Alec was, to all intents and purposes, now apparently totally mobile. Deciding not to mention this, Magnus shook the outstretched hand, then, having asked if McLaughlin had signed in and receiving the affirmative, ushered him towards the lift.

They exchanged the required niceties on the ascent to Magnus's floor – focusing on the weather and work in general, wherein Alec professed to rather enjoying his current work-free existence, including no academic classes to take.

'Alas, for me,' Magnus said, 'that is not an option.'

On arrival at his office, Magnus found another two of his first-year female students waiting for him outside. He didn't remember their names, but, listening to their requests for a meeting, asked the two to email him for an appointment.

Once inside with the door firmly shut, Alec ventured, 'I see you're very popular, Professor Pirie. Is your popularity confined to your female students or does it cross the boundaries of gender?'

'My popularity at present depends on what grade I gave them on their last paper,' Magnus said firmly, ushering Alec to a chair.

'I take it they think you scored them too low?'

'No one comes to complain about a mark that is higher than they anticipated,' Magnus confirmed. 'Can I offer you a freshly brewed coffee?'

'Yes, please.' Alec's eyes lit up. 'I could smell it when I came in. Good coffee is one of the many joys of being free. That and being able to walk for miles in a straight line. Something I haven't been able to do for fifteen years.'

Magnus busied himself pouring the coffee, while his inner voice screamed his distaste that McLaughlin should feel sorry for himself, since his victims were unlikely ever to be free of the past he'd inflicted upon them.

When he returned with the coffee mugs in hand, he found McLaughlin's piercing eyes studying him.

'You think I have no right to feel sorry for myself,' he suggested, as though he'd been reading Magnus's thoughts.

Magnus, unsure how to answer, decided not to.

McLaughlin smiled. 'You'll be pleased to hear that I did well in my finals and am soon to graduate with a first-class honours in Forensic Psychology. Not bad for a boy who left school at fifteen.'

'I thought the school leaving age was raised to sixteen in 1973?'

A dark look crossed McLaughlin's face, but it passed so swiftly Magnus might almost have imagined it.

'I see you've been doing your homework on me, Professor. As for the leaving age, it mattered little to me as I spent more time out of school than in.'

'All the more reason then to congratulate you on your degree success,' Magnus said, somewhat belatedly.

McLaughlin smiled. 'Thank you, Professor Pirie. Coming from such a distinguished criminal profiler, that's high praise indeed.' He paused, then setting down his coffee, said, 'Now we've got the niceties over, shall we discuss the real reason why I'm here?'

Magnus nodded. 'I understand it relates to the body recently discovered on the moors?'

'Found buried on the moors,' McLaughlin corrected him. 'I lived two doors up from wee Mary McIntyre, Professor. And for a while I was a suspect in her abduction. I wasn't the culprit, but the detective at the time, McCreadie was his name, had it in for me. Gave me a hard time. In fact, nowadays *I* could have *him* up for sexual assault.' He continued, his eyes fixed on Magnus, 'McCreadie was determined to pin it on someone and I fitted the bill.' He gave a cold smile. 'So I expect, if they do identify the body as Mary, someone will be back knocking on my door again.'

McLaughlin looked as though he expected a response to that statement. When none came, he continued his story. 'McCreadie's a famous crime writer now, name of J. D. Smart.' He smiled again. 'I've read his books. They're excellent, especially the one in which I feature – or a poorly disguised version of me.'

Magnus was at a loss as to how to respond to any of this. What McLaughlin had said about his place in the Mary

McIntyre story was a revelation. As was the J. D. Smart connection. What Magnus didn't understand was why he was being told all of this.

'McCreadie was already writing fiction, even back then,' Alec said. 'And it's not only me who could tell you that. Problem is, most of the folk involved will be dead, so who's going to tell the truth?'

He looked sorrowful at that, or maybe just sorry for himself, Magnus couldn't tell which.

'If you're looking for advice,' Magnus finally said, 'then I suggest I put you in touch with one of the detectives I've worked with and trust, and you could tell him what you know, before . . .' He halted, wondering how exactly to put this.

'Before they come for me,' McLaughlin finished for him.

17

In the grave, her colour had become one with the soil in which she'd lain. A process similar to tanning had made the soft tissue leathery and hard, the skin discoloured to a brownish hue. In many ways what had taken place in the bog was probably more akin to chemical preservation by embalming, rather than mummification which involved drying or desiccation.

The partially reddened hair was a result, according to the pathologist Dr Richie Walker, of the acid in the peat, which had bleached out the original colour and dyed it via the iron in the soil, giving it the colour spoken of in the Seamus Heaney poem.

Since the victim was a child, Dr Walker was being assisted at the post-mortem by a corroborating pathologist trained in paediatric pathology. Dr Catriona Wang wasn't that much taller than the child they were examining, making Dr Walker's height even more pronounced.

Dr Wang had introduced herself to Rhona with a wide smile. 'We haven't met in person before, Dr MacLeod, but I am familiar with your work.' Her quiet yet melodious voice reminded Rhona of a songbird, and the hands encased in gloves appeared as delicate as wings.

'Please call me Rhona. I assume you're on first-name terms with Richie too?'

'I am, although had Dr Sissons been here, such familiarity with Dr Walker wouldn't of course have been allowed.'

Rhona and Richie exchanged amused looks.

'I see you're familiar with Dr Sissons's ways.'

'I haven't been here long, but I learned the protocol right away.'

With Dr Sissons missing from the equation, the post-mortem had already taken on a different tone. Dr Walker was as respectful and thorough as Dr Sissons when working with the dead, but sarcasm definitely wasn't his thing. In Rhona's opinion, adding in a female forensic pathologist improved things even further. She suspected Richie felt the same.

McNab appeared as Dr Wang began recording a description of the body. His blue eyes above the mask acknowledged Rhona's presence, followed by a raised eyebrow to Rhona when he realized two things at the same time: Dr Sissons, his bête noire, wasn't present, and a woman was.

Dr Walker immediately made the introductions. 'DS McNab. This is Dr Wang. As we believe the victim is a child, Dr Wang is presiding as a consultant paediatric pathologist.'

McNab gave Dr Wang a warm smile, noticeable despite the mask.

'So,' Dr Wang continued in her light voice, 'we have a young female. Length from top of head to heel 54.5 inches or 138.4 centimetres. So her height would likely be within an inch either way. As Dr Walker mentioned earlier, her hair has been bleached by the acid, the red coming from the iron in the soil. However, there is enough of her original colour to suggest she had long dark hair.'

'Age?' McNab said.

'For that we would study the teeth and look at the sites

of bone development and bone length, which of course will take a little time.'

'At a guess?' McNab persisted.

Dr Wang looked a little perturbed by this, but then conceded. 'Between ten and fourteen years.'

McNab came in again. 'Anything to indicate the way she died?'

'The body is well preserved, with no disarticulation. The skull is intact with no obvious evidence of blunt-force trauma. Although,' Dr Wang moved to study the genital area, 'these look like puncture marks.' She looked to Rhona at this juncture.

'I noted those as well,' Rhona said. 'I counted five, perhaps six of them. We have only just begun to test the soil we collected from above and below the body, so we don't know if she died elsewhere and was brought there to bury, or whether she was still capable of bleeding when put in the ground.'

'So the wounds may have been inflicted after her death. Once we open her up, we'll hopefully have a better picture of what happened here.' Dr Wang turned to McNab. 'Do you think you might know who the child is?'

'There's a chance it's Mary McIntyre, aged almost twelve, who disappeared after her confirmation ceremony at her local chapel, a few miles north of the deposition site. She had long dark hair and was wearing a white dress and veil at the time.'

Dr Wang's eyes expressed the sorrow she felt at that piece of news.

'Also, we did find a confirmation frock, veil and shoes in a plastic supermarket bag in the grave,' Rhona told her.

'Which would point to Mary McIntyre as your victim,' Dr Wang said.

'Except,' Rhona looked to McNab, 'I believe the clothes I recovered from the grave wouldn't be a good fit for this girl.'

'What?' McNab looked bemused by this revelation.

'Dr Wang's just confirmed the measurements to be the same as those I recorded at the crime scene,' Rhona said. 'However, the frock and the shoes we retrieved from the grave may be too small to fit a child that size.'

'So they aren't the clothes the victim was wearing when she was abducted?' McNab said.

'They are smaller than we would have expected,' Rhona tried to explain.

McNab was studying Rhona's expression. 'Can we go have a chat, Dr MacLeod?'

Rhona nodded. 'If you'll excuse us, Dr Walker, Dr Wang?'

'What the hell, Rhona?' McNab said as soon as they were in the changing room. 'Why didn't you tell me this earlier?'

'I wanted the measurements to be confirmed by a pathologist.'

'Well, now they have been.' McNab, dumping his scrubs, ran his fingers through his hair. 'Fuck. Mary's big brother, Robbie, got in touch with me. He's already convinced the body is his sister. As are most of the tabloids, even though we have consistently said we haven't ID'd the victim.'

'It might yet be Mary McIntyre,' Rhona said.

'If so, why bury her with someone else's clothes?'

They'd both imagined the scenario. It was impossible not to. Mary McIntyre being abducted in her white frock, stripped of her clothes either before or after her death, in all probability sexually assaulted, then brought to the moor to be buried. Nowhere in that likely story was there a role for another set of clothing.

'I don't know.' Rhona hesitated. 'But the most important thing now is to identify the remains. Retrieving DNA from the body won't be easy.'

'Why?' McNab demanded.

Having finally been convinced by DNA sampling, McNab, like many others, believed it could always be delivered.

'Bogs are acidic. They mess up the DNA pattern. Advice from a forensic anthropologist is that we go for somewhere that's really protected, like the petrous part of the temporal bone in the skull.'

McNab looked perturbed by this. 'But you can do it?'

'Hopefully. If we do, then, provided you can take a buccal swab from Mary's siblings, we'll know the answer. There's also something else that might help.'

'What?'

Rhona explained about yesterday's swim and the discovery of the bracelet. 'These particular bracelets were fairly common in the sixties and seventies and hopefully there might be an inscription when we clean it up.'

'Good work,' McNab said cautiously. 'So,' he went on, reading Rhona's expression, 'if the confirmation outfit doesn't turn out to be from our victim, then who does it belong to?'

'Another victim?' Rhona finally voiced the thoughts she'd had up on the moor.

By McNab's expression, he'd been thinking the same thing.

'The boss has ordered a trawl across the UK for missing kids within the time frame. If we consider even five years either side of 1975, there are plenty of possibilities.'

'We also need to take a proper look at the surrounding area with a UAV and imaging camera,' Rhona said. 'If there are anomalies not consistent with the general ground terrain we need to take a further look at those. And in the case of a buried body, heather is replaced by grass.'

McNab looked thoughtful. 'So that explains what Ellie said when we visited Culloden Moor on that trip north she took me.'

'That no heather will grow on a Jacobite grave?' Rhona said. 'It has some basis in scientific fact, but it's also a good story for the tourists.'

'If we start doing a survey of the surrounding moor, we can count on our own influx of tourists,' McNab said. 'I take it you intend to bring this up at the next strategy meeting?'

'It was the plan, yes.'

'I'll see you there then.'

Rhona reapplied her mask and headed back inside.

A standard post-mortem took around four hours and involved if not a small army, then definitely a subdivision, including forensic biologists, SOCOs, a photographer, a crime scene manager and a note-taker. On the other side of the screen you would normally find the senior investigating officer and the procurator fiscal, for a time at least, although not all fiscals liked to attend.

When in the midst of the procedure, the numbers were hardly noticeable as everyone went quietly and efficiently about their various jobs. McNab didn't like the parts that involved opening up the body. Rhona, used to dealing with the scent of death, preferred to stay throughout. As the one who had been the first witness to the deceased and having seen the context in which she had been laid to her rest, everything Rhona had catalogued at the locus might now be explained.

As it was, Dr Walker's careful and thorough examination couldn't definitively determine how the child had died, although he suspected she had been smothered. The puncture marks round her genitals, he thought, had occurred after death. Something Rhona also believed to be the case.

The tests being done on the grave soil might yet confirm that blood had already stopped flowing when she'd been laid in there. If so, the grave was the deposition site but not the place the child had died.

The signature of a killer emerges out of an offender's fantasies, which develop long before killing their first victim, and often involve mutilation or dismemberment of the victim's body. There was little doubt in anyone's mind that abducting a child who was subsequently killed was a sexual fantasy being played out. The puncturing of the child's sexual organs might serve to confirm this.

As they were finishing up the autopsy, Richie asked if he might speak with Rhona before she left the mortuary.

'If you can spare time for a coffee?' had been his exact words.

Showered and changed, her hair still wet but at least smelling better, Rhona joined him in his office, where he too looked freshly showered.

'There's not much room in here, but I make good coffee,' he announced as she walked into what was little more than a cubby hole.

'It definitely smells good,' Rhona said, relieved now to be back in the land of the living.

He poured her a large mug from the cafetière. 'Milk?'

'Black, please,' Rhona said.

Once they'd both had time to savour the coffee, Richie said, 'I was interested in what you were saying about the

clothes buried with the child, and what that might mean?'
When Rhona didn't immediately respond, he added, 'I
couldn't help but notice McNab's reaction to that information.'

'McNab doesn't like to miss out on anything,' Rhona said.
'I hadn't mentioned this yet because I wanted to be certain
my measurements were correct.'

Richie was waiting, Rhona knew, for an answer to his
original question.

'My concern is that there is another body which we
haven't yet found.'

He looked perturbed by this. 'In the same vicinity?'

'Killers have been known to favour a particular location
for burial.'

The blue eyes darkened. 'Like Saddleworth Moor, you
mean?'

Rhona nodded. 'Yes.'

'Was there anything discussed today that reinforced the
idea it might be Mary McIntyre?'

Rhona shook her head. 'We'll have to wait for dental
reports and DNA samples for that. Thankfully, we have
other family members to compare with. Her older siblings
are still around.'

'Might they identify the clothes?'

'They were both teenagers at the time so who knows if
they registered the outfit in detail. And, as far as I'm aware
from DS McNab, there were no photographs taken of Mary
wearing her confirmation frock.'

Rhona finished her coffee. 'Talking of frocks, I'd better get
going. Chrissy and I are about to start work on the clothing.'

Richie looked as though he had something else to say, so
Rhona waited.

'Okay, I'll just come out and say it. I'm so very pleased you're back at work. We missed you.'

Surprised by this heartfelt declaration, Rhona found herself momentarily at a loss for words.

'I'm glad too,' she said, realizing she truly meant that.

He looked so relieved by her reaction, Rhona thought for a moment he was about to hug her.

'Oh, and I wondered if you were planning on attending the dinner for the end of the diploma course tonight? I've been invited because I gave that talk on autopsies.'

Rhona hadn't been planning to go, and that must have been obvious, because his own face fell.

'I could go along if you need some moral support,' she conceded.

He said a grateful thank you. 'The after-dinner speaker looks good,' he offered with an apologetic look.

'It'll be good to hear Professor Watt speak again,' Rhona assured him. 'He's highly entertaining, as I remember.'

'Great.'

Rhona made her excuses and left at this point, not sure she had made the right decision. It hadn't sounded like a proposal for an actual date, but as she didn't know what the current protocol on that was, she probably wasn't the best judge.

She could, of course, run the scenario past Chrissy and see what she thought, but having agreed to go, she could hardly back out now – anyway, it was work, after all.

18

When Karen had confessed to Marge and the others about the diary and her fears she was going 'doolally', Marge had announced, 'We're all doolally, hen. It's all the drink and drugs we've consumed over the years.'

Everyone had laughed at that point, because if they couldn't see the funny side of things together, what was the point of the cafe?

After her honesty with the others, Karen had felt a little better. The tea, home baking and banter had helped, of course. Added to that, Marge and the others had agreed to help her work things out.

Pat, one of the recovery development officers who'd been visiting them regularly, had encouraged them all to write a poem about themselves and what they'd been through. From each of their poems, they'd developed a short story, and Pat had then suggested they try writing a play about their experiences.

It had been Marge who had proposed that instead of a play, they try to solve the mystery of what had happened to Karen's pal, Mary McIntyre.

'A mystery play,' she'd said, her eyes lighting up at the idea. 'Where we're the detectives.'

Even if the body didn't turn out to be Mary, Marge thought it was a good idea if they helped Karen remember as much as possible of the mystery. That way it wouldn't continue to prey on her mind and she could put it to rest.

To this end they'd begun a mind map, using a big sheet of paper tacked to the back of an old discarded cupboard door. They'd got as far as writing up all the names of the families that had lived nearby and their connections with one another.

Karen had even surprised herself by remembering everyone.

'We had to talk about what happened to make us take drink and drugs,' Marge had reminded them as they'd worked. 'We had to be honest with our stories. This is part of your story, Karen. You have to own it.'

While she was with the others, this all made perfect sense to Karen. Unfortunately, when she was alone again in an empty house, the old fears surfaced like shadows, creeping ever closer until they threatened to suffocate her.

The worst time was when the news came on the radio or TV. Without fail, the presenter would mention 'the body on the moors', as it had come to be known, and the possibility that it might be eleven-year-old Mary McIntyre from East Kilbride.

She was almost twelve, Karen inevitably found herself telling the TV. *It was just before her birthday and we were planning a wee party at the den.*

Mary had wanted a real birthday party, but her mum had said they couldn't afford it.

So me and Mary decided to have one on our own. They'd already bought some sweets and a bottle of ginger with the week's pocket money, and had hidden it at the den ahead of the big day.

Returning from her thoughts to the news broadcast,

Karen would inevitably hear the same police spokesperson stating that the deceased hadn't been identified as yet, and that their enquiries were still continuing.

It was the most recent news programme that had compelled her to revisit the diary, despite her nervousness about doing so. If she was going to try and remember the events surrounding Mary's disappearance, as Marge had urged her to do, then surely this was the way to do it?

It was understandable that as a child of eleven in troubled times, she should have chosen to write down what was happening. In particular the things she didn't understand. The question was, why had she kept hold of this diary that catalogued her friend's disappearance all these years? Through adolescence, her time as a student at Stirling University, her marriage to Jack, the sadness of not having any children of their own. Then Jack's descent into dementia and death.

Karen knew the answer to that question, even though she couldn't voice it. Not out loud anyway.

It was because she'd hoped eventually to figure out what had really happened to Mary.

And maybe the part I played in it?

The diary open now, Karen registered that after the entry on the third of May there was a blank page. Why had she not written down what had happened on that day? The emptiness stared back at her like an accusation. Something had to have happened.

Was that the first day the detective had spoken to her? If so, why hadn't she written what he'd asked her?

Karen turned the page to find the visit of the detective had happened on the fifth of May, not the fourth. So what had happened on the fourth, and why hadn't she written it down? She flipped through more pages, only to find other blank spots. Why had she chosen to leave days empty? Was it because nothing had happened? Or – and a swift and suffocating feeling swept over her – was it because she wanted to forget what had happened on those particular days?

She returned to the fifth of May to read what she'd written there.

The policeman came today, just like Dad said he would. He asked me about Mary. Was she happy? Was she frightened of anyone? When did I last see her? I told him Mary was happy about her dress. She wasn't afraid of anyone, except her dad a little bit if she didn't come when he whistled for her. I told him I had seen her the afternoon before her confirmation when she showed me her dress. I didn't tell him I was jealous.

Karen realized she'd written something after that, but then erased it. She held the diary up to the light, but all she could see were the indentations.

What did I rub out?

She fetched a pencil and began to lightly shade that area of the page to see if the words might be revealed. Then she realized she hadn't written words, rather she had drawn something.

It looked like two stick figures with racquets, a ball high in the air between them. On the hill behind sat a figure watching them.

Karen stared at the drawing, a sick feeling churning her stomach, remembering.

Whenever we played tennis he was there, watching us. Shouting stuff. Stuff I didn't understand . . . but Mary did. Mary understood everything.

19

McNab had initially requested that Robbie McIntyre come to the station to speak to him. Robbie said he'd been in already to give a DNA sample and would rather they met in a nearby cafe.

McNab conceded that it wasn't an interview as such, so okayed Robbie's request. If, or when, the body was ID'd as Mary, everyone who'd been connected to her would become a suspect, just as they had been the first time round. And that would include her brother.

Ollie's research on Robbie had revealed his early convictions after his wee sister had gone missing. Stealing cars being one of them, that and running with a gang. However, by the age of twenty he appeared to have cleaned up his act. McNab only had a photograph of Robbie McIntyre from back then, so was unsure of what he might look like now.

The cafe Robbie suggested wasn't a greasy spoon, but rather a cool, upmarket place. On entry McNab could find no one sipping a latte that he thought might be the man he sought, so he headed for the counter and ordered two double espressos, to save him returning after the first was consumed.

Carrying them to a seat near the window where he might keep an eye on the door, McNab settled down to wait, hoping the description he'd given Robbie of himself would be sufficient. He was giving his mobile his undivided attention, like most of the others in the room, when a deep voice beside him said, 'Detective Sergeant McNab?'

McNab looked up to find a fit-looking guy, dressed smart-casual, who McNab would have taken for late forties, early fifties. His hair was still predominantly dark, with only a sprinkling of grey. In fact, McNab decided, the current version of Robbie McIntyre surprised him.

Ollie had only investigated police files on the younger Robbie, so McNab had no idea what the man did now. Whatever it was, it looked as though he'd made his way up in the world.

McNab rose. 'Robbie McIntyre?'

'I call myself Robert now. Or at least my partner, Andrew, and my work colleagues do,' he said, a little stiffly.

'Can I get you a coffee?' McNab asked.

'I ordered one, then spotted you over here,' he said in an accent that bore no resemblance to McNab's obvious Glasgow tone. 'It should be ready by now.'

McNab watched as McIntyre fetched his coffee, which turned out to be the largest latte available. The strange juxtaposition of McNab's tiny espresso cup next to the newly arrived soup-size bowl struck McNab as rather absurd. He only hoped their conversation didn't turn out to be the same.

McNab waited for the extra-large coffee to be lifted, drunk from, then replaced on the saucer prior to saying, 'Before we talk, I should stress that the body found on the moors hasn't been identified as yet.'

'Oh, it's Mary all right,' Robert McIntyre told him. 'I know it and so does the man who searched for her all those years ago.'

'We're talking about DI Jimmy McCreadie?'

McIntyre nodded. 'We've kept in touch. It was McCreadie who helped me get back on the straight and narrow as a teenager. No doubt you've looked up my chequered history? Stealing cars, gang fights, drugs?'

When McNab didn't respond, McIntyre continued anyway, the neutral voice disappearing, replaced by something more akin to McNab's own accent.

'I lost the head after Mary. The whole family did. Dad used to do that fucking whistle out the window, like she would suddenly come running back. Mum's life ended the day her wee girl disappeared. And my sister married Sammy Barclay just to get out of the house. As for me . . . I hated the police because they fucked up so badly.'

McNab didn't mind the man's anger or his accusation. He'd seen what such a loss could do to a family. It wasn't only the victim who died. The impact was devastating on everyone around them, especially when it involved the loss of a child. And it was even worse when they never got a body to bury.

Back in the seventies, the lack of a body usually meant no one would be charged. Now things were different and there had been convictions for murder despite the victim's remains never being discovered. Plus the advances in forensics were bringing killers to justice in spite of past failures.

McNab sat in silence for a minute, watching as McIntyre regained his composure. 'So, what did you do after your teenage brushes with the law?'

'I went to night school, encouraged by DI McCreadie. Got my Highers and went to college to study accountancy. Now I'm a financial adviser.'

McNab tried to prevent his eyebrows from rising, and not

just because it sounded a better and more lucrative career path than the one he'd chosen.

'Are you in touch with your sister?'

'Not so much. Me and her husband don't tend to hit it off, but I see her kids sometimes, especially now they're in Glasgow.' He gave McNab a studied look. 'But you probably know all this already.'

McNab didn't comment one way or the other. 'What did you want to tell me, apart from us having fucked up?' he said instead.

'McCreadie was close to finding out what had happened to Mary. That's why the men at the top got rid of him.'

'That I don't buy,' McNab said firmly. He had his own gripes with the police force, and corruption was always an undercurrent, just like in any other profession, but that sounded like McCreadie's words put into McIntyre's mouth.

'I've done my homework too, Detective Sergeant McNab. I know your history in the police force. You've sailed close to the wind a few times. The Stonewarrior case for one. The powers that be didn't take that very well, even though you solved the case.'

True enough. And it still rankled.

'Plus,' McIntyre met his eye, 'DI McCreadie recommended you.'

'*Former* DI McCreadie. He hasn't been an officer for a very long time,' he reminded McIntyre.

McNab recalled McCreadie's manner. He hadn't taken to the man. Maybe it was because he'd used his police background to write fictional accounts of the job. Or, as Janice had suggested, 'You don't like him because he's just like you.' When McNab had retorted, 'I deal in facts,' Janice had merely raised an eyebrow.

'So,' McNab went on, 'you and McCreadie have a theory and, I assume, not one in which you present as a suspect?'

'You think I would kill my own sister?' McIntyre looked genuinely astonished.

'It wouldn't be the first time such a thing had happened. Happy families are rarely happy.'

'I never said we were a happy family, but we were as happy as anyone else on that street.' McIntyre had regained his composure. 'You've read McCreadie's notebooks?'

McNab had only looked at the first one as yet, but didn't confirm this. Instead, he said, 'Why don't you tell me why you wanted to speak to me?'

'The priest's still alive. That's where you should go first. Father Joseph Feeney.'

McNab had every intention of interviewing everyone still alive on the list McCreadie had made, but he was keen to know why he was being directed to the priest in the first instance.

'You weren't around in the seventies,' McIntyre said. 'They rarely asked the kids. And if they did, they didn't believe the answers anyway. They didn't listen to me or to Jean either. Jeez, even my father wouldn't hear anything bad said about Father Feeney. My mum . . . I told her some stuff about him but she wouldn't believe it. DI McCreadie was the only one who listened. And they got rid of him when he tried to take it further.'

'Take what further?'

'Father Feeney was a paedophile, although we didn't know that word back in the day.'

'And you believe he abducted your sister?'

His face darkened. 'I never said that. But whoever took

Mary had the priest's help, I'm sure of it. Mary's best friend, Karen Marshall, was the lucky one. She got away.'

'You think both girls were targeted?'

'They were joined together at the hip. Outside of school and church, that is. Karen was a Proddy.' He threw an apologetic glance at McNab. 'Sorry, old habits die hard. Karen's family were Protestants.'

McNab didn't need the terminology of the great sectarian divide explained to him.

'Wee Karen was really freaked when Mary went missing,' McIntyre went on. 'She never came out to play in the street the summer after it happened. We thought her dad, who was in the police, was worried that the bastard who took Mary might come back for Karen.'

'You think Karen might have known him?'

'McCreadie said the first time he spoke to her she kept talking about the confirmation dress and that Mary was happy. The next time he saw her she said nothing. Just sat there, terrified. Nowadays they'd have people trained to deal with a possible child witness. Back then they thought kids just told lies. That's how the paedophile bastards got away with it for so long. The good old days, eh?'

'The day Mary was being confirmed . . . Did you see her in her confirmation dress?'

McIntyre stared at him. 'Why?'

'Would you recognize the dress again?'

'You've got her dress? Jesus Christ. I knew it was Mary. The fucking bastard. I'll kill him myself.' McIntyre rose, his face ablaze.

'Sit down,' McNab ordered.

McIntyre glowered at him but made no attempt to comply with the demand.

'Sit the fuck down or I'll invite you to accompany me to the station for threatening to kill someone.'

McIntyre sank back into the seat.

'If you were presented with a photograph of a dress, would you be able to identify it as the one Mary was wearing?'

McIntyre absorbed this, then eventually shook his head. 'I was a fourteen-year-old boy. So the answer is no.' He looked distressed at having to say that.

'What about jewellery?' McNab tried.

'Jewellery? What d'you mean? A ring?' He halted there, a light dawning in his eyes. 'A bracelet. She had a bracelet. A silver one. Loads of wee girls had them back then. She begged and begged my dad and eventually he appeared home with one. Christ knows where he got it. The pawn shop probably.'

'So this bracelet. Did it have an inscription?'

'You have to be fucking kidding me,' McIntyre said. 'We were poor. God knows how my mother found a dress for Mary's confirmation and you're asking if my dad got a bracelet engraved?' He sat back in his seat. 'It *is* Mary they found on the moors, whatever you're saying about dresses and bracelets. I know it is.'

'How do you know that?' McNab said.

'You have a brother or a sister, Detective Sergeant?'

McNab shook his head.

'She was my wee sister. It was my job to make sure she was okay. I fucking failed that day. I won't do that again.'

McNab glanced at his watch to signal he'd heard enough for now.

'I'll be back in touch once we've ID'd the remains.'

Robbie countered that. 'Once you've confirmed it's my

wee sister.' He thought for a moment. 'Jean would know about the dress. You need to talk to Jean.'

McNab left him there, hunched over his coffee. What the hell was going on in Robert McIntyre's head, McNab didn't want to imagine.

He'd dealt with a child abduction before. It had begun with a road traffic accident during a snowstorm. A wee girl called Emma had left an upturned car with her unconscious mother inside and made her way into nearby woods, because she maintained she'd heard a child's voice calling to her.

It turned out that what she led them to were the remains of a long-lost child.

When they'd found Emma, after a desperate search, she'd been sitting next to a pile of offcuts from the surrounding forest, holding a skull in her hands. She'd told McNab that the skull she'd found in the nearby mound belonged to a child like her.

And she'd been right.

McNab didn't like what had happened during that particular investigation, although they had listened to what Emma had had to say, weird though it had seemed at the time. Plus, they never would have tracked down the killer had it not been for Emma's supposed conversations *with the dead*.

He wasn't comfortable around children, but nine-year-old Emma Watson had been different. They'd formed a bond, which Claire, her mother, had been surprised by, and grateful for.

Outside now, McNab took a deep breath. The sooner they discovered the identity of the victim on the moors, the sooner they could deal with the fallout from the find. One thing was certain: human pain never went away. Never even diminished. It was always there, lurking behind a wall the sufferers built, just waiting to rear its head again.

As he walked away, his mobile rang. Glancing at the screen, he saw Magnus's name. Did he really want to talk to the Orcadian professor now? At that moment, Rhona's imagined voice sounded in his head telling him that he should, which to McNab's mind was ridiculous. Why did his subconscious always need to know what Rhona thought at moments like these?

Nonetheless, McNab found himself driven to answer.

'McNab,' he said gruffly.

'Magnus here.'

As if he didn't know, McNab thought. 'Professor. What can I do for you?'

'It's about the body on the moors.'

'What about it?' McNab said, surprised.

'There's a guy, Alec McLaughlin, I interviewed him in Barlinnie.' Magnus hesitated, as though he was considering giving more details about why he was visiting an inmate, then didn't. 'He says he knows something about it.'

20

The dress had an embroidered top and a full net skirt together with what had once been a stiffened petticoat. There was also a satin bow to be tied at the back. Although badly stained, the style and pattern were distinctive. If a missing child had disappeared wearing this dress, then surely there was a chance that remaining family members might be able to recognize it?

According to McNab, Mary McIntyre's parents were dead, but her sister and brother, who had been teenagers at the time, were still alive. The horror of what Mary's siblings had faced then, and now, wasn't lost on Rhona, whether the body on the moor turned out to be their sister or not.

'I wouldn't want to be shown a picture of her dress looking like that,' Chrissy said. 'All they'll think about is what happened when their sister was wearing it.' She glanced at Rhona. 'Okay, I know it's maybe the wrong size for the body we dug up, but still . . .'

It was for the police to decide whether they showed Mary's siblings a photograph of the dress as it was now, or alternatively an artist's reconstruction of how it would have looked on the morning of Mary's confirmation.

'Anyway, what fourteen-year-old male would remember his wee sister's outfit from forty-odd years ago? The big sister might, though,' Chrissy added. 'Can you remember your favourite dress when you were a kid?'

Rhona could and said so. 'A pink gingham sundress when I was eleven. But I have a photo of me wearing it to remind me. I take it you remember your confirmation outfit?'

'Too right I do. Innocent and virginal in a white dress and veil, we were the little brides of Christ,' Chrissy said. 'Anyway, that's what they told us. Sounds a bit creepy now. I remember wondering what the boys were supposed to be in their wee suits and ties. Maybe the best man at the wedding?' She made a face. 'They don't lay it on as thick nowadays. Just dress demurely, they tell you, preferably in white. But folk in Glasgow like to dress up. Demure is not for them.'

Rhona knew Chrissy was talking like this because the story behind the image was so disturbing. Plus to examine the dress properly would require it to be taken apart, bit by bit, so that they might test any area which appeared optimum for evidence-gathering. Just as the pathologists had done on the child's body at the PM.

Laid out for closer examination, the full set of clothes was even more poignant than when Rhona had first removed them from the plastic bag at the graveside.

'So,' Rhona said, 'do you want to tackle the dress?'

Chrissy thought for a moment. 'You take the dress and the veil. It feels too close to home for me. I'll do the shoes.'

'Jen will want whatever residue you scrape from the soles.'

Chrissy nodded. 'Roger that.'

Back in the seventies, the idea of soil forensics hadn't existed and neither had DNA profiling. Rhona recalled an image she liked to use in the Diploma in Forensic Medical

Science course she lectured on at Glasgow University, which showed a body on Gullane Beach, east of Edinburgh, in 1977. In it, a row of black-booted police officers stood only inches from one of the female teenage victims in what became known as the World's End Murders. The current students were so used to seeing carefully protected scenes of crime, peopled by white-suited personnel, that this particular image always brought a gasp of horror from the audience.

Fortunately, soil from one of the girls' shoes, preserved for future analysis, despite the fact they'd had no idea back then what soil and pollen could reveal, had proved vital in the subsequent historic conviction of the World's End killer.

With most of the afternoon now gone, Rhona's detailed and prolonged examination of the underskirt had identified several possible areas of interest, to be cut out and studied in more detail later. As for the actual dress, her initial taping had produced a few dark hairs and unidentified fibres.

'Coffee time?' Chrissy called from the office doorway.

Rhona gave her the thumbs up. Progress had been made but there was no doubting the length of time it would take to do the job properly.

The coffee poured, Chrissy now surprised Rhona by producing a box of iced doughnuts.

'What happened to the healthy diet?' Rhona said, cheerfully selecting a chocolate-coated delight.

'Everything in moderation,' Chrissy announced, choosing one topped with multi-coloured hundreds and thousands. 'Besides, I needed a sugar rush right about now.'

'Did you find anything of interest?' Rhona said.

Chrissy looked solemn. 'There was soil and pollen on the shoes and material that looked like the remains of gorse flowers. All of which Jen Mackie can give you a better analysis on.'

'Gorse blooms in May here,' Rhona said. 'But Jen's the expert.'

'The fingernails snipped at the PM are proving fruitful,' Chrissy continued. 'There were deposits of skin and blood on the underside.'

'So she could have fought her attacker?'

'Let's hope so. I've retrieved fibres and hairs from the plastic bag, but better than that, a fingerprint.'

Now that was good news.

'What about the cigarette butt?' Rhona said.

'Done. We wait now for the DNA result. Let's hope whoever did this offended again after we started the DNA database. Otherwise it doesn't help until we have a suspect.'

They decided to work on for a further hour, and then go for a drink.

'You never told me what happened with your handsome guitarist,' Rhona suddenly remembered.

'All may be revealed over a glass of wine,' Chrissy promised with a smile.

'Oh,' Rhona suddenly remembered. 'I have to go to a dinner.'

'A dinner? Where?' Chrissy demanded.

'It's the university dinner for participants on the forensic course,' Rhona explained.

Chrissy assumed an amazed expression. 'You never mentioned it before.'

'I wasn't going, then Dr Walker asked if I'd go along to keep him company.'

'You're going on a date with Dr Walker?' Chrissy's voice rose at the end to a surprised squeak.

'It's not a date,' Rhona said, knowing it sounded like one.

Chrissy gave her one of her all-knowing smiles. 'Okay. Whatever you say.'

Rhona, realizing there was no winning this one, headed for the shower.

21

'You have a visitor,' Janice informed McNab as he approached his desk.

'What visitor?' McNab said, made immediately suspicious by the look on Janice's face.

'*She's* with the boss.'

'Who the hell is it?' McNab said, now aware that everyone in the room was interested in their interchange. Maybe even amused by it.

'The boss says you're to go right in,' Janice told him.

McNab contemplated continuing his attempt to extract more information about the surprise visitor, then decided the quickest way to find out who 'she' was, was to take a look.

Aware that at least a dozen pairs of eyes were on his back, he approached the door in what he hoped was a nonchalant manner, only to hear the words, 'Come in, Detective Sergeant,' before he could even knock.

When the door swung open, McNab was rewarded with the sight of someone he hadn't thought to ever see again, even though he'd just been thinking about her earlier.

Emma was taller than he remembered, but the smile was just as bright.

'Michael,' she said in delight. 'Michael Joseph McNab.' She laughed, reminding McNab of the moment he'd revealed his real name in order to try and put her younger self at ease.

116

McNab thought she might run to hug him and was momentarily concerned at the possibility, but she didn't. Instead, she came forward and offered her hand in a grown-up gesture. The nine-year-old Emma Watson he remembered was on her way to becoming a teenager.

'Detective Sergeant McNab.' Her mother, Claire, also in the room, advanced with an equally welcoming look. 'It's so good to see you again. You're wondering why we're here,' Claire answered McNab's bemused look.

McNab glanced at the boss, wondering if DI Wilson already knew the answer to that.

His superior officer was on his feet. 'I'll leave you three to talk. It was good to meet you again, Ms Watson, and you, Emma.'

McNab tried to catch the boss's eye on his way out, wondering what his take was on all this, but DI Wilson's expression suggested it was up to his detective sergeant now.

Once the door was closed – and McNab could only imagine the faces outside at the emergence of the boss – Claire said, 'Emma has something she wants to talk to you about, Detective Sergeant.' Her expression suggested she wasn't totally comfortable with what Emma was about to say but had been prevailed upon to come to the police station by her determined daughter.

'Okay,' McNab said cautiously.

From Emma's expression, she had no such doubts. 'It's about the body on the moors,' she began firmly.

Listening to what Emma now said was like going back in time. McNab had dismissed what he believed were fantasies back then, only to be proved wrong. Listening to her request again now, he had the same misgivings.

In every murder investigation where a body hadn't been

found, inevitably Police Scotland were contacted by psychics who claimed to be able to 'see' its location. As far as McNab was aware, no search had reached a satisfactory conclusion because of such information.

Except in the case of Emma Watson.

That night in the snowy forest she'd located a child's remains under a pile of branches. She'd told McNab that she'd heard the dead child calling to her. At first he'd put it down to an overactive imagination and the shock of the car crash, but Emma had gone on to locate other burial sites, with no explanation as to how such a thing was even possible.

Something McNab had never found a satisfactory explanation for.

Emma was watching him, awaiting his response. McNab knew he had to choose his words carefully.

'Did you tell DI Wilson this?' he said quietly.

'Yes. He told me to speak to you.'

It was a simple enough request. Emma wanted to be taken to the grave site on the moors. Her reason being she wanted to be sure there was only one.

As he watched, McNab saw the fear in her eyes that he was about to refuse such an appeal. Perhaps if he and Rhona hadn't spoken at the PM of the likelihood of another victim, McNab would have told Emma that it wasn't possible. That in such an ongoing enquiry, members of the public couldn't visit the locus of a crime, or words to that effect.

Despite his deep misgivings, he found himself now contemplating the alternative.

Claire came in at that point. 'Detective Inspector Wilson recalled everything that had happened the night of the crash,' she said. 'And what Emma found afterwards.'

So the boss wasn't averse to such a request.

'He thought Emma should speak to you first, since you were directly involved,' Claire added, for emphasis.

'Please,' Emma said.

By the look on Claire's face, McNab realized if he said no the likelihood was Emma would make her mum take her out there anyway. When he said, 'Okay, let me discuss it further with DI Wilson,' he was rewarded with a delighted smile from Emma, and a relieved sigh from her mother.

'It's important we go as soon as possible,' Emma said determinedly.

McNab didn't want to hear why that might be. He pulled out his card and handed it to Claire. 'If you text me in the morning, I'll let you know what's been decided.'

Emma didn't look happy about the partial brush-off, but appeared to decide not to persist.

All eyes turned towards them as they exited the boss's office. A quick glance at Janice found a raised eyebrow and an enquiring look. McNab decided immediately that there was safety in numbers and paused to introduce Emma to 'my partner, DS Clark'.

'I remember Michael talking about you,' Emma said with a smile.

'I'll just show Emma and her mum out,' McNab said, keen to leave the room full of inquisitive faces. 'I'll be back shortly.'

All three were silent as they headed downstairs. McNab was conscious again of the intensity of Emma's presence. She was thinking something but wondering if she should say it. McNab found himself wishing, whatever it was, it would be kept until tomorrow.

Reaching the main entrance, he opened the door and prepared to say his goodbyes.

'They said on the news that it might be a girl called Mary McIntyre,' Emma said. 'Is that true?'

'We haven't confirmed who it is yet,' McNab said, taken aback by the direct question.

Emma nodded. 'Because I'm not sure they're right.'

22

'So what's your plan?' Janice said as McNab opened the box of notebooks.

'You're my right-hand woman. You tell me.'

They'd vacated the incident room and moved instead to an interview room because McNab had got fed up with the whistled snatches of *The X-Files* theme tune that had followed Emma and her mother's departure, her history with McNab being common knowledge.

Janice had been more circumspect when McNab told her what had actually happened in the boss's office.

'Some folk think they know it all, and that includes my colleagues.' She'd darted McNab a look that had included him in the subset she was referring to. 'When the only thing we really know is that we don't know anything.'

'What the hell does that mean?' McNab had said tetchily.

'It means the kid helped us before and she may do it again,' Janice said. 'Right, let's see what we can glean from the notebooks.'

McNab hadn't been convinced. 'You heard it from the author's mouth. J. D. Smart makes things up to entertain his audience.'

'Not back then,' Janice had said. 'Back then he was trying to understand.'

'You bought all his crap,' McNab had retorted. 'When in fact he tells lies for fun and profit.'

At that point Janice's eyebrows had disappeared behind her fringe. 'Where did you get that line?'

McNab wasn't sure. He hoped he'd thought of it himself but was inclined to believe he'd just read it somewhere.

'We can't dismiss the notebooks,' Janice was now saying.

'Who said we were?'

McNab grabbed the top one from the box. It was the one he'd already glanced through. The tight writing, almost formed so that no one but the author might be able to read it, reminded McNab of doctors' prescriptions before the computer was invented.

'How many have you looked at?' Janice was asking.

'Just the first one,' McNab admitted.

'So let's get started.'

She lifted number two and, opening her own bona fide notebook, sat them side by side. Her brow creased as she began to read, or more likely decipher, the close writing within.

McNab opened the first of Smart's books with a flourish, then his own police notebook to emphasize his intention. Whatever response he'd expected from Janice, he didn't get it. To all intents and purposes she was already deep in the words.

As far as McNab was concerned, McCreadie's almost il-legible scrawl seemed to flow like choppy waves across the page. As soon as he began to try to interpret the words, the remainder of the line started to dance before his eyes. It looked to McNab's eye more like music than writing.

After five minutes or so, he announced, 'This'll take too long when I have other things I should be doing. We'll get them transcribed. Then we can see what J. D. Smart has to say.'

Decided, McNab rose. Janice, on the other hand, didn't take her eyes off the page.

McNab, suddenly finding a need to further justify his change of plan, announced, 'I'm off to talk to Dr MacLeod about a possible return visit to the locus.'

At this, Janice did glance up. 'So you are taking the girl there?'

'It's what the boss wants.' McNab attempted an expression suggesting that was the only reason it would happen.

'Okay,' Janice said. 'I'll get someone to help transcribe these.'

She looked for a moment as if she would say something further, then chose not to.

McNab, relieved to be away from the notebooks and their illegible scrawl, made for the coffee machine, from where he called Rhona.

'You just caught me. Chrissy and I are finishing for the day.'

'Where are you headed?' McNab said.

'Usual place. Why?'

'We need to talk about something before the strategy meeting.'

'Okay,' Rhona said. 'D'you want to give me a heads-up on what that might be?'

'I'll tell you when I see you,' McNab said, and rang off.

He was aware that Emma's intervention would intrigue Rhona. After all, she and Magnus had been the ones to give credence to Emma's fanciful ideas back then, whereas he'd dismissed them out of hand. He suspected Rhona would be supportive of the child's request, while he would love for it never to have happened.

McNab checked his watch. He was due to go off shift shortly, as was Janice, so he wasn't actually skiving. And he did need to talk to Rhona. Even as he convinced himself of this, he acknowledged that Janice was unlikely to stop working just because her shift was over.

By the look on her face when he'd left, studying McCreadie's diaries was akin to reading Smart's detective novels. If she did go home, the likelihood was she would take them with her for her bedtime reading.

McNab shuddered at the thought.

His own view was that his time would be better spent interviewing everyone left alive, especially those listed as suspects by McCreadie when he was a cop, rather than a storyteller.

McNab drank his shot of coffee, sure now of his plan for the evening. Even as the certainty presented itself, his mobile buzzed in his pocket.

Hoping it might be Ellie, he checked the screen to find Pirie's number there. The 'decline' button attracted his finger, but he found himself pressing 'accept' instead.

'DS McNab,' he said formally.

'Professor Pirie,' Magnus responded, with what McNab imagined as one of the professor's annoying smiles.

When McNab didn't respond, Pirie continued, 'I wondered if you'd made contact with the former inmate I spoke about?'

'Not as yet,' McNab said cautiously.

'Would it be helpful if I spoke to him further regarding what he knows?' Magnus continued. 'As I said, he was one of my interviewees at the prison for my latest research—'

McNab interrupted. 'And what might that research have been, Professor?'

There was a pregnant pause before Magnus told him. 'Sex offenders and prison education services.'

'So that they can outwit us next time with their increased knowledge of the law and forensic services?' McNab said sharply.

The response that followed exhibited neither annoyance nor distress at the anger in McNab's voice, although he would know full well why it was there. Rhona's run-in with just such a character in the sin-eater case was still fresh in both their minds.

'What I didn't mention in our earlier call was that Alec McLaughlin was a convicted sex offender involving young children. My contacts in the prison don't expect him to have reformed despite having recently been awarded a first-class honours in psychology. Any interview with him, I suspect, might be better conducted by someone who understands that.'

'And that would be you?' When silence followed, McNab added, 'I suspect there'll be quite a few folk wanting to star in the story. If he's on our list, he'll get an interview. If you want to go on talking to him in the meantime . . .'

Magnus sounded relieved by this. 'Thanks. I'll be in touch.'

'You do that,' McNab muttered as he rang off.

At this point McNab recalled how hard Magnus Pirie had worked on the sin-eater case, and how much the professor's insight had played a part in its solution, and was momentarily sorry he'd been so sharp with him. There was just something about that calm, knowledgeable voice that got right up his nose. And it was nothing to do with the Orkney accent.

Despite the fact Chrissy loved it so much.

As he was about to depart the building, his mobile sounded again.

'What now?' he growled at the screen. But this time it was Janice. 'I'm just on my way out,' he told her.

She ignored his exasperated tone. 'Alec McLaughlin,' she said. 'The former inmate you asked to have checked out?'

'Yes?'

'It turns out McLaughlin was a teenager living two doors up from Mary McIntyre when she went missing. Plus he was serving fifteen years in Barlinnie for raping his partner's kids.'

23

Karen checked the time and decided she had at least an hour before darkness fell. Enough time for a short walk to clear her head.

Obsessing about what she'd written in the diary all those years ago was growing into an addiction. Just like her reliance on alcohol, when Jack was ill. One page, like one drink, was no longer enough. Even worse, the more she read, the more jumbled her memories became.

It was like a jigsaw, with each day's entry a piece of that terrible time in her life. But she couldn't fit them all together to form a complete picture.

'We'll help you do that when you bring it in,' Marge had said, when Karen had called her in her distress. 'Leave it for now. Take a walk. Go to one of Jack's favourite places, where you can feel close to him.'

Heeding Marge's advice, Karen now donned her jacket and, locking the front door, set off down the garden path.

She would tackle a walk she and Jack had often taken together of an evening, before the onset of his illness. Even after the dementia had been diagnosed, they'd kept to their routines, until Jack eventually forgot what any of those routines were.

Music from around the time they'd met had helped for a while, bringing him out of his stupor, putting life back into his eyes. They said that music awakened areas of the brain seemingly lost to the illness. Karen believed that because she'd seen it happen.

I should start listening to music again, she mused.

But the sudden thought of listening to their songs without Jack brought such a swift rush of horror, she immediately dismissed the idea.

She would try a familiar walk first, just as Marge had suggested. She would, she decided, head across to King's Knot. Charlie, their dog, had always loved being taken to the former king's gardens at the foot of Castle Hill.

As she entered the large grassy space, a man appeared with a little brown dog. He nodded a hello, but Karen didn't recognize him, so didn't respond. Seemingly unperturbed by this, both man and eager dog walked on. The image of the two of them on their, probably regular, evening walk made Karen wonder whether she should get a dog again.

Charlie had died shortly after Jack got noticeably ill. In truth, Karen had been relieved. She could no longer walk the old black lab because she couldn't leave Jack alone in the house, even for a minute.

Now she could leave the house, she no longer had a companion to go with her.

Trying not to think along those lines, Karen chose the path that hugged the steep wall of imposing grey rock, spotting the man just ahead of her. The dog had been let off the lead and was tearing after a ball. Its owner had stopped, no doubt waiting for the dog to bring the ball back to him.

As Karen drew near, the man turned and, realizing who it was, looked as though he might speak to her.

Dealing with people was still a problem for Karen. All those months shut in with Jack, wondering who was going mad the quickest, she'd lost the knack of casual conversation.

Of any conversation.

True, the recovery cafe had helped, but even that had taken time and a great deal of effort on the part of the other women before Karen had been able to join in the conversation at all.

'Mrs Johnston?'

Heart thumping, her eyes fixed on the ground, Karen willed herself not to look as though she'd heard him.

Maybe he would think her hard of hearing. Lots of folk her age were.

But he didn't give up.

'Mrs Johnston,' he said again.

At this point the dog came hurtling towards her and, stopping in front of her, deposited the ball at her feet.

She might manage to ignore the owner, but not the wee dog, who gazed up at her now, tail wagging in anticipation of her throwing the ball again.

'Sorry,' he said. 'Benji's a bit demanding. He and Charlie got on well together.'

Charlie's name disarmed her. She couldn't walk on now. It would be more than rude to do so. Karen stood helpless, unsure what to do next. To cover her confusion, she lifted the ball and threw it, focusing as it bounced across the grass with the wee terrier scurrying after it.

'I was terribly sorry to hear about Jack.'

There, the dreaded words had been said.

'We used to meet him occasionally with Charlie.'

Karen still hadn't looked at the man's face. She forced herself to do so now.

He was tallish, older than her, probably closer to Jack's

age, with thick grey hair and blue eyes. For a moment he reminded Karen of someone, then the memory melted away. She nodded her thanks, then willed her wobbly legs to move on.

See, Jack's imagined voice told her. *You can do it.*

'Who was he?' she muttered out loud.

Karen thought Jack laughed in response. *No idea. Never seen him or the dog before.*

Jack's imagined remark prompted Karen to stop and look back, only to find neither man nor dog were now anywhere to be seen. In fact, King's Knot was deserted apart from her.

Where had the man gone, and so swiftly?

Karen checked the various tracks, certain that there hadn't been sufficient time for him to head up the back path that wound its way through the tree-lined slope below the castle walls.

Yet, apparently, he had.

Perhaps you imagined him, Jack offered quietly. *Like the crow and the dead cat.*

'The crow was in the sitting room,' Karen said out loud. 'And I did see Toby.'

Jack had always managed to find a logical explanation for what he called 'her intuition', and most of the time Karen had accepted his take on it.

Not this time.

'I saw him,' she muttered as she set off for home. 'I most definitely did not imagine him.'

Despite the odd encounter, Karen found herself buoyed up by her walk and the fact that she'd engaged with someone, however briefly, besides the women of the recovery cafe. She also found herself looking forward to the meeting tomorrow, where they would all get a chance to read her diary and help her remember everything she could about Mary's disappearance.

Even as she thought this, a memory of what Jack had always said sprang to mind.

No use digging up the past, Karen. None of us are perfect and bad things happen. Better to forget it.

A sliver of fear crept in. The problem was, she wasn't entirely sure whether she had actually chosen to forget some things, and questions from the women in the recovery cafe might reveal those she didn't want to remember. Was she making a mistake discussing the past with Marge and the others?

'No.' She shook her head. She wanted to be prepared for when the police came calling. She wanted to be clear what had happened, so she could tell them.

But what if you did something wrong? a small voice said. *What if you were responsible in some way for what happened to Mary?*

Back at the house now, fear engulfed Karen as she shakily tried to put her key in the lock, desperate to get inside and away from the encroaching darkness. When the hall light snapped on, she stood for a moment, breathing in, waiting for her heart to slow in the safety of familiar surroundings.

'I'm back, Jack,' she called, attempting to sound cheery. 'Safe and sound.'

In the silence that followed, Karen imagined she heard his grunt of approval.

'I'll put the kettle on,' she announced. 'We could both do with a cup of tea.'

Hanging up her coat, she spotted something lying on the mat. At first, she thought it might be a slip from the window cleaner, saying he'd done the windows for her while she was out.

As she retrieved it, she immediately knew she was wrong. The note wasn't from the window cleaner, but from someone else entirely.

There was a single line which read:

I know who you are.

24

'Word is another girl went missing in her confirmation dress, from York, in 1974,' Chrissy told Rhona.

'When did you hear that?' Rhona said.

'I have my sources.' Chrissy's left eyebrow rose to reflect that fact.

'Bona fide?'

'Of course.' Her forensic assistant sounded peeved that Rhona might think otherwise. 'There's a list of possibles being produced at the strategy meeting. Only one was abducted wearing a white dress.'

They were seated at the bar of the jazz club, awaiting their wine. It arrived just as Chrissy made her announcement. Rhona lifted the cold glass and took a sip, giving herself time to contemplate Chrissy's latest piece of news.

'Well?' Chrissy was looking for a response to this interesting update.

'At the moment we have one victim and we haven't yet established who that victim is. But hopefully we'll know soon,' Rhona said. She was saved from Chrissy's reply because her assistant had just spotted the figure of McNab coming down the stairs.

'Plus,' Chrissy said in a loud whisper, 'I know why McNab wants to speak to you.' She smiled her success.

Before Rhona could react to this, McNab joined them and, hailing the barmaid, ordered a beer.

'Dr MacLeod.' He suddenly took note of Rhona's evening outfit. 'You look very nice.'

'She's going on a date with Dr Walker,' Chrissy immediately told him.

'It is *not* a date,' Rhona said. 'It's work.'

'Nice work if you can get it,' Chrissy said, before turning to McNab. 'And *I* know why *you're* here.'

'The spy network you have in the station is legendary,' McNab admitted. 'So does your boss know?' He indicated Rhona.

Chrissy shook her head. 'I preferred to wait and watch you tell her.'

'Tell me what?' Rhona now demanded.

'Emma Watson,' McNab said, 'came with her mother, Claire, to the station today.'

At the mention of Emma's name, a flurry of memories swept over Rhona. The first of which was the image of a little girl in a winter wood, frightened, yet determined to help them in their search for the body of a missing child.

'How is she?' was her first response. 'She must be . . .'

'Almost a teenager,' McNab said. 'Taller, but just as intense.' He halted, perhaps looking for the right words to explain the visit.

Rhona was already ahead of him. 'She came to speak to you about the body on the moors?'

McNab nodded. 'She wants—'

'To check that there isn't another body buried there,' Rhona finished for him.

'How weird is that?' Chrissy, big-eyed, came in. 'It's just what we were thinking.'

'*You* have a reason to suspect there might be—' McNab began.

'Emma was right once before, remember?' Rhona said.

McNab's sudden attention to his pint suggested he didn't want to acknowledge that fact.

'Cool,' Chrissy said. 'Rhona can take her up there. That's what you wanted to ask, wasn't it?' She looked pointedly at McNab.

'The boss thinks it's okay,' he offered cautiously.

'Then we'll take her there before the strategy meeting.' Rhona finished her wine and stood up.

'So that's you off on your date?' Chrissy said.

'See you tomorrow,' Rhona said, lifting her bag and making for the stairs, but not before she'd caught McNab's voice saying, 'Does Sean Maguire know about this?'

Rhona didn't hang around long enough to hear Chrissy's reply, just said a silent thank you that she hadn't agreed to meet Richie in the jazz club, even though he'd suggested it.

The bustle of Ashton Lane enveloped her. Puddles from an earlier shower, patchworked by the strings of coloured lights, glistened between the cobbles. She headed up University Avenue towards the towers of the university. The sky above the city was a metallic blue broken by bloodied streaks. She felt a sudden surge of pleasure to be back at work and back in Glasgow.

And Skye will always be there when I need it, she told herself.

She'd reached the main gate where Stan, who Rhona was well acquainted with, was manning the entry post.

'Evening, Dr MacLeod,' he said with a smile. 'Looking forward to a nice dinner and some speeches?'

Rhona was about to answer Stan's query, although in

what manner she wasn't sure, when a tall figure stepped out of the shadows behind him.

'Stan told me you weren't here yet, so I decided to wait for you,' Richie said, almost apologetically.

'I told him these events definitely require a partner in crime,' Stan said with a conspiratorial smile.

'And you should know, Stan. Come on, Dr Walker,' Rhona said, 'it's time to face the fray. For a man who dissects dead people,' she continued as they walked together towards the main building, 'functions like this one should be a walk in the park.'

'I prefer dealing with the dead rather than the living. They don't expect small talk.'

'I'm inclined to agree with you on that,' Rhona said.

The entrance hall was buzzing, the echo of a myriad voices like a wall they had to penetrate. Rhona felt Dr Walker flinch and realized that crowded places such as this were anathema to the pathologist. Hence his desire for moral support.

Released from the idea that this might be construed as a date, Rhona urged him on. 'Think of the crowd as a thick layer of blubber you have to cut through before you get to the interesting part.' She pointed ahead at a clear space next to the door leading to the dining area. 'Plus there's a tray of drinks over there waiting for us.'

Rhona led the way, nodding at those she knew, but not stopping for the usual small talk. Eventually they reached the waiter and lifted their glasses.

'I'd rather have a dram,' Dr Walker said, sipping the usual fizzy offering.

'Me too,' Rhona assured him. 'Whisky will be on offer after dinner. We'll have to wait until then.'

'I take it you've been to a lot of these events?' Dr Walker offered.

'I try to avoid them.' Rhona told him the truth. 'But I'm glad I came to this one.'

'I should have warned you about my reaction to crowds, although it's not always as bad as tonight,' Richie said.

Agoraphobia was known to present itself after a bad experience. Rhona wondered if Richie might tell her when or why the feeling had begun, but he didn't.

Rhona shrugged. 'I can't face closely packed trees, never mind humans. I discovered that on Skye. Shall we find our seats?' She didn't say that they were unlikely to be sitting together, because that could be easily remedied. She had it in mind that they would simply switch place cards.

However, before she could put her plan into action, a voice hailed her from across the room. Rhona recognized the voice immediately and felt her stomach turn over.

Please God it isn't him.

But it most definitely was.

'Fuck,' Rhona said, loud enough for Richie to hear.

'Who is it?' he whispered.

'Just an arsehole I once had a child with,' Rhona told him.

Edward Stewart was heading towards them, blue eyes twinkling, a wide smile on his handsomely tanned face. Rhona wondered if Fiona, his wife, was with him, but couldn't spot her blonde coiffured presence among the melee.

'I apologize in advance,' Rhona warned Richie. 'This won't be pretty.'

And then Edward was there. Offering a hug which Rhona declined.

'Rhona, it's so good to see you.'

'Why are you here?' Rhona responded. 'At a university forensic event?'

Edward's white smile grew wider. 'We're about to become a sponsor for the Diploma in Forensic Medical Science programme. Isn't that fabulous?'

Rhona could think of many words to describe such a link, but fabulous wasn't one of them, so she remained silent.

Edward's studied look moved from Rhona to Richie and back again. He held out his hand. 'Edward Stewart. Rhona and I go way back.'

Richie gave Edward the ghost of a smile. 'Dr Walker, forensic pathologist.'

At this point the gong sounded for dinner, which Rhona immediately saw as an escape route.

'We'd better go in before the rush,' she suggested, keen now to escape Edward.

'No rush,' Edward informed her. 'I spotted earlier that we're on the same table.'

Rhona swore silently at this, utilizing an internal string of expletives Chrissy would have been proud of. Their own seating plan scotched, she turned to give Richie an apologetic look, only to discover he'd already headed through the archway and into the dining hall.

'Shall we?' Edward offered Rhona his arm, which she pointedly ignored. With that symbol of ownership denied him, Edward made an attempt to usher her onward by placing his hand on the small of her back. Rhona quickly sidestepped this and indicated he should go first.

On arrival at their table, they discovered Richie already there.

'Isn't this good?' he said. 'I'm next to you both.'

He might have said 'between you both', which would have been the truth. Edward, Rhona noted, was definitely nonplussed by this sudden demolition of his plans (no doubt he'd already been riffling with the seat placements). However, he quickly regained his composure and, being Edward, immediately said, 'There was something I wanted to chat to Rhona about, so perhaps I might sit next to her for a bit?'

And so they sat down, Rhona casting a grateful glance at Richie for trying.

The hall became a babble of movement and noise as the crowd took their seats, including the other three people at their table. As the introductions began, Rhona was already planning her escape from both the table and, even better, the event.

Her best bet, she decided, was the arrival of a call-out to an imaginary crime scene. If Richie played along, she might be able to rescue him too. Even as she planned this, she realized she was nonetheless curious as to what Edward wanted to say to her.

They hadn't been in contact for some time, although she was aware that he and Fiona were still together and that Jonathan, their son, was at art school. Jonathan was nothing like his father. Rhona knew this because she and Jonathan had been to hell and back together.

She would always wish Jonathan well. His sister, Morag, however, she feared was a perfect combination of both her parents.

'It's good to see you looking so well, Rhona,' Edward was saying.

'What do you want, Edward?' Rhona finished off the wine in her glass.

He made a troubled face, as though they were the best of

friends and yet she'd chosen to fall out with him over some unknown trifle.

'Our son, of course,' he said.

'We don't have a son. As I recall, you wanted him aborted and I gave him up for adoption.'

The smile never faltered.

'We were young and stupid.'

'I was certainly stupid having anything to do with you.'

Rhona's voice had risen and she noted that Richie was looking over at her with a worried expression on his face. She forced herself to stay calm.

'What is it you want?' she tried again.

'I want to get in touch with Liam,' Edward said.

'But why?' Rhona was genuinely perplexed. 'You've never wanted to before. In fact, when you were running for parliament, you asked me – no, warned me – that Liam's existence should never be revealed.'

'That was then. Now is now. I want to make contact with him.'

'How is your own son, Jonathan?' Rhona changed tack.

'Oh, you know. Living the life of an art student.' Edward managed to make it sound as though Jonathan had joined a religious cult.

'Has he come out as gay yet?' Rhona said.

Edward's face became like stone. 'As I said, Jonathan is fine. I'll send him your regards. Back to Liam. I understand he's back in the UK and looking for a job?'

Now that was news to Rhona, so how did Edward know? Rhona tried to remember when she'd last had a communication from Liam. Had he mentioned coming home and getting a job here? Unsure, she simply waited, knowing Edward didn't require an answer. In fact he never required an answer.

'I may have an opening for him, but I need his contact details.'

If Edward knew Liam was coming home and wanted work, how was it he didn't know how to contact him?

At that moment her mobile rang. Rhona made a point of answering it, only then noticing that Richie was missing from his seat.

'Emergency call,' Richie's voice said. 'If you need to escape, meet me at the front gate.'

'Of course, DS McNab,' Rhona said. 'I'll be right there.' Ringing off, she apologized to the table, but sadly she was required at a crime scene.

Ignoring Edward's furious expression, she rose and made her way swiftly through the tables just as the first course was arriving. Wherever she and Richie went now, she decided, it had to offer food, because she was starving.

25

Janice had refused to phone Professor Pirie to tell him they were bringing in McLaughlin for questioning, so McNab had had to do it himself. He'd finally made the call from the jazz club, after Rhona had left on her date with the blue-eyed pathologist and Chrissy had departed to tell her son a bed-time story.

McNab had required a second pint before he'd got down to the job of calling the professor. (He would have preferred whisky but was still rationing himself on that front.)

Pirie, acting surprised to hear McNab's voice, had been cautious but positive in his response.

'Are you contacting Mr McLaughlin or shall I?' he'd said.

'DS Clark has already been in touch with him,' McNab had responded. What he didn't repeat were DS Clark's words: 'McLaughlin was very keen, and stressed he'd like Professor Pirie to be there.'

'So I'm officially on the case?' Magnus had said, sounding self-satisfied to McNab's ear.

'You're on for McLaughlin's interview,' McNab had conceded, knowing full well that meant the boss wanted the professor fully involved. 'Can you be here tomorrow morning at nine?'

McNab had chosen the time, hoping that Professor Pirie might well have a class then. There had been a moment's

142

pause, in which McNab celebrated the fact that the professor wouldn't make it after all, before his hopes had been crushed.

'That's fine, Detective Sergeant. Shall I come in earlier to discuss tactics?'

Discuss tactics? Fuck's sake, McNab had almost said, but had managed not to.

The time they'd agreed was fast approaching. McNab had had to miss his workout this morning just to meet it. One bonus at least.

As he contemplated this, DS Clark arrived with the professor and, thankfully, coffee.

'You'll be behind the observation glass, Professor,' McNab said. 'No doubt your star pupil will be giving his best performance.'

'Are you planning a standard cognitive interview focusing on the day of the girl's disappearance?' Pirie asked.

'Yes,' Janice came in quickly. 'We'll start with free recall around the day Mary McIntyre disappeared. We have some images of the street layout to help with context reinstatement.' She halted there, noting McNab's expression.

'I expect McLaughlin will know all about this method, Professor,' McNab said, 'seeing that his degree is in Forensic Psychology?'

'He will,' Pirie nodded, with no sense of taking offence at McNab's obvious dig, 'and in depth.'

'So, Professor,' McNab said. 'What do you suggest?'

'Mr McLaughlin loves the sound of his own voice so getting him to talk won't be a problem. However, despite his knowledge of psychology, I suspect getting him to recall backwards rather than in chronological order, since lies are usually rehearsed that way, may prove useful. Another

143

thing. He's narcissistic, so perhaps get him to try and recall the day from someone else's point of view. Say Karen Marshall's, Mary's best friend. The girls were apparently joined at the hip, metaphorically speaking.'

'How did you know that?' McNab said, recalling Robbie, Mary's brother, using the same expression.

'I've been reading old newspaper reports,' Magnus told him. 'Why?'

'Nothing,' McNab said as his mobile buzzed. Answering, he listened, then said, 'Someone will be up for him.' Ringing off, he looked at Janice. 'Me or you?'

'I'll go,' Janice said. 'Let's see how he deals with a female officer. Fifteen years ago there weren't many of us around.'

Pirie had moved next door to the viewing room. McNab was already conscious of being watched. That sensation was the only psychic phenomenon he accepted, mainly because it had saved his life on a couple of occasions. Once upon a time, Pirie had tried to explain the psychological reasons for thinking that someone was watching you. McNab had started listening but had soon grown weary. All those words for something he simply knew to be true.

The other thing McNab knew, from instinct or intuition, was when he was in the presence of evil.

He glanced up as the door opened and Janice stood aside to let McLaughlin enter. In that moment, McNab felt the hairs on his arms rise in warning. Evil, it seemed, had many forms. In this case, it had taken on the role of Santa Claus via a red jacket, fastened over a large belly, fluffy white hair with beard to match, and rosy cheeks.

McNab found himself wanting to say 'Ho, ho, ho'.

McLaughlin immediately came forward, hand outstretched. 'It's a pleasure to meet you, Detective Inspector . . .

oh sorry, Detective *Sergeant* McNab. I've been following your career quite closely during my studies.'

McNab did not accept the handshake, which he knew was a wrong move since it then put McLaughlin at an advantage. Although his head had told him to shake hands, his arm, with the hairs still standing, had simply refused.

McNab glanced at Janice to check how she was faring but couldn't read her expression or body language. As for McLaughlin, he gave an avuncular laugh and sat down.

McNab began the formalities but McLaughlin interrupted him to ask in a puzzled fashion where Professor Pirie was. 'I understood he would be present.'

'That wasn't possible,' Janice said coolly. 'Professor Pirie has classes all morning.'

McLaughlin raised a quizzical eyebrow. 'Not according to his online timetable.'

McNab could almost see Pirie shaking his head in the next room at the way things were going. Perhaps even memorizing the scene for the subject of future lectures.

'How Not to Start an Interview with a Psychopath' seemed an appropriate title.

Eventually they were ready.

McLaughlin, McNab thought, looked keen. Unsurprising really, the way things had transpired up to now. He sat relaxed in the chair, a small, contented smile on his pink lips.

Trying to ignore the self-satisfied air emanating from McLaughlin, McNab said, 'The purpose here is for you to tell us everything you remember.'

A cognitive interview normally began with a free recall. Something McLaughlin would know. From the look on his face he had his story all ready and waiting.

LIN ANDERSON

'No bother,' McLaughlin replied.

'So, Mr McLaughlin,' Janice said, 'where were you exactly when you first heard that Mary McIntyre was missing?'

McLaughlin's reaction to this was a joy to behold. Whatever he'd thought they might start with, it certainly wasn't that question. He looked nonplussed, but only for a moment.

'My exact location?' he said slowly.

McNab could almost see the wheels turning as McLaughlin restructured his no doubt well-rehearsed story.

'As near as you can remember.'

McLaughlin shut his eyes, supposedly recreating the image of that day, which was all part of the cognitive handbook. Eventually he said, 'I was sitting on the hill in front of the Catholic primary school.'

'Why there?'

His eyes still shut, McLaughlin continued, 'It was where we hung out. You could see all up and down the street and onto the houses opposite.'

He went on, 'I was sitting there watching all the kids coming down the road from the chapel. Two by two, girls in white dresses and veils. Boys in suits. They were heading for the school. Mary McIntyre's mum came into the garden to watch for Mary. But Mary wasn't among them. When she couldn't see her, Mrs McIntyre ran up to the teacher who was at the front. Then they both looked through all the kids. There must have been eighty of them. But Mary wasn't there.'

He paused for a moment, focusing his now-open eyes directly on Janice.

'That's when I saw Karen Marshall, Mary's pal. She lived in the house opposite the entrance to the school. She was in the front garden. I thought she was waiting for Mary too. But Mary never came. That's when I knew she was missing.'

'Tell us about Karen,' McNab said.

'Her dad was like you, a police officer. A detective constable.' He eyed McNab. 'Better not screw up again, Detective Sergeant, or you'll be back at that rank.' He smiled at his own little joke.

McNab felt Janice's slight nudge under the table, warning him not to rise to the bait. He didn't, mainly because he was having a mental picture of doing a lot worse than that to the creepy bastard.

'What happened next?' Janice asked.

'Well, things got a bit heated. Mary's dad arrived. He was a mean bastard at the best of times. Had a big thick belt with a buckle that hung on a hook in the kitchen. He would whistle his kids in for the night and if they didn't come right away, they got that belt.'

He paused, looking for a reaction. When there was none, he went on, warming again to his story. 'Mary's dad went off up the road towards the chapel to look for Mary and the rest of the kids went into the school. Karen came out of the garden and set off to where she and Mary had a den they'd made. They thought no one knew about it, but we all did.'

'Where was this den?' McNab said, revealing the map they'd prepared of the area in 1975.

McLaughlin drew it towards him and, after studying it with interest, pointed to a wooded area which lay beyond the open ground between the two schools.

'You said *we* all knew about it,' Janice said. 'Who's we?'

'Me, Mary's brother Robbie. He used to go up there with one of his pals. What they were up to, who knows?' He smiled as though he knew exactly.

Thinking back to his discussion with Robbie, McNab suspected he knew what McLaughlin was implying, so he didn't ask.

'What happened next?' he prompted instead.

'I followed her. She was running. Then she suddenly stopped. Something had spooked her. I couldn't see what it was. Then she ran on. I didn't take the path, I cut round the back through the trees.' He stopped there for a moment, looking at them both. 'That's when I saw him.'

McNab and Janice both waited, knowing he'd set them up to ask who he'd seen. When they didn't rise to the bait, he looked irritated, but only briefly.

'Robbie McIntyre was there, and he was carrying something.'

Something tweaked in McNab's brain. *He's lying*, McNab thought. *The fucker is lying. Maybe just this part. Maybe all of it.*

'Describe what he was carrying,' Janice said.

'I was too far away to make it out, but it was definitely white.'

At this point McNab considered whether McLaughlin knew about the confirmation dress in the grave. But how? It hadn't been released to the press and general public, although he had asked Robbie if he might be able to identify the dress his sister was wearing when she'd disappeared. Robbie might contact McCreadie about it, but McNab couldn't for a moment imagine a link between either of those two men and the creature that sat opposite him.

'Please carry on, Mr McLaughlin,' Janice said.

'I went home then.'

'Did you see Karen again that day?'

He shook his head. 'Folk came out and looked about the place, including Karen's dad. The police did the round of the houses and garden sheds. Asking when we'd last seen Mary.'

'When did you last see Mary?' Janice said.

This time McLaughlin was ready with his answer. 'The night before when she was whistled in. She didn't show up at first, so she must have been at the den or in the woods. When she did appear, her dad was livid and dragged her inside the house. She got the belt that night. I heard her crying.'

'Did you tell the police all of this when you were interviewed?' McNab said.

'Of course I did, but DI McCreadie didn't like me. He thought I did it, and made sure everyone else thought that too.'

So that's why he's here, McNab thought, *to plead his innocence*.

But McLaughlin wasn't finished yet and he'd kept his bombshell for the end.

'Wee Mary McIntyre was pregnant when she disappeared. Did McCreadie tell you that, Detective Sergeant?'

26

She's taller, Rhona thought. Tall and gangly, although her face had barely changed, nor had the intense look McNab had mentioned.

Emma had been nine when they'd last met and, as McNab had said, she wasn't far short of a teenager now. She'd greeted Rhona with a delighted smile, although once the subject moved to why they were meeting, the serious look had returned.

Her mum, Claire, had delivered Emma to the police station at midday as agreed, but had chosen not to accompany them on their trip to the moor. It was, she'd explained, too big a reminder of what had happened to her daughter the last time they'd met. Rhona didn't blame her for that.

'Just text me when you're on your way back,' Claire had said with a forced smile, 'and I'll be waiting for you.'

McNab too had chosen not to accompany them but had seemed relaxed about Magnus going. Rhona had been given the impression that he was glad to see the tail end of the professor, who'd apparently been observing an interview McNab and DS Clark had been conducting. Emma, on the other hand, had greeted Magnus with great warmth. It had been Magnus, together with Rhona, who'd persuaded McNab to acknowledge the child's role in the earlier investigation.

Magnus had to sit in the back, so that Emma might sit next to Rhona, although no one spoke as they headed southwards out of the city. The rain came on to match their mood, streaming the windscreen, with the only sound being the soft thump of the wipers.

As they began their climb up onto the moor, Emma roused herself, as though in preparation for what was to follow. Rhona couldn't imagine what was going through the girl's mind, but couldn't dismiss the thought that, by bringing her here, she might be making Emma relive her previous trauma.

A quick sideways glance revealed the opposite. Emma, alert now, wore the determined look Rhona remembered.

The rain had stopped by the time they took to the dirt track that led to the excavation site. As a watery sun broke through the clouds to fashion a rainbow, Rhona couldn't help but wonder, if it *was* a sign of luck, what that luck might mean. That Emma wouldn't locate another body nearby? Or, alternatively, that she would?

Rhona parked in her usual place, and they all climbed out. The rain clouds were now scurrying across the sky, hurried by a brisk wind. Underfoot was muddy and a walk through the sodden heather wouldn't be a pleasant experience.

Rhona glanced at Magnus. How did he want to play this?

Picking up on her signal, Magnus indicated with a nod towards Emma that they should leave it up to the girl to decide.

It seemed Emma had done so already.

'I'd like to be taken to where you found her.'

Rhona nodded. 'Okay. If you're sure.'

Rhona led the way, followed by Emma, with Magnus bringing up the rear. The path she and Chrissy had made with their trips back and forth to the forensic van was still visible, and taking it again now brought an instant recall of what they'd unearthed in this place.

The lochan came into view first, its peaty waters brightened by rays of sunshine, then a glimpse of a tattered crime scene tape that had broken free from its moorings.

Rhona halted for a moment, until all three of them were together.

'The grave is a little ahead. It's not been filled in,' she warned. 'That's distressing in itself, plus—'

'It's okay,' Emma said firmly. 'I'd like you and Magnus to wait here. It's better if I go on alone.'

Rhona glanced at Magnus and he gave an almost imperceptible nod.

Emma, it seemed, had not waited for their approval, but had set off in a determined fashion towards the flapping yellow tape.

'We'll wait in the car,' Magnus called after her.

As Emma raised her hand in acknowledgement of this, Magnus said, 'We have to talk.'

'Okay,' Rhona said, struck by Magnus's expression.

They turned and headed back on the beaten-down heather path and climbed into the car, this time with Magnus in the passenger seat.

'What's wrong?' Rhona said.

'Before I begin, I have permission from DS McNab to tell you this.'

'Okay.' Rhona waited.

'DS McNab and DS Clark interviewed a Mr Alec McLaughlin this morning, on my recommendation. I know Mr McLaughlin from Barlinnie where he took part in my research on the take-up of educational classes by prisoners.

Just released from prison himself, he contacted me and when we met he told me he had information about the disappearance of Mary McIntyre. DS McNab then arranged an interview with him, which I observed from the neighbouring room.'

'Go on,' Rhona said, realizing from Magnus's expression how significant he felt this interview had been.

'Before I tell you what he said, I should point out that he took an Open University degree while incarcerated and achieved a first-class honours in Forensic Psychology, so he's well versed in interview techniques. He was also convicted of raping his partner's three children, for which he's been incarcerated for fifteen years.'

'So whatever he told you could have been a lie,' Rhona finished for him.

Magnus nodded. 'However, he was a neighbour of Mary's whilst a teenager, so knew her and her family well.' He paused as though they'd reached the crunch of the story. 'McLaughlin told us that Mary McIntyre was pregnant when she went missing. In fact he said he thought that's why she disappeared.'

Rhona attempted to assimilate what Magnus had just said. Dr Wang, at post-mortem, had recorded what she believed to be a female of around eleven. The age of course couldn't be exact, and numerous females as young as ten were recorded as having given birth in various countries around the world, including the United States, although not in the UK.

In many of the listed cases, the one to make them pregnant had been someone close to the child, either a relative or a family friend.

'What d'you think?' Magnus said.

'If you're asking me if that was discussed at the post-mortem, it wasn't. Also, like the spleen, intestine and stomach, a pregnant uterus decays early. Plus we're not yet certain that the victim is Mary McIntyre, and won't be unless we can extract DNA.' Rhona explained further, 'Bogs are acidic and they tend to strip the base pairs off the DNA, so although you can see the DNA, you can't read it. Think of letters scattered about a page. You can see them but, because they aren't strung together, there are no words to recognize.'

The rain had come on again with a vengeance, the wind whipping it against the windows.

'She'll be getting soaked out there,' Rhona said, opening the car door. 'I'm going to get her.'

Dark clouds had now obliterated the earlier sunlight, although Rhona could still make out Emma's bright blue coat, which suggested the hooded girl was seated near the grave.

Pulling up her own hood, Rhona began the trudge over the heather against the driving rain. Letting Emma do this once before, in not dissimilar circumstances, had proved fruitful. At this moment in time, it seemed not only ludicrous, but also dangerous. To take an imaginative girl like Emma, on the cusp of womanhood, or maybe already there, and put her back in an environment where she might relive all her own trauma had been a mistake.

As Rhona neared the figure, Emma stood up, but didn't indicate that she'd noted Rhona's approach.

'Emma,' Rhona called, her voice whipped away by the wind. Reaching out, she took the girl by the arm. 'Emma, let's get you back to the car.'

The buffeting wind was catching the slender figure, almost lifting her off her feet.

She turned suddenly, as though just waking up to the fact that Rhona was there, and without saying anything, moved to make her own way back along the path.

Magnus met them en route and, placing his arm about Emma, sought to shield her from the worst of the wind.

Once inside the car, Rhona started up the engine. Their breath had steamed up the windows, obscuring what lay beyond their metal cocoon.

'There's something wrong,' Emma said.

'Wrong how?' Rhona asked, fully expecting Emma, like before, to suggest the grave they'd uncovered wasn't the only one on the moor.

'Two people were in that grave. Not one.'

27

Karen had lain awake most of the night and what snatches of sleep she'd grabbed had been fuelled by nightmarish images of a blood-splattered Mary in her white dress. Moments of elucidation during these dreams convinced her, however fleetingly, that she knew what had happened to her friend, but each time she forced herself awake to write it down, the memory had deserted her.

Had she had any alcohol in the house, she would have drunk it. All of it. Regardless of the consequences.

Eventually Karen had risen, gone downstairs and put the kettle on, Jack's answer to every problem being, *Let's have a cup of tea*.

From the kitchen window, Karen had a clear view of the castle. The image of the rock formation with its hilltop fortress had become so familiar that she no longer paid it much attention. Today was different. Today, she thought of her own memory as being as inaccessible as the castle itself, with no hope of ever penetrating its defences to discover what lay within.

As for the delivery last night when she was out walking the length of Castle Hill . . .

The piece of paper contained what? An accusation? A threat?

And from whom?

The note still lay on the kitchen table where she'd tossed it in her horror. It was crumpled because, after the first reading, she had screwed it up into a ball and thrown it in the bin, only to fish it out again for a second and third reading.

The diary was sitting on the kitchen table, awaiting its trip to the recovery cafe. The question was, could she go there now after receiving the note? Could she go there at all?

The diary now reminded Karen of a scary book she'd once taken out of the library. The horror story had been about an evil house that had preyed on its owners, finding out all their secrets and using those secrets against them. The book had disturbed Karen, so much so that she'd taken it back to the library without finishing it. She'd even put it in the garden shed until she could return it.

Jack had laughed at her fears, but then things had started to go wrong in the house. Little things, inexplicable things. Jack thought she was just being forgetful, like when the gas ring was left on and a tea towel lying close by caught fire. But Karen knew she'd turned all the rings off when she'd finished making the meal. She was always careful about that. So the very next day she'd taken the book back to the library without finding out whether the family had defeated the evil presence in their house, or whether they'd sold up and moved away.

Staring at the diary, Karen suspected she was in the same scenario. The evil from forty-five years ago had never really gone away, it had been lurking there all those years just waiting for her to pick up that diary again.

I should have burned it like Jack told me to, she thought. She'd intended doing that, but for some reason never could. If she did, she'd reasoned, she would never be able to fill in the blanks of what had happened.

Your parents took you away from that street so you wouldn't be reminded of what happened there. They wanted you to forget.

Karen had done what Jack had advised most of the time, but not with the diary. There she had defied him. And that decision had come back to haunt her.

But I can at least get it out of the house, she told herself. She would give it to Marge. The house would be free of it. The diary could no longer taunt her by its presence.

But what about the note? a small voice said. Should she show them the note too?

Karen immediately knew that if she did, she would appear guilty of something.

And she didn't know what that something was. Or did she?

She reached for the diary, and in that moment in her head she heard a frightened voice repeating the same words over and over again.

You have to help me.

28

McLaughlin had read his statement and signed it. The flourish with which he'd done the latter reminded McNab of the way celebrities gave their autographs, certain in the knowledge of their own fame.

By that stage, McNab was finding it increasingly difficult not to kick McLaughlin under the table, or even better, in the balls. However, he'd done such a thing once before in a not dissimilar situation and the boss had taken the blame for it.

Had DI Wilson not done so, you would have been out on your ear, McNab reminded himself.

DS Clark had looked relieved when they'd eventually shown a preening McLaughlin the door.

'Any more help I can give you, don't hesitate to get in touch, officers,' had been his farewell gift.

McNab had hoped as he'd watched McLaughlin depart that the next time they met would be when he arrested him.

He'd had only a short exchange with Pirie before the Prof set off with Rhona and the girl on their paranormal escapade, although he had told Pirie to share McLaughlin's revelation that Mary McIntyre had been pregnant when she'd disappeared. At least when Rhona arrived at the strategy meeting, she'd be up to date.

'So,' Janice was saying, 'what d'you think?'

'Give me your take on it first,' McNab said, handing her a coffee.

'He's intelligent. I can see how he got that degree.'

'Okay, he's a clever, scheming and manipulative bastard who managed to ply his trade for a long time before we caught him. So why present himself back in front of us now?'

'We would come knocking on his door again, and soon?' Janice tried.

'So he gets in first. But how much did you believe of the story?'

'I'd like to know how much Professor Pirie believed.'

'You've got more experience of liars than the Prof.'

He'd always considered Janice a thinker and an astute judge of character. After all, she had him down to a T. Of course, he'd never actually told her that.

Janice gave an amused smile. 'Is that praise, DS McNab?'

McNab didn't respond to the question but repeated his own instead. 'How much?'

'I think we wrong-footed him when we asked where he was when he heard that Mary was missing. *And* when we shifted the focus to Karen Marshall. I wondered about what he said about Mary's father. Whether he didn't like the man in general, or whether it was more personal. Then there was the remark about the brother, which I noted you didn't pursue.'

'Robbie, or Robert as he gets called now, is gay. He made a point of telling me by reference to his partner, Andrew. I think that's what McLaughlin was implying when he talked about Robbie at the den.'

Janice gave a little laugh. 'And you showed no interest, much to his annoyance.'

'Robbie-turned-Robert was keen for us to talk to Father Feeney, who's apparently still alive,' McNab said. 'Claims he was a paedophile and probably protected from on high – and not by God.'

'Which was McCreadie's take on things too,' Janice reminded him.

McNab raised an eyebrow. 'You angling for another trip to see your famous author?'

'So will you when you've read the transcripts of the notebooks,' Janice said.

'Is it legible this time?'

Swivelling in her chair to come alongside him, Janice brought up a document on his screen. 'My advice is to read as much as possible before the strategy meeting.'

'I would rather do interviews,' McNab said.

'Better to know as much as we can about what went on back then before we do.'

Janice was right, McNab knew that. Getting as much info as possible before meeting those still alive was the sensible way to go.

Never the big reader, McNab now looked at the filled screen with a degree of trepidation. He would, he realized, much rather have had Janice give him a summary of the leading points. He was planning to say as much, but she'd swivelled back to her own monitor before he could suggest such a thing, announcing that she was on to notebook three and keen to get back to it.

It's funny, McNab thought as he began to read, *how much you can hear an author's voice in your head when you read his words.* In McCreadie's case, McNab could also see him in his mind's eye saying the words in front of him now.

He wasn't a book fan, but if he was, McNab decided, he

would never want to meet an author in person, even if he did enjoy their books. But hey, in McCreadie's case, he already had, and every word he read would likely be coloured by that meeting, never mind his opinion of the man who'd written them.

Yet McNab was surprised to find that, after the first few sentences, things changed. Perhaps it was because of his own obsession with the case, but he found McCreadie's personal take on what was happening back then compelling, in particular the fact that he'd opened with his notes on Mary's friend, Karen Marshall.

The child, Karen, is terrified. Of me. Of everything that is happening around her. She's stopped talking about how much Mary loved her dress. How her friend was happy. Now she says nothing. I think she's blotting out something from her memory. Something too terrible to contemplate, let alone say out loud.

McNab thought back to what McCreadie had said when they'd met, which pretty well mirrored his thoughts on Karen all those years ago.

He read on.

Karen's family –

Her father, a DC (who I don't know personally but apparently he's sound enough), maintains his youngest daughter has always been quiet. Liz (the mother) is inclined to mollycoddle her, being a late baby. Mary, her pal, is the opposite. More grown up and worldly wise. Probably because of her family who are a bit wild. The mother doesn't approve of Mary as a friend for Karen. The father allows it.

The mother is nervous, fearing if Mary can be taken so can Karen. She is disapproving of Mary. She doesn't come from a good home, she says. The father hits his children. Karen was innocent before she became pally with Mary. Mary is old beyond her years. When I asked what she meant by that, she flushed and told me to ask Mary's mother. I wondered if Mary might have already had her period, or that she knew more about sex than Karen?

Eleanor, the sister of sixteen, was next. Her mother offered to stay with her, but Eleanor declined, saying she'd manage alone. She appeared nervous, clasping and unclasping her hands. She asked what Karen had said. I explained it was better that we just concentrate on her and what she could tell me about Mary. She said she was sorry but she didn't like her. That she bossed Karen around and upset her wee sister by saying there wasn't a seat in heaven for her because she was a Protestant. She thought Mary was just hiding somewhere, so that everyone would look for her. Mary likes to be the centre of attention. And she flirts. With Alec up the road, even Eric. She halts there as though she's said too much. Who's Eric, does he live nearby too, I ask? She shakes her head. Eric's my boyfriend. And he knows Mary? He doesn't know her, she says firmly. But when he comes to collect me, she talks to him. Eleanor insists she isn't worried and that Mary will turn up and get her picture in the papers, which is what she wants.

McNab paused there. He hadn't met Karen's big sister yet, although a couple of uniforms had taken an initial statement from her, the bare bones of which were that she hadn't seen Karen or spoken to her since their parents' funerals and she had no idea where Karen was living now.

She thought Karen had married, although she hadn't been invited to the wedding.

McNab recalled Robbie's declaration that his family had been as happy as anyone else's on that street. It seemed that wasn't far from the truth.

The next piece, he realized, was McCreadie's emotional take on the situation. McNab rarely, if ever, spoke about how the job affected him. Forty-five years ago, when the nature of policing was more gung-ho, he couldn't imagine any officer openly revealing the personal impact of some of the horrors they'd had to face.

Yet here was McCreadie, doing just that.

I wish I could have met Mary McIntyre. (Let's hope I will.) In the few photos taken of her, she seems to challenge the photographer. Bright, according to her teacher, Miss Stevens, likely to do well at secondary school, where she would go in August. There are some issues at home, her teacher says. A father who uses the belt on his children. Miss Stevens disapproves of using the belt in her classroom. Miss Stevens walked them to the chapel and she's sure Mary was with them.

How the fuck do you talk to the parents of a missing child? They think you're going to find her because you have to make them believe that. You're determined to do that, while all the time you know. You just know that some bastard has her and is doing something to her right now, if he's not already killed her. How do you keep that thought off your face?

The father, Dave, is the boss. No doubt about that. Evelyn, the mother, hovers round him, expecting to be swatted away like an annoying fly, but determined to be in his vicinity anyway. I suspect it's a relationship I've seen often as a beat policeman. The one you walk past, despite the screaming. A domestic. Not our business. The famous belt is hanging there on the kitchen wall. He glances at it occasionally, as if to assure himself he's still in charge.

He said he would kill whoever had taken his wean. I didn't admonish him for that. I felt the same way at that moment.

He sounded honest in his answers. Mary went off with her class to confirmation (just as Miss Stevens had told me), dressed in her finery. She never came back. He almost broke down as he said this. I thought in that moment, here's a guy who thought he was in control of his family, belt and all. Then some unknown fucker blows it all sky high.

I asked to speak to Mrs McIntyre alone. He didn't like that, but I insisted. She changed when he left the room. She looked me straight in the eye and said, 'Whoever took her will kill her, won't they?' What could I say to that? I said something stupid like, 'There's time yet to find her.' Her eyes went misty then. I thought she would cry. Then she pulled herself together and that same direct look was back. 'My boy Robbie doesn't like Father Feeney. He says he does things to kids. Robbie's different.' She indicated the closed door. 'I know that. His father doesn't.' She looked frightened. 'You mustn't tell him.' I asked if she trusted Father Feeney. 'He's a priest,' she said. 'A man of God. It would be blasphemous not to.' I asked about Karen. 'She's a nice wee girl,' she said. 'Quiet. Her dad's strict with her, being a policeman. The girls get on well together.' I wanted to ask about what Mrs Marshall had said, but put it a different way. Did Mary have a boyfriend? She gasped at that. 'She's only eleven, well, almost twelve,' then she looked away. So no boys hanging around? 'Dave would never allow that,' she said.

Robbie was next. A fourteen-year-old, he gave me a look that suggested he thought I was a likely enemy. I thought, this boy can go either way, and if his mother's right about him, whatever road he takes it will be a hard one. He resembled his missing sister, with a wild head of dark curly hair on top, and cut short round the sides. He sat hunched and defensive, giving a swift glance now and again at the belt, which was the only thing on the wall apart from a crucifix. I wondered how soon the boy would reject the beatings and turn on his father. Not long.

When I asked him what he knew, he told me to check out the priest. 'He likes altar boys.' He gave me a look that suggested he did more than just like them. And girls? He laughed then. 'Not so popular,' he said. So why ask the priest about Mary? He sat up at that. 'Father Feeney has friends. Fancy friends.' When I asked who, he shook his head. 'That's for you to find out, detective.' I asked if Mary had a boyfriend. 'She's fucking eleven.' Nearly twelve, I said. Any boys or men hanging about her? 'There's a weirdo at the shops flashes her and Karen,' he says. 'And smart Alec up the road talks dirty when the girls play tennis in the street. I told them to ignore him. Plus one of the altar boys, Gerry Ryan, had a notion on Mary. I sorted him out too.'

When I asked for his version of what had happened to his sister, he said to ask Father Feeney. Could Mary just be hiding, I asked him. He glanced again at the belt. 'Mary was never afraid to come home, even if she got a belting. My wee sister wasn't afraid of anything or anyone. But someone's got her, and I'd start with the priest.'

McNab thought about McCreadie. How he'd kept in touch with Robbie over the years. A penance for not finding his sister? Or guilt at doing things badly? Bad outcomes usually came from a botched investigation. Maybe Mc-Creadie had got the shove because he simply messed up and his tale of those at the top trying to hide something was a cover-up for his own failings.

Robbie McIntyre didn't think so back then, or now.

McNab remembered the boss's opinion about the case and about DI McCreadie. If the boss had some questions about those in charge back then, McNab was inclined to believe him.

His mobile buzzed as he prepared to move on to McCreadie's piece on Mary's sister, Jean.

'DS McNab? Can you come see me? Now, if possible.' Ollie sounded pleased with himself. 'I believe I've located Father Feeney.'

29

The bulletins on TV and radio, the acres of coverage in the newspapers, had got it right after all. The remains discovered in the raised peat bog close to Advie Lochan were those of Mary McIntyre, aged eleven, who had disappeared on 1 May 1975.

Rhona leafed through the accumulated results. It had taken time to get everything they needed to confirm the identity of the remains. Their first problem had been the fact that the body has been in the bog for so long. As she'd tried to explain to Magnus, bogs were acidic and thus tended to strip the base pairs off the DNA, making it difficult to 'read'. Success had come when they'd had to go for the petrous part of the temporal bone in the skull, which was well protected. Having managed to extract DNA, it was then a simple process to compare the profile from the deceased with a buccal swab taken from the surviving siblings.

To add to this, they'd located Mary's dental records and digitally reconstructed her face from the skull of the remains. That image of the girl now sat beside the photograph given to the police by her parents all those years ago. Parents who hadn't lived long enough to find and bury their small daughter properly.

'At least the brother and sister are still around to give her a proper funeral,' Chrissy said.

If the siblings had managed to put what had happened to their sister to the back of their mind, then this discovery would bring it all back with a vengeance, Rhona thought. Add in the resulting re-opening of the case, the trawling over the past, plus the interest from the press and public, and things wouldn't be easy for them.

She wondered if the outcome of the discovery might prove worse for Mary's remaining family than never knowing what had happened to their sister.

'I'd always want to know,' Chrissy responded when Rhona said as much. 'If anything like that happened to wee Michael, I'd want him back with me. And I'd want whoever did such a terrible thing to be brought to justice.'

Rhona felt the same. However, the fallout for the families involved would be great. They would become the focus of much scrutiny. As would all their erstwhile neighbours in that small community.

'Does the press know?' Chrissy said.

'Bill is holding a press conference shortly with the sister and brother. They'll no doubt be appealing to anyone who's still alive from that time who might know anything to come forward for interview.'

'Social media's going to love this. I'll bet there's a true crime podcast already in the making,' Chrissy said.

Despite spending her day forensically examining crime scenes, Chrissy's current favourite pastime was listening to crime podcasts and either finding fault with them or avidly solving the crime.

'There's still the puzzle of the clothes buried with her,' Chrissy said.

The Tech department had digitally restored the dress, veil and shoes. According to Bill, the image had been shown to the sister of the murdered girl, who'd said she couldn't be sure of the dress, it was so long ago. She did say she thought the shoes were a bit small, but then again they were poor back then, and confirmation outfits were usually passed from one family member to another.

'Well, mine certainly was,' Chrissy said, 'and the fancy white shoes pinched.'

The supposition was that the dress and shoes were on the small size for Mary, but they had no exact record of her weight and height, just their estimation from the remains. If her mother had still been alive, things would have been different. She would have been able to explain what seemed like a discrepancy.

If they'd had a photograph of Mary taken wearing the dress, that would have helped, but according to McNab there were none in the little evidence they'd found in the police store.

'My mum sewed me into my borrowed dress, because the buttons kept popping,' Chrissy recalled. 'My boobs were the problem. My cousin didn't have any.'

As for the bracelet Rhona had retrieved from the loch, there had proved to be no inscription, although McNab said that Robbie, the brother, told him his father had bought Mary one, probably from a pawn shop. However, Jean, the sister, couldn't recall that event at all. So even siblings a couple of years apart didn't share the same memories.

'How much do you remember from your childhood?' Rhona said.

'Mostly the fights with my drunkard of a father.' Chrissy's hard gaze suddenly softened. 'The best memory was when my only sane and gay brother Patrick took me to the pictures.' She went quiet for a moment. 'Traumas usually stick the longest, like when I got my first period. Jesus, I thought I was dying.'

'You weren't warned?' Rhona said.

'Sex and anything to do with it wasn't a topic for discussion in our good Catholic house. What about you?'

'I remember when my mum told me I was adopted and who my birth mother and father were.'

'Wow.' Chrissy made a face. 'That's a biggie.'

'It didn't feel like it at the time,' Rhona said honestly.

Her mum had volunteered the information one day while they chopped vegetables for the soup together at the kitchen table. Just in case Rhona wanted to know, she'd said, and couldn't ask.

'Your mum was my cousin Lily,' she'd explained. 'She was a traveller.'

It had sounded romantic.

'She's travelled all round the world.' Her mum had continued grating the carrots as she'd talked. 'She brought back this nice boyfriend once. That was your dad. He wanted to marry her, but she always said no.'

'Why?' It was the only question Rhona had ever asked about her real mother.

'Our Lily was her own woman. "Give a man a bit of paper and he'll think he's bought you." That's what she used to say.'

'So you never met your birth mum or dad?' Chrissy asked.

'No, although I have their photograph, taken on a trip to Millport. My dad died in Venice. Lily came back, but she only stayed long enough to have me, and then she went. Couldn't stand the weather here. It was the greyness, Mum said. She died in Istanbul and is buried there.'

Chrissy looked thoughtful. 'I like the sound of Lily.' She gave Rhona a hard look. 'I think you've inherited some of her traits, especially the own woman bit. Your adopted mum did a good job on you, though. Lily probably knew she would.'

Rhona realized that Chrissy was right about her mother. So why had she hidden Liam's existence from both her parents? Looking back, it was something she couldn't explain, even to herself.

What we chose to forget, it seemed, was more significant than what, through time, we simply couldn't remember.

'Teenage years. Now I remember them,' Chrissy was saying with a grin. 'And the first time I had sex, which was pretty shite by the way.'

Rhona held up her hand when Chrissy looked as though she might tell her the whole story. 'Please, I don't need to know the details.'

Chrissy looked affronted. 'I was about to ask you about your first time.'

'Some things,' Rhona said, 'are better left unsaid.'

'That bad, eh?' Chrissy said sympathetically.

'Not at all,' Rhona said with a suggestive smile. 'Anyway, I have to head for the strategy meeting. You'll text me if anything more comes back on the tests?'

Chrissy said she would. 'Are you going to mention your visit to the locus with Emma?'

'No. But I will suggest an aerial examination for anomalies.'

The conference room was filling up, initially to watch the appeal go out on national TV, after which the strategy meeting would go ahead.

As yet there was no sign of McNab or Magnus, both of whom Rhona had expected to see there, but she did spot DS Clark and headed over to her. They exchanged pleasantries while Rhona reminded herself how lucky McNab was to have such a partner, hoping he appreciated it.

'So where is McNab?' Rhona eventually asked.

'He got a call from IT just before we headed here,' Janice said. 'I believe the remains have been ID'd as Mary McIntyre?'

Rhona nodded. 'There are anomalies, which I'll enlighten everyone on.' She halted there as Janice's attention was drawn elsewhere.

'Well, well, well,' Janice was saying, amazement in her voice. 'Look who's here.'

Rhona turned to see a tall, imposing elderly bloke with grey hair enter the room.

'Who's that?' Rhona said, genuinely interested.

'*That* is bestselling author J. D. Smart, aka former Detective Inspector Jimmy McCreadie, who was in charge of the original abduction case. Until, that is, he was shown the door, the reasons for which are unclear. You want to meet him?'

'You know him?' Rhona said, interested.

'The boss sent us to interview him when there was a suspicion that the remains might be wee Mary McIntyre. Needless to say, DS McNab wasn't impressed.'

'What about you?'

'I like his books, so I was interested in meeting him in whatever context.'

'And?' Rhona urged her on, realizing there was more to come.

'Turns out he kept personal notes about the investigation,

173

which he handed over to us. Since the original police note-books are missing from the stored evidence, they're proving very useful, once you decipher the handwriting,' Janice explained as she and Rhona began to weave their way towards the gentleman in question.

Spotting Janice and obviously recognizing her, a big smile spread across the former detective's face.

'DS Clark, I was hoping to see you here.' He held out his hand. 'And this is?' He gestured to Rhona.

'Dr Rhona MacLeod,' Janice gave the introduction.

'Ah,' he said, taking Rhona's hand this time. 'I am very pleased to meet you, Dr MacLeod. I am an admirer of your work, so much so that I took the forensic course you're involved in. Very enlightening, especially for a detective from the old school.'

'A lot of things have changed since your time in the force,' Rhona said.

'They have indeed, and for the better. Hopefully, with your help, this one,' he gestured at the current evidence on display, 'will finally be solved.'

'Will you be contributing today?' Rhona said.

'DI Wilson asked me in to give an overview of the initial investigation. I hope that what I can offer helps. It's such a long time ago and many of those close to the case are dead and gone.' He paused, his look darkening. 'In truth, the story of Mary McIntyre never left me, even after I left the force. Thank God I had the wit to write it all down at the time, so that I would never forget.'

They said there was always at least one unsolved or un-resolved case that haunted every detective. By his tone and expression, the disappearance of Mary McIntyre was the one forever on McCreadie's mind.

At that moment the large screen at one end of the room came on and the babble of chat quickly died away. Bill introduced the man and woman on either side of him as the brother and sister of Mary McIntyre, who had been abducted on the first of May 1975.

'The investigation at the time found no trace of Mary after she had, we believe, taken part in her confirmation ceremony in the local chapel. The remains discovered south of Glasgow have now been identified as Mary. We appeal to anyone with any information on the case, however small, to get in touch with Police Scotland.'

The sister looked more nervous than the brother, and it was he who spoke first.

'The original investigation was flawed,' Robert McIntyre told the camera, 'mainly because back then kids like us,' he nodded at his sister, 'weren't listened to. In fact, when DI McCreadie, who was in charge, did take heed of what we were saying, he was hounded out of his job. This cannot happen a second time. Despite the intervening years, the memory of that day and what led up to it has never left me. And this time we will be heard.' He paused for a moment to collect himself. 'Anyone with knowledge about what happened back then, please come forward to the police. Mary's killer could still be out there, and we want to find him and bring him to justice.'   .

The married sister, Jean Barclay, spoke next. She asked for the children who walked with Mary to the church that day to come forward. 'Also,' she said, 'the police would like to trace Mary's pal Karen Marshall. Mary and Karen were very close,' she said. 'Back then, Karen was in a state of shock when Mary disappeared and could hardly speak. She moved away with her family shortly afterwards and we lost contact with her. If she's alive and listening to this, I urge her to make contact with the police. Maybe there's something she remembers now about what happened on that day.'

Bill brought the session to an end with a final request for everyone who remembered anything regarding Mary's disappearance to come forward.

The chatter in the room started up again as the picture snapped off.

'That was being pre-recorded to go out later today,' Janice said, 'so the boss should be here shortly.'

At that moment Rhona spotted DI Wilson's entry, along with McNab and Magnus.

'That's the criminal psychologist who lectures on the diploma course,' McCreadie remarked. 'To my recollection, he was given a hard time by the unbelievers in the audience, most of them serving officers.'

'There was a time when forensic science got the same response,' Rhona said. 'It still does when something new is developed.'

McNab had spotted them. At first it looked as though he would head over, then he noted who they were standing next to and seemingly changed his mind.

Janice made an exasperated sound which expressed her thoughts perfectly. 'Excuse me, folks, but I need to speak to my partner.' She turned to McCreadie. 'Just to say, your notebooks are making very interesting reading for both of us. So thank you.'

Deserting them, she threaded her way towards a disgruntled-looking McNab.

McCreadie smiled at her retreating figure. 'I suspect DS McNab and I have much in common,' he told Rhona.

'In what way?' Rhona said, thinking she already knew the answer.

'He trusts his guts and, until proved otherwise, he suspects my part in this case is a publicity stunt.'

'And is it?' Rhona asked.

'It won't do the sale of my books any harm, that's for sure,' McCreadie said. 'But I would also like the ghost of Mary McIntyre to be finally laid to rest.'

30

Marge had accepted the job of looking after the diary, while playing down Karen's feelings towards it.

'Have the police been to see you yet?' she'd asked when Karen was buttering the scones in the wee kitchen that led off the room they all met in.

'No,' Karen had said.

'Have you contacted them?'

'They're not even sure it is Mary. This might all be for nothing. Anyway, I was just her pal. It's her family they should be talking to.'

Part of Karen wanted it not to be Mary. They were already talking on TV about other wee girls who'd gone missing around the same time in England.

Marge had looked at her kindly at that point. 'We don't need to talk about it, you know?'

'I know,' Karen had told her. 'But the others are keen and it gives them something to think about other than their own worries.'

'That's true,' Marge nodded. 'So you don't mind the questions?'

'No,' Karen had assured her.

In fact it was going better than Karen had expected. The women, excited by what they thought of as a mystery, had begun by getting Marge to draw a map of the street under

Karen's instructions, with the two schools and the open ground between them. Karen was surprised to find she could remember who lived where and could match the names she'd talked of in the earlier meeting to their appropriate houses.

'And it was against the lamp post there,' Karen pointed to a spot next to her own house, 'that we used to play kick the can.' Even as she said it, she could remember the excitement of hiding in the rough ground opposite only to run out as fast as possible to kick the can before the pursuer could reach you.

'And what came after the open ground between the schools?' Marge was saying. 'More houses?'

'No,' Karen said slowly. 'There was a wood.' Even as she said this, she could see the wood in her mind's eye and the path they'd forged through the long grass to enter it. For kids who'd come from tenement flats with only the street and back courts to play in, the open ground and surrounding woods had been a revelation. 'It was in there that me and Mary built our den.'

It was while watching Marge add the stick-like trees to the map that something broke in Karen. She could almost hear the splintering of the door inside her mind, beyond which, she knew, were the feelings and memories she'd worked so hard to lock up.

'Are you okay?' Marge said, shushing the women's excited chatter.

'We were in the woods,' Karen said, suddenly remembering. 'Before she went to the chapel.' She remembered the moment precisely, plus what Mary had told her that day.

How could she ever have forgotten?

'What is it, Karen?'

To Karen's ears, Marge's voice sounded strange and far-away.

'Karen. Are you okay?' Marge's hand was on her shoulder. 'You're as white as a sheet.'

'I remember,' Karen said. 'I remember what she said.'

'What did she say?' one of the women prompted.

There was a pause before Karen answered.

'Mary said she shouldn't be wearing a white dress at all.' Karen looked round the circle of faces, some eager, some excited, some fearful, some already shocked. 'She asked me if God would forgive her.'

There was an explosion of sound as the women worked out what that might mean.

Karen suddenly understood what Mary had been trying to tell her, although back then she hadn't. She'd thought that Mary had committed a sin like not saying the right number of Hail Marys. She didn't even know what being a virgin meant.

She rose, not wishing to have any more questions asked of her. Talking about Mary like this, even after all these years, seemed like a betrayal of her promise to her friend.

She had to leave, and now.

Karen went through to the kitchen to fetch her jacket. Spotting the diary next to Marge's things, she put it back in her own bag.

She was out of the church and getting into her car when Marge appeared.

'Karen, wait! I'm sorry. Don't go. We won't ask any more questions. I promise.'

Karen said, 'There's something I have to do.'

'You'll come back?'

Karen nodded, although she wasn't sure she would.

Maybe it was up to her now. The door in her mind had opened, just a crack, but if she tried hard enough, she might manage to push it open further. Then she might recall all that had happened on that day forty-five years ago.

The drive home passed in a blur. Nothing more came back to her regarding Mary; instead, fleeting memories of other things around that time did. Her father telling her they were flitting. That they could no longer stay in this house. That her mother would always worry that the man who took Mary might come back for her.

The moment when her sister, Eleanor, told her she was getting married and that Karen would be her bridesmaid. 'You'd like that, wouldn't you? You'll get to wear a white frilly dress after all,' Eleanor had said.

Just like Mary's.

Karen remembered screaming at her sister that she didn't want to wear a white dress like Mary. That she couldn't, because God would never forgive her either.

31

He makes an impressive figure up there. Rhona could think of very few police officers who might captivate an audience such as former Detective Inspector McCreadie was doing at this moment.

Mary McIntyre was coming to life again as McCreadie told her story. He painted a picture of a little girl living in a different era from the one they were experiencing now.

'Where children's stories were not treated as truth. Where the rights of the child were not protected. Where domestic abuse was considered the norm rather than a deviation from it. Where the sectarian divide was wider and deeper, and the control of the Churches more significant in people's minds.

'Despite all of this, Mary McIntyre appeared to have been a lively, happy child, whose best friend, Karen Marshall, was from across the sectarian divide.'

McCreadie described the two families in some detail. Mary's father, who controlled his family via a leather belt. Karen's father, a detective constable, who couldn't conceive of hitting his children. However, in his opinion, Mary's father loved his daughter and was destroyed by her abduction. The power he thought he wielded in the protection of his family proved to be worth nothing after all.

'Mary was in effect in the hands of the Church when she

disappeared. She had joined her classmates to walk to the chapel for confirmation. However, there were around eighty children that day, more girls than boys, all of whom wore white dresses, and many who were wearing veils, covering their faces.

'Mary's teacher believed Mary was among them, although Miss Stevens couldn't say she had spoken directly to Mary. The children had amassed in the school playground. They'd had a roll call, then walked in lines to the chapel.

'The priest, Father Feeney, said he could not say for definite that Mary had been one of those who had been confirmed.

'There were no sightings of Mary after the service. Her best friend, Karen, being Protestant, wasn't with Mary . . . an unusual occurrence. It was said during the investigation that they were joined at the hip outside school hours. Karen was in a state of shock and withdrew into herself, not speaking at all. The child was severely traumatized, we can recognize that now, but back then there was little to be done about it.

'During my time with her, she was literally terrified. I always believed that Karen knew something that frightened or horrified her so much she had shut down because of it. Nowadays Karen would have had the psychological care and attention she required, much like officers affected by frontline duties. Back then, that wasn't an option.

'I understand that the historical evidence taken, i.e. the police notebooks and interviews, have been destroyed or lost over the intervening years. However, I kept personal notes on the interviews I conducted, including my suspicions and questions regarding the disappearance of Mary McIntyre, which I have now handed over to DS McNab and

DS Clark. I believe my illegible script has been transcribed and they are to be made available to those involved in the case.

'I thank DI Wilson for responding to my offer to relate what I know. I am, of course, open to any questions and am happy to help in any way I can.

'However, I should also say my own involvement in the case was cut short as I left the force, or was asked to leave. The Chief Constable, Peter White – Sir Peter White, as he later became – did not agree with the direction I was taking with the investigation, his prime concern being that I paid heed to the fears of Mary's fourteen-year-old brother, who had accused their local priest of sexually abusing young boys. We are, of course, talking of a different era. One in which homosexuality was a crime and the Church held much sway in public life and institutions. Those in power in Scotland were not yet ready to face what was to eventually become by the eighties a worldwide scandal of biblical proportions.

'The argument from on high was that even if Robbie McIntyre's accusations were true, and my superior officer had basically dismissed them as lies, they did not offer any enlightenment in the Mary McIntyre case. For my own part, I believed a cover-up was happening, of what exactly I don't know, but it did involve people in power who had to be protected, even if that meant Mary McIntyre's killer would never be found and brought to justice.'

McCreadie halted there, the anger present in his voice echoed by his expression.

'What about Father Feeney?' a voice asked from the gathered officers. 'Did you pursue him on the question of a cover-up by the Church?'

'I did and not surprisingly he denied it. However, he was

moved to another parish shortly afterwards, which was the norm then if complaints were made against a priest.'

McNab now indicated he had a question and McCreadie nodded at him to go ahead.

'Alec McLaughlin, who was a teenager living a few doors up from the deceased at the time of her disappearance, has recently been released from Barlinnie after fifteen years for raping his partner's three children. McLaughlin volunteered some information recently, believing that the remains were those of Mary McIntyre. He maintains that the girl was pregnant at the time of her disappearance and this in fact led to her having to disappear.'

Rhona watched McCreadie's face as he digested that information.

'Was there any suggestion that that might be the case during the investigation?' McNab said.

'No. None,' McCreadie stated. 'As for McLaughlin's word on this, it's not to be trusted. McLaughlin was a suspect but had an alibi for the time during which Mary disappeared.'

McNab came back in then. 'McLaughlin also said he followed Karen after he heard that Mary was missing. She was going to the den and stopped when she saw Robbie McIntyre leaving there with a white bundle.'

McCreadie assumed a bemused expression. 'McLaughlin was and I suspect still is an inveterate liar, who took great delight in being in the midst of the investigation then and wishes to be the star turn again.'

'So he didn't tell you any of this at the time?' McNab persisted.

'If he had, then it would be in the diaries,' McCreadie said firmly. 'However, it is clear from the diary entries that, without stating it categorically, both Karen's mother and Mary's mother intimated that Mary had started menstruating and thus she would have been capable of becoming pregnant.'

McCreadie searched the audience in case there were any other questions.

When there didn't appear to be, he said, 'Sadly, our forensic knowledge was minimal. Plus we had no sightings and no body, despite a large-scale search and an appeal to the public. Mary McIntyre had simply disappeared without trace.' He paused. 'But she is no longer lost, and you have the forensic knowledge we could only dream about back then to discover what happened to her, and hopefully bring her killer to justice.'

At this point, DI Wilson came to the front to thank former DI McCreadie for his input, then asked that Dr MacLeod bring them up to date with the forensic results.

Rhona had managed a few words with Bill before McCreadie's talk, so he was aware where they were with regard to the forensic evidence. She hadn't intended mentioning the pregnancy story, but now that it was out in the open, she decided as she approached the front to explain their subsequent findings.

Rhona began by outlining their difficulties in extracting recognizable DNA because of the acidic nature of the burial site, and the length of time the body had been there. Then she described how it had been achieved via the petrous part of the temporal bone in the skull, and their eventual match with the buccal swabs from Robert and Jean, Mary's siblings.

'So this is Mary McIntyre's body we are dealing with. As to a possible and discernible pregnancy,' Rhona said, 'the acidic nature of the bog means that bones tend to be leached away and, of course, the very fragile nature of any foetal remains would be challenging to find should they actually survive.

'The first bone to form is the clavicle, or collar bone, and by week eleven of pregnancy it has become tiny but recognizable. We found no evidence of a foetal clavicle at the post-mortem examination.'

McNab came in then. 'But she could have been less than eleven weeks pregnant, and we would never know that from the remains?'

'We have no definitive proof of an early-stage pregnancy, but that doesn't mean there wasn't one,' she confirmed. 'However, it can't be proved either way.'

Rhona now moved on to the clothing.

'First of all, the dress has not yet been identified as the one worn by Mary. Neither of her siblings could confirm this. Also, the dress buried with the victim was of a smaller size than would have comfortably fitted Mary.

'We are still working with the clothing. However,' Rhona indicated the screen display, 'as of now we have isolated one source of DNA from the dress, identified as an unknown female. So not the victim. An explanation for this could be that at the time of Mary's disappearance, money was scarce, and confirmation outfits were often shared between friends and family. Again, Mary's siblings could not confirm whether the dress she wore on that day had been bought new or borrowed.

'We retrieved a cigarette butt from the grave, the DNA of which was compared to the database and found no match. Neither did the fingerprint retrieved from the plastic bag, suggesting whoever was involved hasn't been arrested since the database was up and running.

'I can confirm that Dr Jen Mackie is working with soil

deposits found on the shoes, which may help pinpoint where the girl whose outfit it was last walked. Finally, we believe Mary wasn't killed at the locus, and was already naked when transported to the moor.'

McNab came back in. 'Are there any more bodies up there, Dr MacLeod?'

'I've requested an aerial search to look for any anomalies in ground cover. If there are any in the vicinity, we'll decide then whether we investigate further.'

32

Magnus had slipped out part-way through Rhona's contribution. In normal circumstances he would have ignored the vibrating mobile, but when he saw the name on the screen he decided he should take it. His instinct had proved right. From Pat Robertson's voice when he'd answered, it was obvious this wasn't just a friendly call, but something more urgent.

'Magnus. Thanks for picking up. It's with regard to the appeal that was broadcast earlier about the body they found on the moor. The little girl. Are you involved in any way with the case?'

'Why?' Magnus asked cautiously.

'It's just that the recovery group you spoke to in Stirling . . .' Pat hesitated at this point. 'Marge there – remember Marge? Big, loud . . .'

'And very friendly. I remember,' Magnus said.

'Marge says that Karen Johnston, who's part of their group, is Karen Marshall, the dead girl's best friend. Marge says she was convinced the body the police found was Mary, but was too scared to go to them about it.'

'That's good news,' Magnus said. 'Can you convince her to come in? The police are very keen to talk to her.'

'That's just it,' Pat said. 'Marge says she was at the recovery cafe today before the TV appeal. The women were trying to help Karen remember what happened on the day Mary disappeared, because it worries her so much that she can't. Marge says she suddenly freaked out and left in a weird state. Marge doesn't know if Karen has seen the TV appeal confirming the body was Mary McIntyre and asking folk – in particular Karen – to come forward. They've tried calling her mobile, but it just goes to voicemail. So Marge got in touch with me.'

'Was Karen the woman whose husband had died of dementia?' Magnus said, recalling the lively exchange among the women at the table. All except one.

'Karen was sitting almost directly opposite you,' Pat said. 'Small, fairish hair. She listened but didn't ask any questions.'

Magnus did remember her. He'd even spoken to Marge before he left, concerned about how withdrawn Karen had been during their session. Most of the other women had wanted to question him about the psychology involved in many of their troubles, although not Karen.

Marge had told him then about the husband's illness, explained how Karen had been completely isolated when caring for him. 'She had her food delivered. She never even went to the shops. Said she couldn't leave Jack, even for a minute. She would probably have drunk herself to death if she hadn't come here. That's what she told me.'

'So,' Magnus said to a waiting Pat, 'what can I do to help?'

Finishing the call, Magnus noted that Rhona must have completed her contribution as the meeting room was beginning to empty. Magnus waited, wondering who he should speak to regarding Pat's phone call.

Ideally, DI Wilson, but glancing in at the door, Magnus

saw that Bill was deep in conversation with McCreadie and Rhona at that moment. However, both McNab and DS Clark were heading his way, so Magnus made up his mind to approach them in the first instance.

Catching DS Clark's eye – McNab wasn't acknowledging his presence – Magnus called her name.

With a quick aside to McNab, who seemed intent on going somewhere, and swiftly, DS Clark approached Magnus.

'Professor Pirie, you heard what was said about Alec McLaughlin at the meeting?'

'I did. May I have a word with you?'

She looked unsure. 'Is it about the McLaughlin interview, because it's probably better if DS McNab's there too, and he's had to go out.'

Magnus briefly wondered whether that was true or McNab was in fact just set on avoiding him.

'It would be better if we three sat down together about that, although I thought it went very well,' Magnus said. 'I'll send you both my thoughts via email. However, what I wanted to say is some new information related to the Mary McIntyre case.'

Janice looked interested. 'Shall we get a coffee in the canteen then?'

Magnus was happy to agree, preferring the cafeteria to an interview room.

Collecting their coffees, Janice led Magnus to a quiet corner.

'So,' she said, once they were seated. 'Fire away.'

Not for the first time did Magnus think how much easier it was to talk to DS Clark than McNab. And not for the first time did he try and analyse why that was. Dysfunctional relationships went both ways. Magnus found McNab's sharp edges and cynicism difficult to handle at times. As for McNab, Magnus wasn't sure whether the detective didn't like him personally or whether he didn't like what Magnus represented – the world of forensic psychology.

And yet, he thought briefly, when they did work together, like in the sin-eater case, their combined knowledge of the criminal mind often resulted in success.

'What did you want to run past me, Professor?' DS Clark's enquiry broke into his thoughts.

'I've been visiting a number of recovery cafes over the past couple of months,' Magnus told her. 'I assume you know about these?'

DS Clark nodded.

'Well, while visiting Barlinnie recently, actually to interview Mr McLaughlin, I bumped into Pat Robertson, who was there with three colleagues to run the in-house cafe.' Magnus checked to see if DS Clark was following him.

'Go on,' she said.

'Anyway, I hadn't seen her since she'd taken me for a session at the women's recovery cafe in Raploch in Stirling.'

At the mention of Stirling, DS Clark's interest seemed to grow.

'Anyway, I exited the strategy meeting to take a call from Pat.' Magnus paused. 'It turns out that Karen Johnston, who is part of their group, is in fact Karen Marshall, Mary McIntyre's best friend at the time of her disappearance. She married a man called Jack Johnston and lives in Stirling.'

DS Clark's eyes lit up. 'That's excellent news. Is she going to make contact with us?'

'That's not a certainty,' Magnus said. 'According to Pat and the group's leader, Marge, Karen's been in a very delicate and often confused state since the death of her husband from dementia, and she left the meeting abruptly before the TV appeal with Mary's siblings. They don't know if she saw it, but up to now she has refused to put herself forward, suggesting it wasn't necessary, since they hadn't identified the body as Mary's.'

'But we have now, and she's a key witness,' DS Clark said. 'Do you have this woman's contact details?'

'I have her mobile number, which she isn't answering, according to Pat. The group don't have her address.'

DS Clark considered this. 'We can trace her through her mobile.'

'It's a pay-as-you-go,' Magnus said.

'Okay. There are other ways. You said her husband died recently?'

'Within the last year, I believe.'

'So we contact social services, check funeral parlours, find her doctor's practice.'

It all sounded straightforward, yet Magnus could foresee the difficulties even after they'd located Karen.

'This woman is already traumatized,' he said, 'and from what Pat says, the discovery of Mary's body could have made things worse.'

Janice waited as he explained further.

'Apparently she was having flashbacks about Mary's disappearance even before the body was discovered. Finding out it was her friend might have brought back terrible memories.'

'Memories we are keen to ask her about.' DS Clark rose. 'I need to get started on this, Professor. Thank you for bringing it to us.'

'If or when you find her, I would urge caution on how you question her. Childhood traumas are deep-rooted, often buried well down in the psyche and devastating when they finally surface.'

DS Clark gave him a studied look. 'I have every intention of asking the boss to bring you in on this. The help you gave us regarding the McLaughlin interview was invaluable.' She raised an eyebrow. 'Even though my partner may not have given that impression.'

Watching her leave, Magnus was conscious that, having been entrusted with the information about Karen Johnston, he had now just handed it over to the police.

Was that what Pat, or even Marge, had intended?

He'd asked Pat what he might do to help. Her advice had been to find Karen whatever way he could. Pat knew he would go to the police, because that was the quickest and most efficient way to contact Karen, but still Magnus wasn't sure it was the best way.

He pictured Karen again, sitting opposite him at the meeting. Magnus could see, looking back now, the struggle it had taken her to get herself there. If she was so fragile back then, what might her state of mind be now?

He pulled out his phone. As requested, Pat had texted him Marge Smith's number, with the message,

She knows more about Karen's state of mind than me. I only visit the cafe on occasion.

Magnus contemplated the number briefly, then rang it.

'Marge here,' answered a booming voice he recognized.

'Marge, it's Magnus Pirie.'

'Professor. How are you?'

'Well, Marge, thanks . . .' As he hesitated about what to say exactly, Marge rescued him.

'I take it Pat got in touch about Karen?'

'She did.'

'Something's happened to her, Professor. I just know it. That bloody diary was haunting her.'

'What diary?' Magnus asked.

'She had a diary she wrote around the time of her pal's abduction. It was creeping her out and she asked me to look after it for her. Of course, I said yes. Then after the session earlier today, she runs off with the diary again. And I don't think she's planning to come back.'

Magnus realized from the brief words spoken that there was more to this tale than Pat Robertson had been aware of.

'Can I come and speak to you about this, Marge?' he said.

There was a moment's silence before, 'Sure thing, Professor.' Marge started to give him her address in Raploch, then said, 'Or better still, we can meet at the community hub. There's a great wee cafe there with good coffee and scones. How long will it take you to get here?'

'I'll be there in an hour,' Magnus promised.

33

They had moved into Bill's office. Rhona noted the familiarity of the room, which she hadn't been in for a while. The old swivel chair that Bill had rescued when, during renovations, someone had been foolish enough to throw it out.

It had been in here that Bill had tried to convince her to go to Castlebrae to recuperate and it was in this place that she'd thanked him for his concern and said no. That she would go to Skye instead.

In the end she'd needed both places in order to heal. One hadn't been enough.

Bill was offering them coffee or tea, and urging them to take a seat. Rhona chose coffee, as did McCreadie, and both sat down. Rhona realized she wasn't sure how to refer to the former detective. In her head, she thought of him as former DI McCreadie, but that had been a long time ago. She wondered whether he now preferred the Smart surname.

As Bill dealt with the coffees, Rhona posed the question.

He bestowed a smile on her. 'Just call me J. D. That's what my readers call me, and it's also my autograph when I'm asked to sign books.'

'Why did you change your name when you became an author?' Rhona asked.

'I started writing when I came out of the forces. It seemed sensible to have a pseudonym after both my previous occupations.' He gave a half-smile. 'I still have enemies from the past. What police officer doesn't? Same could be said for Special Forces.'

Bill came over then and handed them their coffee.

'I thought it important that you two meet in person, since this case may hopefully be helped by forensic developments in the last forty-five years. And since we appear to have no record of what was done back then in forensic terms, you,' he nodded to J. D., 'would seem to be our only known source of information on that front.'

Rhona watched as J. D. considered this. 'You've not found the evidence boxes?'

'Not as yet, but we're still looking,' Bill said.

'I don't think Dr MacLeod needs me to tell her how primitive it was in terms of forensics. She deals with it in her lecture on the World's End case, specifically with that startling image of the row of plods standing six inches from the body on the beach. Now that made me grue when I saw it, although it was standard practice at the time.'

He continued, 'Bear in mind it was a missing child and not a crime scene or a deposition site we were dealing with.' He looked to Rhona. 'So all we could really do was map out her movements and interview any suspects.'

'What, if any, material was taken from the suspects?' Rhona said.

'If it had been a murder enquiry, then fingerprints, blood type, maybe fibres. But this wasn't a murder. So fingerprints only, which apparently we no longer have.'

Everything he'd said just confirmed what Rhona already suspected. The dress found with the body was the only real link they had with the killer.

'What you said in the strategy meeting about the dress

and the DNA you've located so far not being from Mary . . .' J. D. said.

Rhona waited.

'It reminded me of something I'd forgotten.'

'Go on,' Bill said.

'It was odd, but her mum said the school clothes Mary was wearing before she got dressed up for the confirmation were missing from her bedroom.'

'And you never found them?' Rhona said.

'No. We assumed she'd taken them with her to change into later.'

'But she was coming back to the school, which was across the road from her house,' Rhona said. 'Why would she take a change of clothing with her?'

J. D. nodded. 'We wondered if she'd planned to go to the den she had with Karen and maybe change there, so as not to mess up her dress.'

'Did you ask Karen about this?'

'When she did talk, she just kept saying how much Mary loved her dress. Then she shut up altogether.'

Karen was key to all of this, if they could locate her, Rhona thought. Even down to the actual dress Mary had worn that day.

'I'm not convinced Mary was wearing the dress we found in the grave, either when she was killed or even when she was moved to the deposition site,' Rhona said. 'So maybe she was dressed in her normal clothes. Did her mother describe them?'

'Her usual school clothes: a hand-knitted blue woollen jumper and grey pleated skirt, white ankle socks and leather sandals.'

Rhona thought back to the trace samples they'd retrieved

from the clothes and, in particular, the body. The taping she'd done in the grave before they'd taken the body to the mortuary had resulted in mostly peaty deposits, as she'd suspected, but not only that. There had also been microscopic pieces of hair, like shavings.

'What?' J. D. said, seeing her expression.

Rhona shook her head, indicating she'd been absorbing what he'd just told her.

'So,' J. D. said, 'it looks like it's up to you, Dr MacLeod.' He assumed an apologetic air. 'Let's hope you have more luck than I did.'

J. D. said his goodbyes then, reminding Bill that anything more they needed from him, they only had to ask. Rhona stayed, keen to get Bill's feelings on both the strategy meeting and their tête-à-tête with J. D. Smart.

'So,' Bill said, 'what do you think?'

'The new information on Mary's clothes was important,' Rhona said. 'When I taped the body in situ, I picked up a lot of peat, but mixed with it were tiny bits of hair. I couldn't think what that meant, but then I remembered a case from way back, in England. The murder of a young girl. She was found naked, but there were microscopic stubby hairs which turned out to come from her killer, who'd recently had his hair razor cut. Are there any photos of the suspects taken at that time?'

Bill shook his head. 'It's as if the case files disappeared just like Mary McIntyre did.'

'J. D. mentioned Sir Peter White as being his superior at the time. Is he still alive?'

'No. We're trying to chase up anyone else involved in the case, or with knowledge of it. Our best sources of information at the moment would seem to be former DI McCreadie and the siblings of Mary, and Karen herself of course.'

Rhona wondered if J. D. was also keen to keep it that way.

'What?' Bill said, reading her expression.

'Does it strike you that he only tells us what he wants us to know, and at a time of his own choosing? It's like dropping clues in a crime novel,' Rhona said.

'In which we're the players and he's directing the plot?' Bill suggested.

'Exactly.' Thinking on from that, Rhona added, 'I'll take a bet he's writing a book about the Mary McIntyre case. One in which J. D. Smart leads us to the killer.'

'You think our former DI may already know who killed Mary?'

'I think it's a distinct possibility,' Rhona said.

34

'What took you so long?' McNab enquired when Janice appeared. 'Don't tell me, Professor Pirie had loads to say about McLaughlin's interview, mainly featuring how shite we were at doing it?'

Janice bestowed a look on him that would have curdled milk.

'Okay, okay, what did our friendly forensic psychologist have to say then?'

Janice relented. 'He thought the interview with McLaughlin went well, and we could meet sometime and talk about it further. Plus he would email us his notes.'

McNab raised an eyebrow but kept his mouth shut, because his partner's expression defied him to do otherwise.

'Also,' Janice continued en route to the vehicle, 'he thinks he's located Karen Marshall, married name Johnston, via a recovery cafe in Raploch, Stirling.'

'Jesus!' McNab said, coming to an abrupt halt. 'That's good news.'

'Yes and no. It appears she was pretty freaked at the body's discovery and is uncontactable by mobile, and the other women don't know her address.'

Having reached the car, McNab made his way swiftly towards the driver's door, just in case Janice was considering taking the wheel again. However, Janice seemed unperturbed by his move, and opened the door on the passenger side.

'So,' McNab said, once safely in his seat of choice, 'you've got someone looking for the address?'

'Yes.'

McNab started the engine with a smile. He was feeling good about all of this, including being back in charge of the car.

'So where is Father Feeney residing now?' Janice said.

'Father Joseph Feeney, aka Declan Walsh, left the priest-hood ten years ago. He now lives in a flat in the West End of Glasgow and is aware of our forthcoming visit,' McNab said.

'You spoke to him?'

'He called us on the number given on the TV appeal, although Ollie had already located his whereabouts prior to that.'

'Do we know anything about him over the time between then and now?'

'According to Ollie's trawl, Father Feeney was transferred to a diocese in Belfast after the Mary McIntyre case, where he served until he decided to leave the priesthood. Why he did that, we don't know.'

'Well, we can always ask,' Janice said in her usual forth-right manner.

McNab hadn't been strictly accurate about not knowing any more than he'd told Janice. It was just that Ollie couldn't confirm the other stuff he'd told McNab, so it could of course be online porkies, and McNab preferred to carry his cards close to his chest anyway.

Having a partner on the job was fine, even good at times (all that stuff about having your back), but it wasn't that different from personal relationships. Better to keep a few secrets.

*

Father Feeney now lived in the converted former Notre Dame Chapel in Victoria Crescent. McNab chose not to mention this, interested as he was to see Janice's expression once they arrived.

He wasn't disappointed.

'He lives in a former chapel?'

'Once a priest, always a priest?' McNab said. 'Pretty impressive and expensive surroundings.'

'I thought priests didn't earn any money?' Janice said.

'You're right, plus they're not meant to leave or retire. After all, they made a solemn promise to God.'

'You're very knowledgeable about all of this,' Janice said, somewhat sarcastically, McNab thought.

'I did some research before we came.'

McNab drew into a parking space just short of the gated entrance to the chapel and its associated former school buildings, also now converted into luxury flats.

Auto-locking the car, he headed for the entrance, Janice following.

The buzzer to the right of the metal gate had the flat numbers but no names. When McNab chose the one he'd been given, a voice swiftly answered.

'Who is it?'

'DS McNab and DS Clark, here to speak to Declan Walsh,' McNab said.

'Very good. Come on up. The pedestrian gate's open. Use the steps by the underground parking. Our entrance is there.'

'Our entrance?' Janice said, throwing McNab one of her looks. 'Is there something you're not telling me about Declan Walsh?'

McNab found himself having to confess to the possibility

of that. 'Ollie dug up some further information on the former Father Feeney, which hadn't been confirmed, until maybe now.'

A second buzzer ring brought them into the building, which McNab thought still boasted of its former life. Chapels were chapels, he thought, whatever folk did with them.

Reaching the front door, they found it already open. In the doorway stood a slim, grey-haired man, who, to McNab at least, looked younger than his seventy years. The eyes behind fine-rimmed spectacles were a bright blue and the smile he wore as he ushered them inside the apartment looked genuine enough.

'I'm so glad you're here, although I did offer to come down to the police station and save you the bother.'

He led them through a hall and into a sitting room dominated by arched windows and a fine view.

'Can I get you tea, coffee?' he offered as he showed them to a seat.

'Thank you, that would be good,' Janice said.

When Walsh disappeared to wherever the kitchen was, they both took a proper look at their surroundings. The way people lived was a good indicator of their current view on life. Whatever the last ten years had brought to the former priest, it wasn't poverty.

There were a number of impressive semi-religious paintings adorning the walls, prompting Janice to stand up and take a closer look.

'They're all by the same artist,' she told McNab as she reassumed her seat. 'Jordi Ferrer. Isn't there a Catalan footballer called Jordi . . . Jordi – what's his second name?'

'Alba,' McNab finished for her, wondering how the hell she knew that. The arrival of their host prevented him from asking.

'Here we are,' Walsh said brightly, laying a tray down on a polished coffee table. 'I've made a pot of reasonably strong coffee and a pot of Earl Grey tea, so you have a choice.'

Having sampled the excellent and strong coffee, McNab now relaxed back in the leather chair he'd chosen, already suspecting, if Ollie was right, that it was the one normally occupied by the said Jordi Ferrer.

'So,' their host said, 'I was distressed to hear that the remains found on the moor were those of wee Mary McIntyre. I always hoped –' he shook his head – 'no, prayed we would find her, although I feared she wouldn't be alive.' He took off his glasses at that moment and wiped them on a handkerchief he brought from his trouser pocket. 'Her disappearance haunts me still. As I'm sure it does her remaining family.'

The small and poignant sermon over, McNab nodded to Janice to go ahead.

'Can you tell us where you were when you first heard Mary was missing?' Janice said.

It wasn't the question he'd perhaps expected, but Walsh's reaction definitely wasn't the same as McLaughlin's had been.

'I remember that moment very well. Mary's father appeared at the church, frantic with worry because Mary wasn't with the others when they arrived back at the school. We immediately searched the chapel, the toilets and my living quarters next door. My housekeeper was there. She hadn't seen Mary. There were some grounds, mainly at the back. We checked them too.'

This time it was McNab who posed the question. 'Did you notice Mary that day at all?'

Walsh answered immediately. 'No, I cannot in all honesty

say I did. Each child gave me their chosen confirmation name, usually a saint's name, and there were popular ones, which were often repeated. The school helped them choose their name and sent a list.'

'What was Mary's confirmation name?' Janice said.

'It was Anne, as far as I remember, after the sainted mother of the Virgin Mary.'

Now he sounds like a priest, McNab thought, before asking, 'What about Robert McIntyre?'

Walsh nodded as though he'd been expecting such a question. 'I saw Robbie on the news. He's grown into a fine man. I'm glad things worked out for him. Mary's disappearance hit him very hard. He always thought he was her protector. Against his father and that belt of his.'

'And you?' McNab finished for him.

Walsh looked pained and rather sad. 'Robbie was struggling with his sexuality back then. It's difficult to describe to people who haven't lived through those times how frightening it was to be different. The Catholic Church was, of course, the biggest bigot of them all.'

'Robert McIntyre gave a statement back then to Detective Inspector McCreadie, and to us more recently, accusing you of the sexual abuse of minors,' McNab said bluntly.

'I know, and I forgave him back then, as I do again now,' Walsh said, with no apparent anger in his voice and demeanour.

'Why would Robbie say such a thing?' Janice asked.

'I caught Robbie and another boy having sex. I spoke to them, perhaps too forcibly, regarding the sin. Robbie accused me of being the same, which was true, although I was denying it to myself and the Church at the time.'

He hesitated there, his thoughts, or so it seemed, having

drifted back to the past. 'I eventually saw that the greatest sin was in my own denial, and so I left the priesthood.'

'Robert mentioned you moved in important circles,' McNab said.

'Back then the Church was held in much greater esteem than now. I was often invited to civil events. I was also trying to start a junior sports club which involved asking for money. Many of the wealthy men I approached were generous enough to donate, including the Chief Constable at the time, Peter White.' He paused there. 'I hope Robbie eventually admitted to who he was. I feel guilty looking back that I didn't support him. He has every reason to be angry with me.'

When McNab didn't enlighten him on that, Walsh continued unburdening himself. 'It took many years before I could face the truth. Even then, when I approached the Church about it, I was told to continue with my relationships, but just not broadcast it. So basically to live a lie.' He nodded as though remembering. 'Then I met Jordi when visiting Barcelona and found the courage to be truthful.'

'That's when you left the Church?' Janice asked.

'Yes. Jordi and I now share our time between here and Barcelona.' He waved at the paintings. 'He's an artist, quite famous in Europe. We'll be heading back there for the summer.'

McNab wanted to say, better stick around until we give that the okay, but glancing at Janice, decided not to.

'We've taken note of what you've said, Mr Walsh,' she was saying. 'Although we may require you to provide a formal statement at a later date.'

'Of course,' he said with a smile.

'We also require a DNA sample for elimination purposes, which you can give now or when you come in to provide your statement,' McNab offered.

His reply was swift. 'I'm happy to give one now.'

Was the former priest relieved or discomfited by all of this, McNab wondered, as Janice produced the kit and duly did the mouth swab, but found he couldn't tell.

Thinking it was all over, Walsh now rose to show them out, but it seemed Janice had something more to say.

'Do you remember Karen Marshall, Mr Walsh?'

He looked perplexed. 'I don't believe I do.'

'She was Mary's best friend. They were joined at the hip, or so people say, except when in school or church, since Karen was a Protestant.'

McNab saw something – he was unsure of what – flicker across Walsh's face.

Walsh shook his head. 'If she wasn't one of us, I'm unlikely to have met her.'

'What about Alec McLaughlin then? He lived two doors up from Mary.'

His look darkened. 'I remember Alec. A most unpleasant character. I thought he ended up in prison?'

'He did,' McNab said, 'but he was released recently.'

'I take it you're interviewing him?'

'You think he has information regarding Mary's abduction?' Janice said.

Walsh was fighting himself on what he should or shouldn't say. Eventually he told them, 'Alec wasn't of the faith, so I didn't know him personally, but there were a lot of rumours about his attitude to girls even back then.'

They departed after that, staying silent until they were clear of the grounds.

'So,' McNab said as they got into the car. 'When did you decide to bring up Karen Marshall?'

'Probably around the time you decided to mention McLaughlin.'

'Robbie never talked about McLaughlin in any context other than that he shouted things at the girls when they were playing tennis in the street,' McNab said as he drove away.

'We should be used to folk telling half-truths and lies,' Janice said.

'We are,' McNab assured her. 'How much of what the priest said do you believe?'

Janice didn't answer.

'Well?' McNab insisted.

'Pretty well none of it,' Janice said. 'Except maybe for Jordi Ferrer. I saw a letter addressed to that name on the hall table.'

'Well spotted, partner,' McNab said, delighted.

'Plus, I believe he was in the flat during our interview.'

McNab waited for the reason.

'There was a smell of cologne or aftershave, and it wasn't coming from Walsh.'

'Or me,' McNab said.

'Definitely not you.'

35

Karen locked the front door behind her and went through to the kitchen, but not before she'd checked there had been no further notes put through her letter box.

Once in the kitchen, she placed the diary on the table.

'I'm sorry I'm late,' she told the chair opposite hers at the kitchen range. 'Things got a little awkward at the recovery cafe.'

'Really?' she heard Jack say. 'I thought it was doing you good to go there. You're not back on the drink again?' His voice sounded panicked, so Karen put him straight.

'Of course not. I haven't touched a drop.' She didn't add that she'd wanted to.

'Good. So are you making a pot of tea or will I?'

'I'm on it,' Karen told him. 'The diary's proving a problem,' she said as she filled the kettle.

'I thought you'd thrown that out when I told you to.' Jack's voice sounded angry.

'I didn't,' she admitted, 'because it might help me remember.'

'But you don't want to remember. You must never remember. That's what your father told you. Forget all this, Karen. Forget what happened and live your life. That's what he said.'

'And it worked for a while, but not any more.'

She poured the hot water into two mugs, popped a teabag in each and a drop of milk, stirred them, then put the teabags into the food-waste bucket.

'Hope it's not too weak,' she heard Jack say. 'I don't like dishwater tea.'

Karen plonked the mug on the edge of the range next to him. 'Just as you like it.'

'So,' he said, 'you're back talking to me all the time. Not a good sign.'

It wasn't and Karen knew it. She lifted Jack's mug, took it through to the scullery and tossed the dark tea into the sink, telling herself to get a grip. She wasn't going back there, talking to a dead man who hadn't even recognized her as his wife for the eighteen months before he died.

It was ridiculous.

Noting the time, she switched on the radio to catch the news, and sat down with her own tea to listen, both praying and dreading that there might be news about Mary. It came at the end of the bulletin, just a short clip from a news conference. The detective's voice sounded both serious and kind. He explained that the body found on the moor had now been identified as . . .

Mary's name echoed in Karen's head, stripping away all the years between then and now.

'They've found her,' she whispered to Jack. 'They've found Mary.'

Then she heard her own name being spoken. The detective wanted her to come forward and speak to them. Karen was Mary's best friend, he said. We need to talk to her. We will find the person who did this, he said, but we need your help. Anyone who lived on Hill Street at that time, who knew Mary, should contact Police Scotland.

'That's you,' a voice told her, only it wasn't Jack's voice any more, but Mary's.

'Mary?' Karen said. 'What should I say?'

'*Tell them. Tell them everything.*'

36

It was good to get out of the city. Although it was surprising how swiftly the urban landscape changed to open fields, speedily turning spring green. Glasgow was renowned for its parklands, but one of its attractions apart from the river was how quickly you could come within sight of the Scottish Highlands.

Magnus stayed on the dual carriageway until the round-about north of Stirling, which allowed him a spectacular view of the castle atop its rock on his way past, the light catching the bright colour of the restored Great Hall. The beauty of the castle pointed to it as a royal residence, whereas Edinburgh Castle, although imposing, was in reality a military barracks built to house the Queen's garrison in Scotland.

Heading back now towards town, he gained a closer view, the green of the foliage on the west side of the castle rise making clear they were heading for summer. There was a magical path there, he remembered, called the Back Walk, a way he'd like to take again.

Turning left before the grassy spread of King's Knot, he passed to the left of the castle and headed into Raploch. He'd visited the community campus before, having met Pat Robertson there, after which she'd taken him to the church building that housed the recovery cafe meetings.

Finding a parking space, he locked the car and headed inside, turning left towards the cafe, drawn by the smell of coffee and the chatter of customers.

The room was busy. Looking around, he didn't spot the imposing figure that was Marge, so he got himself a coffee and, since the scones came highly recommended, ordered one. Carrying his tray to a high table by the front window, where Marge might see him on entry, he took a seat and surveyed the clientele.

It was a professional habit of his, this fascination with people. DS McNab did it too. Magnus had watched him in action, although he felt that their desires to observe came from different perspectives. His being psychological, whereas McNab was eternally looking for lawbreakers, past and prospective.

Currently in the room were a group of women round a table dressed as though they might work in the building. Two younger women, dressed in workout gear. A couple of elderly men in conversation. A group of teenagers on their mobiles and a mother with three children. A good cross-section of the community.

'Professor Pirie,' a voice now boomed out across the room, much to the interest and amusement of those gathered there.

Whereas he'd been recently studying them, now Magnus became the centre of attention. It was obvious from the greetings that followed Marge's advance that she was a 'weel kent' figure, and a popular one.

Magnus stood and extended his hand in greeting, which she ignored, giving him a hug instead.

'What can I get you?' he offered.

'No need,' Marge told him. 'They know what I like and it'll be here in a moment.'

She was right. Her tea and scone arrived soon after she'd taken her seat.

'I work here part-time on a voluntary basis, so there are perks. Like these scones.'

She proceeded to butter hers.

'So have you found Karen yet?' she said as she sipped her tea.

'The police know,' Magnus said, 'and are seeing if they can locate her.'

'Her pals at the cafe are also on the job. We didn't ask for her address, but that doesn't mean we can't find it out, probably quicker than the polis.'

She checked Magnus's reaction to this and, finding it positive, continued. 'In her state, a couple of uniforms turning up at her door will likely terrify her. It should be one of us, me probably.' Marge hesitated. 'Or maybe me and you, Professor?'

'They've agreed that I sit in on any interview,' Magnus told her.

'That's a start, but it doesn't help if she's topped herself first.'

'You think that's a possibility?' Magnus said, shocked.

'It's always a possibility with folk as traumatized as Karen.'

'I'll see what I can do,' Magnus promised. 'You mentioned a diary?'

'The diary's not the only thing we need to talk about,' Marge said firmly. 'There's something else you've got to see.' She finished her tea. 'And for that we need to go back to the church hall.'

And so they walked round to the hall, where Marge brought out a big, hand-drawn map of the street Karen had grown up on, together with a chart they'd made up of all folk living nearby at the time of Mary's disappearance.

'When she first told us about Mary, she was keen to get the others to ask questions, because it might jog her memory. She said it was like a door had been shut and locked on a room she needed to see. We've all been there, Professor, you saw that when you visited us. We need to face up to what we've seen, what we've done, otherwise it's like being haunted. Karen was truly haunted. She'd been having nightmares, seeing things, talking to her dead husband. She thought she was going doolally. I told her we were all doolally. So . . . we decided to play it a bit like a mystery game. We would solve it for her. That was even before they found the body.'

She continued, 'She liked that idea, because she thought she was getting somewhere. But that bloody diary scared her. It was like it was cursed, that's what she said. She wanted it out of the house.'

'Did you get to see what was in there?'

Marge shook her head in a determined manner. 'No. Today when she asked me to keep it, I thought I would take a look. Maybe photograph the pages.' She looked at Magnus. 'Was that wrong, Professor? We were all so worried about her.'

'You were trying to help,' Magnus said.

'Anyway, I drew the map as she described it. She was quite cheery at that point.' Marge pointed to the left of the map. 'I asked what was after the rough ground. I thought it was maybe other houses. Karen said no, it was a wood where she and her pal Mary had built a den, so I made an attempt at trees. That's when it all kicked off.'

Magnus waited for her to go on.

'She went white as a sheet. I thought she was going to

216

faint and then she said they were in the woods before Mary went to the chapel.' Marge looked at Magnus. 'She said Mary told her she shouldn't be wearing a white dress at all. She asked Karen if God would forgive her. You know what that means, Professor?'

Religion wasn't a contentious issue in Orkney. Mostly Church of Scotland residents, with a very small percentage of those of the Catholic faith, sectarianism didn't exist and the kids all went to the same school, just like in the Highlands. Unfamiliar with the ways of the Catholic Church, Magnus had had to look up the whole confirmation ritual to understand the significance of the child's dress and veil.

Mary, it seemed, had known exactly what wearing it meant.

Marge was looking at him, her eyes filled with tears. 'Some man got to her, Professor, and made her ashamed to wear that dress.'

Magnus recalled Alec McLaughlin's words that Mary McIntyre had been pregnant and that was why she'd had to disappear. Maybe he was right.

'After she said that, everyone was talking about what it meant. That's when Karen got up and went out. I thought maybe she just needed to collect herself, but when she didn't come back, I went looking for her. She was out in the car, ready to go, plus she'd taken back the diary.' Marge looked at Magnus, her distress at this obvious. 'I asked if she'd be back, but I knew she wouldn't.'

Magnus looked again at the map. The names were all there on the street that Marge had drawn. The McIntyres, the Marshalls, Alec McLaughlin. And across the road the two schools, one Catholic, one Protestant, and the hidden den in the woods.

A broken line showed the path from the den to the school and on to the chapel, represented by a cross at the top of the map.

Mary had walked that way and apparently never came back.

The ominous silence while they both considered all of this was suddenly broken by the ring of Marge's mobile.

Checking the screen, she said, 'It's Beth from the recovery cafe.' Answering with a quick, 'It's Marge', she then listened carefully, her expression moving from pleasure to concern. 'Okay, me and the Prof will take a look.'

Ringing off, she broke the news.

'We've found out where Karen lives.'

37

'So,' said Chrissy, sticking her head round the door. 'Time to shut up shop?' Her voice held the traces of an appeal in it. 'My eyes are crossing.'

Rhona understood the feeling. She'd been focused entirely on the dress since her return from the meeting. Now cut up into areas of interest, it lay on the surface like a giant jigsaw puzzle, its pieces promising to complete the picture of who or what it had been in contact with. But as yet they were just that. Promises.

'Any luck?' Chrissy said.

'Every contact leaves a trace,' Rhona repeated Locard's famous words.

'And we can find more traces now than back when it happened,' Chrissy said.

Which is what everyone, police and public, would expect them to do.

'So,' Chrissy said, 'are you up for a drink? Then you can tell me what happened at the strategy meeting.'

'You mean you don't already know?' Rhona shot Chrissy a look of disbelief.

'Well, I might know something that happened outside the meeting room at the end when you were talking to DI Wilson and J. D. Smart.' Chrissy looked pleased with herself. 'Which I'm happy to tell you over that drink. Plus you can tell me how it went with Dr Walker last night, which I note you have not yet revealed.'

Chrissy was right: Rhona had avoided a discussion of last night's event, mainly because she was still pissed off and unnerved by Edward's sudden reappearance in her life. After she and Richie had walked out together, having missed the meal, they'd gone for a curry. Richie hadn't asked her any more about Edward, which she was glad about. They'd eaten, and she'd gone home alone in a taxi to brood about Edward and his desire to offer Liam a job since he was coming home. Something Liam had not informed her about.

'What's up?' Chrissy was saying as they got changed. 'You look like thunder. You don't have to go for a drink if you don't want to.'

Rhona decided there was no point keeping it a secret.

'Edward turned up last night at the dinner.'

Chrissy's mouth fell open. '*The* Edward?'

'That's the one,' Rhona said, slipping on her coat. 'He even managed to sit at our table. So we left early.'

'He spoke to you?'

'Too right, he did. Made a point of asking me for *our* son's contact details, so he might offer him a job on his apparently imminent return to Glasgow.'

'What did you say?' Chrissy was goggle-eyed.

'I told him *we* didn't have a son, since he'd denied Liam's existence and that was after he'd wanted him aborted.'

'Jeez,' Chrissy said in admiration. 'Wish I'd been there.'

'Not sure Dr Walker felt quite the same way, although he did save me by quietly exiting and fake-phoning me from the lobby to ask me to attend a crime scene.'

'I like that man,' Chrissy said, impressed. 'By the way, you never mentioned that Liam was coming back?'

'That's because I didn't know.'

'Ah . . .' Chrissy now saw possibly the true reason for the anger. 'You'd better contact Liam. See what's happening.'

Rhona knew she should, but she hadn't. If she did, how could she ask the question she most wanted the answer to? *Why did you not tell me?*

They were at the back of the jazz club, cutting down the path onto Ashton Lane. The evening was spring warm, and some folk were brave enough to sit at the rear outside tables.

'No way,' Chrissy informed Rhona when she saw her looking over at them.

Heading downstairs, Rhona asked Chrissy to order the usual while she went to check if Sean was about. They hadn't spoken to one another since the night he'd stayed over – although her real reason for seeking him out was to find out if Liam had been in touch with Sean, and he hadn't got round to telling her.

She found the office empty but heard sounds from the back room where artists hung out before performances.

'Sean,' she called and waited. If whoever was playing tonight was in there, she didn't want to just walk in un-announced.

The door opened and Sean, looking surprised at her appearance, said, 'We were just talking about you.'

'Who's we?' Rhona said, noting what she read as his slight discomfort.

Sean threw open the door for her to see.

'Liam?'

The tall figure of her son stepped forward. 'Hi, Rhona. I just got in from the airport. Thought the chances were you'd come here after work.'

'You never said you were coming back,' she heard herself saying.

'A sudden decision,' he said.

'Why don't we head upstairs and get a drink?' Sean said.

It was always thus, Rhona thought. Sean coping when she couldn't. Part of her longed to ask Liam why he hadn't told her of his arrival when obviously Edward knew, but she managed to restrain herself. Liam owed her nothing, apart for the fact she'd given birth to him. He had a mother and father, she reminded herself, and it wasn't her and Edward Stewart.

Sean was urging her on with a slight nod, which if deciphered might mean, *We'll speak about this later.*

Emerging into the bar, Liam stood unsure for a moment, until Chrissy, spotting his presence, shouted his name in delight and immediately headed his way for a hug.

'It's so good to see you, and you're even taller and more handsome than ever.'

The awkward moment over, for Liam at least, Rhona sought refuge in her waiting drink, while all she could think about was why he was back here, and where he was planning on staying, at his real parents' place or with her? And the most horrific thought of all . . . was he seeing Edward?

She found out shortly afterwards, because Liam told her.

He'd come to stand next to her. At close quarters she couldn't stop herself from noting aspects of Edward, especially when she'd first met and fallen in love with him. For she hadn't always hated Edward Stewart. And she didn't dislike his son, her son, for looking so like him.

'I came back because I heard what happened to you,' he said quietly.

Rhona studied his face. What did he know and who had told him? She couldn't bring herself to ask either question.

'I wanted to see for myself that you were all right.'

He had done that once before. Come looking for her to check if she was okay after the arson case in Edinburgh. *And* he'd come to her when *he* had needed help finding his missing friend, Jude.

'I'm okay . . . now,' Rhona said. 'But thank you for being concerned.'

'In case you're wondering, I found out about the sin-eater case when I met a pal from uni. I got in touch with Sean and he told me a bit about what had happened, said that you'd gone to Skye to recuperate, but were back now and working.'

'When did you contact Sean?' Rhona didn't like how quickly and shrilly she'd asked that question.

'Firstly, when you were in Skye. Then today when I landed.' He hesitated. 'I should have come sooner, I'm sorry.'

'No,' Rhona said. 'You shouldn't. But I'm glad you're here now. How long are you here for?'

'A week. I'm going to see Mum and Dad after this, then I'm staying with a mate in town.' He hesitated. 'I thought we could eat together while I'm here? Sean says he'll cook. What d'you think?'

'I'd like that.' She paused, and then came out with what she really wanted to know. 'Has Edward Stewart been in touch with you?'

He looked startled by the question. 'No, why?'

'He asked me for your contact details. For some reason he knew you were coming back.'

Liam thought about that for a moment. 'He has a son called Jonathan?'

Rhona nodded.

'We have a mutual acquaintance. He must have heard that way.'

'He says he wants to offer you a job,' Rhona found herself saying.

Liam laughed out loud. 'You're joking? Why?'

'Who knows if it's even true?' Rhona said.

'And who cares,' Liam told her.

'I'll drink to that,' Rhona said, raising her glass.

'So,' Sean said later, after Liam had said his goodbyes, 'when's our meal?'

'Tomorrow night if that works for you?'

'Sure thing,' he smiled. 'Everything go all right with Liam?'

Rhona wanted to ask why he hadn't told her Liam had been in touch when she was in Skye, but then again how could he, when she'd told him not to call her, but to wait for her to contact him. Sean had stuck by her wishes and, she assumed, Liam's too.

'It went well.' She touched his arm. 'Thank you.'

'You give me too much credit. He's a fine kid.'

'Well, I can't take any credit for that,' Rhona said.

'Hey, according to my forensic friend, a child takes fifty per cent DNA from each of their biological parents.'

'With Edward and me as his biological parents, I'd say that Liam turned out the way he has because of nurture, not nature,' Rhona said.

Seeing Chrissy giving her goodbyes, Rhona indicated she would go with her.

'You're not sticking around then?' Sean sounded sorry.

'I'll see you tomorrow night for dinner at my place,' Rhona promised.

Once out of the crowd downstairs, Chrissy said, 'I'm assuming you still want to hear what happened after the strategy meeting?'

'Why else would I follow you out when we're going in opposite directions?' Rhona said.

'Well,' Chrissy began, 'Magnus had coffee with Janice and told her that Karen Marshall's married name is Johnston and he believes he's met her at the women's recovery cafe in Raploch, Stirling.'

38

When Rhona let herself into the flat, the cat came bounding to meet her as usual. She'd set up a timer on his food bowl, which meant Tom got to eat when she wasn't around, but he still associated her arrival with food, or maybe it was now more about company and affection.

Running before her into the kitchen, he sprang onto the table, waiting for whatever treat she decided to give him. Checking his food bowl, Rhona found it was by no means empty, so he certainly wasn't starving. Nevertheless, she fished in the cupboard for the treats that Sean had introduced during her sojourn on Skye and, quite delighted by this, Tom bounded away with his prize.

Now what was she going to eat?

Rhona checked the fridge, but sadly the food Sean had bought was finished, which meant she was back to the delivery menus. She grabbed the Italian one and, calling the number, ordered a seafood pizza, while suddenly relishing the thought that tomorrow night someone would be cooking for her.

Having been assured that her pizza would be with her in twenty minutes, she decided to have a quick shower in the interim. Standing under the hot water, she allowed herself to think of tonight's events, re-imagining her first sight of Liam standing taller than Sean. How her eye had immediately assessed him against the last time they'd met, noting the squarer chin, the still-thick mop of blond hair (one good feature he'd got from Edward), his tentative smile when he saw her.

I was too quick with the questions, she admonished herself. *I let Edward get to me. When will I ever learn about that?* This thought led to another, equally unpleasant: Edward Stewart, once he wanted something, was unlikely to give up until he got it.

When she'd announced her pregnancy with Liam, Edward had immediately decided he didn't want a child. When she'd ignored his orders to have an abortion, he no longer wanted her. Later, when she'd already had the baby boy adopted, he'd made sure she would at no time reveal him as the father should she ever broadcast the fact that as a teenager she had borne a child and given it up for adoption. He'd denied Liam before he was born as he'd denied him after.

Why the sudden interest now?

Rhona stepped out of the shower and towelled herself dry, annoyed that her pleasure at seeing Liam again was being marred by the thought that Edward had some sort of plan for the son he'd previously denied or ignored.

Stop it, she told herself. Liam had laughed at the idea of a job with his non-father and that was unlikely to change – or was it?

Edward had money and power. Who knows what he would do to get what he wanted? Fiona, his wife and the power behind the throne, immediately came to mind. Edward would never have made that move at the university dinner were Fiona not aware of it.

Maybe it was Fiona she had to worry about?

The buzzer went as Rhona was pulling on her clothes and she headed through to answer it.

'Great to have you back, Dr MacLeod,' Stevie, her pizza delivery bloke, announced. 'I thought you'd given up on us or moved away. Or even worse, you were sticking to curry and Chinese,' he added with a grin.

'Not when you make the best pizzas around here,' Rhona told him.

Carrying the box through to the sitting room, she lit the gas fire. By then the scent of hot food had brought Tom through to take up his place next to her on the sofa.

While she ate her pizza, Rhona continued to contemplate what the reason for Edward's interest in Liam might be. And then a thought struck her. Could it have anything to do with Jonathan, his son with Fiona?

Edward had made it plain on a number of occasions that Jonathan was a disappointment to him. His manner of response to her enquiry at the dinner had echoed that, when he'd muttered something about art school, then shifted the focus. He'd been furious when Jonathan had chosen not to go to university . . . unlike Liam.

God, what was he thinking? That he could somehow choose Liam as the favoured one? She could almost hear him at the press conference. How he'd found his son again and was so pleased to put things right between them.

Get a grip, Rhona told herself as she went through to the kitchen to fill up her wine glass. Liam had too much sense to take anything like that on board.

Heading back through, she took her laptop with her. The only thing that would stop her thinking about Edward was concentrating on work instead.

Former DI McCreadie had given a pretty full picture of

the previous investigation at the strategy meeting. His talk had now been made available online for those involved in the investigation, together with the transcribed notebooks he'd handed over to the police. Putting her concerns about J. D. Smart and his actual role in the investigation to one side, Rhona settled down to read the material.

Her first impression of the contents of the notebooks was that McCreadie, or J. D., wrote the way he spoke. It was as though you were right there with him in the interviews, sharing his thoughts and his observations, especially on the emotional impact of dealing with a child's abduction. She wondered if McCreadie had ever been married or had had kids of his own. Was that why this particular case haunted him so?

She recalled again that terrible room with the body of the seventeen-year-old boy, mutilated and abused. The horrifying thought that the victim might turn out to be her own son. It was that discovery that had set her on the path to finding Liam.

A missing child, a murdered child, like Mary, became like one of your own, at least until you found their killer.

McCreadie had never had that release, coupled with the fact that he hadn't been permitted to continue to pursue the case. How difficult that must have been for him. No wonder he had never forgotten it.

As she continued to read McCreadie's account of the disappearance of Mary McIntyre, a notification arrived indicating a result was back on a DNA test she'd submitted. Opening it, Rhona saw another bit of the jigsaw puzzle snap into place. The dress, despite being small in size, had also been worn by Mary McIntyre.

So, two girls had worn that dress, or been made to put it on.

The question now was, who was the other girl, and was she still alive?

39

Marge, now they knew Karen's address, seemed puzzled when Magnus urged her to wait before rushing round there.

'Why? We need to check she's all right. I know what state she was in when she left here, Professor, and with respect, you don't.' The strength of Marge's feelings was obvious on her face and in her stance.

'We have to inform the police first,' Magnus said.

'But they can't get there before us.' Seeing Magnus perhaps wavering, she added, 'Can we call them when we get there?'

Magnus considered this suggestion and found it sat well with his conscience. He would call McNab once they were sure they were at the right house.

'Okay,' he said. 'My car's parked back at the Community Campus.'

'Right.' Marge had already donned her jacket. 'I just need to lock up and we're off.'

'Has anyone tried calling Karen in the last hour?' Magnus said as they walked swiftly in the direction of the car.

'Beth tried her mobile number again as soon as they found the address. It went to voicemail.' As they reached the car, she added, her voice grim, 'It wouldn't be the first time I've been too late to help someone, Professor. I don't want that to happen again.'

The daylight was beginning to fade as they made their way back to the roundabout from where Magnus had admired his view of the castle. He'd already programmed in the postcode Marge's friend Beth had sent them, and a female voice was telling them where to go.

The voice directed them to a turn-off from the main road which took them towards what looked like a row of farm cottages.

'She did say she had a view of the castle,' Marge told Magnus, 'but then who doesn't round here? Oh, and they had a dog that Jack walked round Castle Hill, which is right there.' She pointed across the road.

'Does she still have the dog?' Magnus asked.

'It died when Jack got really ill. Karen was relieved, because she said she couldn't leave Jack alone to walk it.'

The way grew narrow here, more of a farm track than a road. Magnus could only hope a vehicle didn't appear coming the other way. Eventually the track did a ninety-degree turn and ran along in front of some houses, then came to a dead end.

There wasn't a number on any of the cottages, just names, and none of them matched the one that Beth had texted Marge.

'Maybe we got it wrong,' Marge said, her voice heavy with disappointment.

'Or we missed an entrance on our way up here.' Magnus began to turn the car round. 'Let's take another look.'

With the encroaching darkness, the distant castle was now lit up, the golden Great Hall looking like something out of a fairy tale. Retracing their route, Magnus tried to watch both the road and the hedges to either side. Still, he would have missed the entrance had it not been for Marge's eagle eye.

'There, just ahead, the sign,' she said. 'Rowan Cottage.'

Magnus made an abrupt turn left onto a gorse-lined track, the dark buds just waiting to open.

They trundled on and, like the other route, the track eventually turned left and came to an abrupt halt outside a house. A house which was in darkness, apart from one light to the left of the single-storey building.

'She's there,' Marge said. 'Thank God.'

Magnus was saying the same thing internally, although at the same time reminding himself that wasn't necessarily true.

'What about her car? Is it there?'

There was a carport to the right side of the cottage.

'It is,' Marge said in delight. 'Karen didn't drive all the time Jack was ill. But she's back driving now. She comes to the meetings by car.'

Magnus was beginning to allow himself a sigh of relief.

'Okay, I'll phone DS McNab before we go in.'

But Marge was already out of the car and heading for the front door as Magnus dialled the number. It rang long enough for Magnus to think McNab had seen his name on the screen and had decided not to answer.

Then, 'What's up, Professor, cos I'm about to eat?'

'It's Karen Johnston. I've found her – or at least the recovery cafe women did.'

There was a moment's silence, through which Magnus heard music and perhaps a woman's voice.

'You found her address or you've actually found her?' McNab eventually said.

'I'm outside her house now. Marge from the recovery cafe is with me.'

'Great. Send me the address and ask the lady to get in

touch with Police Scotland in the morning and someone will be round.'

He couldn't blame McNab for not knowing the intricacies of this story, because he'd only recently learned of them himself, so Magnus chose not to try and fill him in. Instead he said, 'I'll let you know how I get on.'

'The morning will be fine,' McNab said, obviously keen to get off the phone and back to his evening's entertainment.

As Magnus got out of the car, Marge suddenly appeared back.

'She's not answering the door. I've knocked and called for her. Something's wrong, I can feel it.'

Magnus followed her back and added his attempt at getting an answer. When that didn't work, he said, 'Try her mobile again. See if we can hear it ring.'

Marge did as requested and they both listened. At first all they could hear was the distant rumble of traffic from the main road, then Magnus did hear something.

'That's it,' Marge agreed. 'That's her mobile. God, why isn't she answering?'

Lots of possibilities flitted through Magnus's mind, most involving suicide, but he didn't voice them.

Instead, he headed for the lit window but found the curtains drawn. 'I'll check at the back,' he told Marge. Using his phone torch, he picked his way along a gravel path and round to the back door. A small scullery window shared light from what he now assumed was the kitchen.

He tried the back door, expecting it to be locked like the front. It wasn't. He shouted to Marge. When her own phone torch turned the corner, he could make out her face, which now appeared more determined than frightened.

'This door isn't locked,' he told her.

'I'll go in first, Professor,' Marge told him in no uncertain terms. 'Karen won't be afraid of me.'

Marge pushed open the door.

'Karen,' she called. 'It's me, Marge. I just wanted to check you're okay. The girls are worried about you.' Her voice, firm and clear, seemed to resonate in the emptiness.

Magnus followed a little behind, conscious that the scene that could meet Marge might be worse than terrible. As he entered the kitchen proper, he saw with relief that it was empty. There were two high-backed easy chairs, one on either side of an oil-fired range. A mug stood on the right-hand corner within reaching distance of whoever had sat there. Beside it sat the mobile.

The other chair housed a jumper spread out against the seat back, the sleeves along the arms. Below, a pair of trousers had been placed as though someone was wearing them, a pair of slippers below.

He turned, hearing a small distressed sound from Marge.

'She can't let him go,' she said.

Magnus pulled himself together. 'I'll check the other rooms.'

He entered the hall, with its porch leading to the outside world. Crossing it, he opened the far door and clicked on the light. His immediate impression was of abandonment and cold. The open fireplace, he guessed, hadn't been used for some considerable time. The room was empty.

What about the bedroom?

Off the hall was another smaller passageway, leading towards the back of the house. Magnus followed it past a bathroom to a final door at the end.

He hesitated. If Karen was in the house, it had to be in here. Gently, he turned the handle and opened the door.

From where he stood he could clearly see the bed and the humped shape of a duvet, which, he knew, would have to be checked.

In that moment, Magnus wished he had left this to the police. Then, gathering himself, he flicked on the light and tugged the duvet off the foot of the bed. It slid to the floor, its shape crumpling to nothing. Exposed, the bed did hold a figure, or the stuffed version of one.

A pair of men's pyjamas, filled with what looked like more of Jack's clothing, had been arranged on the right-hand side of the otherwise empty bed.

The psychology of loss Magnus knew about, but he had never seen this form before. The clothes on the chair, the stuffed figure in the bed. At that moment he fully understood Marge's fear for her friend's state of mind and her safety.

'Professor.' Marge's urgent and definitely frightened voice broke into his thoughts.

Magnus retreated, closing the bedroom door behind him.

On entering the kitchen, he found Marge in the doorway of the scullery, her normally ruddy complexion drained of all colour.

'Something's happened in there. There's blood splattered all about the place and there's a knife lying in the sink.'

Magnus took Marge's place in the doorway.

They had passed through the scullery without giving it a second thought, keen to check the kitchen and the other rooms. With its own light now on, Magnus could clearly see what Marge had described. His first thought was that they had entered via a crime scene.

'We don't touch anything else,' Magnus said. 'I'm calling 999.'

40

The call from Professor Pirie had interrupted the sequence of planned events for the evening, but only briefly, and only during the meal. McNab had even managed to be upbeat and civil in his response to the professor's phone call, mainly because Ellie had been watching and listening to the interchange and McNab knew she liked the Orcadian.

Having dispensed with the interruption satisfactorily, McNab had got back to his plan, which had involved him serving up spaghetti from a local Italian restaurant together with an Italian red wine recommended by the proprietor.

They'd completed the meal with a whisky, a fine malt from the Spey Valley. Aroused more than inebriated, they'd then swiftly made their way to the bedroom, where McNab had got to examine the wonderful artwork on Ellie's body close up. After which he'd fallen into a sound and satisfying sleep.

Which had lasted until now, when it was being shattered by the incessant drill of his mobile.

Reaching out groggily, McNab glanced at the screen to find an unidentifiable number.

'DS McNab,' he said, rising swiftly and heading for the sitting room.

'DS Jones here, Stirling. It's with regard to Karen Johnston, or Karen Marshall, who I understand you're looking for?'

'Go ahead,' McNab said.

'Professor Magnus Pirie called 999 last night and was sub-sequently put through to us. He'd been attempting to make contact with Mrs Johnston and found evidence of a possible assault at her cottage.'

'And Karen?'

'She wasn't present. We're searching for her now.'

'Karen Johnston is a potential witness in the Mary McIn-tyre murder enquiry. I should have been informed of this last night,' McNab said. 'Is Professor Pirie still there?'

'The professor went home after he and Ms Marge Balfour had given their statements. I believe he's expecting you to call.'

I bet he is, thought McNab.

Ringing off, McNab listened for a moment in case his raised voice had wakened Ellie, but when all was quiet, he went and closed the bedroom door. Now wide awake, he realized the thing he needed was coffee, so he set about putting on the machine. Then he had a swift shower.

Dressed, with one strong coffee drunk and another poured, McNab decided he was now able to talk to Pirie.

The call was answered immediately, suggesting Pirie was not only up and about, but already had the mobile in his hand.

McNab got in first. 'Why didn't you call back when you found a crime scene at the house?'

There was a short silence as though Pirie was working out the least confrontational thing to say.

'I explained to the local police about Karen. They said they would deal with it and contact you, which I'm assum-ing they did?'

'I would rather have heard last night,' McNab said, although that wasn't strictly true.

238

'I apologize. I should have called when I got back, but it was very late and you sounded as though you had company.'

McNab couldn't argue with that. Plus he'd been drinking so would have had to organize a driver to take him to Stirling. None of which he told Pirie, of course.

'We need to talk,' Pirie said. 'There are things Marge told me about Karen that I believe may be pertinent to the investigation.'

'Okay,' McNab said cautiously. 'Where?'

McNab sent a message to Ellie, indicating he had to go into work and he would see her later, then slipped quietly out. The Merchant City was quiet at this hour, so parking wasn't a problem, although the cafe, where they'd arranged to meet, was open and reasonably busy. As McNab entered he spotted Pirie in conversation with two young women, student types like most of the others in there.

The females were smiling and nodding at whatever words of wisdom Pirie was bestowing on them. Not for the first time, McNab wondered why he'd never heard of Pirie having a partner, since the Orcadian was obviously a big hit with the women.

Spotting McNab's entry, Pirie said his goodbyes and came across.

'What's with the fan club?' McNab said.

'Students in my forensic psychology class,' Pirie said. 'I've ordered for us.'

They took a seat near the window, McNab conscious of the fact that the two girls' interest in their professor also now appeared to encompass him.

'They knew you were a police officer as soon as you walked in,' Pirie said with a small smile.

'Maybe I've just arrested them, or one of their pals,' McNab offered, taking a mouthful of the strong Americano that Pirie had chosen for him.

'You underestimate your effect on the ladies,' Pirie countered.

McNab could have said, 'Much like yourself, Professor', but didn't. Instead he said, 'So what do I need to know?'

The tale Pirie told him featured a child's diary written by Karen at the time of Mary's disappearance. It continued with the trauma of a woman who had apparently foreseen the discovery of her pal's body, only for that to come true. Then the recovery women's attempts to help Karen Marshall remember more about the day on which her pal had disappeared, only for Karen to run from them, taking the diary with her.

'You've seen this diary?' McNab finally interrupted.

'No, but Marge has, although she hasn't seen its contents. Karen asked Marge to look after the diary for her, as its presence in the house was haunting her. Then she changed her mind and took it back.'

'So no one has read it?'

'Correct. Although Karen says what she wrote down back then isn't the whole story. There are days she left empty. Days when something happened that she can't remember. That's why she was getting the women to ask her questions, to help her try.'

'So why did she run away from the meeting?' McNab was trying to absorb what was beginning to sound like a visit to a therapist.

'You know how McLaughlin told you that Mary was pregnant when she disappeared?' Pirie was saying.

'That wasn't identified at the PM,' McNab reminded him.

At this point Pirie began to tell a story about white dresses and virginity and whether God would forgive Mary. With every word spoken, McNab felt his distaste rise.

Pirie was watching him, waiting for a response.

'You're saying there's a likelihood that Mary McIntyre was being sexually abused when she went missing?'

'Marge thinks Karen believes that.'

McNab contemplated all of this, then got back on firm ground. 'Tell me about the possible crime scene.'

Pirie began to describe his arrival at the cottage, how he'd found the back door unlocked and had entered via the scullery.

'The light wasn't on in there, so we didn't spot the blood at that point.'

He talked about the kitchen. The mobile phone, which they'd heard ring from outside. The chair dressed in Karen's husband's clothes.

McNab interrupted him there. 'How long ago did he die?'

'Sometime within the last year, I believe. Dementia. Karen never went out of the house towards the end.'

McNab stopped Pirie again when he reached the bedroom scene. 'She'd created models of her dead husband on the chair and in the bed?'

'The clothes were laid out on the chair as though he was wearing them. The dummy in the bed was a pair of stuffed pyjamas . . .'

McNab cut him off there, mainly because the last image he'd conjured up was just too powerful. Plus he was already wondering, when or if they found Karen Marshall, whether she could be regarded as a reliable witness.

'What about the blood splattering?'

'Only in the scullery. I wondered if she might have cut

herself with the kitchen knife that lay in the sink. When the police arrived they checked for a 999 call, in case she'd been taken to A&E, but no. Plus her car's still there.'

So Karen Marshall had walked out of that house of her own free will or she'd been removed by someone.

'Did she take anything with her, a bag, the diary?'

'I only noted that her mobile had been left behind.'

'And no signs of a break-in?'

Magnus looked distressed, as though he hadn't taken sufficient care in recording the scene. 'The front door was locked, the back door open.'

'So, what do you think's happened to her, Professor?'

'Karen hasn't got over the loss of her husband. Added to that, a horror in her past has resurfaced, which she feels in some way responsible for. I think Karen is in a great deal of danger. Most likely from herself.'

41

Janice had been circumspect when McNab had called her with the news.

'I assume you have plenty to occupy yourself and don't want another trip to Stirling?' McNab had added.

There'd been a brief interruption as someone had demanded DS Clark's attention, then she'd come back on.

'I've made arrangements to interview Karen Marshall's sister. Will you be back in time for that?'

'Is she coming into the station?'

'I thought we would go to her. She lives in Strathaven.'

McNab had taken note of when he was required.

'Okay,' he told Janice, 'if I'm not back at the station by then, you go ahead and I'll meet you there.'

It was just as well Janice hadn't wanted to accompany him, McNab thought, since he was only fifteen minutes from Stirling when he'd made the call and taking great pleasure in being alone in the car.

Not being a fan of the countryside, scenery wasn't something McNab usually noticed, although the trip to Skye with Rhona after the sin-eater case had altered his thoughts on that a little. However, back then he'd been riding his Harley with Rhona on pillion, which had made it special, despite the circumstances.

McNab now acknowledged the approaching view of the

city of Stirling, with its castle and the distant pinnacle that was the Wallace Monument. On their previous visit Janice had suggested it was a large phallic symbol, like most of the monuments dedicated to men.

McNab had never thought of it like that until Janice's declaration. Checking the monument again, he now suspected his partner might be right.

The satnav, set to direct him to Karen's address, was taking the same route as it had on their visit to McCreadie's house, which suggested the former detective and Karen Marshall lived on the same side of the city.

After circling the same roundabouts and bypassing the sign to Raploch as before, McNab now found himself leaving the main road that ran alongside the castle rock just short of McCreadie's street, and taking what appeared to be a farm track, just as Pirie had described.

Despite the Prof's warning, he almost missed the dilapidated sign for Rowan Cottage, partly hidden as it was by gorse bushes. The gorse continued to shield his view until the track turned abruptly left and he saw the police vehicles lined up outside what he assumed was Rowan Cottage.

It was obvious his arrival had been spotted, because an officer approached as soon as McNab stepped out of the vehicle, introducing himself as the DS Jones who'd made the morning phone call. They shook hands and Jones said, 'If you want a look inside, there are suits in the van.'

'Any sign of Mrs Johnston?' McNab asked as he kitted up.

'None. We've done a house-to-house in the vicinity and are currently scouring open land up to and including Castle Hill, although that's a bit of a problem.'

'How so?'

'I take it you've never walked in the woods that surround the castle?'

'You guess right.'

'Heavy undergrowth, jumbles of huge fallen rocks, really steep and rough ground. Almost impenetrable in parts.'

Glancing across, McNab could imagine what he was talking about.

'Police dogs?' he said.

DS Jones nodded. 'Even they can't get to some of the steeper spots.'

Dressed now, McNab indicated he was ready to go inside. The front door lay open, but he chose instead to walk the path taken by Pirie. Metal treads had been laid throughout, the SOCO team still moving around the interior. The local police were obviously treating this as a probable crime scene, rather than a straightforward disappearance.

When he entered the scullery, McNab could see why. Something had happened here, whether accidental or otherwise. McNab tried to imagine a scenario that fitted the blood spill.

He'd once caught his hand in the front door as a child, the snib practically removing the tip of his left forefinger. His mother had pressed it down, bound his hand up and taken him to A&E, where they'd swiftly sewn it back on.

When they'd returned home, the young McNab had been pretty impressed by the bloody mess he'd made. The place had definitely looked like a crime scene.

In this case, the abandoned knife in the sink could be the culprit. Whatever had happened here hadn't been carried through to the kitchen, where two SOCOs were still at work. McNab introduced himself, took a good look round, in particular at the dressed chair Pirie had mentioned, then went to check out the remainder of the house.

First came the sitting room, surprisingly cold after the warmth of the kitchen, and obviously abandoned. The hearth had some ash in it, plus scattered soot on the fireplace and nearby carpet. McNab took a closer look and found the markings of birds in the sooty deposits. It looked like Karen had had an intruder . . . one of the winged variety.

He saved the bedroom until last. The door was open and from the doorway he could see the stuffed pyjamas lying on one side of the bed, the duvet on the floor where Magnus had pulled it off.

The reality was even more powerful than he'd imagined. Karen Marshall, as Magnus had indicated, was most likely not of sound mind. The Prof's concern that she may have been trying to harm herself was beginning to look more likely. Add in the blood in the scullery . . .

McNab had been involved with many lost-and-found scenarios. When a young woman disappeared on a night out, you just knew the likelihood was she was lying dead somewhere. With elderly mispers, they were usually suffering from dementia and had just wandered off. But, thankfully, they were highly noticeable, so usually safely retrieved, only to wander off again at some later date.

Karen, as far as he was aware, wasn't suffering from dementia, but had been looking after someone who was, and this had clearly taken its toll.

As he re-entered the kitchen, a thought occurred. He'd seen two small skylights on the roof, which indicated a loft. He checked with one of the SOCOs.

'Has anyone been in the loft?'

She nodded an affirmative. 'All clear.'

'So how'd they get up?'

'There's a pull-down ladder in the cupboard in the back corridor,' she told him.

Feeling foolish that he hadn't checked the cupboard, McNab went back for a look. The ladder was still down, so he climbed up to emerge into a low-ceilinged, floored loft.

McNab didn't have a loft himself, but he knew if he did, it would bear no resemblance to this one, which was neater than his living room. Shafts of sunlight from the two windows lit the carefully stacked boxes with labels attached. Checking a couple of these, he realized the loft space was split in two. On one side, the labels were inscribed with a description of contents and Karen's name. The other, Jack's.

He made his way across to Karen's side where a box marked KAREN MISCELLANEOUS, and dated five years after Mary's disappearance, lay open, with some of its contents, mainly books, scattered outside.

Magnus had said Karen had found her old diary and been reading it again. So maybe that's what she'd come up here for?

If he'd hoped to find it back in the box, McNab was to be disappointed. It looked like Karen, whether she'd left Rowan Cottage under her own free will or otherwise, had taken the diary with her.

Exiting the cottage, McNab hailed the CSM.

'We'll need the mobile ASAP,' McNab told him. 'Plus we're looking for an old diary of Karen's, which could be somewhere in the house, or maybe the car. So if you find it . . .'

'We'll let you know immediately,' DS Jones said.

'Any sign of her handbag, purse, et cetera?'

DS Jones confirmed that none had been found.

As McNab retreated to his own vehicle, his mobile rang.

This time the screen revealed the caller's name, although it wasn't someone he particularly wanted to talk to.

'It's Jimmy McCreadie. I hear you're in Stirling and not too far from me?'

McNab wondered how he knew that, then admonished himself. Smart McCreadie would have his local contacts, especially in the world of crime detection. After all, he had to keep up to speed on research for his books.

When McNab admitted he was right, McCreadie said, 'If you have time, I'd like to speak to you about Karen Marshall, or Karen Johnston as she was known here.'

McNab considered this for a moment. He didn't want to give McCreadie more power in this case than he already had. Still . . .

'I can spare half an hour,' he offered.

'Good,' McCreadie said briskly. 'Come over. I'll get Lucy to put the coffee on.'

As McNab headed there, he had a simple yet profound thought, which seemed to make ever more sense the nearer he got to McCreadie's house.

What if the former DI, now crime writer, had known all along that Karen Marshall lived just along the road from him?

He was obviously being watched for, as the door of the big stone villa was opened before McNab could even ring for attention.

Lucy greeted him with a smile, fashioned as though for an old friend. 'Good morning, Detective Sergeant.'

'Good morning, Lucy,' McNab reciprocated.

'Mr Smart is in the conservatory. Coffee, strong?'

McNab nodded his agreement. He might not be fond of McCreadie, but he was definitely partial to his coffee.

McCreadie greeted him with the same enthusiasm as his housekeeper, which immediately put McNab on guard. He wasn't at all happy with McCreadie playing a part in the investigation, despite the usefulness of the information he deigned to give them.

'Have a seat, Detective Sergeant. Coffee should be here shortly.'

McNab took a seat, but said nothing, although he was keen to know how McCreadie had been aware that he was in Stirling.

As though reading his mind, McCreadie said, 'I know about Karen Johnston's disappearance. News travels fast in Stirling, and we don't live that far from one another. Plus—' He halted there as Lucy came in with the tray.

Once she had departed, McCreadie supplied the end of his sentence.

'As I was about to say, I know Karen.'

McNab almost spilt his coffee at this point.

'You knew Karen Marshall was here in Stirling and you didn't inform us?'

McCreadie looked pained by the accusation. 'I know Karen Johnston, or more correctly, I knew Jack Johnston. He and I used to meet on occasion when he walked their dog on King's Knot. I don't have a dog, but Lucy does, and I sometimes take Benji out with me. Walking is good for plotting. It frees the mind.'

He checked on McNab before continuing. 'Of course, when Jack got ill, he stopped going on walks. I never saw him again. Then I spotted Karen a few days ago. She was walking alone through King's Knot. Charlie, their black lab, had died, or so I'd heard. I had Benji with me and of course he went up to her with his ball. She looked a bit uncomfortable about it, but she threw the ball, although she definitely didn't want to speak to me.'

'Did you recognize her?'

'As Karen Marshall? Definitely not.'

'Did she know you?'

'I'd only met Jack in person, so no to my current persona. If you're referring to the last time we met officially, that was forty-five years ago, when she was an eleven-year-old traumatized kid and I was a young detective inspector, so I suspect not.'

He looked concerned. 'Word is, she's very troubled, perhaps even suicidal?'

McNab didn't respond, mainly because he had no intention of feeding McCreadie any more information, when it should be the other way round.

At that point, thankfully, his mobile rang. Seeing Janice's name on the screen, McNab said, 'Sorry, I have to take this,' and went out into the hall.

'Are you on your way?' Janice said briskly.

'Just leaving Stirling now,' McNab promised.

'Change of plans. Eleanor, Karen's sister, is coming into the station. You have one hour to get back here.'

When McNab rang off, he found McCreadie watching him from the conservatory door.

'I have to head off. Thank Lucy for the coffee,' McNab said.

'If I hear anything more about Karen, I'll let you know,' McCreadie promised as McNab let himself out.

'I'm sure you will,' McNab muttered to himself as he made for the car.

42

Rhona was in the shower when she heard the phone ring. Jumping out and grabbing a towel, she went in search of where she'd left her mobile, eventually discovering it under Tom on the sitting-room sofa.

It was McNab. 'Morning, Dr MacLeod. Did I get you out of bed?'

'No. What's up?'

'Some good news and some bad,' he told her. 'The Prof located Karen Marshall's current address in Stirling via the women's recovery cafe there. Bad news is, when the Prof went to visit her last night with Marge, one of her recovery pals, they found what might be a crime scene.'

McNab explained about blood in the kitchen and the fact that Karen had seemingly left without her mobile or her car.

'You think she's just walked out or was abducted?' Rhona said.

'It could be either. Whichever way, we need to find her.'

'Do you want me up there?'

'The Stirling lot are dealing with it on the ground, but I'll make sure you get sent whatever forensic evidence is collected.'

'You're heading there now?'

'I took a look first thing. I'll text you the CSM's number there, so you can speak to him yourself if need be.'

251

Minutes later Rhona heard the ping of the promised text. Checking it, she found DS Jones's name and number. Rhona had dealt with the detective sergeant before, and knew him as an excellent Crime Scene Manager, although that didn't altogether dispel her misgivings about not being there herself. Context was everything at a scene of crime, and this one was at the residence of a key witness in the Mary McIntyre case.

As she dressed, Rhona contemplated how Karen Marshall might provide the answer to many of their questions regarding the dress, and Mary's implied pregnancy. Assuming the adult Karen could remember what had happened on that day over forty years ago.

McCreadie had implied that the eleven-year-old Karen had been severely traumatized, to the extent of not being able to speak at the time. Magnus believed that Karen could have buried the trauma so deep that it might never be recovered. But perhaps simple images, like the reconstructed dress or the bracelet Rhona had retrieved from the lochan, might help jog her memory.

Of course, none of that was possible if Karen had disappeared again.

When Rhona reached the lab, Chrissy was waiting for her, freshly brewed coffee at the ready. Sniffing the air, Rhona thought she also caught the aroma of filled rolls, but didn't remark on this for fear of jinxing it.

'Good, you're here,' Chrissy said. 'Have you heard the latest?'

'McNab called me first thing,' Rhona said, assuming Chrissy was discussing Karen's recent appearance and subsequent disappearance.

Chrissy looked puzzled. 'I mean the result on the DNA sample you sent. It was a match for Mary, which means she did wear the dress.'

'Sorry,' Rhona said, pouring herself a cup of coffee. 'I saw that last night.'

'So that wasn't why McNab called?'

Rhona explained about Magnus locating Karen's home address and turning up to find her gone in what looked like suspicious circumstances.

'Bloody hell,' said Chrissy. 'Shouldn't we be there?'

'McNab says the local team is on site. He's checked it out himself, plus all samples will come here.'

'So what was suspicious about the scene?' Chrissy said.

'Blood in the kitchen, her mobile left behind and she didn't take the car. Photos should be through soon. And I intend giving the CSM there a call.'

'If we had a sample of Karen's DNA . . .'

'We could compare it with the unknown female,' Rhona finished for her.

'Emma did say there was more than one girl in the grave,' Chrissy reminded Rhona.

'Well, there wasn't, not literally.'

'Perhaps she meant the dress had been worn by two girls,' responded Chrissy, who was a keen proponent of Emma's powers, having seen them in action before.

At this point, she produced the filled rolls, which felt like a minor miracle, so Rhona accepted hers without comment, for fear of prompting the return of the porridge pots.

'Any results from the aerial scan?' Chrissy said once she'd consumed her roll.

A hyperspectral imaging camera could pick up anomalies

not consistent with the general ground terrain, which might in turn indicate the possibility of another grave.

'No anomalies, at least not enough to send in the cadaver dogs or request an excavation,' Rhona told her. 'When I was talking to J. D. Smart about that . . .'

Chrissy interrupted her. 'I can't believe J. D. Smart was there and I never got to speak to him properly.'

'So you *are* a fan?' Rhona said, with a smile. 'I thought you were having McNab on.'

'I like his crime podcasts. He examines old unsolved cases and—'

Rhona stopped Chrissy there. 'He's not made a podcast of the Mary McIntyre case?'

'No,' Chrissy assured her. 'Although it might have been useful if he had.'

Rhona reminded Chrissy about her chat with Bill after the author's departure, and their perception that J. D. was in fact attempting to control the proceedings.

'So McNab has a rival,' Chrissy said with a smile and a shake of her head. 'I look forward to seeing that pair go head to head.'

'The other thing he told us, having somehow just remembered,' Rhona said, 'was that the clothes Mary had been wearing before her confirmation were missing from her home.'

'That's weird. Could she have taken them with her? But why would she do that?' Chrissy mused further. 'Her house was opposite the school.'

'Maybe she didn't plan on going straight home,' Rhona said, 'and didn't want to spoil her dress?'

'God, I was terrified of messing my frock. Mainly because my mum had warned me to within an inch of my life that my Aunt Annie would have my guts for garters. And, believe me, Annie was one scary woman.'

'If Mary had planned to go to her den . . .' Rhona said.

'Karen, her bosom buddy, would know if that was the case.'

Rhona nodded. The idea of not going to Stirling, having irked her from the beginning, now became major.

As usual, Chrissy was observing her thought processes.

'You're going up there,' she said.

'Can you manage on your own?'

'Of course. But before you go, describe the missing clothes,' Chrissy said.

'A hand-knitted blue woollen jumper, a grey pleated skirt, white ankle socks, plus a pair of leather sandals,' Rhona told her. 'All circa 1975.'

'I'll make a start on the fibres you took from the body.'

'And I'll let DS Jones know I'm on my way.'

Now past mid-morning, the road out of Glasgow was quiet, which gave Rhona the opportunity to think. For Karen Marshall to disappear so swiftly after she'd just been located suggested she didn't want to be found, or alternatively, someone hadn't wanted her to get in touch with the police.

Rhona wondered how many people outside those in the recovery cafe had known about the diary. The press certainly hadn't learned about it or it would have been a front-page splash, whether the diary contained key information on Mary McIntyre's murder or not. The fact that the press hadn't got hold of the diary story was a tribute to the support group who'd stayed loyal in their silence.

But, Rhona thought, as she approached the single-track road that led to Rowan Cottage, Karen Marshall's home address couldn't be kept a secret any longer. That was obvious from the existence of the barrier at the road end, together with the attending police officer.

She rolled down her window and told him who she was.

'DS Jones said you were on your way, Dr MacLeod. Go on up. I'm just keeping the local press and other interested parties at bay. Although we've already had a drone from King's Knot come for a look.'

Thick gorse bushes, some already starting to bloom in the milder weather of the last few days, blanked any view Rhona may have had of the cottage and its immediate surroundings. Only the castle rose like a sentinel in the near distance. Assuming Karen had left either on foot or in a vehicle, it was unlikely that she'd been seen on this road.

Meeting an abrupt corner, Rhona swung hard left to pull up behind a police car.

DS Jones came forward to greet her. 'Dr MacLeod, you made it through the barrier?'

'I did, thanks.' Rhona looked up as the hum of a drone overhead caught her attention. 'I see we're being observed?'

'It's been around most of the day. We think it's being launched from Castle Hill, but we haven't located where yet. Still, if it spots our missing person, it'll be doing us a favour.'

'I take it there's nothing back from the search party?'

He shook his head. 'If she did walk into town she could have headed anywhere by bus or train. We're checking out both possibilities and asking the public to help with possible sightings.'

'So you have a recent photo of Karen?'

'Fortunately, one was taken at the recovery cafe by Marge Balfour, when Professor Pirie visited the group. It's not a great photo, but it's the best we have.'

He walked Rhona to the front door. 'Take as long as you like, Dr MacLeod. We've finished in there for now. I should say they've taken a few items for DNA purposes, which will come through to you. Here's a list of what they took.'

Rhona viewed the cottage from the outside first. A traditionally stone-built single-storey house with a front porch, a window on either side and two skylights indicating a loft.

Stepping into the porch, she found a couple of potted plants on ledges, below which were two pairs of wellies, different sizes, and an umbrella. An inner door led into a hall with two doors leading off, plus a narrow passageway heading towards the back of the building.

The temperature in the hallway was comfortable, despite being near the front door, the warmth coming from her left.

The house had a familiar scent Rhona had noticed in other old buildings. It wasn't unpleasant, more like lived in. Maybe it was the weathered stone or the wood finishes via the doors and floorboards.

She stood for a moment, deciding where to look first. On her left, the door lay half open. The one her right was firmly closed.

She chose to go right. As the clasp released and the door swung open, a rush of cold air caught her in its grasp. Now she understood why the team working on the cottage had kept this particular door shut.

Despite the time of day there was very little light, so she flicked on the switch. The room had the air of not having been disturbed for some considerable time. Even the visit from the SOCOs hadn't changed that. The fireplace was empty apart from fallen soot, and Rhona's nose caught a fleeting smell of damp, suggesting there hadn't been a fire lit in that grate for some time. She stepped forward via the metal treads set out by the forensic team, intrigued by what looked like impressions on the soot.

Closer now, she made out the shape. Three lines meeting together to form a fourth, it looked undoubtedly like the footprint of a bird. Standing by the empty grate, Rhona was fairly certain she could hear the possible culprits cawing above her.

A three-seater sofa, two armchairs and a TV filled the small room. Marks left by the SOCOs told a tale of finger-print dusting, but Rhona doubted, as they must have, whether this room had been visited recently at all.

Closing the door behind her, she now chose to walk the narrow passageway to its end, passing a neat bathroom on the way, together with an access point for the loft by way of a narrow set of steps.

The end door led into a bedroom, just big enough to hold a double bed, a wardrobe and a small dressing table, housing some toiletries. The saddest thing about the room was the bed. The duvet had been pulled back, exposing an indented pillow where someone had lain. On the other side, a pair of pyjamas stuffed with clothes had been placed to face the sleeper.

The poignant image told the tale of a marriage cruelly ended by death. It also painted a picture of Karen's current state of mind.

Rhona stood for a moment, taking in the scene, then turned and headed for the scullery which had prompted Magnus to call 999.

Entering the kitchen, her first view was of two high-backed armchairs, sitting on either side of the source of the heat, an old-fashioned range. The room was cosy and obvi-ously the most lived in in the cottage.

Rhona imagined Karen and her husband sitting there companionably on either side of the range. Just as in the bedroom, Jack's absence had been replaced by his clothes, arranged as though he still sat in his chair. Apart from this oddity, nothing else looked out of place. Rhona checked the evidence list again, to find that a tea mug had been removed from the range next to Karen's chair. Plus her mobile from the table.

If there had been an intruder it didn't look as though they'd been in here.

Rhona now stepped into the scullery to view what had caused Magnus to call the emergency services.

Depending on the injury and its location, blood left the body in a variety of ways: flowing, dripping, spraying, spurting, gushing or simply oozing. Minor injuries could produce more blood than you might expect. Head wounds, for example, or slicing your finger with a sharp knife whilst cooking.

According to the forensic list DS Jones had given her, the knife found in the sink had been removed for further examination. It was the blood pattern on the surrounding surfaces, plus the faint bloodied footprint on the floor, that now interested Rhona.

Her initial reading suggested that Karen, presuming it was her blood, had been cut at the sink and, turning quickly, perhaps in shock or looking for something to stem the flow, had caused both the splattering and the drops to the floor, resulting in the footprint.

But if she had simply cut her hand, why was there no evidence of her stemming the blood in the form of a cloth or paper towel?

The bloody footprint faced the back door and not towards

the kitchen, which suggested whatever had happened had sent Karen out of the cottage.

Why?

It was at this point that Rhona noticed another mark, this time on the window ledge behind the sink. Using a magnifier, Rhona took a closer look.

It was a bird print like those she'd seen among the soot in the sitting room. Rhona took a photograph, then went looking online for a possible match to confirm her suspicions from earlier.

It didn't take long.

It appeared that a crow had been both in the sitting room and in the scullery. In here it had perched on the window ledge next to the sink. Had the crow escaped the sitting room to enter the scullery, its sudden appearance startling Karen, causing her to accidentally cut herself?

Or maybe it had strafed her.

It wasn't uncommon for a single crow or a flock to strafe humans. It had happened quite recently to students on a campus in Cork in Ireland. The actual reason had been difficult to decipher, although it was thought to have occurred because a nestling had been on the ground nearby and they were protecting it. An alternative explanation could have been that they were demanding food. Perhaps, in this case, that's what the crow had been after?

So a roof crow had appeared, either from the sitting room (what about the closed door?) or perhaps entering via an open back door?

Rhona stepped outside.

Treads were here too and there were photos already accessible taken by the investigation team looking into the scullery, although none capturing the bird footprints.

The back door was surrounded by ivy and, examining the foliage more closely, Rhona located three dark congealed spots on the glossy leaves, plus some spotting on the gravel of the path.

So Karen had still been bleeding when she'd come outside.

Standing looking towards the open door, Rhona now spotted another item of evidence of what might have driven Karen outside.

Tucked in at the edge of the path was a black feather, a match, Rhona suspected, for the crow that had caused Karen to flee her home.

There was no further blood spill to provide a trail, which suggested Karen's wound had stopped bleeding. So why didn't she go back inside and clean up the mess?

It seemed out of character for her not to have done that.

Perhaps something had happened to prompt her to leave. In her hurry, she'd grabbed her bag, leaving the back door open. Perhaps significantly, she hadn't taken her mobile with her.

It was described on the evidence list as a pay-as-you-go, which couldn't be traced, but maybe she didn't want calls of any description. And the car? It too could be traced, so better to leave it behind.

Karen Marshall, Rhona thought, had run away, or someone had made her do so.

She now headed for the attic stairs, flicking on the light switch at the top of the ladder.

Just like the rest of the house, the loft space was tidy and well organized. Only one box lay open and that had Karen's name on the side. A few well-thumbed books had been unpacked, their titles and the date on the side suggesting this box held Karen's childhood. Is this where she'd kept the diary?

Rhona began to methodically unpack the remaining items, laying them out carefully in order of appearance. Apart from more books, there was a doll with a red dress and balding blonde hair, and, at the bottom of the box, a plastic bag. Lifting it out, she realized it wasn't just there as lining, but in fact held something soft.

Opening it, she extracted the contents.

Moths had been hard at work, despite the plastic cover. Little holes patchworked the wool but, removed and shaken out, there was no doubting it had once been a blue hand-knitted jumper, of a size to fit an eleven-year-old girl.

43

'She's here already,' Janice informed McNab when he walked in.

'Well, so am I,' McNab said. 'Has the Prof arrived?'

Janice eyed him. 'No, why?'

'I called him and told him we were about to interview Karen's sister. What?' he added, taking pleasure in his partner's bemused expression. 'After which we can discuss his thoughts on today's interview *and* the previous one.'

Janice gave him a sideways look of disbelief. 'You've changed your tune,' she said.

He hadn't, he was just following the boss's orders. Of course, he didn't tell Janice that. At this point McNab noticed the coffee on his desk.

'I don't want us going in there with you needing a caffeine fix,' Janice told him.

McNab smiled his thanks. 'We'll tell the front desk to put the Prof in the observation room when he does arrive.'

'So how do you want to play this?' Janice said as they walked.

'Just like with McLaughlin. You start.'

By the gleam in her eye that's exactly what Janice had wanted.

'Why the change of venue?' McNab said. 'I thought you wanted to visit Mrs Jackson?'

'Mrs Jackson asked to come here instead.'

'Really? Most folk prefer not to venture inside a police station.' McNab thought for a minute. 'Maybe she's got something to hide at home?'

'After forty-five years, it'll be well hidden,' Janice told him.

They say you can make up your mind about a person in seven seconds. That first impressions are that important. Even as Eleanor Marshall, now Jackson, summed them up, McNab did the same with her.

She looked like a woman who'd been dragged down to a polling booth against her will and told to vote for the political party she most hated. There was a curl to her mouth and a defiant look in her eyes that didn't suggest she had a mind to co-operate, no matter what she was asked.

After the introductions, she told them exactly what she thought about being questioned on something that had happened forty-five years ago. Particularly since she'd given a statement at the time when it was fresh in her mind. Anyway, Mary's disappearance had blighted all their lives and she didn't want to go back there again, ever.

Waiting quietly, a sympathetic look on her face, Janice let the woman have her say until the litany of complaints came to an end.

While this was going on, McNab simply watched. To his mind, what Mrs Jackson seemed most annoyed about was the fact that they'd found Mary McIntyre's body, whereas she would have preferred that they hadn't.

'It was over and done with years ago,' she was saying with a shake of her head.

'Not for Mary's family,' McNab said. 'Nor for her pal Karen.'

At the mention of Karen's name, Eleanor pursed her lips. 'Karen grew up and got married. She went on with her life, put it behind her. Like we all had to do.' She paused. 'Besides, we gave our statements to the detective when it happened.'

'Back then it was a missing person enquiry,' McNab said. 'Now it's a murder investigation.' He nodded at Janice to begin.

Janice set up the recording, while Mrs Jackson fiddled with the clasp on her handbag, not looking at them.

'What we want you to do is speak freely, Mrs Jackson. Answer the questions with as much detail as you remember. Is that okay?'

The woman gave a brisk nod, as though resigning herself to just getting on with it.

'Right,' Janice said. 'Can you please tell us where you were when you first heard that Mary McIntyre had disappeared?'

The frown between her eyes deepened, and a wave of distaste twisted her mouth.

'Why on earth does that matter?' she said.

'Just answer the question,' McNab told her.

She threw McNab a disapproving look, before saying, 'It was when I came home from work at Boots, the chemist.' She drew herself up in the chair. 'I was sixteen. It was my first job.'

'What time was that?' Janice asked.

'The shop shut at six, so it would be around half six by the time I walked back. The police were out looking for her, plus most of the street.'

'Where was Karen?'

'In her room.'

'Did you speak to her?'

'I stayed with Mum. Dad was out with the search party, and she was upset.'

'What about Karen?' McNab said.

She shrugged. 'She never said anything. She was never a talker, except when her pal Mary was about.'

'Was she upset, crying, in shock?' Janice tried.

'She was silent, that's all I remember.'

'We've put out an appeal for everyone who lived nearby at the time to get in touch, in particular Karen. We've had no response from her. Have you any idea how we might contact your sister?'

She looked annoyed by the question. 'I told the other police officers when they came round. We don't keep in touch. I haven't heard from Karen in years, and I don't know where she lives now.'

'So when was the last time you saw or heard from Karen?'

'Mum's funeral. She came to that,' she said through pursed lips, as though it had been a crime.

They waited for her to continue. Eventually she did.

'Look. Mary McIntyre's disappearance destroyed every family on that street. It was like a poison, eating us all up. Everyone suspecting everyone else. It was evil. My father moved us away because my mum couldn't cope with being there.'

Now McNab took over. Opening up his laptop, he said, 'You spoke to DI McCreadie at the time it happened.'

'I spoke to a detective, yes. I don't remember his name.'

'I have the notes here that Detective Inspector McCreadie took when he interviewed you.'

McNab began to read out the relevant passage.

'*"She"* – that's you – *"said she was sorry but she didn't like her"* – her being Mary. *"That she bossed Karen around and upset her wee sister by saying there wasn't a seat in heaven for her because she was a Protestant. She thought Mary was just hiding somewhere, so that everyone would look for her. Mary likes to be the centre of attention. And she flirts. With Alec up the road, even Eric. She halts there as though she's said too much. Who's Eric, does he live nearby too, I ask? She shakes her head. Eric's my boyfriend. And he knows Mary? He doesn't know her, she says firmly. But when he comes to collect me, she talks to him."'*

There was a moment's silence while her face moved from amazement to anger. 'That's wrong. He's telling lies. I never said such a thing.'

'What thing is wrong?' McNab said. 'That you didn't like Mary? That she told tales about who was allowed in heaven? Or that Mary flirted with your boyfriend?'

She drew herself up. 'I don't remember saying any of those things. In fact I'm sure I didn't. I certainly didn't sign anything like that.'

'Eric, your boyfriend at the time, he became your husband?' Janice said.

She nodded. 'Yes. And we've been married for forty-four years,' she added proudly.

McNab thought at that moment that whoever Eric was, he deserved a medal.

'We'd like to speak to your husband,' Janice said.

'Why?' Mrs Jackson seemed surprised. 'He didn't even know Mary.'

'But you said Mary spoke to him when he came to pick you up?' McNab reminded her.

'I don't remember saying that.'

'Was Eric ever interviewed by DI McCreadie?' Janice said.

'I don't think so. We'd only just met when Mary disappeared. He didn't know anyone in the street except me.'

'Nevertheless, we will have to speak to Eric,' Janice persisted. 'To confirm or deny what you told DI McCreadie back then.'

Eleanor Jackson made a sound of annoyance, or perhaps resignation, McNab wasn't sure which. Then she said, 'Well, he's not here. He's in Europe somewhere with the lorry. He drives long distance.'

'How long has he been doing that for?' Janice said, with an interested smile.

'A very long time.' She sighed as though it wouldn't have been her choice.

'When do you expect him back?'

'In a couple of weeks,' she said dismissively. 'So can I go now?'

'Firstly, we'd like you to write down everything you remember about that day. And the names of anyone you suspected might have been involved in Mary's disappearance.'

'You want me to tell you who I think did it?' She looked surprised and quite pleased about this.

'Yes.'

'Well, you should start with that creepy guy McLaughlin who lived up the street. They jailed him, you know, for raping children.'

'Just write down anything that's relevant. Plus the contact details for your husband,' McNab stressed.

The eager look disappeared and they were back with annoyance.

'Can't that wait until he gets back?'

'We need to make arrangements for him to come in and give a DNA sample,' McNab said.

Annoyance became anger.

'Why on earth would he do that?'

'All men associated with the street at that time will be required to do the same,' Janice said.

'What about the dead ones?' she said sarcastically. 'There'll be quite a few of them.'

'We can always exhume them,' McNab said to annoy her. 'Just one more thing. We did locate your sister, Karen, in Stirling. However, she has since disappeared in suspicious circumstances.' When he checked Eleanor's face for her reaction to this, McNab found it, for once, completely blank. 'We fear for Karen's safety. Should she try and get in touch—'

'She won't,' she said. 'Karen won't get in touch with me.' As if dismissing both the suggestion and them, she picked up the pen and began to write.

44

Midway through the afternoon, the rush hour had already begun, although it seemed most of the vehicles were intent on leaving Glasgow, rather than heading there.

As she drove, Rhona went over what she'd discovered at the cottage, establishing in her mind the possible interpretations the context of the scene had appeared to offer.

In any investigation, there was always a danger of fitting evidence into your own theory of what may have happened. Of seeing patterns where none actually existed. It even had a name. *Pareidolia*. Rhona liked the word, but not what it inferred.

Having studied the context of what had happened at the cottage, she'd come to a possible theory, but not a conclusion. A careful study of the pattern of the blood splattering and spotting, at close quarters in the lab, might suggest something entirely different.

The bird footprints were certainly solid evidence of a crow having been in the house. When exactly it had been there, she couldn't determine. However, the bird footprints could have been there for days.

Therefore, the theory that the crow had caused the accident was just that, a theory.

Plus, it didn't shed light on why Karen had left the cottage, leaving her mobile behind. The reason for her speedy departure lay, Rhona thought, in her current state of mind, which didn't bode well for Karen's safety.

It was perfectly possible to imagine Karen in her traumatized state attempting to cut herself at the sink. Failing in this, she could have left, to find another way to more easily and speedily end her life. There were plenty of places to do that nearby.

The castle rock being one.

Off the motorway now, Rhona drew into a petrol station, filled up the tank and bought herself a coffee. Back in the car, she parked up and checked her phone to discover a couple of missed calls, one from McNab, the other from Chrissy.

Swithering which to answer first, she chose McNab, already feeling guilty at it not being Chrissy.

'Where are you?' he demanded on pick-up.

'On my way back to the lab.'

'Don't go there. You're needed at . . .' The address he gave her was the street Mary McIntyre had disappeared from.

'Why am I going there?'

'It's Alec McLaughlin. He's been found dead in suspicious circumstances. Chrissy is on her way.'

Before he could ring off, Rhona told him about her find in the loft of Rowan Cottage.

'I checked that box,' he said. 'In case the diary was in there. You think the jumper's part of Mary's missing clothes?'

'We can test for her DNA, but it's wool and blue and the right size,' Rhona told him.

'If it is Mary's, then Karen Marshall's had it since the day Mary disappeared.'

He didn't say it, but Rhona could hear the words anyway. Karen Marshall had secrets to tell.

Rejoining the motorway, Rhona edged her way past

Glasgow city centre and headed south, using the satnav to direct her to the address McNab had supplied her with.

Eventually she found herself driving up a steep brae she recognized from an earlier Google image, passing a mix of local authority houses and those that looked as though they'd been purchased, probably during the Thatcher era.

To her right, the open ground sketched out in DI McCreadie's notebook was no longer wild, but tamed with close-cut grass and budding yellow and purple spring crocuses. Some of the gardens opposite had become parking places for cars, including number ninety-five, Karen Marshall's old home. Almost directly opposite the house was the drive that led into the Catholic school which her pal Mary had attended.

Rhona halted there for a moment, taking in the scene she'd so far only viewed as a police sketch made forty-five years ago, or as it was now via Google Earth.

On the far side of the school drive was a steep bank, topped by an area of waste ground, not yet cultivated by the council. North of this, on the crest of the hill, Rhona could make out the playground and buildings of the Protestant school. Finally, to the east, the dark shadow of the trees, where the girls had built their den.

Two doors up from Karen's former home had been Mary McIntyre's house, and was, according to McNab, where her older sister, Jean, and her husband, Samuel Barclay, now lived. Here the garden had been well maintained, and it too was bright with spring bulbs.

As she crested the hill, police vehicles appeared in a line in front of a house with a dilapidated air and boarded-up windows, the patch of garden in front home to a discarded mattress and other assorted junk.

According to McNab, McLaughlin's body had been discovered in his teenage home, although he'd been residing in a Glasgow hostel for the homeless after his release from Barlinnie.

So what had brought him back here?

There was no doubt McLaughlin had been keen to inveigle his way into the investigation. Why else contact Magnus and offer himself to be interviewed by the police? Also according to McNab, McLaughlin had been touting himself around the various tabloids with stories of what had gone on in this street forty-five years ago, one of which had given him a front-page special, showing a recent photo of him taken here with STREET OF EVIL as the headline.

Which wouldn't endear him to either the past or current residents.

There was none of the usual group of onlookers that a crime scene tended to attract, although Rhona got the strong impression she was being watched from neighbouring houses as she kitted up. Ducking under the crime scene tape, she was met by the CSM.

'Duty pathologist's been, Dr MacLeod. Your assistant's in there now,' he told her. 'The body's in the living room on the left. It's a bit of a mess in there,' he warned her.

The outer door led into a small porch, which in turn led into a rectangular hall. The glass door between looked as though it had been kicked in, with broken glass scattered over the linoleum flooring. To the right, three steps met a landing, before turning to continue upstairs. Ahead of Rhona, a short corridor gave access to a bathroom and at its end a kitchen.

Rhona entered the living room, although the word *enter* didn't really describe it. *Waded in* would have been a better description, for the floor was ankle-deep in refuse, consisting of empty plastic and glass bottles plus fast-food containers. Whoever had been using the place to meet or doss in hadn't been house proud, that was for certain.

Hearing her entry, Chrissy's white-suited figure rose from the sea of debris.

'And I thought my place was a pigsty,' she declared, with her characteristic grin. 'So what do we do about this little lot?'

'We'll have it bagged and taken to the lab,' Rhona said. 'Where's the body?'

'Back here,' Chrissy told her.

Someone had already moved enough rubbish aside to accommodate the laying of metal treads. Rhona followed that route through, past an old battered settee and two armchairs.

She'd already been aware of the hum of flies, but as she neared, they rose from the body in a cloud, buzzing in anger at being disturbed.

McLaughlin lay naked and splayed out on his front, his head surrounded by a large pool of congealed blood. Ignoring the flies, Rhona crouched for a better view of the gash that had almost severed his head from his body.

Chrissy was swatting the flies from around her own head. 'Time I netted a few of these and took a fly spray to the rest.'

Half an hour later, the room had been cleared of all garbage and the flies had been killed or captured for the purpose of helping establish time of death. Sadly, the removal of the rubbish and the flies hadn't altered the stench in the room. That telltale scent of death mingled with rotting food and urine. But it had revealed some partial bloody footprints, which had produced an excited 'Looky, looky' from Chrissy as she'd filled the last black bag.

'We're going to stink to high heaven after this one,' Chrissy announced, knotting the black refuse bag. 'Plus it looks like I won't make my date tonight.' She pulled a face.

'Who's the date with?' Rhona said as the arc lights snapped on and the locus became startlingly bright.

'Danny, jazz guitarist, of course,' Chrissy told her. 'We were planning a pizza, then back to his place to watch a film.'

'To watch a film?' Rhona repeated in disbelief.

'Whatever.' Chrissy shook her head. 'It won't be happening now, anyway.'

Rhona couldn't dispute that, since the probability was they'd be here well into the night. Twelve-hour stints with a dead body were standard. They certainly wouldn't be leaving before they were sure they'd collected all the forensic evidence they could, before the body was moved to the mortuary for the autopsy.

Context was everything, and now the arc lights were on, the crime scene could be viewed in detail.

From the bedding on the nearby sofa, it looked like McLaughlin may have been dossing here. The accumulated rubbish obviously had a longer time frame. The smell, too, indicated an extended period of illicit habitation and wasn't just occasioned by a dead body in the early stages of decomposition.

During life, the core temperature of humans was normally maintained at around 37 degrees. From the moment of death, the mechanisms that maintained that temperature ceased. How quickly the body cooled was dependent on many factors including the temperature of the environment in which it lay.

It might have been spring, but in this room it was still winter. Plus it appeared the victim had been naked when he

275

died. Hypostasis, the discoloration caused as the blood, no longer pumped round by the heart, sank to its lowest level, was fully developed. In normal circumstances this would have taken three to four hours. From the dark-purple pattern, McLaughlin had lain in this position from the moment of his death.

The eyes were cloudy, as the crystalline structure of the cornea became dehydrated. Rigor mortis was in the early stages, having started in the face, neck and jaw muscles.

Chrissy was bagging the abandoned clothes, which had no sign of blood on them. Further evidence that the victim had been naked when he'd met his death. She eventually voiced the inevitable question, 'Why the hell was he naked? You wouldn't get naked to go to sleep in here. It's baltic. Which suggests he was undressed for sexual shenanigans.'

Chrissy's variety of expressions for sex was expansive, but this was a new one even for Rhona. And much less colourful than usual.

At this moment in time, Rhona was studying the back of McLaughlin's head, in particular at the neckline.

'Take a look at this,' she said, handing Chrissy the magnifying glass.

Chrissy obliged.

'Yeuch. That's saliva. Someone dribbled on him.'

Rhona smiled. 'They did indeed. Probably during sexual shenanigans or as they slit his throat.'

She sampled the material and secured it in a container, handing it to Chrissy to mark up and store. Now she hunkered down to examine the smaller second pool of blood near the thighs. Having by now taped the back of the body, she was keen to examine the front.

Beckoning Chrissy back over, they began together to ease the body up, exposing the reason for the lower blood loss.

'Jesus, Mary and Joseph,' Chrissy muttered from behind the mask. 'They cut his prick.'

The assailant had at least attempted to sever the victim's penis. However, judging by the clean and forceful slice to the throat, Rhona suspected the partial dismemberment of the penis had been intentional and possibly before McLaughlin's throat was cut.

'Looks like my theory of sexual shenanigans was right after all,' Chrissy said.

Chrissy's contribution over, Rhona sent her off to deliver the forensic evidence to the lab, and from there to her late night out with Danny. In truth, Rhona preferred this last stint with the body alone to write up her notes.

Earlier in the proceedings, McNab had popped his head in to establish what they'd learned about McLaughlin's last hours on this earth. Respect for the dead, regardless of your personal feelings about them, was paramount at the crime scene. What the victim had done prior to this moment wasn't the issue. Now he was the victim of a crime, and must be treated as such.

Despite his distaste for McLaughlin, McNab was well aware of Rhona's feelings on this matter. He therefore showed neither relief nor pleasure that the world was rid of a man who'd raped children in his care for over a decade before being brought to justice. A man who, if given the opportunity, might well have done the same again.

'How was he discovered?' Rhona said.

'An anonymous tip-off. Untraced.'

'The killer?'

'Or one of the dossers who've been using the place,' McNab said. 'Bit of a nasty find, when you're looking for a place to lay your weary head for the night. McLaughlin must have known if he came back here and spouted the stuff he did in the tabloids that he was taking a chance,' he went on. 'Even in prison, isolated and guarded round the clock, he was attacked on a regular basis.'

He studied the mangled penis. 'So is that because of what he's been up to recently or what he did fifteen years ago . . .'

'Or maybe forty-five years ago,' Rhona had finished for him.

Eventually relinquishing the body to the mortuary van, Rhona went outside and discarded her oversuit. The night air was chilly, but she breathed it in with gusto, knowing that when she climbed into her car, she would still take the smell of that room with her.

Seated now, with the car window open, she retrieved her mobile, only to discover a list of missed calls from Sean. In that moment, Rhona knew why he'd been continually phoning.

It hadn't only been Chrissy who'd had a dinner date tonight.

She'd also had one, with Sean and her son, Liam. One she'd completely forgotten about.

45

McNab opened the garden gate and stepped inside. He wasn't a garden lover, but even he could tell that this one was well cared for. The daylight was fading, but there was enough left to show off the spring flowers, none of which McNab knew by name, but they smelled nice. Certainly better than the house of death a few doors up.

He'd called ahead to ask if it was okay to visit, and Jean Barclay had said of course. McNab wondered if she just wanted to know what had been happening up the street, or whether she knew already. News travelled fast in small communities and McNab suspected this street was likely as much a community now as it had been half a century ago.

Jean opened the door to him and, with a cautious smile of welcome, invited him in.

McNab had met Jean Barclay on a couple of occasions. When she'd given her initial interview and confessed to not being able to identify her sister's confirmation dress. When she'd been asked to give a DNA sample to check against the body they'd found. And, finally, when she'd been told that it was her sister.

'The family liaison officer has just left,' she told McNab as she ushered him to a seat in the comfortable living room.

'They're looking after you then?'

'I can't thank them enough. If only we'd had that level of support when Mary disappeared . . .' She tailed off.

'Different times,' McNab offered. 'Hopefully we're improving.'

She nodded. 'Can I make you a tea or a coffee?'

McNab asked for coffee. 'Strong,' he said.

'I remember.' She gave a little smile. 'You're addicted to caffeine?'

'It's better than the drink.'

His joke fell flat, but, maybe worse than that, McNab caught a fleeting glimpse of fear, as though he'd touched a nerve somewhere.

A quick glance around caught the portrait gallery on the sideboard. He already knew the set-up. A family photograph of Jean with her husband and two children. Plus one of each of the kids graduating from college or university.

On his earlier visits, there hadn't been one of Mary. Now there was. A single small framed snap had appeared at the front, perhaps because she'd finally been found.

Jean Barclay's swift return with the coffee suggested she'd already had a pot warm and waiting. McNab accepted the large mug and took a mouthful.

'Sam's a lover of strong black coffee too,' Jean told him.

'Is your husband about?' McNab said.

She shook her head. 'He's out.' She didn't venture to say where.

Samuel Barclay hadn't appeared to have been on the scene when the wee sister went missing, so had stood back from the family appeals and the investigation in general. McNab had got the impression of a man of few words, who was concerned about the horror his wife was being put through again after forty-five years. He always spoke quietly, his Irish accent undiminished in the forty-three years since he'd arrived here from Donegal.

Jean was waiting patiently for McNab to reveal the reason for his visit, if it wasn't about the stramash at the top of the street.

'I know about the body you found in the old McLaughlin house,' she eventually said.

McNab nodded, wondering how much she knew.

'Folk are saying it's Alec McLaughlin,' she said tentatively. 'He's been hanging about here, so I wondered.'

McNab considered whether it was worth just spilling the beans. The body had been identified as Alec McLaughlin. In fact he'd been the one to confirm it himself.

She came in again. 'He gave a story to the papers about Mary. About all of us. Said this was a street of evil back then.' She looked distressed and angry about that.

McNab didn't respond, judging it was his silence that was prompting Jean to talk.

'He was a pervert back then and he went on doing that until they caught him. Think of all those children he got to in between.'

'Was Mary one of them?' McNab said quietly.

Jean looked shocked by the suggestion. 'No. Definitely not. Robbie would never have allowed Alec near Mary. But Alec used to sit on the hill and shout things at her and Karen when they played tennis. Poor Karen, have you spoken to her?' she added.

'Karen Marshall has disappeared from her home in Stirling,' McNab said.

'Was this after our appeal?' Jean said, concerned.

McNab nodded. 'Karen didn't approach us, but a friend in

Stirling went looking for her after the TV appeal and found her missing from her home.'

A flurry of worry crossed her face. 'Did we put her in danger?'

'Why do you say that?'

'All this time I prayed Mary was still alive. That someone had stolen her. Like women steal babies from the hospital. Like those snatched children in America who turn up years later. Maybe she'd just run away. Mary didn't like getting belted, but at times she seemed to invite it. Always coming in ages after Dad had whistled for her. I nursed that notion all these years, until you found her in that bog.'

McNab had heard this before from Jean, but he was still moved by it.

'Karen Marshall kept a diary at the time Mary disappeared,' he said. 'We haven't seen it, but we believe it might throw some light on what happened that day.'

'Is that why Karen's missing? Oh God.' She covered her mouth. 'Is Mary's killer still alive? Has he finally got Karen too?'

McNab didn't want to register just how strongly that thought haunted him. He changed the subject.

'The former DI McCreadie on the case, he remembered that Mary's school clothes went missing around the time she did. He said a hand-knitted jumper, a grey skirt, white socks and sandals?'

Jean thought for a moment. 'I remember our school clothes. Mum hand-knitted our jumpers, to match the school uniform. Mary's was blue. Mine, being the secondary school, was maroon. But I don't remember anyone saying they were missing.' She looked at McNab. 'Have you found these clothes? Is that why you're here?'

'We found what might be the jumper.' He brought up the image Rhona had sent and passed the phone over.

Jean stared at it as though willing herself to recognize it. 'It could be,' she said finally. 'Where did you find it?'

McNab wasn't about to reveal that, not until Rhona checked it for Mary's DNA. Instead he said, 'If Karen comes here, it's important you let us know immediately. You have my card?'

Jean nodded. 'I hope she's all right. When I think back, I realize that Mary disappearing was terrible for all of us, but for a child Karen's age, who didn't understand what men were capable of, it must have been the end of innocence.'

The air outside had sharpened. McNab breathed it in, trying to clear his head. Someone was still on duty at the locus, just one vehicle left outside the door. Tomorrow there would be house-to-house enquiries, just like there had been all those years ago.

Back then they'd started out with hope. The golden hour they called it, when everything was fresh in people's minds. The hour immediately after a child disappeared. The hour in which they held out hope that the child would be found alive and returned to their family.

There had been no golden hour result in the case of the missing Mary McIntyre and no peace for her traumatized friend. Not then. Not now.

As he climbed in the car, McNab realized he was already too late to meet Ellie at the Rock Cafe as arranged. He would have to text her, blame the fact that he'd had a call-out. In that moment, McNab knew he couldn't be bothered excusing himself or explaining.

He was a detective, that was the job, and Ellie should

know that by now. His silence, of course, might mean that she didn't come back to his place tonight.

Did he mind?

He realized he didn't but couldn't explain why. If he went home alone, he would be free to brood. Maybe even take the whisky bottle out of the kitchen cupboard. McNab contemplated that thought for a moment, before switching to an image of himself in the shower. Hot and at full blast.

As for food, he could pick up a fish supper on the way. He sent Ellie a brief text, *Out on a murder case*, then headed for home.

46

Rhona stood at the door listening.

The faint aroma of something delicious had met her on the stairs. Being so late, she doubted there was the remotest chance the dinner party wasn't yet over. That they were extending it, in expectation of her imminent return.

The silence that met her suggested Liam had departed for his parents' house. As for Sean, since she hadn't returned his calls, he had likely gone back to his own flat.

Part of her was disappointed and part of her was relieved that she wouldn't have to make conversation with either of the men in her private life. McNab she could have managed, since they'd just shared a crime scene. Even Magnus would have taken little effort.

Arriving back in the real world, when you've just been at the scene of a brutal murder, wasn't dissimilar to a soldier coming home from the front line. You needed time to switch clothes and your mindset.

Rhona slipped her key in the lock. As the door swung open, the one occupant she didn't mind meeting came slinking towards her, tail straight up in the air, the tip flicking back and forth. Tom threaded through her legs and graciously allowed her to pat him before dashing off again.

The silence in here was heavy, as though the flat was all talked out. Sean and Liam got on really well. In any previous meal, she had been the odd one out, watching in pleasurable silence as her blond son held his own against the dark-haired Irishman.

Such a rapport could never have existed between Edward and Liam. Rhona had viewed the relationship Edward had with his other son first-hand. The son who'd been planned. The son he'd wanted.

Truth was, Edward didn't really want a son as an individual. He wanted a younger version of himself, and he'd spent a lot of time trying to mould Jonathan in that model. Jonathan had rebelled, of course, and the result had been worse than anyone could have imagined.

Rhona hung up her coat and kicked off her shoes.

The door to the spare room was open. She glanced inside, but there was no Sean asleep there. She checked her own bedroom now, to find the same. Relaxing into the realization that she was alone, Rhona headed for the shower. She was hungry, ravenous in fact, but the biggest desire was to shed her body of the smell of that room.

Turning the setting up to the hottest she could handle, she stepped under the spray. At first she just let the water beat on her head and shoulders. Then she soaped every inch of her body and shampooed her hair.

Only once she could smell nothing but the scent of cleanliness did she emerge to towel herself dry. It always amazed her that a shower did not just clean the body, but also seemed to clear her mind as well.

Sauntering through to the kitchen, she noted that the slow cooker was still on and the aroma she'd caught on the stairs might just come from it.

A note on the table from Sean said 'Call me!' with no mention of Liam or expressions like 'Where the hell were you?'

Rhona helped herself to a plate of vegetable curry and, grabbing a fork, headed for the sitting room. The shutters were closed, the lamps lit as though in welcome. Rhona put on the gas fire and, reclaiming the couch from Tom, stretched out on it with her plate on her knees.

After which, she purposefully thought of nothing until she had cleared her plate.

Depositing the plate in the dishwasher, she fetched her laptop and mobile and took them back through with her. Head clear now, hunger satisfied, her first decision was to text both Liam and Sean.

She began with Liam, explaining about the call-out and her extended stint with the body, together with an apology for forgetting what day of the week it was. If Liam had time maybe they could meet for a drink at the jazz club tomorrow night, otherwise he could get in touch next time he was in Glasgow.

It was strange, Rhona mused, how much easier it was to say things in a text, rather than face to face. As for Sean, she sent a similar excuse/apology and promised to make it up to him. What if she took him out to dinner at a restaurant of his choice, no expense spared?

She didn't promise him sex afterwards, but Rhona hoped that had been implied.

Conscience assuaged, Rhona now checked for any updates on the investigation that had arrived in her absence. Finding nothing of significance, she switched back to the transcript of McCreadie's interviews, looking specifically for those he'd conducted with Alec McLaughlin.

McNab had questioned McCreadie at the recent strategy meeting about McLaughlin's reappearance and his suggestion that Mary had been pregnant. McCreadie had been dismissive of anything McLaughlin had said, calling him an inveterate liar, who also had an alibi for the time Mary had gone missing.

McCreadie's notes on this were easy to find, because they were frequent. He'd obviously spoken to McLaughlin on a number of occasions but had been unable to disprove his alibi. The first mention of McLaughlin was shortly after the interviews with the two families.

McLaughlin was sixteen, but he seemed way older, both in looks and attitude. I confess I didn't like him from the outset. He didn't like the police either. He also didn't like most folk on the street. He knew the missing girl 'to look at', but not any more than that. 'She's too young for me, anyway.' He repeated that a few times. He was living with an aunt after abandonment by his mother at three, followed by time in the care system. 'Fucking Catholic orphanage. You should be jailing them for what they did to kids like me. After that my mad auntie and her drunkard husband. I'm there to keep him off her.' When I asked him to elaborate, he wouldn't, just made a gesture that suggested they were 'doing it'. I've met young blokes like him before and it always ends badly. For women in particular. I think he's predatory. I know he's been watching Mary and Karen when they play outside. Robbie the brother hates him, but is adamant that the priest is implicated, not creepy Alec. And he's got an airtight alibi.

'What is it?' Rhona found herself saying. Whatever it was, it wasn't mentioned here. Rhona did a word search and, jumping back in the document, she found it.

Alec maintains he was in the woods at the time Mary went missing. Robbie confirms he saw him there.

So Robbie McIntyre, later championed by DI McCreadie, was McLaughlin's alibi. Rhona assumed McNab was aware of this; after all, he'd asked the former DI about McLaughlin's announcement that he'd spotted Robbie in the woods that day.

Did Robbie acknowledge McLaughlin's presence in the woods back then in exchange for his silence about what Robbie and his mate were doing there? Did Robert, as he now called himself, still maintain Alec McLaughlin's alibi for that time? And had he stayed certain in his belief that the priest was the one to hold the truth of Mary's abduction and death?

Whatever role McLaughlin had or hadn't played in Mary's disappearance, he was no longer capable of either lying or telling the truth about it now.

A further word search on McLaughlin's name just repeated in some form what had gone before. Rhona abandoned McCreadie's notes and, fetching a coffee, now began to peruse the photographs she'd taken of the victim at the scene of crime.

The results of the taping of the body would be looked at more closely tomorrow in the lab, followed by the further tapings done at the autopsy. As well as the severed penis, evidence of anal penetration (although no semen deposit) had also suggested a sexual motive in the death of McLaughlin, which might be a revenge attack for the rape of three minors or earlier sexual assaults that he hadn't been brought to justice for. Or even all the way back to what he'd been up to on that street forty-five years ago.

According to McNab, there had been a number of attacks on McLaughlin's life in prison, and once he'd made his presence known to the outside world via the tabloid story, anyone who wanted revenge knew where to find him.

Rhona didn't envy the investigation team their job. In her case, the forensic trace evidence she found and identified didn't involve truth or lies, just facts with their associated probability. For the team on Mary's murder, McLaughlin's death just added a further complication.

It would also involve many more man hours, which officers would rather have seen used in the search for Mary's killer. Assuming that killer wasn't McLaughlin himself.

Rhona transferred her thoughts to the image currently on the laptop screen. A close-up of the throat showed a homicidal wound to the neck. Deeper on the right, suggesting perhaps a left-handed killer, it was classically asymmetrical, with no tentative marks.

There were also no defensive marks on McLaughlin's forearms, hands or fingers, so he hadn't been attempting to defend himself at the time. A forensic pathologist would report how this might have been played out.

Rhona's unpleasant mental picture was of McLaughlin forced onto his hands and knees before both wounds and the rape were inflicted. A man of his age, bulk and mobility would have been unlikely to have had the strength to resist.

Unless, of course, it hadn't been rape, and he'd adopted that position willingly.

As for the size and shape of the knife, and the direction of the cut, the forensic pathologist would register their opinion on that at the autopsy.

From a trace point of view, the killer had engaged with McLaughlin's naked body. Perhaps also his clothes. On average, human beings lost 50 to 100 hairs from their head per day. It was no different with pubic hair.

The killer had spent a considerable time with his victim, and every contact left a trace.

They just had to identify that trace.

47

Since she'd left the cottage, she'd begun to fill in the blanks, although she wasn't sure what was the actual truth or what she imagined to be the truth.

She remembered her childhood as happy, yet bad things had happened. Her time with Mary she remembered as good. They'd laughed a lot. Or Mary had made her laugh. Mary knew about the world. How, Karen didn't know, but Mary knew more about it than she did. Mary had told her there had once been a volcano in Edinburgh. How could that be right? Volcanoes were in other places in the world, not in Scotland. But she'd believed her.

Sometimes Mary said she didn't believe in God, but she still went to chapel all the time, and she worried about God forgiving her.

That was why it happened. Why it had all happened.

And she was as much responsible as Mary. She'd seen her chance and took it. If she hadn't, Mary would be alive now.

That's what she knew to be the truth. What Mary had asked her to do that day had made her happy. She'd jumped at the chance, because it would get her what she wanted.

She should have told Mary that God forgives. They tell you that in the church on Sunday, but there's also a lot about hell and damnation. And that had frightened her.

It wasn't until later that she'd realized it wasn't Mary who was likely to go to hell. It was her.

The uphill track through the trees had reached its steepest part. Karen took a seat on the carved wooden bench that awaited her at the next fork in the path.

From here she could see the layered green of King's Knot through the budding branches of the ancient woodland. This walk up Castle Hill to Stirling's famous Old Town Cemetery had been a favourite with her and Jack, and the dog, of course.

Before life had gone to hell.

Karen glanced down at the self-inflicted wound on her wrist. Swollen and seeping, its throbbing sent a wash of perspiration to bead her brow. The smell when she raised the wrist to her nostrils reminded her of Jack's final days. It had been the signal that it would soon be over. Just like now.

She waited until her head stopped swimming, then restarted her climb, hoping to have reached the top before another wave of weakness hit. She was entering by the open gate that led into the Old Town Cemetery just as it did.

Determined to reach the grave before it swamped her, Karen tried to up her pace, stumbling like a drunk through the gravestones.

Then she was there, her hand on the cold granite. Jack's headstone her support.

'What now, Jack?' she whispered.

'If you tell them, you know what will happen?'

'Mary told me too.'

He sounded surprised by that. 'But the killer might already be dead, and what about all the innocent folk who'll be made to suffer?'

But the killer wasn't dead.

Her mind made up, Karen gathered her strength. If she could make it up the hill, then she could make it down again.

Gravity and momentum were helping her descent, but maybe a little too fast. The trees were rushing past and Karen experienced the pleasurable sensation that she was running through the woods towards their den, where Mary would be waiting for her.

It was at that point that a man stepped out in front of her downhill race.

'Found you at last, Karen,' he said.

48

McNab had been woken by the alarm. The one set to get him out of bed and off to the gym for his daily workout (which hadn't been exactly daily). He reached out as usual only to discover the place beside him empty. Then last night's events rushed back to explain Ellie's absence.

Had she been there, McNab would have cheerfully doused the alarm and achieved his workout in a more pleasurable way. Since he was so obviously alone, he decided to head for the gym instead.

Two cups of coffee, a workout and a motorbike ride later, he arrived at the station, surprisingly on time. And upbeat. McNab would never openly admit it, even to himself, but McLaughlin's recent demise felt like a positive in the Mary McIntyre case.

That didn't mean they wouldn't engage in finding his killer, or killers. It did mean, however, that McLaughlin could never abuse (or kill) a child again. By getting his name and story in the papers, McLaughlin had set himself up and someone had taken a shot at that target. McNab couldn't believe he'd taken that chance unless there was big money or some other reward in the offing such as notoriety, something McLaughlin was inclined to court.

Despite his early arrival, he found Janice there before him. 'Jeez, DS Clark, do you sleep here?'

'You look happy,' she said, not answering his question.

'Just well rested,' McNab told her.

'I take it Ellie didn't stay at your place last night then,' Janice said.

McNab assumed a shocked expression. 'I'm certain that's a sexist remark, I'm just not sure why.'

'I'm your partner. I can say what I like to you.'

'How come you know stuff about my personal life and I know nothing about yours?' McNab said, suddenly realizing that was true.

Janice stuck out her left hand.

'What?' McNab said.

'My personal life. I'm engaged.'

'Since when?'

'Since last night.'

McNab mastered his surprise. 'Who's the lucky bloke?' he said, glancing around the room as though the said bloke would suddenly walk up and announce himself. 'I didn't even know you had a boyfriend.'

'I don't. I have a girlfriend, Paula, soon to be my wife,' Janice told him, a smile playing her lips.

Was she having him on? Then again, Janice wasn't a big joker. McNab, conscious that his mouth hung open, closed it. 'I didn't know you were . . .' He stopped, unable to finish that particular sentence.

'You didn't wonder why your male charm never worked on me?' Janice was grinning now, obviously enjoying his discomfort.

McNab rallied. 'Well, congratulations. Can I take you and your partner out for a drink tonight to celebrate?'

'There's a few of us heading for the Merlin after work. You can come along if you like.'

McNab nodded absent-mindedly, while his brain wondered how many other folk knew when he hadn't wised up to it. Rhona and Chrissy? Surely Chrissy would have told him?

He thought back to all those times he'd definitely flirted with Janice. In particular when she'd first appeared on the scene. He'd taken offence when she'd turned him down, to the extent that the boss had had to have a word with him.

Was it possible just not to notice? He shot Janice a sideways glance. Well, it wasn't as though the word was tattooed across her forehead. Maybe he hadn't registered her sexuality because it didn't matter. She was his partner, a good one at that. After their initial misunderstanding, that's what she'd become.

But then again, if he was that shite at reading people, why was he a detective?

'So,' Janice was saying, 'I've taken a look at last night's crime scene. Pretty rough.' She made a face. 'Are you planning on attending the autopsy?'

'Not my responsibility,' McNab said firmly. 'I was only called in to identify the victim and because he was one of our suspects.'

'Any thoughts on who did it?'

'Let me count the possibilities.'

'What if it was our killer, because McLaughlin knew too much?'

'If it was, then we've rattled somebody's cage.'

They'd continued with their enquiries with respect to other known paedophiles and child murderers across the UK. There were plenty who would have fitted the timing, including the notorious Robert Black. But the consensus among the team was that this had been local. McLaughlin's demise might be a further signal that they were right.

McNab told Janice about the blue sweater. 'There's no guaranteeing it was Mary's, but I called on Jean Barclay last night and she thought it might be. According to Jean, her mother knitted a blue one for Mary and a maroon one for her.'

'Karen Marshall could provide the answers to a lot of this,' Janice said.

'If we find her.' McNab didn't add 'alive', although that's what they were both thinking. 'Rhona reckons the wound in the kitchen could have been self-inflicted,' he added.

'So she may be in danger from herself as well as someone else.' Janice glanced at her watch. 'The Prof's bringing in Marge from the recovery cafe to speak to us about exactly that.'

They went via the coffee machine. Armed with a double espresso, McNab held the door open for his partner to enter first, which resulted in a strange look from Janice and a whispered 'Stop it.'

Slightly rattled by this, he wondered if he'd never done it before. The truth was, he had no idea.

Magnus rose on their entry and shook both their hands, before introducing the woman who sat next to him as Marge Balfour, from the Raploch women's recovery cafe.

McNab examined the formidable-looking woman, who was also eyeing him up with the same interest.

'I'm not o'er fond of the polis,' she declared. 'But the professor tells me I can trust you,' she told McNab.

'We all want to find Karen,' Janice said. 'Anything you can tell us with respect to that, we'd be very grateful.'

The firm set of Marge's mouth eased a little. 'I take it he's your partner?' She gestured to McNab.

When Janice nodded, she said, 'If you can trust him, then I suppose I can.'

That settled, Janice set up the recording, then asked Marge to tell them everything she could about Karen.

It was a sorry tale, interspersed with hope. She spoke of Karen turning up at the recovery cafe, like a waif and stray. How the women had welcomed her but hadn't hounded her about her reasons for being there.

'She'd been on the drink,' Marge said. 'Although not on that day. She looked more like she could have done with a drink.' At this point she eyed McNab, as though reading him like an open book. 'She eventually told us about her man, Jack, and the dementia. Christ, anyone who hasn't seen that fucking awful illness in action has no idea the way it hollows you out, you and the folk caring for you.' She paused. 'The drink had got her through it, but she'd stopped that before coming to us. "Jack told me to," she said.

'Things were going well for a bit. The Prof came to speak to us as a group, and she listened, but said nothing. Karen could do that, you know, retreat into herself, but she was coming back, until . . .' She paused, looking round at their intent faces. 'Until the bloody crow arrived. The crow and the dead cat.'

She then proceeded to explain about the invasion of the crow via the chimney, followed by a vision of Karen's dead cat passing the window. 'She said she was having nightmares. That it was about her pal Mary who had disappeared all those years ago. She thought she was going doolally. I told her we all were. That's why we came to the cafe.'

Marge halted a moment to see if they would say anything. When they didn't, she continued.

'Then she heard on the bloody radio about the body you lot found on the moor. She knew right away it was Mary, so that made matters worse.'

'And the diary?' Janice prompted.

'She still had the fucking diary she'd kept around the time her pal disappeared. Imagine keeping it all those years. Apparently Jack had told her to get rid of it. To forget the past. But it haunted her because she couldn't remember that day. Not properly. She'd gone into a dwam apparently, stopped speaking altogether when it happened.'

'Go on,' McNab urged.

'Then stuff started coming back. The day she brought the diary in for me to look after because she wanted it out of the house. We were drawing a map of the street. She told me there was a wood where they'd built their den. When I started drawing it, she suddenly freaked out.' Marge paused to look directly at them. 'She said Mary was upset. She wondered if God would forgive her.'

'Forgive her for what?' Janice said in surprise.

'Some bastard had been interfering with Mary, and she thought because of that she couldn't get confirmed.'

'Jesus,' McNab mouthed under his breath.

'That's when Karen made off. I thought she'd just gone to the bathroom, but when I went looking for her, she was out at the car and she'd taken back the diary.' She paused again. 'That's the last I saw of her.'

The silence that followed was heavy with thought. For McNab the possible admission by Mary that she'd been abused was the most significant part of the whole speech. McLaughlin had suggested Mary had been pregnant when she'd disappeared. The truth of that, considering the time lapse and the state of the remains, couldn't be determined. But this memory of Karen's suggested someone had been preying on Mary before she'd disappeared.

'The woods,' Marge said. 'Something happened in those

bloody woods. Something Karen's buried so deep, she can't bear to have it resurface.' She looked round at the faces. 'What me and the Prof saw at the cottage – did Karen hurt herself, or has some bastard got at Karen to stop her telling you the truth?'

Janice didn't answer the question but posed one of her own instead. 'If Karen wanted to hide, where do you think she might go to do that?'

Marge thought for a minute. 'I can't see Karen leaving Stirling, because that would mean leaving Jack. She still talks to him, you know? That's what the chair was all about in the kitchen. So . . .' She paused. 'She spent a long time alone, no one noticing her. I'd say she stayed around Stirling somewhere. Or else she's dead, just like her pal Mary.'

49

'Well, how'd the date go?'

Chrissy smiled. 'Very well, thank you.'

Rhona waited, expecting a bit more than that. When nothing was forthcoming, she added, 'So what film did you watch?'

'By the time we had our pizza, it was a bit late to watch a film.'

Rhona said nothing, just met Chrissy's grin with one of her own.

'What about you?' Chrissy said as they continued to kit up. 'What time did you get home?'

'Too late for my dinner party,' Rhona admitted.

'Fuck,' Chrissy said, suddenly remembering. 'You were supposed to be eating with Liam.'

'It would've been better if you'd reminded me of that last night,' Rhona said.

'Sorry.' Chrissy assumed a pained expression. 'So what happened?'

'I found six missed calls from Sean as I was leaving the locus. I met the lingering aroma of something delicious in the stairwell, but the party was over and they had gone.'

'Shit,' Chrissy said in sympathy. 'Was there any food left?'

'Yes, in the slow cooker, with a note from Sean telling me to call. It was too late for that so I sent both men a text apologizing,' she said.

'You're going to have to make it up to them,' Chrissy advised. 'In different ways, of course.'

Rhona nodded. 'Liam's with his parents now, so it'll have to be when he next comes to Glasgow. As for Sean, I've asked him out to dinner at a place of his choice. No expense spared.'

Chrissy nodded approvingly. 'Nice. Followed by a film afterwards at your place?'

'Could be,' Rhona agreed, before changing the subject. 'Anything else come back on the evidence?'

'Oh, I almost forgot,' Chrissy said. 'There's an email through from Jen Mackie. I haven't opened it yet, though the title suggests success of some sort.'

There were a couple of paragraphs and a request to look at the three attachments for further details.

Hi Rhona,

I've attached a soil map of the area of interest, including the woodland where the girls had their den, together with an Ordnance Survey map circa 1975. Note on the OS map there is a track running behind the wood, which has since become a tarred road. I believe it would have been possible to drive a vehicle along this track at that time.

As to the soil recovered from the outer sole of the shoes, it is an inorganic sandy loam mineral soil with high phosphorus, and contains well-preserved fragments of deciduous leaf material (beech, birch) and a pollen profile reflecting the understory of a wood (beech, birch, many mixed grasses, etc.), which has definitely not come from a peat. This likely indicates that she had walked last in a deciduous woodland. There's no trace of fibrous peat, nor is there any of the pollen I would expect to find if the contact location was peat, such as Cyperaceae (sedges) or Sphagnum (mosses) – there were none found.

The trace of pollen recovered from the edges of the dress. This corroborates the results from the footwear – showing direct contact of the fabric with brushings of ash and birch pollen into the weave of the fabric, both of which peak in pollen numbers from April to May . . . I'd say that's been the last place she visited alive in the late spring.

If you want to discuss further, just give me a call.

Jen XX

Chrissy had been reading alongside her. 'So Mary did return from chapel?'

'And she went to the den or the woods,' Rhona said, 'still wearing her confirmation outfit. Doesn't that strike you as odd? If the dress was borrowed or even if it wasn't, going to a den in the woods would likely get it dirty.'

'She was going to meet someone?' Chrissy tried. 'Maybe her pal?'

'Her pal's house was across the road from the school. Karen was probably waiting for her there. Why go to the woods?'

The most probable answer was that she was going to meet someone. But if not Karen, then who?

'Whoever it was, they were either the last person to see Mary alive . . .' Chrissy said.

'Or the person who abducted and killed her,' Rhona finished for her.

They were convinced by the evidence that Mary had been naked when she'd died. So her abductor had managed to subdue her as far as his vehicle. Whatever happened then probably sealed Mary's fate.

'What if it was a stranger?' Chrissy said. 'Paedophiles like Robert Black stalked their victims all over the UK.'

Rhona had considered that too. But how would a complete stranger know about the confirmation or the fact that Mary was going to the den, when she should have been at the school with the other newly confirmed kids? This felt closer to home. She told Chrissy so.

As for the blue jumper she'd found in Karen's attic, if it was part of Mary's missing outfit, how had Karen come by it?

'And so we come round to Karen again,' Chrissy said.

'We have Karen's toothbrush from the cottage, so we'll soon have her DNA,' Rhona said. 'At least then we can establish if she was the other wearer of the dress.'

'You'll have to watch your time,' Chrissy reminded her. 'The autopsy's at two o'clock.'

'I'll set an alarm,' Rhona promised.

50

The screen was divided into half a dozen different images, so fuzzy that to McNab's mind the CCTV footage might not even contain humans, let alone ones he might recognize.

'These are all from the city centre,' Ollie told him. 'One in a corner shop, a cafe, in the queue for Greggs, the rest in various streets. She's in them all.'

'Where?' McNab said, narrowing his eyes as if that would make any difference.

Ollie patiently went through all the images, pointing specifically at the figure he claimed was Karen Marshall.

'This woman ought to have been a spy. She's practically invisible,' Ollie said, sounding impressed. 'It's as though she knows no one is aware of her existence, even a security camera. She's hiding in plain sight.'

In plain sight. McNab remembered someone else from his past who had been hiding in plain sight during the Stonewarrior case. Eventually McNab had realized that, but it had taken too long and cost more than one life.

'You're telling me Karen Marshall is alive?' he checked.

'She was alive until late afternoon yesterday.'

'Nothing from last night or today?'

'Not so far.' Ollie took a bite from the iced doughnut McNab had brought him.

So Karen Marshall wasn't dead or in the hands of a

kidnapper after the scene at Rowan Cottage. At least until twelve or so hours ago. McNab tried to take this as a positive, though a lot could have happened in those missing hours.

Ollie continued, 'Also, I think there's something wrong with her left arm. Look –' he pointed again to the screen – 'she's holding it oddly.'

'We think she was injured in the cottage,' McNab said. 'A knife wound, perhaps self-inflicted.'

Ollie nodded. 'That could be it. But there's something else about these images.'

'What's that?'

'Both in the queue and the cafe, there's a guy, the same guy, in the background of the footage.'

'Show me,' McNab demanded.

'He has his back to us, so I can't show you his face, but I can recognize, as you know, more than just faces.' Ollie indicated who he was on about, prompting McNab to go through his peering routine again.

'His stance is the same.' Ollie endeavoured to explain his reasoning. 'The set of his shoulders, the form of what we can see of his body. He's tall, maybe close to six feet, and he's not young, not by the clothes he wears and the way he moves.'

'What age?' McNab said, desirous of something more concrete.

'Over fifty,' was all that Ollie would offer.

'Where were these sightings?'

Ollie showed him the locations on the street map.

'So he could just live or shop in that area?'

'He could,' Ollie agreed, 'but . . .'

'But what?'

'I spend a lot of my time "recognizing" people. I can tell if they're in the scene for a purpose. Stalkers in particular.'

'And you think the purpose here may have been Karen Marshall?'

'I do.'

'And we have no shots of his face at all?'

Ollie shook his head. 'I've gone through a lot of footage of the city centre and found none.'

As a detective, McNab would have called it a hunch. In Ollie's case, it was something more. As a super recognizer, he was rarely wrong, but without a face that folk could identify, it didn't really help them.

Still, the guy in the images might just be an ordinary punter whose interest in Karen came from seeing her on the police appeal.

Or something more threatening than that, a small voice told him.

'So we keep checking for Karen from last night and throughout today. And for her stalker.'

Ollie nodded his agreement. 'Now for the lorry guy,' he said.

They'd tried the mobile number Eleanor Jackson had given them, to no avail. Mrs Jackson could have messed up the number. Perhaps even on purpose, by switching a couple of digits. After all, she'd been pretty pissed off by the end of the interview.

Ollie brought up a photograph. 'This is an Eric Jackson, long-distance lorry driver with—' He quoted a company name. 'He's been doing that for a while. Forty years or so with various firms. Initially in the UK and Ireland, then abroad.'

McNab studied the image, which looked like a recent

passport photograph, all washed out, with staring eyes and definitely no smiling permitted. Jackson didn't look like anyone you might welcome into your country. McNab suspected his own passport photo would fall into the same category.

Ollie continued, 'Mr Jackson can be away from home frequently and for long periods, as his wife stated. He isn't, however, out of the country on a job at this particular moment in time.'

'You're telling me she lied?' McNab said sharply.

'Not necessarily. Maybe his schedule got changed or he came back earlier than expected,' Ollie suggested.

'Or maybe she didn't want us talking to him,' McNab offered a different explanation. 'You've tried making contact again?'

Ollie nodded. 'With no success.'

'But he is in the UK?'

'According to his company, he is.'

Maybe the marriage of forty-four years wasn't as perfect as they'd been led to believe, McNab thought. He recalled the anger Eleanor Jackson had shown at, as she put it, the dragging up of things from the past. The way in which Mary's disappearance had broken up families.

Eleanor Jackson had never explained why she'd hadn't kept in contact with her younger sister, but she'd alluded to the disappearance of Mary McIntyre as being connected to it.

McNab thought back to his reading of McCreadie's interview with Eleanor as a sixteen-year-old. She'd sounded like a stroppy teenager, duly pissed off that her life had been disrupted by the disappearance of a girl who she didn't even like and who she believed was simply hiding to get attention.

And that may well have been the case. Mary had crossed her dad and his belt threat a few times, according to her sister, Jean. Even Jean had considered the possibility – or false hope – that Mary would suddenly appear, safe and well.

Would he like to be reminded about some of the things he'd said or done aged sixteen? Back when he thought being handy with a chib was a useful skill on the road to adulthood?

That was a question that didn't need answering.

Plus it had come from McCreadie's notes. A crime fiction guy. Who was to say it wasn't fiction he was writing back then too? If it was, then no wonder Eleanor Jackson was so angry about it.

Something had happened to the Marshall family that had made them move house and split up. And that something seemed to rest with their youngest daughter, Karen. Maybe that was why Eleanor didn't want anything more to do with her sister.

What was it Robbie McIntyre had said? *We were as happy as any other family on that street.*

McNab checked the time. Robbie McIntyre would be coming in shortly. He'd rung the station as soon as he'd heard from his sister Jean about the death of Alec McLaughlin.

McNab had a few questions for Robbie too. Regarding McLaughlin's musings. Plus the interesting fact that it had been Robbie who'd been McLaughlin's alibi for Mary's disappearance.

51

She was dreaming. Either that or she was dead.

She was running towards the den because Mary was waiting there for her. They would be together again. She would say she was sorry. She would make amends. Her sins would be forgiven. She couldn't bring Mary back to life, but she could join her in death.

But just as she ran faster and faster, a figure stepped out to stop her.

A man whose voice sounded familiar, although it came from long, long ago.

Then she was back at the wedding, watching, waiting. She wasn't wearing the white dress her sister had wanted her to put on. Her mother and sister had pleaded with her, shouted at her, threatened that she wouldn't go to the wedding at all unless she wore that dress.

Then she'd screamed at them the reason why she wouldn't wear the bloody dress.

Her shocked mother's face floated in front of her. Eleanor's voice called her a liar. After that they'd retreated and her father had been called.

Sending the two women away, he'd come and sat beside her on the bed.

'It's because of Mary, isn't it?'

It was, but not the way he thought.

She wanted to tell him everything, but horror and shock closed her throat again.

The dream, for it was a dream, abruptly ended there and her eyes sprang open to darkness. She was lying somewhere in the dark. Her searching fingers touched something soft and Karen realized she was in a bed.

Was it her bed? Was she back in Rowan Cottage?

She reached out for Jack, but of course he wasn't there.

He would never be there again.

She dragged herself up and cried out in pain as her left wrist buckled under her.

She was hurt. Why was she hurt?

An image appeared, shocking in its power. She was ducking as the crow flew at her, cawing, its claws catching in her hair. The knife, already in the act of slicing her wrist, clattering into the sink. Then the spray of blood like a filigree fan. She smelled metal, tasted it on her lips.

The bird wouldn't let go. Wouldn't let her pick up the knife again. Wouldn't let her finish the job.

So she'd run outside, flailing, trying to get free of the crow. She was running along the path and then . . . nothing . . . until the woods and Jack's grave. And what he'd reminded her of.

The innocents.

What had she been planning to tell the police? Who had killed Mary? But she didn't know. Or she couldn't be sure.

But you suspect, a small voice said. *You suspect you know.*

I was a child, she heard herself repeat. *I didn't understand what was happening. I didn't know.*

A line of light appeared in the darkness and Karen realized a door had just opened. Someone was here with her, but who?

A voice spoke her name.

So it was him. He was here.

52

Robbie – or Robert – didn't look as good as the last time they'd met. In fact he looked terrible. McNab realized he was gazing at a mirror image of himself when he'd last been on a bender, which he was glad to say had been some time ago.

'So someone killed the old bastard,' Robbie said. 'And not before time. How did the fucker die? I hope it wasn't quick?'

'Where were you last night?' McNab said.

'With my partner, having too much to drink, as you can tell from my demeanour. Can't hold it the way I could when I was younger.'

'So you have an alibi,' McNab said. 'Just like the one you supplied for Alec McLaughlin forty-five years ago.'

Robbie's face shifted through a series of emotions.

'Why did you do that? Protect McLaughlin?' McNab said.

Robbie came back at him immediately. 'I told the truth. McLaughlin didn't take Mary. He couldn't have. He was a creep, but he had no access to a vehicle. The priest did. Father Feeney had a van, owned by the parish. That van was at the chapel. Mary was at the chapel and she disappeared from there.'

'So Alec didn't see you having sex with a male in the woods?'

Robbie stared at him, then shrugged his shoulders. 'It wouldn't matter if he had. He was there so he didn't take Mary.'

'This guy you were with?'

'I told McCreadie where I was and who I was with. He wasn't a suspect.'

It couldn't have been easy back then to give McLaughlin that alibi, knowing that McLaughlin could well report Robbie for what he'd been witness to. Robbie had been a minor at the time, which had made what he was doing doubly illegal in the Scotland of 1975.

Robbie had told McCreadie the truth back then, even though it had been dangerous for him to do so. So why would he lie now?

'Okay,' McNab said. 'Write down the full details of where you were last night and who saw you there, and sign it.'

As he rose to go, he felt his mobile vibrate in his pocket. Without reaching for it, he said, 'One more thing. What do you remember about Eric Jackson?'

'Eric who?' Robbie said.

'Eleanor Marshall's boyfriend at the time.'

Robbie looked lost by the request. 'Eleanor had loads of guys after her. She was a looker. I don't remember any of their names.'

McNab left Robbie to it, fairly certain he'd had nothing to do with dispatching McLaughlin. Once outside, he checked his mobile to find a missed call from the man he'd just been talking about. Smart McCreadie.

Did he have time for Mr Fiction to pump him for some more police info, or alternatively to be handed a small clue at a time of J. D. Smart's choosing?

McNab swithered and then came down on the side of any further information being always welcome, whoever it came from.

'Detective Sergeant. Thanks for getting back to me. I really appreciate it.'

'What's up?' McNab said cautiously.

'Can you spare the time to come up to Stirling?'

'Not really,' McNab said. 'As you can imagine as a former detective, we have our hands full here.'

'Yes, I heard about Alec McLaughlin.'

McNab didn't ask how he'd heard, since he was aware McCreadie had a network of probably more informants within Police Scotland than Chrissy.

'I've asked Professor Pirie to come, and Marge, Karen Marshall's friend from the Raploch cafe.'

McNab felt the hairs stand up on the back of his neck. *Why the gathering? Was there something he was missing?*

'I'm in regular touch with Professor Pirie,' McNab said, almost truthfully. 'Can he inform me about whatever you're discussing?'

'It's better if you learn this first-hand.'

McCreadie's insistence was beginning to jar. 'I believe I'm of more use here,' McNab told him.

As he was on the point of killing the call, McCreadie's voice broke in again.

'Please, DS McNab, this is vitally important.'

'But not so important that you can't come to Glasgow?'

A moment's silence, then, 'I can't leave her alone in the house.'

'Can't leave who alone?' Was he jabbering on about his housekeeper?

'I have Karen Marshall here, but she's in a poor way.'

McNab was almost speechless. 'You have apprehended Karen Marshall, without informing the police?'

'I have just informed you. She's agreed to see Professor

Pirie and Marge. She is in a poor state mentally and physically, and very frightened by the prospect of the police. However, I think she'll respond to you, especially since you and Professor Pirie work so closely and well together. Hence the call.'

McNab didn't believe the last part of his pretty speech. As for the rest . . .

'I'll be there as soon as I can,' McNab said and cut the call.

McCreadie's announcement still ringing in his brain, he went in search of Janice, finally locating her in the canteen with a mug of tea and one of the ring doughnuts Ollie liked so much. He ordered a large black coffee and joined her.

'What's happened?' she said, spotting his fraught expression.

McNab led with the news that wasn't freaking him out.

'I've spoken to Robbie McIntyre, who came in after hearing about McLaughlin,' he told her. 'He's writing down what we talked about. Can you check on him and let him go? Unless, of course, you have anything you want to ask him yourself?'

'He has an alibi for last night?' Janice said.

'Out drinking with his partner. He looked like that was true.'

'You get which places they drank in?'

'He's supplying a list,' McNab said.

'So that's not what you're pissed off about?'

'McCreadie says he's found Karen Marshall.'

'That's good news, isn't it?' Janice sounded bewildered by his reaction.

'He's keeping her at his place. Smart says she's only willing to speak to the Prof and her pal Marge. Not the police.'

'But you're going anyway?'

'According to McCreadie, I'm to blend into the background and await further orders.'

Now Janice could see where the annoyance came from. 'That doesn't sound like you,' she laughed.

McNab realized she'd been doing that a lot today. Must be the engagement, he decided. Seeing he wasn't going to rile Janice regarding Smart's capture of their prime witness, he changed the subject.

'So we're still on for a drink tonight?'

'I'll have to check with Paula first.'

'About what? Me or the drink?' he joshed.

'Oh, she's well keen to finally meet *you*,' Janice said with yet another laugh.

McNab retreated at that point, wondering if meeting his partner's significant other was a great idea after all. On his way to the bike, he considered inviting Ellie tonight as his own significant other. Although asking Ellie to an engagement drinks party might not be a good idea. Plus there was no guarantee that she would act as an ally.

At this point McNab checked his mobile, but there still hadn't been a response to this morning's apology for his no-show last night. It seemed a murder wasn't a good enough excuse.

53

Dr Walker glanced up as a suited Rhona entered, acknowledging her arrival with a welcoming nod and a pair of smiling blue eyes.

The SOCOs had finished the initial taping and photographing of the body, and Dr Walker was now examining and recording his thoughts on the wounds they'd located.

Rhona had never met Alec McLaughlin, though she'd seen his photograph at the strategy meeting and heard all about the man from both Magnus and McNab.

Magnus's psychological reading of the deceased had been close to a recognized psychopath with a strong narcissistic streak, who was likely to re-offend in his chosen sphere, the sexual abuse of children. Because of this, he hadn't been safe in prison. It seemed he hadn't been safe as a free man either.

Lying on his back, the two major wounds were clearly visible. Dr Walker identified and measured the wounds and began to describe how he thought they'd come about.

For Rhona, the main reason for coming here was to have her own reading of how McLaughlin had died either verified or disputed, via a forensic pathologist's interpretation of the wounds and how and when they'd occurred.

'The fatal neck wound was done swiftly and without any tentative early cuts,' Dr Walker was saying. 'By someone who knew what they were doing. I would therefore conclude that death was caused by the severing of the carotid artery causing him to bleed out.

'The attack on the penis may have come before. Perhaps even during the sexual act,' he recorded. 'As there were no injuries in the area of the anus, it's not possible to establish whether the sex was consensual or not, but it did occur.

'There is also no bruising on the arms or upper body to suggest the victim was physically forced to his knees and then onto all fours. If a knife was used to threaten him, then that may have been sufficient encouragement. Again, he may have conceded to undressing and getting into this position by choice.

'McLaughlin, as noted earlier, was not a fit man. Once down on all fours, getting up again wouldn't have been an easy movement. The likelihood was that he collapsed forward on death, and was found in that position.'

'So,' Richie said as they disrobed and stuffed their suits into the waiting basket, 'did that help point the finger at anyone in particular?'

'Someone who can wield a knife and who perhaps had a desire for revenge,' Rhona said.

'Was he a suspect in the Mary McIntyre case?'

'Everyone who lived on that street in 1975 is a suspect. McLaughlin submitted to a DNA swab and it didn't find a match on anything we took from Mary's remains or the grave,' Rhona told him.

'Though he may have known something that he wasn't willing to share with the police?' Richie said.

'That was always a possibility,' Rhona agreed.

'I saw that he was giving interviews to the press about the *Street of Evil* he was forced to live on as a child.'

'He had, according to Magnus, a fine conceit of himself,' Rhona confirmed.

'So where does that leave you with the Mary McIntyre case?'

'We continue with our examination and tests from the body, clothes and the locus, and hope we find a way to identify Mary's killer.'

'Which will take a lot longer than an autopsy.'

'A lot longer. Not that I'm disputing the skill involved in forensic pathology,' Rhona said with a smile.

'I'm sorry the forensic dinner didn't go so well,' Richie said, changing the subject.

'No matter. I caught up with my son, Liam, albeit briefly,' Rhona told him. 'Fortunately, he feels the same way about Edward as I do.'

Richie looked pleased by that. 'So do you maybe want to try for a second meal without such a table companion?' he offered.

Rhona now realized that this was what the conversation had been leading up to. Richie was a nice guy, obviously available, and keen to get together. She should, of course, be straight with him, and tell him she was in a relationship.

Which wasn't strictly true, she admonished herself.

Instead she said, 'DS Clark got engaged last night to her partner, Paula. She's having a drinks party tonight to celebrate. Chrissy and I are going. Would you like to come along, meet a few more of Police Scotland and the forensic service?'

Richie looked pleased by the invitation. 'I would,' he nodded.

Rhona told him where and when.

'I'll see you there then,' he said with a smile.

*

On her way back to the lab, Rhona considered the wisdom of the invitation, then decided it was kinder than turning him down flat. Plus Dr Walker needed to get to know as many of the police and forensics team as he might work with in the future.

Chrissy, when told, of course had a different take on things. One Rhona should have anticipated.

'Poor Dr Walker's got the hots for you, Dr MacLeod. You know that and yet, and yet, no mention of Sean?' Chrissy shook her head in admonishment.

'What was I supposed to say? That I'm taken? Which I'm not,' Rhona added.

'True.' Chrissy contemplated this. 'Maybe you could have said you didn't want to be in a relationship right now?'

'Who says I don't?' Rhona countered.

'A steady relationship then,' tried Chrissy, who wasn't normally at a loss for words.

'Dr Walker asks me out to a simple dinner and I turn him down by declaring I'm not ready for a steady relationship at the moment? I don't think so.'

'Okay, it's a minefield, but he is dishy.' Chrissy assumed a wide-eyed look. 'Those blue eyes.'

'Then he's all yours to charm tonight,' Rhona told her.

Chrissy, judging that the dating discussion was over for the moment, asked how the autopsy had gone.

'Just the way we thought,' Rhona told her. 'Any developments here?'

'Karen also wore the confirmation dress. The DNA results confirm this.'

Rhona nodded. She'd been expecting that. The girls were real pals. If Mary had a dress like that, Karen would likely have been allowed to try it on. It could be as simple as that, or it could mean something more. What that something was, she had no idea.

'Also, McNab was looking for you. He's headed back to Stirling.'

This was far more of a surprise. 'Again? Why?' Rhona said.

'It appears they've finally located Karen Marshall.'

'Did she come back to Rowan Cottage?' That had always been Rhona's hope.

'No. It seems she was found by J. D. Smart and she's currently at his house.'

Rhona could imagine McNab's reaction to that. Much like her own, perhaps. Still, she was glad Karen had been found, and alive.

'It seems she's in a bad way mentally. She's asked to see Marge, her friend, and Magnus,' Chrissy said. 'McNab's just there to observe.'

'Before he hears Karen's story, he needs to be made aware of the soil evidence from Jen, placing Mary last alive near the girls' den,' Rhona said. 'And the fact that both girls have worn that dress.'

54

The call from Rhona arrived just as McNab passed by the drive that led to Rowan Cottage. McNab listened to what she had to say regarding Karen having worn the confirmation dress, plus the startling news that the forensic evidence put the last location Mary had been alive and wearing the shoes at or near the girls' den.

So Mary had gone there after the ceremony at the chapel.

'I thought you'd want to know that before you speak to Karen,' Rhona said. She followed that with a good luck, suggesting he might need it.

As he turned off the main road, McNab spotted Magnus's vehicle already parked in front of the McCreadie villa. Easing his bike in behind, he removed his outer clothing and stored it with the helmet in his panniers. He had no idea what Karen Johnston felt about the biking fraternity in general, or biker-clad policemen in particular, but decided not to take the chance that it might be negative.

The housekeeper was there before McNab even reached for the bell. This time Lucy's expression was sombre rather than welcoming.

'They're in the conservatory. I've taken through a tray already, Detective Sergeant.'

McNab followed the scent of freshly brewed coffee to find

Magnus and Marge seated on the large couch, with McCreadie poised above them in his high-backed chair.

'Ah, Sergeant. We were hoping you were on your way.'

Magnus cast McNab a glance which he didn't try to interpret. As for Marge, she appeared genuinely pleased to see him.

Once McNab had his coffee, McCreadie related his story.

'I was taking my usual walk in the woods by the castle and I saw a woman's figure ahead of me. There are multiple woodland paths criss-crossing one another on the Back Walk, some much steeper than others. They all eventually lead you to the Old Town Cemetery at the top.

'The woman was climbing, but slowly, and kept stopping to draw breath. I was much the same. She reached the top before me and I assume went into the cemetery. I took a rest on one of the benches. From there I caught several glimpses of her, threading her way through the gravestones. She was obviously heading for a particular grave.

'That's when I realized who it might be. I'd decided to go and check if I was right, when she suddenly came rushing down the slope towards me. I was fearful she might fall, so I stepped out in front of her. That's when I saw it was Karen Johnston.'

He glanced at McNab as though for permission to go on. McNab remained silent, so he did.

'She seemed confused and was rambling, but she appeared to recognize me from our encounter earlier on King's Knot with Lucy's dog. I suggested I walk her home, since she didn't look well.

'It takes a much shorter time to walk down that brae than up, although I feared she wouldn't make it much further than the foot of the hill.'

McNab interrupted him at that point, his tone verging on the sarcastic. 'So you steered her towards your house instead of her own?'

McCreadie ignored the insinuation and nodded. 'Luckily Lucy was here and took charge of Karen. She advised I call my doctor because she thought that a nasty cut on Karen's arm had turned septic. Dr Wills came and dressed the wound, gave her an antibiotic injection and some pain-killers, after which she thankfully slept.'

'When did all this happen?' McNab asked.

'Yesterday evening.'

'And you only let us know now?'

McCreadie had obviously been waiting for the accusation and was ready for it.

'Karen begged me not to tell anyone she was here. She appeared very frightened and made me promise. This morning she was more lucid and I got her to agree to meet with Marge and Professor Pirie. She is not aware that I invited you here, Detective Sergeant.'

Being an ex-cop, McCreadie was all too aware that keeping Karen Johnston's whereabouts from the police could be a punishable offence, but he hadn't hesitated to do it anyway. The look he fastened on McNab read as: *You would have done the same, would you not?*

'I'm assuming Karen Johnston isn't a suspect in this enquiry, but a witness?' McCreadie said to emphasize his point.

That was a step too far for McNab. 'You can't assume that about anyone in this case.'

A shocked Marge looked as though she might intervene at this point, but wisely didn't. As for Magnus, he knew what McNab had just stated was in fact the truth. Children did kill other children. Sometimes on purpose, sometimes by accident.

With that possibility on the table, McNab said, 'I need to hear everything Karen has to say. And I need to be the one to ask the questions.'

There was silence as McCreadie considered this.

'What if Professor Pirie and Marge go in first?' he eventually offered. 'See how things are with Karen. Then we bring you in, Detective Sergeant?'

'Before this happens,' McNab said, 'I'd like to see the diary.'

'You can ask Karen for it,' McCreadie said. 'She's got it next to the bed.'

McNab suspected McCreadie had already seen the famous diary, and probably photographed its contents too. After all, he'd had all night to do so.

McCreadie now led them all upstairs. The upper landing proved to be a rectangular balcony with a number of doors leading off. McCreadie chose one and, knocking quietly, said, 'Karen, Professor Pirie and Marge are here to see you. Is it okay to come in?'

She must have answered in the affirmative, because McCreadie ushered them inside, then indicated that McNab should wait by the open door. 'You'll hear everything that's said from here, Sergeant.'

McNab caught Marge's voice first. She was greeting her friend warmly, and although he couldn't see their interchange, he guessed they were hugging. Magnus came next and their exchange was equally positive.

Then he heard Magnus speak.

'We have my colleague DS McNab with us, who's keen to talk to you, if you feel up to it. He's been very concerned for your welfare and has spent many hours, probably without sleep, looking for you. May we let him come in?'

It was a good try on the Prof's part. McNab had to give him that.

There was a long and silent pause, in which McNab found himself holding his breath. He had every right to walk in, regardless of Karen's response, but he didn't want their meeting to begin like that.

She must have nodded, because he heard no words spoken before McCreadie came to usher him inside.

The room was spacious with a big bay window overlooking the green layers of King's Knot. In the bed a diminutive woman lay propped against the pillows. McNab thought Karen Marshall looked as though a puff of air might blow her away.

Up to now, he'd only viewed the photograph from the recovery cafe where Karen had made a point of disappearing into the background.

He felt an overwhelming sense of relief that Karen Marshall was still alive.

Stepping forward, he offered what he hoped was an encouraging smile. 'We've been very worried about you, Karen. I'm glad to see you're safe.'

A pair of bright, perhaps still feverish eyes stared out at him from a white face.

'May I talk with you alone?' McNab tried.

She observed him intently for a moment before saying, 'I'd like that.'

McNab didn't look round to see McCreadie's reaction to this, just focused on Karen as he heard the others file out of the room. As soon as he judged they were alone, McNab drew up a chair and sat beside Karen.

'What do you want to know, Detective Sergeant?' she said in a weary, haunted voice.

'Everything,' McNab said. 'Tell me everything.'

55

McCreadie was right. Karen Johnston – who he would always think of as Karen Marshall – appeared barely well enough to be interviewed.

Noting her wan face, and the heavily bandaged left wrist, McNab wondered whether this should indeed be postponed. Knowing he hadn't even considered her mental state, McNab suggested they could delay their talk until she felt better.

'I've waited long enough. I told myself I couldn't remember, but maybe the truth was I wouldn't remember. Or it was easier to forget.' She lifted her downcast eyes and observed McNab. 'The women at the cafe know all about covering up the bad things that have happened to you. They know it just eats away at you. Hollows you out.'

She halted there and gave him an apologetic smile. 'When you found Mary's body, I knew it was time for this to happen. You see, up to that point I'd always hoped that Mary had run away, and that she would come back one day.'

McNab brought out his phone. 'Can I record our conversation, rather than write it down? That way I can listen again later?' he requested.

'Go ahead,' she said.

McNab set it up, pressed record, then nodded at Karen to continue.

'Mary was my pal.' She smiled, as though remembering the happy times. 'We were the same age, but she was much braver than me. That belt her dad had? She wasn't scared of him or his belt.'

Karen gave a little laugh, then her face darkened. 'But she was afraid of God. Religion did that to you in those days. Priests and ministers told children they were full of sin. I didn't even know what that meant. Turns out it was mostly about sex, something I also didn't know much about.' She looked at McNab. 'Mary knew more about it all than me.' She shook her head. 'But I found out soon enough.'

McNab waited for Karen to continue.

'We were at the den when Mary told me that she couldn't be confirmed because God wouldn't forgive her. I didn't ask what he wouldn't forgive her for. I didn't say don't be silly, Mary. All I could think about was the dress. Did that mean she wasn't going to wear the dress?' Karen gave a hollow laugh. 'I wanted a dress like that. I was a Protestant, so I would never have one. All the white net, and a veil, just like a bride. So when Mary asked me, I said yes.' She looked to McNab, willing him to understand what she meant.

And he did.

'She asked you to go instead of her? You were the one confirmed that day?'

'Yes.'

It all came out in a rush now.

'We arranged to meet at the den, where Mary changed back into the school clothes she'd brought from home. I put on the dress and veil and went to the chapel. When I got back, Mary wasn't there waiting like we arranged. I thought she was probably hiding in case someone spotted her and realized she hadn't gone to the ceremony. I changed back into my own clothes and left the dress, the veil and shoes in the plastic bag as she'd asked.'

She halted there, her face stricken with remorse.

'It was my fault she died. If I'd said no that day, she wouldn't have been there. He wouldn't have got her. She would have been safe.'

McNab waited, although his brain was working overtime on what she'd just told him. For the confirmation clothes to be buried with Mary, her killer must have been to the den, before or after he'd taken Mary.

'We found a blue jumper in a box in your loft,' McNab said quietly. 'Was that Mary's?'

Karen seemed startled by the question, then said guiltily, 'After everyone said she was missing, I ran back to the den to look for her. The dress and the bag were gone. I wondered if she was hiding somewhere in the woods. I went looking, shouting her name. That's when I found the jumper.'

She hesitated. 'I should have given it to the police, I know, but I hoped she'd come back. I was a wee girl who'd lost her best friend and it was the only thing I had of hers.'

'Did you ever wash the jumper?' McNab said.

'Oh no. My mother never knew I had it. I kept it hidden. Like the diary.'

If Mary was wearing the jumper when she'd met her assailant, then evidence of that contact could still be on it. In 1975, forensic science, in its infancy, would likely have gained little from it. And considering other evidence had disappeared during the years in between, maybe the jumper would have done the same.

If the confirmation outfit had remained in the bag, then chances were it had never been handled by the killer, which was why they'd only found Mary and Karen's DNA on it. As for the jumper . . . McNab allowed himself a small glimmer of hope.

And now to the tricky question.

'Who do you think sexually assaulted Mary?' McNab tried, knowing this might prove the key to everything.

Karen didn't or couldn't meet McNab's eye. 'I didn't ask. I didn't want to know. All I wanted was to wear that dress.'

'But you think you might know now?' McNab tried.

'I don't *know*,' she repeated.

'But you suspect?' McNab tried again.

Her response, when it came, didn't answer his question.

'My dad told me I had to forget everything that happened that day. Everyone in the street suspected everyone else. My dad said we had to protect the innocent and not listen to gossip or repeat it. My mum was terrified that whoever had taken Mary would come back for me.'

'What about Eleanor?' McNab said.

Karen gave a small laugh. 'My sister hated it most of all. She blamed Mary for everything.' She reached for the school jotter and handed it to McNab. 'I was just a wee girl,' she said. 'I didn't understand what was going on. Except that if Mary was dead, it was my fault.'

'Well,' McCreadie said as McNab re-entered the conservatory. 'How did it go?'

McNab ignored the question and addressed Marge. 'I think Karen needs a friend. Maybe you could go and sit with her for a bit?'

'I'll go right up.'

Marge having departed and shut the door behind her, both Magnus and McCreadie were waiting for whatever McNab had to say. By the former detective's expression,

McNab suspected what he'd just been told by Karen wasn't likely to have reached McCreadie's ears between Karen's arrival here and this morning. Not unless she'd been talking in her fever-filled state.

The diary, however, was a different matter. Once Karen had fallen asleep, there had been ample time for McCreadie to take a look at what was in the jotter that McNab now had in his hand.

McCreadie must have ordered more coffee, because just at that moment Lucy arrived with a tray. McNab was delighted. A caffeine fix was just what he needed at this point in time.

He told Lucy so, and was rewarded with a glimmer of a smile.

After Lucy left, McCreadie took his chance, his voice fierce and impassioned.

'I know I'm not officially on the case, but I was the investigating officer forty-five years ago. I screwed up big time back then, so I'll do everything in my power to get it right this time.'

McNab listened to McCreadie's little speech in silence, then said, 'So you'll be happy to answer a few questions regarding Karen Marshall's recent disappearance?'

McCreadie looked slightly taken aback by this, but nodded anyway. 'Of course.'

'Had you already seen Karen in Stirling since her disappearance, and before you met her in the castle woods?'

When McCreadie didn't immediately answer, McNab repeated the question.

'No. I had not,' he said cautiously.

'What if I told you that you were captured on CCTV in Karen's presence at least twice in the time since her disappearance?'

'Then I'd say you were mistaken.'

'You haven't asked where this might have occurred,' McNab said.

'Because I haven't left the house for weeks, apart for my short walks on King's Knot and Castle Hill,' McCreadie said, seemingly on solid ground now. 'I have a deadline to meet on the next book, so a quick walk is all I can spare at the moment. Ask Lucy, she'll tell you.'

McNab could see that Magnus had no idea where all this was going, but he finally came in on the action.

'You suspect from this footage you're referring to that someone, a man, was stalking Karen?' he said.

'Our super recognizer thought so.' McNab laid it on thick, just to be sure. 'If he had an image of you for comparison,' he said, looking pointedly at McCreadie, 'then Ollie would be able to eliminate you.'

McCreadie never flinched. 'Well, of course I'd be happy to supply an image. As I said, I've barely been out of the house. Assuming it's true that someone is stalking Karen, then that's a worrying development. There's no chance it was McLaughlin before his demise?'

'What do you know about McLaughlin's demise?' McNab said.

'Just what's been released to the press.'

McNab didn't believe that, but let it go anyway and asked his final question.

'Have you read or photographed the contents of Karen's diary?'

'I have not,' was McCreadie's immediate response.

'So it won't turn up on one of your true crime podcasts?'

McCreadie gave a wry smile. 'Not until after it's been

presented in court *and* if I have Karen's permission, Detective Sergeant.'

So that was it. McNab rose to go. 'I'll be in touch,' he said.

McCreadie came back in then. 'I was planning to ask Karen to stay here until she's feeling better?'

'I think that would be wise,' Magnus intervened.

McNab okayed this and made to leave. 'There's a strategy meeting tomorrow, first thing,' he told Magnus. 'We'll talk there, Professor Pirie.'

Pulling on his waterproofs at the bike, McNab had another quick look at the note Karen had given him along with the diary. A note she'd said had been posted through her letter box.

It said, *I know who you are.*

When McNab had asked Karen what she thought it meant, she'd said, 'Someone around here knew that I was Karen Marshall, Mary's friend.'

Even Marge and the women at the cafe weren't aware of that until Karen had told them. But . . . perhaps one of her not-so-far-away neighbours had already worked it out. The guy who'd known Karen's husband, and who'd met Karen on King's Knot, then miraculously encountered her again as she visited her husband's grave in the Old Town Cemetery.

Former DI Jimmy McCreadie, now crime writer J. D. Smart.

The rain came on as he left Stirling, reminding McNab just how wet you could get when riding a Harley. And going fast only made it worse.

56

'Well,' Chrissy said as she elbowed her way through the crowd, 'it looks like a good turnout for the lovebirds.'

Rhona, following in Chrissy wake, had to agree. Police officers, she thought, were easy to spot, even out of uniform. Why, she wasn't sure, but it was true. Paula's friends and probably co-workers definitely did not look the same. Or maybe it was because the groups were at this moment clearly delineated. Hopefully once the drink flowed, there might be more of a mingling.

'What does Paula do?' Rhona said, aware that even if she didn't know, Chrissy likely would.

'She's a GP, I believe,' Chrissy said, confident as ever with her answer.

Having now got them to the bar, Chrissy asked Rhona what she wanted to drink. 'Not the white wine,' she advised.

'Why not?'

'Because, take it from me, the white in here is shite. What about a cocktail instead?'

At this point Rhona noted that the board behind the bar was offering two cocktails for the price of one, which may well have prompted Chrissy's suggestion.

'Okay. Get me what you're having.'

Rhona wasn't planning to stay much past one drink to

toast the happy couple, so taking a chance with Chrissy's choice seemed okay.

While Chrissy got the drinks, Rhona sought out the couple, spotting them standing together in a corner. She headed their way.

Janice, seeing her approach, looked pleased, and immediately did the introductions. Paula, Rhona discovered, was from Inverness originally, but knew Skye well. In fact she'd been a locum in Broadford for six months.

'You're from the Misty Isle, I hear?' she said.

'My adoptive parents were,' Rhona explained. 'That's where I got the MacLeod name.' They chatted for a while, exchanging names of people they might both know, including Jamie, the undertaker, and the famous Blaze, the Border collie that had aided Rhona on her last case on the island.

By that time, Chrissy was back with two French 75s, which she assured Rhona was only gin and prosecco, 'although it should really be champagne'.

They toasted the happy couple.

'How did McNab take your announcement?' Rhona said.

'With complete mystification,' Janice said. 'Said he didn't even know I had a boyfriend.' She mimicked McNab's surprise.

They all laughed.

'And him a detective,' Chrissy said, shaking her head.

'I think he's a bit perplexed that he never worked out the gay part. Seeing as he's always right about everything,' Janice said. 'He was quite sweet, to be honest.'

'I'm dying to meet this man who's my partner's other partner,' Paula declared.

'Not as much as he'll want to meet you,' Chrissy said. 'In fact,' she looked around for the umpteenth time, 'where the hell is he? Surely he must be back from Stirling by now?'

There was a sudden silence as the three who knew why McNab had been in Stirling registered that they couldn't speak about it. Not in mixed company. Perhaps, sensing this, Paula informed them she was off to the Ladies. 'I'll be there a while,' she added.

'You've got her well trained,' Chrissy said, impressed.

'I do the same thing when we attend doctors' functions. Folk like talking about their work, but if it's not your work, it's a lot less interesting,' Janice said.

'So how'd it go in Stirling?' Chrissy said. 'Have you heard?'

'Nothing since we spoke before he left,' Janice told her. 'However, I do know McNab didn't like being summoned by former DI McCreadie, even if it was because he'd located Karen Marshall.'

'It did sound a little convenient that he should be the one to find her,' Rhona said.

'D'you get the feeling the former detective likes to be just one step ahead of us?' Janice ventured. 'Even to the extent of managing the story?'

There was a murmur of thoughtful agreement on that.

At that moment, Chrissy spotted the subject of their conversation. 'Here comes McNab in his biker gear. And he's wet.'

McNab had no difficulty threading through the throng as they all stepped back to avoid him.

'Ladies,' he said cheerfully. 'Sorry I'm late. And that I'm very wet.' He halted there, adopting a worried expression. 'I am still allowed to refer to you as ladies?'

'Fuck off, McNab,' Janice told him with a grin. 'How'd it go with J. D.?'

'I spoke to Karen alone. She gave me the diary. She's

338

staying with Smart until she feels better,' McNab summed it up in three sentences, before turning to Rhona. 'We need to have words about the jumper, Dr MacLeod. And soon.'

At this point, Paula returned. Rhona watched as Paula and McNab realized who they each were, while Janice winked at Rhona.

'So,' said Chrissy, 'Paula . . . McNab. McNab . . . Paula.'

'Don't I get a first name?' McNab said.

'You have one?' Janice retorted, her expression astonished.

'Yes,' Chrissy said, 'it's Michael. My wee boy's named after him.'

Paula looked taken aback at this, glancing between them, the question *Is he McNab's?* etched on her face.

'He's not the father,' Chrissy put her right. 'I'm one female he hasn't bedded.'

'Hey,' Janice intervened. 'Not the only one.'

Rhona kept her mouth shut, as did McNab. And they did so without looking at one another.

Chrissy explained further. 'McNab saved wee Michael's life before he was born.'

'I'll tell you the story later,' Janice promised Paula.

'I'm delighted to meet you, Paula,' McNab said. 'And when I get a drink, I'd be happy to toast the pair of you.'

'So where's Ellie?' Rhona enquired when McNab arrived back with more drinks for everyone.

He shrugged his shoulders. 'No answer to my texts since I stood her up to go to McLaughlin's murder scene.'

'You did let her know why?'

'I did. But a little late,' McNab admitted.

'So you went home alone with a carry-out meal and brooded in the shower?'

McNab's face broke into a grin. 'You know me too well. What about you?'

'I stood up two men. One of whom was my son who I haven't seen in six months or more.'

'Okay. You win.' McNab raised his glass to her.

The group had split up as Janice and Paula moved round the room, greeting everyone. McNab glanced over at their progress.

'You really had no idea?' Rhona said.

'Nope. Never thought about it for a moment,' McNab admitted. 'I had a notion on Janice when she arrived. That shows you I had no idea.'

'I remember,' Rhona said. 'But then again you've been known to fancy all new arrivals.'

She thought McNab might dispute that, but he didn't.

'How are things with Ellie?' she said.

'How are things with Sean?' he countered.

The silence from both of us pretty well sums up our relationships, Rhona thought. She moved on to more favourable ground.

'You wanted to talk about the jumper?'

Rhona listened intently to a fuller description of McNab's conversation earlier with Karen, including his thoughts that the killer may not have had contact with the confirmation dress at all.

'Karen blamed herself for her friend's death,' Rhona said. 'No wonder she stopped talking.'

McNab nodded. 'Thing is, I had a quick look at the diary. There's not a lot in there, and most of it contradicts what Karen just told me.'

Rhona considered this. 'Maybe she was writing what she wanted to be the truth back then, rather than what was the truth?'

'So which story do I believe? The one I heard today or what's in the diary?'

'Can I read it?' Rhona said.

'I photographed the pages and sent copies to you and Pirie along with the recording I made of our conversation,' McNab said. 'McCreadie says he's not read the diary, but I don't buy that. He had twelve hours minimum when Karen Marshall was in his house, likely not compos mentis. He would have been desperate to know what was in that jotter. I would have, if I was in his shoes,' he admitted.

'I'll take a look when I get home,' Rhona promised. 'Oh,' she said, remembering. 'We collected a saliva sample from the back of McLaughlin's neck.'

Midway through taking a slug of his pint, McNab grued. 'Not a good image to hold in my head.'

'But it means we have a DNA sample for whoever was breathing down his neck,' Rhona said, thinking if anyone uninitiated was listening into their conversation, it wasn't a pretty picture they were painting. She recalled once before, sitting enthusiastically discussing blood splattering in a pub with Chrissy, only to realize those sitting around them were making moves to get away.

'There was one thing in the diary, though.' McNab returned to their previous subject. 'It sounded like Karen was also being creeped out by some bloke.'

'Did she give a name?'

McNab shook his head. 'She mentioned a bloke hanging about the local shops, exposing himself. But there was also a reference to someone closer to home, I think.'

The conversation ended there with a surprise arrival. Rhona saw Ellie first. She was headed towards them, with a look on her face that suggested trouble.

Rhona called a welcome, to warn McNab of his girl-friend's imminent arrival and hopefully soften whatever she had in mind.

'Ellie?' McNab turned in surprise. 'Hey, you *did* get my message?'

'Which one?' Ellie smiled sweetly, although there was a cold steel in her eyes.

Rhona made her excuses and, silently wishing McNab luck, absented herself from what looked like the impending fray.

57

The heavy rain of the previous night had thankfully cleared and spring returned, making Rhona's walk to work through the park something to be enjoyed, and not endured.

On her way home after the pub the previous evening, she'd picked up a microwave meal and, reheating it, had then settled down to read the diary. It hadn't taken long to see what McNab had meant regarding fact and fiction.

The diary had read like her own made-up stories as a child, where she had starred in numerous imagined mysteries along the lines of *The Famous Five*. Despite this, Rhona had still had a strong sense of reality in some of the diary's detail, like the skipping song and the fear and loss when Mary did not return.

The story Karen had told McNab of what had really happened that day – the switching of outfits, Karen taking Mary's place at the altar to be confirmed – did ring true, because it answered many of the questions they'd had. Rhona had gone over the sequence of events using Karen's story and for the first time it seemed to her that they fitted. It's what had happened afterwards that still had to be made clear.

The killer had taken possession of the bag, so he'd visited the den after Karen's departure. Had he known Karen would return to change and had he been watching for her? Maybe he'd intended to also take Karen?

Rhona wondered if Karen had considered this afterwards, and fear at this happening had kept her silent?

The shaded drawing and what it had revealed showed that Karen had been afraid of Alec McLaughlin, who'd taken to sitting on the hill watching them play tennis, while shouting obscenities. Her father had warned her about bad men. Karen had puzzled over whether she knew of any bad men, then thought she knew one.

Was she thinking about Alec at that point or someone else?

As for the jumper story, that too had rung true. She could only hope that they would recover something from it that might give them a lead to Mary's killer.

For once Chrissy wasn't at the lab before her. Rhona had a silent wish that it was because Chrissy had stopped to pick up their filled rolls on the way. As she thought this, she noted the row of porridge pots staring down defiantly at her from the shelf near the coffee maker. Rhona assured them their days were numbered as she set about making the coffee.

Chrissy entered shortly after, accompanied by a delicious smell, signifying that Rhona's wish had just come true. Trying not to gloat at the porridge pots, Rhona acted as though this was simply normal.

'Coffee's ready,' she announced as Chrissy plonked the two brown paper bags on the table.

'Full works,' Chrissy promised.

Once settled and eating, Chrissy said, 'Where did you disappear to last night? When I came back from my rounds, you were gone,' she added accusingly.

'Ellie arrived when McNab and I were talking. I was avoiding what looked like a possible fight.'

'Wise move,' Chrissy agreed. 'And here I thought you'd

ducked out before Dr Walker arrived. Remember how you invited him?'

'Oh God, did he come?' Rhona said in horror.

'Of course, and he spent a lot of time looking for you. I was no help, since I didn't know you'd left,' Chrissy said. 'Looks like you're on a run of standing men up.'

Rhona had completely forgotten about inviting Richie, but she could hardly tell him that.

As though reading her thoughts, Chrissy said, 'I'd like to be a fly on the wall the next time you two meet up.'

'I went home early to read Karen's diary,' Rhona said. It was an excuse, but a real one. 'McNab had photographed it and sent it through, along with a recording of his talk with her.'

'So you can text Dr Walker and tell him that so as to prolong his agony. Or you can tell him you're not interested in going out with him.'

Neither sounded appealing to Rhona at that moment.

'So,' Chrissy said. 'What about the diary? Did it give us a clue to the killer?'

'I think you should read it yourself, before we start work,' Rhona said. 'Maybe you'll spot something I didn't.'

Leaving Chrissy to do that, Rhona checked to see what they'd had back from their various tests. Although they'd not found semen on the body to check for DNA, Chrissy had extracted skin and microscopic blood spots from under Mary's fingernails. From these they had a DNA profile, but still no match.

McNab was excited about what they might retrieve from the jumper, but assuming they did and it provided the same profile DNA, it still wouldn't give them the suspect's name if he wasn't on the database.

There were other things they could do, though. With two sources of the same DNA, they definitely had a reason to extend their search. Perhaps through a familial search, hoping that a close family member had broken the law. The blond hairs they'd recovered from the body, without roots, weren't ideal for DNA capture, but they could extract mitochondrial DNA from them and confirm if it was a match for the other two sources.

At this point her mobile buzzed, and it had McNab's name on the screen. She answered.

'Dr MacLeod here,' she said.

'I love when you talk dirty, Dr MacLeod.'

'You sound cheerful, Detective Sergeant McNab. I take it things went all right last night with Ellie?'

'Well, she didn't dump me. Just told me she was thinking of having sex with someone else.'

'What?' Rhona said, mystified.

'We agreed at the beginning of this relationship that we would tell one another if that was the case. At least, Ellie proposed the arrangement and I agreed. Never believing it would ever happen.'

Rhona now realized the forced cheerfulness was just a cover for what he was really feeling.

'Apparently when I'm on a murder case like this one, I become obsessed,' McNab added, 'and not with her.'

Rhona finally found something she could agree with. 'That's true of you, me, maybe all of us in this line of work . . . except Chrissy.'

Thank God she had made him laugh.

'Have you read the diary?' McNab changed the subject.

'I have.'

'And what do you think?'

Rhona told him.

'Can you meet with Magnus and me, before the strategy meeting?' McNab said. 'Magnus knows the state of Karen's mind, I hope. You know how what she said fits with the forensics. We need to put everything together before we talk to the team,' he finished.

McNab sounded keyed up. Rhona knew what he was like when something had landed. Something important. But he obviously wasn't yet ready to tell her what that something was.

58

McNab wondered if Rhona had sensed his excitement. This is what he lived for in the job. The moment the scattered pieces started to shuffle into place.

'I'm ready,' he told Ollie.

The initial picture on the screen was Jackson's passport photograph from the last time. McNab thought again that the face looked like a Ukrainian terrorist or a Mafia hitman.

However, the full face wasn't what Ollie was interested in. He'd wanted images of the man's stance, the shape of the shoulders, the way he held his head. Trawling social media and God knows where else, he'd found a selection of such images, and now McNab was watching them spool across the screen.

The software running alongside was doing its job, checking each image by comparing it to the physical attributes of the man in the CCTV images. However, the software, no matter how powerful, wasn't as good as Ollie, and he was just using it to prove to McNab that he was right.

Eventually the program made its decision.

The man in the various images was the missing husband of Eleanor Jackson, who was supposedly somewhere in a truck in Europe. But he wasn't, because he'd been caught on CCTV in Stirling, within touching distance of Karen Marshall.

'I'm checking European police records, in case he comes up in any of them,' Ollie said. 'So far he's clean.'

'Or he's not been caught yet,' McNab added.

'So what now?' Ollie said.

'It's time Mrs Jackson and I had another chat.' McNab helped himself to a ring doughnut from the box he'd brought for Ollie. 'How are things with Maria?'

'She's putting me on a diet,' Ollie said.

'No more doughnuts?'

'She says you're to bring me fruit instead,' Ollie said in a crestfallen manner.

'Irn-Bru still all right?'

'Apparently the new one has less sugar, so she's okayed that, in moderation.'

McNab patted Ollie on the shoulder. 'She sounds like a keeper. I'd do what she says. You'll live longer.' McNab popped the last bit of doughnut in his own mouth.

There was nothing like a sugar rush at times like this.

McNab stopped by the coffee machine to add caffeine to the mix, then went to find his partner. He recalled last night's meeting with the soon-to-be Mrs Clark, or Mrs – what was the lovely Paula's surname? Maybe they didn't do the Mrs thing anyway and just stayed with their own names.

He had discovered since the news of their engagement had been broken to him that he was becoming more obser-vant of his colleagues, not wishing to be caught out again. Criminals he could read like a book. Ordinary law-abiding citizens and their sexuality obviously not so well.

He knew he was avoiding thinking about Ellie and her determined but also questioning suggestion she'd made last night. Shock had been his first and main reaction. So much so that he hadn't slept much afterwards, his brain having decided to replay their conversation like a broken record all night long.

McNab forced himself to focus instead on Ollie's news, and to wonder if he should visit Mrs Jackson alone or take his engaged partner along. Even as he considered this, McNab realized the likelihood was that DS Clark would be the one to decide.

He found Janice at her desk reading Karen's diary, a knot of concentration creasing her brow. She was good at the focused thing, he realized. Good at picking up the nuances in what people said, and how they reacted. In contrast, he was at times the veritable bull in the china shop.

Janice looked up then, sensing his watchful eyes upon her.

'What?' she said.

'A good time last night, was it not?' McNab ventured.

'You mean, what did Paula think of you?'

That was Janice, straight to the point. 'Well, I liked *her*,' McNab tried.

Janice gave him a half-smile, but failed to respond with a reciprocal comment from Paula about him. Having waited slightly for this, McNab delivered his news. 'Ollie has identified the man in the CCTV footage in Stirling as Eric Jackson.'

Janice assimilated this, taking her time. McNab could almost hear her brain working on it.

'So, you're going to see Mrs Jackson and you want to know if I'm coming with you?'

God, she was good. McNab smiled back, acknowledging how right she was.

'I'll stay here,' she told him. 'I want to listen to the

recording again. There's something Karen isn't telling us, in the diary and in the interview.'

'Any idea what that could be?' McNab said.

'Ask me when you get back,' Janice said, returning to her screen.

McNab headed for the Gents, only to have his mobile drill loudly on the way. He answered without consulting the screen to find out who it was.

'DS McNab here.'

'She's gone. Karen's gone.' McCreadie rushed on. 'She was sleeping – or we thought she was. I was writing in the conservatory and Lucy was in the kitchen. Karen must have walked out.'

'How long ago?' McNab demanded.

'We have no idea, it could be up to two hours. I drove to Rowan Cottage and her car's missing from the garage.'

'Have you tried Marge? Maybe she went to the recovery cafe?' McNab said.

It was obvious by the silence that he hadn't.

'I'm sorry. My head's been in the book.'

It sounded like fictional crime had won over fact.

'I'll deal with it,' McNab said and rang off.

Marge answered on the first ring. 'She's gone, hasn't she?' she said before McNab could tell her what had happened.

'I was hoping she'd come to you. Have you any idea where she might have gone?'

There was a moment's silence before Marge said, 'There was something she wasn't telling us. I've seen that too often not to recognize it. She's either decided to do what she tried back in the cottage or she's gone to confront her fears.'

'Gone where?' McNab said.

'That I don't know.'

'You'll call me if she gets in touch?'

Marge assured him she would, although she didn't sound optimistic.

McNab set the wheels in motion for a second search for Karen, the most important thing being to find the car. He'd already discarded his plan to go to see Eleanor Jackson. It was more important to meet with Magnus and Rhona prior to the strategy meeting as previously planned. Eleanor Jackson would have to come into the police station instead.

The biggest question around this was the place of Eric Jackson in the story. Mrs Jackson had maintained from the beginning that she was not in touch with her sister. But what if she'd been lying? What if she'd always known where Karen was?

And why lie about her husband's whereabouts?

Of course, it could be that Eric was the one telling the lies. Perhaps he just liked taking some time out before he came home after a job. Or maybe he rarely came home at all? Maybe the forty-four-year-old marriage Eleanor had so proudly announced didn't exist in reality.

The biggest question of all was why Eric Jackson had been in Stirling, and so close to his sister-in-law.

59

The rain had come on as she'd left Stirling, a steady grey drizzle that matched her mood. Karen hadn't driven this road since her mother's death. How many years ago had that been? She realized she didn't know, or didn't want to remember.

Professor Pirie had been right about the detective. He had been kind. She'd felt bad when the professor had explained how hard DS McNab had been working to find her. That was the problem, she acknowledged. It had been since Jack's illness and death. All that time she'd never considered herself, because she'd had Jack to look after. Now she thought only of herself. What she wanted. What she needed. What might bring her peace.

But mostly of how much she wanted it all to end.

Marge had told her that her recovery would play out like this . . . until, that is, she faced up to the truth, no matter how difficult that was. Until now, she hadn't known what that truth was, or pretended she hadn't.

Remember the innocents in all of this, her father had told her. *Whispers and innuendo are evil things. If you don't have something good to say about someone*, her mother had told her, *then say nothing at all.*

Mary didn't believe that. Mary said what she thought. Mary was braver than she, Karen, could ever be.

And Mary had died because of that, a small voice reminded her.

Her arm burned under its dressing but Karen welcomed the pain, because it kept her focused, both on the road and on what she had to do. Turning on the radio, she almost expected to hear her name again, to discover the police were already looking for her, but there was no mention of it on the hourly news, although she was pretty sure they would be searching for her car.

It took a lot less time and effort than she'd imagined to travel beyond the boundaries that she had set herself. To go back in time.

As she approached the steep hill of her youth, Karen had a sudden memory of travelling down that brae at breakneck speed on her bike, trying to catch Mary up. Then she was back at the entrance to the Catholic school and the play-ground where she'd first learned to ride the same bike, a second-hand one that she and her dad had painted blue.

The biggest surprise of all on returning to the past was how small the street looked, how small the houses and the gardens out front were. As a child her dad's garden had always seemed so big.

She parked outside her old house and sat for a moment to compose herself, then she locked the car and set off up the path that led to the rough ground. Looking back on the row of houses that had been her world before Mary had disappeared, Karen suddenly remembered who else had stood on the hill looking down as she did now.

Closing her eyes, she could hear Mary's voice shouting at her to 'get the ball' after she'd missed a shot. You had to be fast, because no matter how quickly you ran down that brae, the tennis ball moved faster.

She'd eventually caught up with it and, turning, had seen Alec come down from his perch on the hill and stand close to Mary, no doubt whispering his obscenities.

Turning abruptly to dispel the image, Karen made for the distant trees. Nothing much had changed up here, she noted, apart from the rubbish scattered through the undergrowth.

As she approached the wood, she realized it too had shrunk in size, or maybe part of it had been cut down. The remaining trees seemed scrawny; the old stone wall where the crow had stared down on her was broken, the stones scattered.

She carried on towards where she thought the den had been, only to find nothing of the structure remained. None of the branches they'd pulled together to form a wall and a roof. Nothing to show it had ever existed.

She walked on through the remaining trees towards the distant sound of traffic. Emerging from behind a scrubby hedge, she found a tarred road, where before it had been a farm track. In the near distance, new housing fanned out across the hillside near the small reservoir where the boys had gone fishing for minnows.

He'd used to park the van here, pretending he had come to fish, then wait in the woods to watch them. Sometimes, when they'd been there for ages and didn't want to go home, they'd had to pee among the trees, giggling at how horrified their mums would be if they were to find out.

No doubt he'd watched that too.

A wave of nausea washed over Karen and she had to lean head-down against a stubby tree.

How long had he planned it? When did he decide which one of them it would be? Had he meant to kill or was it a mistake made in that moment?

If he'd come upon me there instead of Mary, he might have left me alive, knowing I would never be brave enough to tell anyone.

Mary would have told if she'd stayed alive, because Mary was old enough to understand what was going on.

It was Mary who told my dad about the flasher at the shops. It was Mary who told Robbie about Alec shouting at us. It was Mary who'd tried to tell her parents about Father Feeney.

Karen turned and walked back to the car. There was somewhere else she had to go on this street. Someone she had to see, before she finished her journey.

She halted at the gate, pleased to see the spring flowers in the neat front garden. Maybe this wouldn't be too bad, after all. Although, too frightened that she might change her mind and chicken out, she hadn't called ahead. Gathering her courage, she pushed open the gate, walked up the path to the front door and rang the bell.

It took a moment or two before she heard footsteps, during which she veered between turning and running away and thinking her heart had stopped.

Then the door opened and the face looking out at her now still held traces of its teenage self. Karen also realized that this was what Mary might have looked like if only she had lived. The face grew puzzled, then the light of recognition flashed in her eyes.

'Karen Marshall, it's you, isn't it?'

Karen nodded and was immediately swept inside.

60

The meeting room was gradually filling up. By the reaction of the crowd it looked like they anticipated something big was about to happen. Rhona wondered if it had anything to do with McNab's mood when she'd spoken to him earlier.

It began to look even more that way when Bill, after a brief introduction, called on DS McNab to come to the front. As McNab passed Rhona, he acknowledged her with a brief nod, but for once she couldn't read his demeanour. Was he about to tell them something good or something really bad?

McNab began by explaining how Karen had been located in Stirling, without placing too much emphasis on the role McCreadie had played in it. Despite this, you could tell by the audience's reaction that they were keen to give the former DI credit for what he'd done.

McNab now played the interview he'd conducted with Karen at McCreadie's home. Rhona thought listening to Karen's wavering and troubled voice, her starts and stops, her pain, both physical and mental, was even more poignant among others than it had been alone.

The story of the dress, and the reason why Mary felt she couldn't be confirmed, had the impact Rhona suspected it would. Most people in the room had no real idea of what life had been like in 1975 for children within the Church, and in wider society, although McCreadie, give him his due, had tried to enlighten the team to those facts in his address at the previous meeting.

Rhona's eyes were drawn back to the screen as McNab brought up the pages of the diary. Many of the team would have already read these, but by the reaction in the room some obviously hadn't.

McNab continued, 'I probably don't need to tell you this, but there are discrepancies in both Karen's answers to my questions and what's written in the diary. And for me, at least, there's a strong sense that Karen may yet know more than she has revealed or remembered.'

Rhona, having been summoned to the fore to do her bit, now brought up Dr Jen Mackie's analysis of the soil on the shoes, confirming that the last place they'd been worn was in the wooded area of the girls' den.

'Karen said she came back from the chapel to the den to meet with Mary, but Mary wasn't there. So she changed back into her own clothes and left the dress, veil and shoes in the plastic bag. However, when she went back later the bag had gone.

'Karen also confirmed that the jumper we found in her loft was Mary's and that she'd found it lying in the woods behind the den when she returned later. There is a possibility that traces of the killer may be on that jumper.'

McNab thanked Rhona, then stood for a moment in silence. By his expression, Rhona knew what was coming next wasn't going to be the good news she'd hoped for.

'Within the last hour, Mr McCreadie has been in touch to say that Karen left his house undetected and is now missing again.'

A babble of shocked chatter burst around Rhona.

McNab carried on. 'No one saw her leave. However, we

believe she made her way back to her home, where she then took her car,' he said. 'So it's likely she intends travelling further than her immediate vicinity.

'Judging by Karen's frame of mind, her friend at the recovery cafe, Marge Balfour, believes Karen may have decided to face her demons. What those demons are we don't yet fully know.'

The murmurings grew again.

'However, according to Professor Pirie, who has also spoken to Karen, she is still in a fragile mental state and may in fact be a suicide risk. So let's find her as quickly as possible.'

As the crowd departed, Rhona caught up with Janice.

'Did you know about Karen disappearing?'

'It was as much of a surprise to me as it was to you,' Janice told her, obviously annoyed that McNab hadn't told her.

At that moment, McNab appeared as though from no-where, causing Rhona to wonder if he'd been listening in.

'I was just talking about you,' Janice said, unruffled by his sudden arrival. 'What's up?' she said, noting his expression.

'Jean Barclay just called me. She's had a visitor. Karen Marshall arrived at her door an hour ago. Confessed to Jean that she was responsible for Mary's death. That she'd replaced Mary at her confirmation, leaving Mary at the den. If she hadn't done that, Mary would be alive today.'

'Did she tell her why Mary didn't go herself?' Rhona said.

'Apparently, Karen babbled a story about wanting a place in heaven, like Mary. Then she upped and left.'

'Why didn't she just tell Jean the truth?' Janice said.

Rhona thought of the recording and what Karen had said

when McNab asked if she knew who'd been interfering with her friend.

'She's protecting the innocent, just like her father told her to.'

61

Had she lived, would Mary have looked like her big sister, Jean? They'd always shared the same dark hair, and Jean's voice had reminded her so much of Mary, Karen had almost wept.

Jean had been pleased to see her. It had showed clearly on her face.

I should have gone back sooner.

But how could she have done that, when she couldn't remember what had really happened that day?

'You didn't tell her the truth,' Jack told her from the passenger seat.

'Protect the innocent. That's what Dad told me to do,' she replied.

'Plus you took the blame. Babbling on about getting your place in heaven.'

Jack's voice annoyed her now. She wanted him to be quiet.

'You're dead,' she replied. 'I don't have to listen to you any more.'

'You're sick,' he shouted back at her. 'You know that, don't you? There's a poison in you.'

Karen turned the radio on to drown out Jack and wiped the sweat from her brow. The radiating heat from her body seemed to rise in waves, which even the car's air-conditioning couldn't help.

Never mind, she didn't have far to go. One last stop and it would all be over.

The radio was playing old hits and Karen recognized a few from her early years with Jack. The music seemed to have calmed him too, because he'd stopped being cross with her and was humming alongside her, just the way he'd done during his illness.

Funny how music memories were still in there, when dementia seemed to destroy everything else.

Karen tried to remember what music Eleanor used to like as a teenager. There had been one she'd played over and over, Karen recalled. What was it?

'"I'm Not in Love" by 10cc,' the music host told her. 'I'm playing it now.'

'I'm Not in Love', that was it. How did he know that was Eleanor's song?

Karen tuned in, humming along with it, and Jack did the same. For a moment she was happy, then another memory intervened. One Karen didn't want to recall. Suddenly she was back at her sister's wedding watching the bride and groom dance around the floor together, Eleanor's dress so white it dazzled her eyes.

The image abruptly changed to Mary trying on her confirmation dress, birling round in it for Karen to admire, even as a green spark of jealousy bit at her heart.

Karen reached out and switched off the radio.

'Why'd you do that?' Jack complained.

'Go to sleep,' she told him.

It would be dark when she got there; the sun was already

turning the sky red. Karen fiddled with the air-con as the sweat broke out again on her brow.

'It doesn't matter,' she whispered to herself. 'I'll soon be there.'

62

There was something wrong in all of this. Something he wasn't getting. He'd kept telling himself that it was Karen who was either hiding something or not remembering clearly. But maybe it was him?

He was supposed to be a detective.

Somewhere in all this material – the statements, the forensic evidence, the interviews, the diary, his talk with Karen – was the truth. Concocted stories were never airtight and this was a concocted story. A web of remembrance, the criss-crossing of multicoloured threads, some strong, others weak.

The past is what we decide it to be.

No one in this was telling the truth. All of them were telling their own truths. The ways in which they wanted to remember it. The ways in which they could cope with that memory.

Karen had buried her story in order to survive it.

McNab chose the one thing he believed didn't happen, then questioned himself whether it had. What had so traumatized Karen that day that she had ceased to speak at all? What had she buried so deep in her subconscious that it had remained hidden there for forty-five years?

Karen had told him she'd always hoped that Mary had run away, and would eventually come back. Maybe that was the lie she told herself in order to survive, because she knew it wasn't true.

Karen, McNab realized with certainty, had always known her friend was dead.

She had known because Karen had seen Mary killed. Or she knew because Karen had killed her. The shocking and possible truth of each of these scenarios began to play out in McNab's head.

Firstly, the one he definitely didn't want to be true. The girls fighting over who would wear the dress. In the struggle, Mary falls badly, hits her head. Karen can't rouse her. Would she do as she said and go to the chapel in Mary's place? Or just run?

The scenario, although possible, required an adult to remove the body and bury it. Would Karen tell anyone about the accident, and if so, who?

It came to him then that if she told anyone, it would be her policeman father. And what would he do? Report his daughter? See her locked up for all her young life? Or remove the evidence? All the evidence that the girls had ever been at the den that day.

The impossible had just become the probable.

But what about the marks on the body that suggested a sexual motive for Mary's death?

DC Kenny Marshall would have known what to do, in case the body was ever discovered. McNab suddenly recalled the gentle way in which the body had been laid to rest, the pillowed head resting on the confirmation dress. Would a sex-crazed killer have done that?

McNab realized he was the one writing the story now. Fashioning it in his own way to fit the known facts.

And yet . . . what was it Karen had said at the completion of their talk?

My dad told me I had to forget everything that happened that day. I was just a wee girl. I didn't understand what was going on. Except, she'd added, *if Mary was dead, it was my fault.*

McNab had chosen to use the car to visit Eleanor Jackson, rather than the bike. The Harley would have got him there faster, but he couldn't think so well when riding it, his exhilaration taking up all of his thoughts.

He'd decided not to give any forewarning of his visit. If Eleanor Jackson wasn't in, he would simply wait for her.

Karen's sister had left East Kilbride sometime after she'd married Eric, moving down the A726 to Strathaven. McNab found the stone villa where they'd apparently brought up two kids who no longer lived at home, according to Mrs Jackson.

The substantial property now looked way too big for a woman on her own, whose husband seemed to spend most of his time working abroad. McNab parked on the road outside, then gave Janice a call.

'I'm here,' he said. 'Any word on Karen?'

'We picked up her car on the cameras heading south through Glasgow – timing suggests that's when she was making for her old address and her visit to Jean. We have nothing yet on where she went after that, either north or south.'

'Make sure someone's watching for her at Rowan Cottage. Let's hope she heads home. Oh, and Janice, have someone at her husband's grave. I have a feeling she may eventually go there.'

Noting a light had come on upstairs, McNab got out of

the car, locked it and headed up the short drive. The villa with its garden looked a bit further up the scale than the police house Eleanor had been brought up in. Which suggested her husband's truck tours on the continent were well paid. Of course, Eleanor might also work. McNab tried to recall if she'd mentioned that in their conversation and realized if she had, he hadn't made a note of it, only being interested in what had happened forty-five years ago.

The doorbell produced chimes that weren't answered, even though McNab was pretty sure they were loud enough to penetrate the entire house. The attached garage was closed and there wasn't a car in the drive. But there *was* the light on upstairs.

McNab rang again and waited, impatient now. Finally, he opened the letter box and shouted through.

'Police. Open the door!'

Eventually, he heard movement, a door opening, footsteps. Then a voice said, 'Who is it?'

McNab repeated, 'It's the police. Detective Sergeant McNab.'

A moment's silence, then the door was unlocked and opened a fraction. Mrs Jackson stared through the crack at him and his ID as though she'd never met him before.

'May I come in, Mrs Jackson?' McNab said.

'Is it really necessary?' Mrs Jackson used the irritated voice McNab had come to know.

'Yes,' McNab told her.

The door was grudgingly opened further and McNab allowed to enter. Mrs Jackson was dressed in slacks and a sweater. Out of the formal clothes she'd worn to the station, she looked younger, although no less cross.

'You should have called before coming here,' she told McNab as he followed her into a sitting room where she switched on a light.

'I was nearby, in fact just up the road at your old home, speaking to Jean Barclay.'

She accepted his lie without surprise, which seemed odd. McNab had assumed she would ask why he should be doing such a thing, in the evening, like this.

'What is it you want?' Mrs Jackson said.

'Shall we sit down first?' McNab said.

She grudgingly took a seat. McNab, as he did the same, was struck by the thought that the room was rarely used, just like the sitting room in Karen's cottage.

'Is your husband back yet?' McNab said.

'I told you already that he wouldn't be back for at least two weeks.'

'That's odd, because his company believe he's already back in the UK,' McNab said, keeping a keen eye on her face as he said it.

'That's nonsense. He called me and told me the date himself.' She looked as though she believed this, or perhaps just wanted to believe it.

'Mrs Jackson, we have CCTV footage showing your husband, Eric Jackson, in central Stirling two days ago.'

Now that statement did throw her.

'That's impossible,' she managed. 'Why would Eric be in Stirling?'

'I was hoping you would be able to tell me that,' McNab said.

'There's been a mistake, of course,' she responded angrily. 'The footage from those cameras renders people unrecognizable.'

McNab was inclined to agree, but obviously didn't.

'It was Eric, that's been confirmed.' He stuck with the plan. 'Your husband was in two images with your sister, Karen, during the time she was missing.'

'That's nonsense. Anyway, my sister isn't missing any more,' she said.

'What makes you say that?' McNab said swiftly.

'It was on the news,' Mrs Jackson said. 'Some former detective found her wandering in the woods at the castle.'

'And that didn't worry you?'

She pursed her lips. 'My sister was always a drama queen. Mary McIntyre encouraged her in that.'

Despite her harsh words, something else had crept into Mrs Jackson's speech. McNab, with years on the job, now smelled fear seeping through. She might be speaking harshly, but something he'd said had frightened Mrs Jackson. Something about her husband or her sister.

'I'd like you to call your husband right now,' McNab said.

'I gave you his number. You can phone him yourself.'

Nice try, he thought. 'Call him on your phone, then give the phone to me,' McNab ordered.

'This is ridiculous,' she said, any fear now masked again by anger.

'Now,' McNab said.

'Then I'll have to fetch my phone,' she said, and already he could read on her face what she thought was her way out.

'I'll come with you.'

That was it. Her face crumpled and McNab found himself staring at a completely different version of Eleanor Jackson. McNab let her cry for a bit, simply waiting for her to stop.

'Your husband doesn't come home, does he?'

She shook her head. 'Not for the last six months.'

'Where does he go, do you know?'

'No idea. He won't tell me.'

'When did this happen?'

'After the last tour. He came back for his clothes. Said he'd met someone else.'

'And the number you gave us?' McNab said.

'He's changed it. I can't get him either.'

McNab knew he hadn't had the whole truth, but he'd had some of it. Maybe now was the time to tell Eleanor Jackson her younger sister's version of what had happened that day all those years ago.

Eleanor listened in silence. She seemed so unmoved by the tale, McNab began to wonder if she already knew it. If so, keeping it from the police would be a criminal offence. He told her so.

'I didn't know, but it sounds just like the sort of thing Karen would do. If she'd told Dad at the time . . .' She tailed off.

McNab caught a whiff of fear again. What was she afraid of? That her husband wouldn't come back or that he might?

He rose to go. 'We never did get that DNA sample from Mr Jackson.'

'I'm sorry. If he calls, I'll tell him you need that and he'll come down to the station.'

'If you had something of his – a toothbrush maybe?' McNab said.

'I told you he took all his things when he left.'

'Then we'll have to put a call out for him to the TV and tabloids. That might be embarrassing for both of you. Especially if it's in reference to a murder case.'

Her face had turned ashen. 'Please don't do that,' she said. 'I'll find a way to speak to him.'

'Good, then I'd better get back. You'll call me if anything should change?' McNab said, making for the front door. 'In particular, if Karen should come here.'

Keen to usher him out, Eleanor now stopped in her tracks. 'Why would she do that?' she said.

'We think Karen is laying her demons to rest. She visited Jean. Maybe you're next.'

63

Jack was sleeping. She could hear the soft snores coming from the passenger seat. The peaceful sound of his breathing brought her a little peace too.

'My sonorous breathing', he'd called it when alive. When he grew ever more ill, Karen had longed for him to go to sleep, for when he did, she had her own peace back again, however short-lived.

Maybe that was why she was conjuring up the sound now.

The flashes of heat had thankfully abated, only to be replaced by shivering. As long as she could manage to keep her hands on the wheel, long enough to get to her destination, she would be okay.

Getting where she wanted to go, however, was proving difficult. She had never been to this town, never mind this house. She had her map, but now that it had grown dark, she had to keep stopping to use the torch to read it. She should, of course, have bought one of those new-fangled mobiles that could direct you to where you wanted to go.

Marge had offered to help her choose one.

In the end she hadn't, because when would she be going anywhere that she needed such a phone? She knew Stirling well enough and she hadn't thought she would ever step out of her house for a very long time, never mind leave the city.

She had the feeling she was lost again. In the dark it was difficult to find the street names.

Karen pulled into the kerb below a street lamp.

Jack had woken up. 'You're wasting your time,' he told her. 'Your sister won't let you in the door.'

'She might,' Karen said.

Jack was right, but she had to try.

Fifteen minutes later, she found the street. The next problem was finding the right house. The house numbers seemed to be all over the place. Some houses had it above the door, some at the end of the drive, but eventually she did locate number seventeen.

Karen stepped out into the coolness of the night, shutting the car door on Jack's last demand that she give up on all this nonsense. Breathing in the fresh air, she found that the shivers had abated and the flush of heat returned. Never mind, she told herself. This wouldn't take long. Then she could rest.

The light was on in what might be the living room. It was a lovely house, she thought, looking up at it. Big. Eleanor had always wanted a big house. *Especially because she had to share a bedroom with me.*

Karen rang the bell and, listening to its musical chimes, waited for her sister to come.

64

He wished he'd taken Janice with him. She might have read the woman better. There was no clarity in McNab's thoughts over what had just happened. The mix of bravado and fear he'd picked up from Eleanor Jackson – had that just been because her husband of forty-four years had left her for another woman?

Or was she hiding something else?

McNab had dealt with many unpleasant domestic scenarios in his time as a police officer. He remembered the smell of fear when you walked into such a home. The results of physical violence were usually obvious on the woman. The 'walked into a door' explanation. But sometimes the perpetrator focused on the hidden parts of the body, the bits covered by clothes. The arms, the torso, the vaginal area.

Last, but definitely not least, the onslaught of psychological violence. Insidious control.

McNab went through all of these possibilities, trying to match one of them to Eleanor Jackson's behaviour tonight. Where had her fear come from?

He still wasn't clear if she was in touch with her husband, and now wished he'd checked the house. Maybe Eric Jackson had been there, or even close by. Her surprise at the Stirling connection had seemed genuine, but . . .

One thing was certain, she did not want her sister to

appear at the door. If Karen did, the likelihood was Mrs Jackson wouldn't even let her cross the threshold.

But what if she looked ill? Jean had said that Karen had looked very poorly when she'd arrived at her place. Would that make a difference? And would Eleanor call him if her sister did appear, as she'd promised?

McNab had an overwhelming desire to turn round and head back, and basically hang around the house just in case. But he'd promised Ellie that tonight he would turn up for her end of shift at the Rock Cafe. If not, he thought, his days as her boyfriend were probably numbered. Or he would enter the world of non-monogamous dating.

When he thought about it that way, it didn't sound so bad. If Ellie could sleep with other men, then he could sleep with other women. That had been the arrangement.

The trouble was, finding those other women.

McNab permitted his thoughts to turn to Rhona. He wasn't convinced that her relationship with Sean was monogamous. It hadn't been at times in the past. In particular, when McNab had risen from the dead after the Russian case.

He allowed himself a brief moment to dwell on that encounter, before returning to the truth, which was, if he had to fight for Ellie, he would gladly do so.

Fifteen minutes later a call came in from Janice.

'They've spotted Karen's car on the Stirling road. It looks as though she's heading for home. What d'you want to do?'

McNab knew the one thing he didn't want to do, which was to head for Stirling himself.

'Make sure there's someone at the cottage to see her arrive. We'll speak with Karen in the morning.'

'Okay. If you're sure. How did it go with Mrs Jackson?'

'Her husband left her, or so she says. Although I'd say she was covering for him. Any more sightings of the guy?'

'Not that I know of. See you tomorrow. Over and out.'

McNab congratulated himself on his decision not to hang about the Jackson house awaiting the possible arrival of Karen. It looked like she'd done what she planned to do and was on her way home.

He had another thought. What if Karen didn't head for Rowan Cottage, but instead went back to McCreadie's place? If Karen was still ill, it might be better if she did go there.

Personally, and from the point of view of the investigation, McNab wasn't keen on extending McCreadie's influence any further than had happened already. Also, he didn't want Karen divulging material to McCreadie until he, McNab, had spoken to her himself.

What if he was right in his earlier thoughts about Karen – or had he been way off target with that? Maybe she wasn't hiding anything and her story had been exactly how it had happened that day.

He switched his focus on to what he'd intended doing tonight, and, ignoring any road signs that might encourage him to take the Stirling route, he got off the motorway and headed into town.

Shedding his detective persona was the problem, McNab decided, as he joined the mostly leather-clad clientele entering the Rock Cafe. Blending in would have been easier had he come on the Harley, but that hadn't been possible. He still felt like the polis as he made his way through the crowd and headed for the downstairs bar. Maybe it was the looks he got or maybe because so many regulars in here would know exactly what he was. Either because they'd met him in that life or they knew Ellie was dating a detective.

McNab realized just how awkward at times this might all be for Ellie. She'd always laughed the idea off, insisting that she could date whomsoever she pleased, but still . . . As for him, the only grief he'd got for dating a biker chick was caused by envy from his fellow officers. Which only grew when or if they met Ellie in person.

At that moment he caught sight of her behind the bar, holding forth with some guy whose dreams of what might be tonight were about to be smashed. McNab called Ellie's name as he made his way over, keen to let the one currently chatting her up know he had competition.

The smile Ellie bestowed on McNab made his heart soar. There might yet prove to be a competition where he was sharing first place with some other bloke, but he intended to win Ellie back, and by a long Scots mile.

'You're here and on time?' Ellie said.

McNab's smile indicated that had never been in doubt. He ordered a non-alcoholic beer, adding that her carriage awaited her outside, when she was ready to go.

'I have an hour until the end of my shift,' she told him. 'You want some food?'

Until that moment, McNab hadn't realized just how hungry he was.

Seeing his expression, Ellie said, 'I'll order your usual. We'll have to be quick. Kitchen shuts shortly.'

McNab carried his pint to the nearest free table and placed his seat so that he could gaze on Ellie at the bar. Her erstwhile suitor had given up and was now, McNab spotted, working his charm on some other lucky girl.

That image made him think about the other bloke, the

one who'd made an impression on Ellie. So much so that she was contemplating having sex with him. Could that bloke be in here now?

He began a sweep of the room, just like the detective he was. No one was in here he recognized. Not like the last time, during the Skye case. He began to relax. He would eat, wait for Ellie, take her home . . . to his place or hers. He would make an impression. A good one, so that her thoughts of striking out elsewhere would diminish. He would do what she wanted . . . become obsessed by her, and not the job.

He might have missed the call, had he not gone to the Gents, where the noise of the music was less loud. He hesitated when he saw the number, knowing it was from work in some capacity, but then again it might be the news that Karen had reached home safely.

McNab answered to find Ollie on the other end.

'What the fuck, Ollie?'

'Sorry, but I thought you'd want to know.'

'Know what?'

'Eric Jackson. I found him online. He's a user of child porn. It's under another name, but it's definitely him. I've been talking to some of my counterparts in Europe. He's on their list. Probably indulges most when he's over there on his truck runs. They were very interested to find out we know him.'

'Jesus . . .' Another piece of the puzzle edged its way into place. How far back did Jackson's predilection go? As far as Mary McIntyre?

Robbie, Mary's brother, hadn't recognized Eric from the photograph McNab had shown him. So he hadn't been on Robbie's radar like the priest and Alec McLaughlin had been.

But in McCreadie's notebooks, Eleanor had told him that Mary chatted to Eric when he came to see her.

Could Eric be the one that Mary had spoken about to Karen?

If so, had Karen told anyone? Is that what she and Eleanor fell out about all those years ago?

McNab didn't see that happening. Karen, like most kids back then, was unlikely to have told anyone about the abuse. The majority kept it to themselves, letting it eat away at them into adulthood.

Staying where he was despite the heavy looks he was getting, McNab checked if Ollie had let Janice know.

'I've only just worked it out myself. You're the first to know.'

'Okay, get the word out. The boss and DS Clark first. We need to find this guy before he realizes we're on to him.'

McNab stood for a moment, contemplating his next move.

'What are you fucking standing there for?' a big guy finally challenged him. 'How many dicks are you planning on looking at?'

'Yours was an easy miss, mate,' McNab told him before exiting.

Back at his table, he wondered who else needed to know the news. Eleanor Jackson maybe? McNab pulled up Mrs Jackson's number and rang it. Then had another thought. Maybe she knew already? Perhaps she'd known from way back.

As McNab went to kill the call, she answered.

'DS McNab.' Her voice sounded relieved. 'I was about to phone you.'

'What is it?' McNab said, wary now.

'I wanted to let you know that Karen did come here and

we talked for a bit. About Jack and his dementia, and her dreams about Mary. Then Eric appeared.' She rushed on. 'I wasn't expecting him. Karen said she felt ill and needed to go home. I wanted her to stay, so we could talk some more, but she insisted she had to get home. That's when Eric offered to drive her.'

Her final words were like knockout punches to McNab's head.

'You let Karen go with your husband?'

Eleanor sounded puzzled by his reaction. 'Karen seemed pleased about it. She asked to use the toilet first. When she came back down, she looked a little better. She said she'd be in touch again soon, then left with Eric.'

'In his car?' McNab checked.

'No, in Karen's.'

McNab rang off then, before he found himself telling Eleanor Jackson more than he wanted to. The last thing they needed was for her to warn her husband.

As for Karen, why would she let Jackson take her, if she'd thought for a moment that he had anything to do with Mary's disappearance and death? Whatever the answer to that, at least they now knew exactly where Jackson was.

McNab looked round for Ellie but she'd disappeared for the moment. He would have to leave. He could try and find her first, or go and explain later.

As usual in this job, he really didn't have a choice.

Back at his vehicle, he alerted everyone necessary to what was going on. According to traffic, Karen's car was now approaching Stirling. There was no reason to suppose it had stopped anywhere in between.

The next call McNab made surprised even him.

'Sergeant McNab, have you found her?' McCreadie's voice sounded worried.

'We believe Karen's on her way back to Stirling,' McNab told him.

'Thank God she's okay.'

'Eric Jackson's with her in the car,' McNab said, wanting to gauge McCreadie's reaction to that piece of news.

There was a heavy silence, then McCreadie came back on. 'You want to know how I feel about that?'

'I do.'

'There was nothing back then to suggest Eric Jackson had anything to do with Mary McIntyre's disappearance.'

'How closely did you look at him?'

'He was away when it happened. He was older than Eleanor. Had his driving licence and worked as a driver for a delivery firm. We checked and he was definitely on the road. Somewhere in the Borders, I believe.'

'So he wasn't a suspect?'

'There was no evidence to suggest he should be,' McCreadie said sharply. 'If we'd had DNA testing back then, we'd have swabbed every male in the vicinity. Him included. But we didn't.'

'There'll be someone at the cottage awaiting Karen's arrival. However, there's always the chance that she might come back to you instead,' McNab said. 'We intend arresting Eric Jackson. I'd be obliged if you could delay him, if they do come there.'

McNab put up the blue light, knowing however fast he drove, he wouldn't be there before Karen.

65

I told Jack to shift to the back seat, but he wasn't happy about it. I explained that Eric was going to drive and I needed to be beside him to show him the way, and that seemed to placate Jack for the moment.

Eric said nothing when I appeared to speak to a dead man. In fact he seemed quite amused by it. I suspect he thought that the police would never take the word of a woman who was so obviously doolally. Especially anything she said about what had happened forty-five years ago.

After getting Jack to stop complaining, I relaxed. It was obvious that Eric wasn't afraid of me. I wasn't afraid of him either. Not any more.

I sneaked a sideways look at him, noting the big hairy hands on the wheel. The side of his jaw, the still-thick blond hair, cut in a stylish way. He looked younger than Eleanor now, although it was the other way round really.

I still had a clear picture of him back then. He'd just had a haircut and there'd been bits of hair on his collar. And that smile, like he knew he could and would have anything he wanted.

I realized he was contemplating asking me something. Just to check if I was really losing my marbles, I suppose.

How would I answer if he did?

I could hear him thinking. His thoughts were mainly

about how he would dispose of me. Or if he really had to. If I was muddled and mad, nothing I said about Mary's death could be used in a court of law. And they didn't have anything else linking him to her murder. He'd been careful about that. Or thought he had.

I didn't hear that exactly, the way I can hear Jack, but I'm pretty sure that's what was going through his mind.

He'd kept his promise. Just as I'd kept mine. But now that he'd left Eleanor, was she still safe?

We were nearing Stirling. I could see the castle lit up on its crag. I thought again how much I liked the golden glow of the Great Hall.

'We're nearly home,' I told a snoring Jack.

I wondered if Eleanor had already called the detective. I hoped she had.

We're sailing past the entrance to Rowan Cottage. If Eleanor did call the detective, then there's likely to be a police car there by now, but I'm not ready for the police yet.

He turns left where I tell him, and I point to the house, clothed in darkness.

'Very nice,' he says admiringly. 'Is anyone home?'

'No. Jack's dead,' I remind him. 'Aren't you, Jack?' I call into the back seat.

He gives a little laugh at my madness, confident now in his power over me. I smile as he releases his seat belt. He doesn't see the knife I take from my pocket. He is too busy thinking of the dark empty house we're about to enter, and what will happen there.

I reach over and, for a brief moment, he believes I am about to fondle him.

'You haven't forgotten,' he says with a smile.

'No,' I say.

My touch in his groin becomes steel. Stabbing and grinding. Now the true madness takes me. The madness of remembering what he did to me. What he did to Mary. He is caught completely off guard. Just as I was as a little girl when he forced his thick fingers inside me.

Now Jack joins me in my madness. Screaming words of encouragement from the back. I have never heard him so elated.

'Again, girl, again,' he screams.

I obey him. Blood spouts to meet my face. Hot and tasting of copper.

He has his big hands round my neck now, hoping to choke the life out of me. But I am a mad woman and I cannot be stopped.

66

McNab saw the flashing blue lights as he approached the Raploch roundabout and knew instinctively that the story had met its conclusion at McCreadie's.

Had Karen directed him there? Or had Jackson thought the nearby woods might be Karen's final resting place?

Turning left into the road behind the King's Garden, McNab drew in behind the line of police cars. The stately row of villas alongside was a blaze of lights, the neighbours keen to discover what had taken place outside or maybe inside the home of the famous crime novelist, J. D. Smart.

What a story this was going to make.

There was no cynicism in McNab's thoughts, just relief. According to McCreadie's brief call, Karen was alive and Jackson dead. That's all he needed to know for the moment.

Emerging from his vehicle, he was met by a familiar figure.

'You got here fast,' DS Jones said.

'Not quite fast enough,' McNab said. 'Do we know what happened?'

'He tried to strangle her. She knifed him in the groin. Mr McCreadie came out and saw it happening. He got Karen out the car and called the ambulance. By the time they got here, Jackson was dead.'

'Did they take Karen to hospital?'

'She wouldn't go. She's in with Mr McCreadie and his housekeeper. SOCOs are working Jackson's body and the car. You can take a look if you kit up or I can show you some photos.'

McNab chose the photos.

Ten minutes later he was approaching McCreadie's front door, which was opened to him before he could knock.

'DS McNab,' Lucy greeted him, her voice a mix of strain and relief. 'Karen's with Mr McCreadie in the conservatory.'

Karen was lying on the sofa, a blanket over her. McCreadie had been sitting alongside but rose to greet McNab on entry.

God, McCreadie looks old, McNab thought, *old and tired, but relieved too.*

'You thought she might come here,' McCreadie said. 'Thank God, you were right.' He stood, making room for McNab to take a seat beside Karen.

She gave him a weak smile. 'Detective McNab,' she said. 'How did you know I'd come back here?'

'Call it a hunch,' McNab said.

Her slender throat clearly showed the grip of Jackson's hands. McNab wondered how she could have survived his obvious attempts to throttle her. Unless . . . she had weakened him already, by making the first move?

From the crime scene photos taken on arrival by DS Jones, the knife Karen had used lay on the floor of the passenger seat. It looked like a bigger version of the one she'd wielded on her own wrist in the scullery at Rowan Cottage. Longer and obviously sharp enough to do real damage. Why have a knife like that with you, if you didn't intend harming yourself or others?

By the quantity of blood inside the vehicle, she'd caught

the femoral artery, weakening Jackson enough to save her own life. But who had struck the first blow?

'Is my Jack still in the car?' Karen suddenly asked him. 'He won't like that, Detective. Not with all that blood. Jack never liked the sight of blood.' She gave him a little smile and McNab could have sworn her eyes twinkled at him before she closed them.

Lucy arrived with a tray, breaking the moment.

'Can I talk to you?' McNab said to McCreadie. 'In private?'

'Let's go into the sitting room.' He led McNab through the hall and into a room that looked out onto the crime scene.

'Of course, you want to know what happened?'

'The truth of what happened.' McNab emphasized the word 'truth'.

'I was in the conservatory, which as you know is at the back of the house, so the front was in darkness. After your call, I came to sit in here in the dark and watch, just in case. I'm ashamed to say I dozed off, albeit I think briefly. When I woke I saw there was a car that hadn't been there before. It matched the description you gave me of Karen's car.

'I went straight out there. As I approached the car I realized there was a struggle going on inside. His hands were round her throat. The doors were locked. I couldn't open them. Then came the blood. It splattered the window and he went limp. Karen unlocked her door and I got her out and brought her inside,' he said. 'Where I called 999.'

'So she was defending herself when she stuck the knife in him?'

'Without a doubt. Had she not done so, I couldn't have got into the car in time and Karen Marshall would be dead.'

He didn't add, 'just like Mary McIntyre', but it hung there between them nevertheless.

It was a good story, and Jimmy McCreadie would stick to it. Who wouldn't take the word of a former detective inspector and famous crime writer? Especially the detective who had served on the original case.

'I assume,' McCreadie said, 'when you told me you planned to arrest him that you have proof he was implicated in Mary's death?'

McNab didn't answer. He felt that to be the case, but now that they had Jackson and his DNA, the forensic evidence would tell them the truth.

'There's stuff Karen's still not telling us,' McNab said.

'She will, though,' McCreadie said. 'I'm sure of that. When she's fully recovered, that is. The doctor's been,' he added. 'Karen's still running a high temperature. That might account for the delirium, he says.'

'So she's not doolally after all?' McNab said.

'Only time and her recovery will tell.' McCreadie gave him a half-smile.

67

*Written evidence relating to the abduction
and murder of Mary McIntyre*

The handwritten note found by Karen Johnston in the hall at Rowan Cottage read, *I know who you are*. This note is believed to have been written by the accused, Eric Jackson.

The following is the letter found by Eleanor Jackson, sister of Karen Johnston (née Marshall), in her bathroom after Karen left the house to be driven back to Stirling by Eric Jackson on the night in question.

> *Eric told me it was our secret. That he would never tell anyone and neither should I. He said it was normal. He did it to my big sister and she liked it.*
>
> *After Mary disappeared, he said that if I told anyone, he would kill my sister. They were going to be married, so it would be easy.*
>
> *My father told me we had to protect the innocent, so I did.*

Statement by Karen Johnston (formerly Karen Marshall):

What I told Detective Sergeant McNab about that day was almost the whole truth. Mary wasn't there when I returned to the den, so I changed back into my own clothes, folded the dress and veil and carefully put them in the bag with the shoes. Later when I returned I found Mary's jumper in the nearby woods.

I had told Mary what Eric had been doing to me. I knew I had committed a sin. She tried to console me. She told me if I went to the chapel wearing her dress, I would be absolved of my sins. She was very angry about Eric.

He hadn't got to Mary. No one had. I made that part up.

She would have told him that day when he came to the den to leave me alone. That she would tell everyone what he was like. What he had done to me.

I believe that's why he killed Mary. To stop her doing that.

He had a van for work, although he never brought it to our house when he came for Eleanor. But Mary and I saw it sometimes up the back track near the reservoir. That's when he used to spy on us.

After Mary disappeared, I tried to tell Eleanor what Eric was really like, but she wouldn't listen to me. She said I was too young to understand about men.

My sister was an innocent in all of this, and he said he would kill her if I told the truth about him. I believed he would because of Mary.

My father told me to forget that day and everything that had happened. Eleanor married Eric and they moved away. I never had to see him again.

I made myself believe Mary wasn't dead. That she'd run away. That it was my fault Eric abused me. That I was the one to blame for everything.

Until I saw the crow and the dead cat walking past the cottage. Then I knew Mary was dead, and she wanted her body to be found.

When that did happen, that's when I started to unravel. Marge and the other women at the recovery cafe tried to help me remember. When they began to succeed, I became very frightened. When I tried to cut my wrists, I failed, because of the crow. It flew at my head and I dropped the knife. I believed the crow was sent by Mary. That she wanted me to stay alive to tell the truth.

Then I saw Eric. He was in Stirling, watching me. Reminding me of my promise. I think the note was from him too. By then I was ill. Everything became muddled. I had stopped talking to Jack for a while, but now I did it all the time, because it helped.

I thought I was dying, so I went to say goodbye to Jack at the cemetery. That's when I met Detective McCreadie again. I didn't recognize him the first time, when he was in King's Knot with the dog, but I did now. I was running down the path in the woods. I thought Eric was chasing me. That's when Detective McCreadie stepped out to catch me. I like to think Mary made that possible.

He took me home and Lucy looked after me. The doctor came and after he treated me I started to feel better. But I couldn't stay there, because of Eric.

If he thought I'd told anyone about him and Mary, he would keep his promise and kill my sister.

So I went to see Eleanor. I tried to tell her, but how do you tell your sister that her husband abused her wee sister? That he'd threatened to kill Eleanor if I breathed a word of it to anyone? That I thought he'd killed Mary and buried her out on the moor?

Eleanor had told me that Eric had left her for another woman. She told me DS McNab had been to see her. He'd told her to call him if I came to visit. I urged her to do that.

Then he turned up. Walked into the house and pretended to be surprised that I was there. I knew then I was right and he had been trailing me. The only other explanation would be that Eleanor called him and told him I was there. I didn't want to believe that of my sister.

He was just like before. Friendly, pretending to be concerned because I looked so ill. He was so glad, he said, that Eleanor and I were friends again. He gave me a look at that point. A look I understood perfectly. When I said I felt ill, he offered to take me home. I accepted to get him away from my sister.

She'd been surprised when Eric had appeared, and not altogether happy. There's something wrong between them.

Getting into the car, I made Jack move into the back seat. Plus I went on talking to him as usual. Eric found that amusing. I could read his mind. He was beginning to think I'd gone a bit mad. So maybe no one would believe anything I said. But could he take that chance?

Or would he decide he couldn't?

I directed him back to the villa. It felt safer than Rowan Cottage because it was close to Detective McCreadie. I don't think Eric believed that I lived there, but he didn't say anything. I hoped Eleanor would call Detective McNab, although I wasn't certain she would.

Detective McCreadie saved me. I'd picked up the knife when I went back to Rowan Cottage for the car. I thought I'd maybe do a better job on myself next time.

When Eric tried to strangle me, I stuck the knife in his leg, although I was aiming for his crotch. I couldn't breathe with Eric's big hands round my neck, and I think I started to pass out, but Detective McCreadie was there at the car window and he saved me.

The next thing I remember is being back in his house with Lucy. He told me Eric was dead. I was glad.

Signed: *Karen Marshall*

A brief summation of the forensic evidence submitted by Dr Rhona MacLeod establishing Eric Jackson as the killer of Mary McIntyre:

Eric Jackson left his mark forensically in a number of ways. He'd handled Mary's school jumper, which was found in the woods after her disappearance. Evidence of his recently cut hair was retrieved from the body of Mary McIntyre. Skin and blood under Mary's fingernails had also come from the accused. The DNA from the cigarette was also a match. The fingerprint extracted from the black bag was Eric Jackson's.

A brief report as to the circumstances of Eric Jackson's death:

There might be a dispute as to when Karen drew her knife. Whether she had struck first, before Jackson began to strangle her. However, there was an eye witness, former Detective Inspector McCreadie, who has declared under oath that Karen Marshall was in danger of her life before she struck her assailant in the leg with a kitchen knife.

That she caught the femoral artery, which had produced the swift bleed-out and death of her assailant, had been something Karen couldn't have foreseen, particularly when she'd been experiencing a high fever at the time.

The report from Jackson's autopsy, plus the forensic examination of the vehicle in which Jackson died, both reinforced former DI McCreadie's version of events.

Dossier on Eric Jackson, 1975 until the present day:

Through his DNA profile and the subsequent digital forensic investigation, Eric Jackson has been identified as a person of interest in a number of child abductions and murders throughout Europe. He is also implicated in the production of child pornography, mainly in Europe, but also in the UK. This investigation is ongoing.

The murder of Alec McLaughlin, a suspect in the Mary McIntyre abduction and murder:

David Ian Willis has been charged with the murder of Alec McLaughlin by cutting his throat on [date given] at [address given]. Willis is the brother of McLaughlin's former partner Anne Marie Willis. In his defence, he said that McLaughlin had raped his sister's three young children over many years and had been locked up for it, but not for long enough.

'I was just waiting for the bastard's release.'

68

Summer had arrived. The view from Rhona's lab window provided proof of that. The trees circling University Hill had burst into life, obstructing Rhona's view of the park below and the red sandstone majesty of Kelvingrove Art Gallery and Museum.

She missed the sight of its Gothic splendour, but, Rhona reminded herself, she would see it soon enough when she left the lab and headed home through the park.

Chrissy had gone already, keen to see her son and use the arrival of the long light evenings of a Scottish summer to play with young Michael in the garden.

Rhona now contemplated how she might spend her own evening. She could enjoy the park for an hour, then maybe pick up some food on her way home. She briefly thought of Sean, and not for the first time since the night of the missed dinner. After that disaster, she'd sent both men a text, apologizing for forgetting to tell them that she'd been called out to a murder scene.

Liam had responded positively, promising to get back in touch the next time he was in Glasgow. As for Sean, her apology and offer to make it up to him by taking him out to dinner had fallen on deaf ears. It appeared Sean had a heavy schedule in the coming weeks, including a trip to Paris to play, so he couldn't fit in a dinner with Rhona at the moment.

She wasn't sure if it was a brush-off or simply the truth. She found herself wondering how many times Sean had felt the same about her own similar responses.

The intercom buzzed as she was making ready to leave.

For a brief moment Rhona hoped it might be Liam, back in Glasgow again, or even Sean deciding he had time for her after all, then the voice told her who it actually was.

On entry, McNab greeted her with a characteristic grin, while Rhona waited for him to explain why he was there.

'Where's Chrissy?' he said, looking around.

'She went home early to play with wee Michael. Why are you here?' Rhona asked outright.

'I was in the area,' McNab began, then stopped when he caught her disbelieving expression.

The grin began to fade and Rhona now caught a glimpse of McNab's true mood. Rhona could read McNab like a book – after all, she'd had enough experience of doing so over the years they'd worked together.

'It's Ellie, isn't it?' she said.

'How did you guess?' McNab said drily.

'What happened?'

'I think she may have dumped me,' McNab admitted. 'After abandoning her the night I was chasing Eric Jackson.'

'You explained why?' Rhona said.

'Yes, but it didn't work. Seems being in a relationship with an officer of the law is losing its appeal.'

'Ditto with Sean,' Rhona said. 'Ever since I missed that meal and went to view Alec McLaughlin's body instead. Even my offer of dinner out at my expense hasn't done the trick.'

McNab was brightening a little. 'So what are you planning for tonight then?' he said.

'A walk through the park, then a pizza probably,' Rhona told him.

McNab hesitated, leading Rhona to believe he might be about to ask if he could come with her.

She got in first. 'You can join me if you like.'

McNab's face broke into a relieved grin. 'Eating out or in?'

Taking McNab home with her didn't seem like a wise move, certainly not in the mood she was in, so Rhona said, 'Let's splash out. Your choice of restaurant.'

'Okay, Dr MacLeod, fancy an Italian?' McNab said, beginning to look like a new man.

'I do,' Rhona told him.

'Then I know just the place.'

69

The crow's back. No more need to fall down the chimney to gain entry. I just leave the back door open and in he comes. His favourite perch is on the back of Jack's chair.

I used to think the crow had come from Mary. Now I'm not so sure. Maybe it was Jack after all. He certainly looks very comfortable in Jack's place alongside the kitchen range.

He also enjoys hearing me talk to him. So much so, he sometimes caws a reply. Which, of course, the clothes, however well laid out, never did.

Mr McCreadie often comes to visit. Plus we meet for a walk when he takes out Lucy's wee terrier, Benji.

We're working on a project together. Him and me and Marge.

They say if you can turn bad things into a story, then you've survived them.

I'm beginning to think that may be true.

Three months later

Local Headliner at Bloody Scotland

International bestselling writer J. D. Smart will talk about his new podcast and soon-to-be-published book, *The Taking of Mary McIntyre*, at Scotland's International Crime Writing Festival in Stirling, mid-September.

The former Detective Inspector and famous Stirling resident, who left the force after his unsuccessful investigation into the disappearance of eleven-year-old Mary McIntyre in 1975, played a major role in the new investigation into her murder after her body was discovered in a raised peat bog south of her home town of East Kilbride.

Appearing with J. D. Smart on stage will be Mary's childhood friend Karen Marshall, who helped identify her friend's killer forty-five years later. On stage too will be Marge Balfour from the Raploch women's recovery cafe, who, together with the other women in the group, helped Karen recall what had happened to her as a child.

Advances in forensic science, together with the retrieval of Karen's memories, were instrumental in solving this case.

Mary's killer and Karen's abuser, Eric Jackson, died earlier this year as he attempted to silence Karen forever.

Acknowledgements

I'd like to thank my sister-in-law for her story of the haunting appearance of her dead cat, and my neighbour for the scary story of the two crows in her sitting room. Both tales gave rise to the idea for the opening chapter.

After I'd written it, I was asked to visit the women's recovery cafe in Raploch, Stirling, where they were reading the first Rhona book, *Driftnet*. They were working on their own writing projects, mutually supporting each other in their recovery. Meeting them and listening to their work was the inspiration for telling Karen's story.

As is always the case, I could not write a Dr Rhona MacLeod novel without expert help from the real practitioners of the world of forensic science. I love the research involved because of the fascinating input from the people below.

So a big thank you to:

Professor of Anthropology at Lancaster University Sue Black DBE FRSE FRCP FRAI, for her advice regarding what we can learn from peat bodies.

Professor Lorna Dawson at the James Hutton Institute for sharing her knowledge of raised peat bogs in Scotland, and her invaluable appearance as Dr Jen Mackie, forensic soil scientist.

Emeritus Professor of Forensic Pathology James Grieve for his advice regarding the autopsy of a peat-buried child.

A big thanks, too, to my wonderful editor Alex Saunders and the team at Pan Macmillan, who I think know Dr Rhona MacLeod almost as well as I do.

Paths of the Dead

By Lin Anderson

Paths of the Dead *is the thrilling ninth book in Lin Anderson's Rhona MacLeod series.*

It was never just a game . . .

When Amy MacKenzie agrees to attend a meeting at a local spiritualist church, the last person she expects to hear calling to her from beyond the grave is her son – the son whom she'd only spoken to an hour before.

Then the body of a young man is found inside a Neolithic stone circle high above the city of Glasgow, and forensic scientist Rhona MacLeod is soon on the case. The hands have been severed and there is a stone in the victim's mouth with the number five scratched on it. DI Michael McNab is certain it's a gangland murder, but Rhona isn't convinced. When a second body is found in similar circumstances, a pattern begins to emerge of a killer intent on masterminding a gruesome Druidic game that everyone will be forced to play . . .

The Special Dead

By Lin Anderson

The Special Dead *is the thrilling tenth book
in Lin Anderson's Rhona MacLeod series.*

When Mark is invited back to Leila's flat and ordered to strip, he thinks he's about to have a night to remember. Waking later, he finds Leila gone from his side. Keen to leave, he opens the wrong door and finds he's entered a nightmare; behind the swaying Barbie dolls that hang from the ceiling is the body of the girl he just had sex with.

Rhona MacLeod's forensic investigation of the scene reveals the red plaited silk cord used to hang Leila is a cingulum, a Wiccan artefact used in sex magick. Sketches of sexual partners hidden in the dolls provide a link to nine powerful men, but who are they? As the investigation continues, it looks increasingly likely that other witches will be targeted too.

Working on the investigation is the newly demoted DS Michael McNab, who is keen to stay sober and redeem himself with Rhona, but an encounter with Leila's colleague and fellow Wiccan Freya Devine threatens his resolve. Soon McNab realizes Freya may hold the key to identifying the men linked to the dolls, but the Nine will do anything to keep their identities a secret.

None but the Dead

By Lin Anderson

None but the Dead is the thrilling eleventh book in Lin Anderson's Rhona MacLeod series.

Sanday: one of Britain's northernmost islands, inaccessible when the wind prevents the ferry crossing from the mainland, or fog grounds the tiny, island-hopping plane.

When human remains are discovered to the rear of an old primary school, forensic expert Dr Rhona MacLeod and her assistant arrive to excavate the grave. Approaching midwinter, they find daylight in short supply, the weather inhospitable and some of the island's inhabitants less than co-operative. When the suspicious death of an old man in Glasgow appears to have links with the island, DS Michael McNab is dispatched to investigate. Desperately uncomfortable in such surroundings, he finds that none of the tools of detective work are there. No internet, no CCTV, and no police station.

As the weather closes in, the team – including criminal profiler and Orkney native Professor Magnus Pirie – are presented with a series of unexplained incidents, apparently linked to the discovery of thirteen magic flowers representing the souls of dead children who had attended the island school where the body was discovered. But how and in what circumstance did they die? And why are their long-forgotten deaths significant to the current investigation?

As a major storm approaches, bringing gale-force winds and high seas, the islanders turn on one another, as past and present evil deeds collide, and long-buried secrets break the surface, along with the exposed bones.

Follow the Dead

By Lin Anderson

Follow the Dead *is the thrilling twelfth book
in Lin Anderson's Rhona MacLeod series.*

On holiday in the Scottish Highlands, forensic scientist Dr Rhona MacLeod joins a mountain rescue team on Cairngorm summit, where a mysterious plane has crash-landed. Nearby, a climbing expedition has left three young people dead, with a fourth still missing.

Meanwhile in Glasgow, DS McNab's raid on the Delta Club produces far more than just a massive haul of cocaine. Questioning one of the underage girls found partying with the city's elite, he discovers she was smuggled into Scotland via Norway, and that the crashed plane may be linked to the club.

Joined by Norwegian detective Alvis Olsen, who harbours disturbing theories about how the two cases are connected with his homeland, Rhona searches for the missing link. What she uncovers is a group of ruthless people willing to do anything to ensure the investigation dies in the frozen wasteland of the Cairngorms . . .

Sins of the Dead

By Lin Anderson

Sins of the Dead *is the thrilling thirteenth book in Lin Anderson's Rhona MacLeod series.*

While illegally street racing in the underground tunnels of Glasgow, four Harley-Davidson riders make a horrifying discovery: a dead man left in the darkness, hands together on his chest as if peacefully laid to rest. The cause of death is unclear, the only clues being a half glass of red wine and a partially eaten chunk of bread by his side that echo the ancient religious practice of sin-eating.

Called to the scene, forensic scientist Rhona MacLeod is perplexed by the lack of evidence. But when another body is found near her own flat, laid out in a similar manner, she fears a forensically aware killer stalks the city and is marking the victims with their unique signature. Even more worryingly, the killer appears to be using skills they may have learned while attending her forensic science lectures at Glasgow University.

There are signs that Rhona is being targeted, and that the killer is playing with her and the police, drawing them into a deadly race against time, before the sin-eater's next victim is chosen . . .

'Inventive, compelling, genuinely scary and beautifully written, as always'
Denzil Meyrick

Time for the Dead

By Lin Anderson

Time for the Dead *is the fourteenth book in Lin Anderson's Rhona MacLeod series.*

When forensic scientist Rhona MacLeod returns to her roots on Scotland's Isle of Skye, a chance encounter in the woods behind a nearby activities centre leads her to what seems to be a crime scene, but without a victim. Could this be linked to a group of army medics, who visited the centre while on leave from Afghanistan and can no longer be located on the island?

Enlisting the help of local tracker dog Blaze, Rhona starts searching for a connection.

Two days later a body is found at the base of the famous cliff known as Kilt Rock, face and identity obliterated by the fall, which leads Rhona to suspect the missing medics may be on the island for reasons other than relaxation. Furthermore, elements of the case suggest a link with an ongoing operation in Glasgow, which draws DS Michael McNab into the investigation.

As the island's unforgiving conditions close in, Rhona must find out what really happened to the group in Afghanistan, as the consequences may be being played out in brutal killings on Skye . . .